BLACK LIGHT
A Novel of Karma

Talbot Mundy (1879-1940) was one of the premier writers of adventure fiction of his day. As his career progressed, his writings also became known for their fascination with the human spirit, mysticism, and the supernatural. Sixtyt-five years after his death, he is best known for his novels *King of the Khyber Rifles* and *Om, The Secret of Ahbor Valley*, as well as his introspective memoir, *I Say Sunrise*.

Books by Talbot Mundy
published by Ariel Press:

Black Light
Caves of Terror
The Thunder Dragon Gate
Old Ugly-Face
Gunga Sahib
C.I.D.
Winds from the East
(an anthology of Mundy stories, articles, and poems
compiled by Brian Taves)

TALBOT MUNDY

BLACK LIGHT
A Novel of Karma

ARIEL PRESS
Atlanta – Columbus

This book is made possible by a gift
to the Publications Fund of Light
by Judith R. Ross

BLACK LIGHT
Copyright © 1930 by Talbot Mundy
        1958 by Dawn Mundy Provost

All Rights reserved. No part of this book may be used or reproduced in any manner whatsoever without written permission, except in the case of brief quotations embodied in articles and reviews. Printed in the United States of America. Direct inquiries to: Ariel Press, P. O. Box 297, Marble Hill, GA 30148.

ISBN 0-89804-200-3

BLACK LIGHT

A Novel of Karma

EVENING HYMN
OF THE ANCIENT SECT KNOWN AS THE BRETHREN
OF THE THORNY ROSE-RED PATH

Souls now astir in mystery of gloaming
Moving to the whisper of the twilight breeze,
Hearts like the doves to their dovecotes homing,
Lo, we beg a blessing on our bended knees.
Gods! Ye were men when the weary world was younger!
Pity us, O pity us, Dwellers in the Light!
Heal, O Compassionate! A blessing for our hunger
Pour from the Silence of the star-hung night!

Priest (solo): Sap of the growth of the greening trees,
Soul of the sigh of the morning breeze,
Cry of the fowl on the lonely mere,
Sadness, aching and old and drear,
Youth of the jungle of grass and thorn,
Laughter and glory of glittering morn,
Mauve of the snow on the mountain peaks,
Infinite azure the eagle seeks,
Milk of the moon on the whitened wall,
These are thy brothers. Come, they call!
These, so long as the sands shall run,
These and thy heart,
These and thy soul,
These and thy life
Are one.

Chorus: Lo, we are answered! Love we each other!
Pilgrims, we are pilgrims on the endless Way,
Tree, beast and man. O Universal Mother,
Brood above dark mystery and bring forth Day!
Dark are night's wings. Death shall be no deeper.
Hail then, hail then, Dwellers of the Night!
Peace be your gifts to us! Comfort ye the sleeper.
Waken us with gladness when ye bring forth Light!

I

> *"Shall I sin, to satisfy your itch
> for what you have no right to?"*

There was no moon yet. The ponderous temple wall loomed behind Hawkes, a huge tree breathing near him, full of the restlessness of parakeets that made the silence audible and darkness visible; its branches, high above the wall, were a formless shadow, too dense for the starlight. Hawkes' white uniform absorbed the hue of smoke, a trifle reddened by the glow of embers.

"Come and try!" he remarked to himself, and retired again into the shadow, muttering: "I'd like to have someone try to buy me—just once."

No purchasers appeared, and he did not appear to expect any among the bearers of lanterns, like fireflies, who came unhurrying from the city—decent enough citizens—silversmiths and sandal-makers, weavers, tradesmen—not so virtuous, nor yet so mean that they might not glean a little comfort at a day's end, from the same hymn men have sung for centuries, until its words mean less than the mood it makes. They took no notice, or appeared to take none, of Joe Beddington who left his horse amid the trees three hundred yards away and strode by himself, so to speak, in the stream.

The citizens of Adana gathered in the clearing amid the trees, filled it and spread outward along the temple wall, extinguishing their lanterns because the priests, who are obstinate people, object to imported kerosene; and anyhow, there would be a full moon presently, so why waste oil? Joe Beddington, staring about him, strode through their midst and presently stood where Hawkes had been. Chandri Lal, a small lean cobra charmer, eased himself out of a shadow and laid his circular basket near Beddington's feet, studying the dying fire, speculating whether to blow that into flame or wait until the moon should rise above the temple wall. Hymn or no hymn, business is business; Chandri Lal had heard that all Americans shed money as clouds shed rain. He hoped Hawkes would not see him. He knew, to half an ounce, the weight of Hawkes' boot and the heft behind it.

Sergeant Hawkes came out of the shadow and saluted Joe, or rather he saluted about a hundred million dollars:

"Your mother decided not to come, sir? Just as well. She'd have got tired standing here."

"No," Joe answered, "mother would have tired us."

Hawkes changed the subject: "Let me tell you about this temple."

"You did. It dates back to a million B.C. Never been entered by anyone not directly descended from somebody named in the Mahabharata. That's nothing. You should see our American D.A.R.'s. They're going to censor the telephone book. Mother, you know, is a D.A.R. My father was more like yours—quite human—no rating, except in Bradstreet. Mother's folk came over on the *Hesperus* and did the red men dirt."

"They're going to start the hymn," said Hawkes.

"What are the words of it?"

"Quiet now. Tell you later. You know, sir, we're not supposed to be here; but the high priest is a decent fellow in his own way. When I sent him word there'd be a foreign visitor to watch tonight's ceremony he merely asked me to be here too."

Joe Beddington believed that no more than Hawkes did. "You don't say."

Hawkes evoked some truth to justify prevarication: "Yes, sir, even natives who aren't Hindus aren't supposed to witness this. Mohammedans, for instance—"

"I get you. Like the accounts of a corporation—keep 'em esoteric. That's a dandy hymn. Hello—who's the man in vestments? Oh, my God!"

The edge of an enormous moon rose over the top of the wall and framed a robed priest in an aureole of mellow light; a platform high above the wall on which his bare feet rested had become a pool of liquid amber. An incredible star, in a purple sky, appeared to draw nearer and pause exactly over the crown of his head; subtly liquid highlights glistened on his robes and the shadows beneath him deepened into velvet mystery in which every dark hue in the spectrum brooded waiting to be born. It was exactly what the Norman stained-glass makers aimed at and almost achieved.

The confidingly plaintive minor chanting of the hymn ceased. Silence fell. One pure golden gong note—absolute A major—stole on the night as if it were the voice of a ray of the rising moon. And then the priest's voice. In a chant that rose and fell like the cool wet melody of tumbling streams, unhurried, flowing because Law insists, he asserted what all Night knows and Man should seek to understand. There was no argument, no vehemence, no question. He propounded no problem—pleaded with neither violable principle nor erring ignorance. Whatever he had to say, it was so absolute that Beddington, to whom the words meant nothing, recognized the beauty and interpreted the essence, so that every fiber in him thrilled to the mystic meaning. It embarrassed him, like the sight of a naked woman.

Then another gong note. Caught into a shadow as if night had reabsorbed him, the priest vanished. The enormous moon wetted the temple roof with liquid light that overflowed until the clearing amid the trees lay luminous and filled with the kneeling forms of humans sketched, as it were, with violet pastel on the amber floor. They sang their *nunc dimittis*. Dark trees stirred to a faint wind, scented with the breath of ripened grain and cows in the smoke-dimmed villages. Leaves whispered the obbligato for the hymn. A little whirl of dust arose and walked away along a moonlit path. Hawkes' voice fell flat and out of harmony:

"They don't come out from the temple until the moonlight reaches a mark in the central quadrangle. They're performing a ceremony in some way connected with astrology—or so I'm told."

"I'd give my boots to go inside and see," said Joe.

"Can't be done, sir. Nobody's allowed in—never. Do you see that Yogi?"

The ascending moon had bathed another section of the temple wall in soft light. Now a gate in the wall was visible and—to the right, beyond cavernous darkness where the wall turned outward sharply and a high dome cast its shadow—there was an outcrop of the curiously layered and twisted green-gray rock on which the temple foundations rested. It formed vague Titan-steps, and a platform backed against the masonry. There was what looked like a giant beehive on the platform. A man sat beside it, naked except for a rag on his loins. He had gray hair falling to his shoulders and a white beard that spread on his breast.

"That man used to be the high priest of the temple. He is famous all over India for his astrology, and that's strange, because he won't tell fortunes; or perhaps he will, perhaps he won't, I don't know; he refused to tell mine."

"How much did you offer him?"

"He won't take money."

"How does he live?"

"Temple people feed him. Pilgrims, all sorts of pious people, bring him little offerings of food. He gives away most of it. That Yogi would surprise you, sir. Talks good English. Traveled—France, England, the United States. Some say he can talk French and German. But there he sits day after day, and says nothing. I'll bet you he'd say less than nothing if he knew how. Maybe he does. How old do you suppose he is? There's records—actual official records."

"He doesn't look so specially old," said Joe.

"The moonlight is a bit deceptive. The natives say he is more than two centuries old. I'm a Christian myself. I believe the Bible all right. But I can't persuade myself that in these days people live to be as long in the tooth as Abraham." *

The moon grew less dramatic—smaller in appearance but more searching, as it rose above the temple; its mellow amber faded; masonry and men's garments took on a grayish hue; the Yogi-astrologer sat motionless—a graven image posturing against the wall, not moving even when a woman, whose black *sari* was hardly darker than her skin, came forth from a shadow and bowed in the dust at his feet.

Joe Beddington strolled toward the Yogi. Chandri Lal, captain of emasculated cobras, stirred himself to seize an opportunity; he followed at a half-run, leaning forward, with his basket in both hands ready to be laid before Joe's feet. Joe scorned him:

"Nothing doing. I've seen scores of snake acts."

Suddenly a foot leaped forth from darkness. The basket went in one direction, cobras in another. Hawkes' swagger-cane descended sharply, semi-officially, as it were, without personal malice, on Chandri Lal's naked shoulders.

"Git, you heathen! Git the hell from here! Use judgment! Showing off snakes in this place is as bad as a Punch-and-Judy show in church. Now mind, I've warned you! One more breach of blooming etiquette, and—"

Chandri Lal picked up his basket and followed the trail of his snakes in the dust. The woman at the Yogi's

---

* Instances of extreme longevity are not unknown among Indian ascetics. See Mukerji's account in the *Atlantic Monthly* of the Holy Man of Benares whom authentic official records certify to have been more than two centuries old. He died quite recently.

feet implored some favor from him, elbows, forehead, belly in the dust, beseeching mercy. Joe watched. The Yogi made no response. Joe spoke at last, producing money:

"Old man, will you tell my fortune?"

The Yogi met his gaze. There was almost a minute's silence, broken at last by a passionate outburst from the woman. Then the Yogi's voice, calm as eternity—only startling because he used such perfect English:

"That is what she—this ayah also wants."

"Why not tell her?"

"If it were good for her to know, she *would* know; there would be no need to tell her."

"Tell mine. How much shall I pay you?"

"Do as you will with your money."

Joe held out twenty rupees. Chandri Lal drew nearer; he could smell money as well as see it through perplexing shadow.

"Give it to that ayah," said the Yogi.

"Why? Oh, all right—here you are, mother, your lucky evening—take 'em." Joe dropped the rupees in the dust before her nose and Chandri Lal pounced, but Hawkes' boot served for a danger signal, so he backed away again. Blubbering, the ayah stowed the money in her bosom.

"Come on, tell," said Joe. "I'm waiting."

"You have paid the ayah," said the Yogi. "Let her tell you."

Joe grinned uneasily. "Stung, eh? Serves me right. I should have known you can't tell fortunes any more than I can."

The Yogi seemed indifferent, but in a sense, Hawkes' honor was concerned since he was acting showman.

"Hell, he can tell 'em. They all come to him—high priests — pilgrims — bunnias — he tells some — some he doesn't. If he tells, it comes true."

"Bunk!" said Joe.

"Why should I tell you?" asked the Yogi suddenly. "Should I sin to satisfy your itch for what you have no right to?"

"How about the ayah, then? You told me to ask her. How if *she* sins?"

"Who shall say she sins? If she tells what she neither knows nor not-knows, what harm can happen? Nothing to strain Karma's entrails. Knowledge is one thing—speech another. There is a time for speaking, and a time for silence. That which brings forth action at the wrong time is not wisdom though it may have knowledge."

"Half a mo', sir, half a mo'—excuse me," Hawkes remarked and stepped aside into a shadow. Suddenly his fist struck like a poleax and a man went reeling backward on his heels—fell—struggled to his feet, and ran, leaving his turban behind him. Hawkes pointed to the turban. "Hey, you—there's a present for you."

Chandri Lal pounced on the turban and thrust it into the basket with the snakes, then changed his mind and tried to sell it to the ayah.

"Bastards!" Hawkes informed the wide world, chafing his right knuckles.

"Possibly—even probably," remarked the Yogi. "But did the blow correct the accident of birth?"

"It weren't intended to," Hawkes answered. "It was meant to cure that swine of sneaking in the dark where he ain't invited. Do you call that sinful?"

"Not a big sin," said the Yogi. "But you shall measure it at the time of payment. Who knows? It may have been a good sin—one of those by which we are instructed. Few learn, save by sinning. He—that man you struck—he may learn also."

"I'll learn him," Hawkes muttered.

"You pack quite a wallop," said Joe. "What had he done to you?"

"Nothing sir," Hawkes took him by the arm and led him to where the temple cast the darkest shadow. It felt like being led by a policeman across Trafalgar Square; in spite of silence and the peculiar vacancy of moonlight there was a remarkable feeling of crowds in motion— unexplainable unless as a trick of the nervous system. On the way, jerkily through the corner of his mouth, Hawkes hinted at a sort of half-embarrassment.

"The Book says turn the other cheek. But that was Jerusalem. This is India."

"So you don't believe in theories from books?"

"Theories, sir? They're funny. Any of 'em might be all right if we all believed 'em. But a one-man theory is like a one-man army—only good if you can keep it quiet. I'm a one-man army. There's a theory I'm a Fusilier, belonging to a battalion at Nusserabad. But I'm no theorizer. So I'm here on special duty, drawing double pay and doing nothing except enjoy life."

"Doing nothing?"

"A bit of everything. I'm supposed to be learning languages. I'm instructor in fencing and fancy needlework to British officers of native regiments. That's to say, I pick out gravel from their faces and forearms when they skin 'emselves riding to pig. They—half of 'em can't ride—but they've all got gizzards; so they fall off frequent. Gravel leaves a bad scar unless it's cleaned out careful. Scars spoil luck with women. So instead of sweating in a barracks I stay here—and to hell with the King's Regulations."

"Don't you do any regular work?"

"Not me, sir. Now and then I'm loaned to teach a Maharajah's butler how to mix drinks—I'm a genius at that. And on the quiet, now and then I do a little propaganda."

"Secret service, eh?"

"No, sir. Not a secret in my system. Quite the contrary. Officers wish for promotion. I'm an expert in promotion. Have to be, since I'm paid by results. I invent ways for making 'em famous—famous, that is, in the proper quarter; it's useless to try to sell a black pig in a white pig market. That's a stool, sir—care to sit down—nautch procession won't be here for half an hour yet."

Beddington sat on the stool and suddenly became aware, by means of other senses than he knew he had, of people near him. The darkness seemed alive with living shadows that he could neither hear nor see—an uncanny sensation that made the hair rise on his neck. However, he controlled himself. "Who are they?" he demanded in a normal voice.

"Troopers from the native Lancer regiment. And I'll

bet they're jealous. Didn't you see me give that bloke from Poonch a bloody nose? They're laying for him. I step in and wipe their eye. You can't beat that for competition. Come here, Khilji—meet a gentleman from the United States."

One after another, seven shadows emerged into the semi-darkness, took shape and saluted—big men—white teeth gleaming in the midst of black beards. He addressed as Khilji, grinning, imitated Hawkes' use of his fist; then, out of sheer politeness, because Beddington might not otherwise understand, he added a remark in English:

"Hah-hah! Saucy bastards are the men from Poonch! You Hawkes, you taught him something."

"Yes," said Hawkes, "I poonched him. He was lucky. You men would ha' killed him. That would have cost you about six months' pay apiece to hire a substitute to take the blame. You ought to pay me a commission for saving you all that money."

"Eh-eh, you Hawkes!"

Men became shadows. Shadows melted into darkness. Silence.

"You seem well acquainted here," said Beddington.

"By nature, sir, I'm like a terrier. I snoot and sniff around and pass the time o' day with all and sundry. Time I'm through, I know the news—and which dog I can lick if I have to—and where the likely pickings are in backyards. Yes, sir, I believe I know these parts as thoroughly as some folk."

"Care for a drink?"

Beddington produced a flask, a self-defensive habit

that he had adopted since prohibition. It enabled him to pose as normal, which he was not. It relieved him of the burden of making conversation. One drink—then straight to the point, although he had noticed that it did not work so well in foreign lands. Hawkes stared, straining his eyes in the dark as he drank.

"Hot stuff, sir."

"Yes, I've no ice."

"Sir, I meant wonderful stuff."

"Have another. Do you drink much?"

"No, sir. Can't afford it. Three or four drinks and I'd lose if I bet to-morrow was Friday. I like drink, but I like prosperity more. When I've time on my hands I snoot around and see things."

"Could you undertake a private investigation for me?"

Hawkes struck a match to light his pipe; he used the match adroitly. Beddington understood:

"It's on the level. But it's personal and private."

"Money in it?"

"Yes. Whatever's fair." It was Beddington's turn to watch Hawkes' face. The first match had failed; Hawkes struck another and cupped it in his hands. But a face is a mask if a man is a rogue. Beddington judged better by the tone of voice and phrasing of the answer.

"All right, sir, I'll be frank too. If it's unlawful, the answer's no. If it's dirty, it's no. If it's merely risky—yes, provided the pay fits the risk. If it's difficult, so much the better."

"It probably is difficult. I want to find some one whose name I don't know, and whose age I can only guess approximately. She may be dead, but if she is I want to see proof. She may know who she is; she may not."

"Woman, eh? White?"

"United States American of Scotch, Welsh and Irish ancestry."

"Age?"

"Roughly, twenty-one."

"Present information?"

"None whatever—except that her parents died in this district, of cholera, about twenty-one years ago."

Hawkes whistled — sharp — flat — then natural. There was a distinct pause. Then, in a normal voice:

"Sounds vague enough. I can try, sir."

"The parents of this child had a Goanese butler—a man named Xavier Braganza—who also died of cholera. But before he died he told a Catholic missionary and several other people that the native wet-nurse—the ayah as he called her—had carried the child away and vanished. But—and this is about all the clue we have—he added that the ayah was an idolatrous heathen without a trace in her of any sort of virtue, who would probably keep the child in hiding until old enough for sale."

"About twenty-one years ago, sir, this district was almost wiped out by cholera. Nearly all the white officials died. Records got lost and stolen—some o' them got burned—the dacoits came down from the hills and plundered right and left, taking the cholera back with 'em, so that it spread into Nepaul. Almost anything a man can think of might have happened."

"There's one reason why I want this search kept quiet. Possibly the child was sold into a harem or something worse. If so, and we find her, it might be a lot too late to help her. Do you understand me? There might be legal difficulties, even if her character weren't rotted to the core. It might be useless or even cruel to give her a hint of who she is."

A quarter-tone change in Hawkes' voice suggested alertness and a vague suspicion: "Any money coming to her?"

"Of her own? No. Her mother, though, was my mother's youngest bridesmaid. There was a very strong friendship between them. If this girl should be found, and should prove to be not too far socially and morally sunk my mother would see to it that she should never lack for money."

"Hell's bells! Fairy godmothers are always other people's luck," said Hawkes. "Myself, I was an orphan once, and butter wouldn't have melted in my mouth, I was that sweet and guileless. Anyone who'd claimed me might ha' raised me for a duke and done a proud job. I could ha' rolled in millions and done credit to the money. However, they raised me in a London County Council Institute, and it weren't a bad place either. When I was old enough I was sent to sea on a training-ship, to the tune of a heap o' blarney about Nelson o' the Nile—and Admiral Sir Francis Drake—and Britain needs no bulwarks. I served three years' apprenticeship, and I'm still wondering what Nelson found that made life tolerable. So I quit the sea and joined the army—and here I am, what might have been a millionaire, if only millionaires had sense and knew a promising orphan when they see one. Hide up now, sir—nautch is coming."

"Why hide?"

"Well, sir, it's like some husbands with their wives. The husband knows—you bet he knows, but all he asks is not to catch her at it; he's conventional, but he's tolerant; so, if she'll give him half a chance, he'll look the other way. Same here; there are about as many eyes in this here dark as there are mosquitoes. They know we're here, and it's against their law and custom; but they're good, kind-hearted folks, so if we act half respectful o' their prejudices they'll take care to seem to look the other way. Get right down in the ditch, sir—no, no snakes, I saw to that—if you should lie on that piece o' sacking and set your elbows on the bank you'll get a good view."

A gong sounded and Hawkes knocked his pipe against his boot to empty it. There came a surging of excitement from the trees, where probably a thousand Hindus shuffled for position. They seemed to try to make believe they were in hiding, as if tradition had made that a part of the ritual; they resembled a stage ambush. The moon had risen until shadow of dome and wall were short enough to leave a dusty road uncovered, pale, with undetermined edges. The temple wall where the Yogi sat beside his beehive hut was already bathed in light and the Yogi no longer looked like a bas-relief, nor even like a statue; he sat motionless, but he looked human, although indifferent to the woman who lay flat on the earth in front of him still sobbing her petition: "Speak, thou holy one, thou man of wisdom!" In a side-mouth whisper Hawkes interpreted her words to Joe.

Music—strange stuff that made Joe Beddington's spine tingle—music with a rhythm no more obvious at first than that of wind in the trees or water flowing amid the boulders of a ford. It was several minutes before the musicians appeared from around the curve of the high wall—a group of about twenty men in long loin-cloths, naked from the waist up, not even marching in step but nevertheless appearing to obey one impulse. On either side of them, in single file, walked a line of lantern bearers with the lanterns hung on long sticks. There were only two small drums; the remainder were weird wind instruments, creating a timeless tune that seemed to have no connection with another system of sounds from an unseen source, which nevertheless insisted on the ear's attention and in some way emphasized the melody.

Then came priests—not less than fifty of them, draped in saffron colored linen but each man's naked belly gleaming in the moonlight. They bore all sorts of mysteries of many shapes, including some that resembled chalices of jeweled gold. There were censers, too, and a reek of incense made from pungent gums whose smell stirred imagination more commandingly than ever pictured symbols did. More lantern bearers in a group, and then the sistra and some things like castanets, creating that sea of sound which underlay and permeated the music. It was pleasing but not satisfying; it stirred an unfamiliar emotion and awakened nerves not normally self-assertive. Beddington spared one swift glance along the lane of moon-white dust and saw that the music had stirred the waiting Hindus to the verge of hysteria; they were leaping like shadows of flames on a wall; he himself felt an impulse to do something of the sort. Only a habit restrained him. His will urged. He wanted to do it.

"Ever hear of magic?" Hawkes asked in a whisper. "That's it. But that's not half of it. Watch what's coming."

In one sense it was utterly impossible to watch what came; the eye refused obedience; it was hypnotic motion controlled with such consummate skill that it stirred more psychic senses than the onlooker ever knew he had. Instead of seeing about a hundred dancing women draped in filmy pale-blue stuff like jeweled incense smoke, and chanting as they danced, their bare feet silent in the dust, their ankles clashing with golden bracelets, Beddington's imagination leaped to grapple with those mysteries the dance was meant to symbolize. It was no dance in the ordinary meaning of the word, and yet it made all other dancing seem like stupid repetition of a common catchphrase. This was as exciting and elusive as the flow of life into the veins of nature. It was as maddening as a fight between strong men or as the sea-surf pounding on a moonlit reef. It was as difficult to watch as one wave in a welter with the wind across the tide. Its movement seemed inevitable—timed—yet so much more than three-dimensional that no one pattern could include it and no eye could define its rhythm. Something in the fashion of the fire-fly dance, it seemed to link the finite with the infinite.

Beddington forced himself to speak. He was afraid of

his own emotions and aware of impulse to obey them. Down the lane of moonlight he could see the Hindus making, as he phrased it, asses of themselves. He did not propose to let hysteria swallow him too.

"My God, Hawkes, I've seen a temple nautch or two, and durbar nautches by the dozen. They were all the bunk. I'd heard of things like this but—this is beyond reason. It's—"

"Impossible, ain't it?" said Hawkes. "But it's true all the same. And it's nothing to what goes on *inside* the temple."

"How do *you* know?"

"Oh, I've heard tell."

Hawkes was lying, and Joe knew it, but he let that pass. He had an eye for line and color and an ear for music; vaguely he had always thought the three were varying aspects of one supersensual phenomenon, but now he understood it—though he could not have told how he did. He was in the grip of excitement that made him want to laugh and cry and swear, all in one meaningless spasm. There was more beauty visible at one time, forced on his attention, than his untrained senses and his prisoned intellect could endure without reeling. He could hear a voice that might, or might not be his own—he did not know, chanting in Greek elegiacs, lines from Homer's *Iliad* that he had not looked at since he left the university. And then climax—perfect and beyond words incomparable.

Borne on a litter by four white bulls, on a throne beneath a peacock canopy formed by the spread of the bird's tail, sat the high priest in his vestments, bearing in his hands a globe of carved crystal containing a light like a jewel. At each corner of the four-square platform of the litter stood a young girl as if supporting the canopy. One breast of each was showing. They were draped in crimson filmy stuff that dimmed while it revealed their outlines. The four bulls and their burden were surrounded and followed by a waving mystery of peacock-feather fans and colored lights that interblended in the smoke of incense and the rising dust. They appeared to be towed, bulls and all, by the stream-like motion of the nautch girls, as if magic had harnessed poetry by unseen traces, guiding it with reins invisible. Then, like a guard of Nature forces, four by four, a hundred priests came marching, each disguised in mask and robe suggesting one of the four mystic elements of Fire, Air, Earth and Water. Silence. Dust ascending in the moonlight. And then Hawkes spoke:

"They'll be back about three in the morning. Would you swap that for the stage o' Drury Lane, sir? It don't mean nothing to me. And yet it means so much that I feel like turning pious. It's the thirteenth time I've seen it. Twice I saw it in the monsoon, with the girls all slick and wetted down with rain until the lot of 'em seemed naked—mud as slippery as oil, and not a foot set wrong—wind and rain in their faces—moon under the clouds and branches blowing off the trees. They liked it, if a grin means anything. What would you say it all means?"

"Damned if I know." Joe crawled out from the ditch and straightened himself, rubbing an elbow that had "gone to sleep" from resting on the sun-baked earth.

"They probably don't know either. The meaning of things like that gets lost in the course of centuries. Do you suppose all those red jewels glowing on the high priest's robe are genuine rubies?"

"So they say, sir. Why not?"

"Who is that?"

Hawkes hesitated, and disguised the hesitation by spitting into the embers of the fire.

"There's all sorts, sir, connected with the temple."

A woman—quite young, if the set of her shoulders and the grace of her motion were any criterion—came along the path the procession had taken. She was heavily veiled. As she passed the Yogi she saluted him with both hands to her eyes, but he took no notice. The ayah knelt to her, murmuring what seemed like praises and, seizing the end of her *sari*, pressed it to her lips. She took a little notice of the ayah—not much. She seemed more inclined to notice Hawkes, but Hawkes deliberately turned his back toward her. Joe laughed.

"Scared of women?"

"Can't be too careful, sir."

Six of the native troopers strode forth from the shadow, halted, formed up two deep, waited for the girl—then, one of them giving the gruff command, they trudged off, two in front of her, four following. She might have been their prisoner, except that the escort looked too proud, and she too sure of herself. It seemed to Joe that she was staring at him through her veil; however, he, too, thought it better to be careful. He walked over to where the Yogi sat as motionless as stone and stared at him instead.

The ayah clutched at Joe's legs, imprecating or else begging, it was hard to tell which. Chandri Lal ran forward to prevent her, but the Yogi stopped him with a monosyllable.

"What does she want?" Joe asked him.

The Yogi answered in English: "She wants instruction."

"Why not give it to her?"

The Yogi stared—smiled—spoke at last, in a deep voice, rich with humor:

"Give? Do you give always what is asked? O man from Jupiter!"

TEMPLE NAUTCH SONG

Moonrise! Moonrise! Symbol thou of seeming!
Old light, cold light, still light streaming!
Earth lies dreaming, earth lies dreaming,
Earth thy daughter, *
Thou, who taught her
Life like tears on trackless water!

Moonrise! Moonrise! Indra's sun is sinking!
Dim light, dim light, earth lies drinking
Thy illusive essence, linking
All that is not,
All that is not,
In a chain of endless thinking.

* (In the ancient Sanskrit scriptures, from which all Indian cosmogony is derived, it is taught that the earth is a child of the moon. The contrary modern opinion that the moon was once part of the earth, seems as absurd to the educated, thinking Indian as the former religious-political western teaching that the earth stands still while sun and stars revolve around it, seemed absurd to Galileo.)

II

"You are an egg that is about to hatch."

Joe stared. The Jupiter Chemical Works, of which his mother owned control by virtue of a trust deed drawn with much more foresight and determination than the Constitution of the United States, is notorious and he understood that perfectly. He was used to seeing his name in newspapers that denounced him one day as a wealthy malefactor and the next day, praised him as a pioneer in the forefront of civilization—so used to it that he had ceased to laugh. He had ceased, too, to concern himself about it, having long ago learned that the son of a trust deed drawn by his mother's lawyers in her favor is as helpless as the husband of a reigning queen. He could not even hire and fire the men who wrecked the company's rivals, bribed and blackmailed politicians, cheated law and obliged him to take public blame for what they did, while his mother banked the dividends. He understood the hatred and the flattery of crowds, and could even sympathize. But it puzzled him that a nearly naked Yogi, all those thousands of miles away from New York, should know his business. It was like a slap in the face.

"Why do you call me that?" he demanded.

"The strongest line on your forehead is that of Jupiter," the Yogi answered. "It is long, strong, straight—and it is deepest when you smile, which is as it should be. But you were born with the rising sign of Gemini. If it had been Aries, no mother, nor any woman, nor any combination of men, however masterful, could have held you fettered. Even as it is, you are no woman's plaything."

Joe shrugged his shoulders. He was not his mother's plaything, simply and only because she did not know how to play. She had no more sense of fun in her than Clytemnestra; no more lyrical delight in unreality than a codfish. Owner of banks and trusts and factories, all did her bidding or else learned the discontent of being toads under a roller.

And he could swear on his oath, as a man who had tried it, that astrology was stark, unmitigated bunk. He had studied it, using Newton's method. For his own amusement he had tried it on the rhythmic rise and fall of stock exchange quotations, and he found it rather less reliable than broker's tips, or than the system with which idiots lose their money at Monte Carlo.

"Smile!" said the Yogi. "Always smile when we ignorant folk offend your honor's wisdom!"

Hawkes intervened. As showman for the night he felt his pride involved again. "Say," he objected, "has some one fed you lemons? Here's a gentleman who's acted generous. He's paid his money, no matter who you gave it to. Now act honest and do what he paid for. Tell his fortune."

"Do you demand that?" asked the Yogi, staring at Beddington.

"Tell hers," he answered. The ayah was clutching his ankles again.

"I will tell it to you," said the Yogi. "It was you who paid, and it is true I accepted the money, although I did not keep it. Should you in turn tell her what I tell you, that is your responsibility. I advise—I warn you not to, that is all."

"How in hell can I tell her? I don't know her language."

"Telling what should not be told—and hell—are as cause and effect," said the Yogi. "She is a fool, that ayah. You will look far for a fool who has greater faith and charity. But who can make a fool wise?"

"Are you wise?" Joe asked him.

"No," said the Yogi, "but wiser than she is—and wiser than you, or you would not have asked me. That fool—that charitable, faithful fool desires to know what shall become of her child, who now no longer is a child, but full grown and aware of the blood in her veins, and of her sex, and of the sin of inertia. A riddle is better than speech misunderstood, so I will speak in riddles. This shall happen to her: a war within herself—one worse than ever soldiers wage with bayonets. She shall be torn between the camel of her obstinacy, and the horse of her ambition, the mule of her stupidity, and the elephant of her wisdom. When those four have pulled her enough apart, a devil may enter into her, or ten devils—or perhaps a benign spirit—who knows? It depends on at least a hundred thousand million influences, each one of which in former lives she wove into her character. Do you understand that? No, of course you don't. Nevertheless, I have answered you. So go away and think about it. Doubt it—deny it—believe it—mock—swear—take or leave it—it is all one to me. I have told you the truth."

Chandri Lal was whispering to the ayah. Apparently he knew English—possibly enough to misinterpret what he heard. At any rate he understood the ayah and her hunger for information, which was hardly keener than his own craving for money. She had money.

"Heavenborn," he began. "Holy one!" Then, seeing that the Yogi took no notice of him, he addressed Hawkes in the vernacular. Hawkes, nothing loath, interpreted:

"He says," said Hawkes, "that ayah wants to know, shall her child be a queen—a royal ranee?"

"Tell her," suggested Beddington.

"She can be," said the Yogi. "I have cast her horoscope. If she is brave, she can be a queen over herself. She has resources and a struggle is impending. Nay—I will say no more. I am in debt to that fool-woman for necessities. Shall I repay her with speech that will stick like a barb in her heart? Shall I use my wisdom to unbridle folly? There is a time for silence."

He relapsed into silence as solid as concrete. He exuded silence. He was its image, its expression. Even the ayah ceased from importunity, since even she in her hysteria could recognize finality. She began to abuse Hawkes, including Joe within the scope of a tempest of words.

"What does she say?"

"She accuses you and me, sir, of having stopped that Yogi just when he was coming to the point. She says for you to take your money back, it's bad-luck money."

Joe turned away. He felt he had had enough of unreality for one night, yet he grudged returning to the real. The ascending moon, grown pale, was whitening walls and blackening the shadows; even he himself felt like a bone-white ghost, the more so because his footfall made no sound in the dry dust. He knew that to talk to his mother would produce a sort of psychic anticlimax that he could not explain, and for which she would have no sympathy. It was at such moments that he knew he hated her; the hatred was kin to fear; the fear, if not pre-natal, something she had fastened on him with her will when he was a suckling. At the age of eight and twenty a man had no right, he knew, to be under anyone's dominance. He had an iron will of his own; he was notoriously uncontrollable by anyone except his mother. Her stronger will, compelling his, was what enabled her, unseen, to guide the destinies of interwoven trusts so intricate that even governments were helpless to prevent.

It was only at night, and at times like this when life seemed like a dream, that he was really conscious of the grudge he owed his mother and of a secret sense of shame that he must obey her always. True, he had often resisted her. He could withstand her tantrums. The bludgeoning abuse with which she browbeat servants, secretaries and even the firm's attorneys to obedience, made no impression on him. He could laugh. It was when she was quiet and determined, when she grew kittenish and motherly by turns, and above all when she pretended to need his advice that he grew aware of the numbness somewhere in his conscience and an impulse to obey her that was irresistible. He had long ago ceased to attempt to resist that.

It had been only to oblige his mother that he undertook this idiotic search for someone who, for all the proof he had, had not been born. They had nothing but rumor to go on; a twenty-year rumor at that. It was one of his mother's incredible lapses into sentimentality that she mistook for philanthropic zeal.

Such thoughts flash through a man's mind in a moment. Habit, as it were, presented them *en masse,* along with their product in the shape of disgust and an impulse to escape from them. Activity of mind or body was the only possible way of escape—learn, discover, do something—now, swiftly. That accounted for Joe's sudden forays at a tangent after odds and ends of stray clues into other people's business—swift questions that made some men think him an inquisitive butter-in; while others thought the habit indicated some form of degeneracy, as if he could not concentrate on one thing at a time.

"Why did you hit that Poonchi?" he demanded, turning disconcertingly on Hawkes. "Who is he?"

Hawkes resented it, yet hardly cared to show resentment—yet at any rate. Only those who meet millionaires every day of their lives understand that there is nothing to be gained by yielding to their arrogance; and besides, as a soldier, the habit of answering all questions promptly was as well developed in him as evasiveness was; he could answer questions fluently and instantly but keep the essential information to himself.

"A spy of the Rajah of Poonch-Terai."

"Has he any right here?"

"Damned if I know. A man's rights in this country

are mostly what he can get away with. If he'd been up to no mischief he'd have hit back, he wouldn't have run."

"Have you any idea what sort of mischief?"

"That's not difficult to guess, sir."

"Guess for me. I'm curious."

"Sir, when a man lurks in the shadows where he's uninvited, and runs when he's hit, you can bet he was after either plunder or a woman. Where's the plunder hereabouts? He'd have hit back, wouldn't he, if it had been his own woman or a woman for himself that he was after? Q.E.D. he was a pimp; it 'ud be sinful not to chase him off the lot."

"Did you say he belongs to the Rajah of Poonch-Terai? But Poonch-Terai is several hundred miles from here."

"Maybe, sir. But the Rajah isn't. He's what they call a Maharajah — a nineteen-gun salute man — so rich he needn't trouble himself to pay his debts."

"You mean that spy was trying to get women for him for his harem?"

"Draw your conclusions. Why not? They're always doing it. The Rajahs haven't much else to think about. They've other folks to collect the taxes for them and rule their district. They can't play polo and get drunk all the time. They pretty soon get weary of a woman, so they're always wanting new ones; and if there happens to be one they can't get, that's the one woman in the universe they've got to have."

"And that's why you're here?"

"Me and those Bengali troopers."

Joe smiled. Hawkes stiffened.

"Which of you loves the lady?"

Soldiers have to learn to sweat their tempers; only generals may grow apoplectic; Hawkes, as a sergeant, grinned appropriate complaisance and instantly made up his mind to take the one revenge available to a poor man faced by a rich man's impudence. He could bleed him. He could act the sycophant and make it pay. The point Joe had missed, and that Hawkes knew he had missed, was a certain vaguely evasive element of mystic chivalry connected with that night-watch by a British sergeant, several Indian troopers and, to make the mixture triply unconventional, a Yogi. What Joe had probably forgotten, if he ever knew it, was that the poor have a way of despising the rich for what they regard as ignorant ill-manners.

"Did you wish me to look for that girl you spoke about, sir?"

"Yes. You've one chance in a hundred million."

"Make it worth my while, sir."

"Very well. A thousand if you find her."

"A thousand pounds, sir—righto, that's fair enough."

Beddington had meant rupees; Hawkes knew that. "I'll have to hire a spy or two as well, sir, and I can't afford to pay them out of my pocket. I suppose you'll pay legitimate expenses? If you can let me have some money now, sir—?"

Joe gave him three hundred rupees in paper money. "Thanks, sir. I'll account for it, of course. The district collector asked me to bring you up to his bungalow afterwards. If you'll wait half a minute while I explain to those troopers, I'll see you on your way, sir."

But Joe had sensed the intention to lay siege to his pocketbook. The rich like being "worked," when they are aware of it, about as keenly as eels like being skinned alive. Generosity is one thing, submission to extortion something else.

"No thanks. I know the way. I'll walk. Will you tell the sais to take my horse home?"

"Very well, sir. Do you mind telling Mr. Cummings that I offered? Otherwise he might not understand."

Joe nodded, too displeased to trust himself to speak. Cummings had ordered him spied on, had he? What did the ass suspect him of? Souvenir hunting? Sacrilege? "I wonder," he thought, "who invented the lie that Government service develops genius? They're most of 'em payroll parasites, who'd be a failure in any other walk of life—grafters or else incompetents—or both."

The midnight of a wave of discontent submerged him. He was far more of a poet than a pirate—hated piracy, from too intimate knowledge of his mother's methods—hated most its subtler intricacies—liked open black-jack methods better as more honest. In such moods a poet is gloomier than any other mortal; and the gloomiest of poets is one who is tied to the chariot wheels of a Jupiter Chemical Works and a bank, by the spidery threads of a trust deed. Worse yet, when the spider in the center of it is his mother, because he must rebel, in despair, against nature herself who has ruled that a filial instinct shall be sometimes overwhelming, and maternal instinct not invariably sweet with the odor of selflessness.

"Damn!" he remarked aloud, and turned toward the Yogi for a last stare. Suddenly he strode into the pool of moonlight in front of the rock where the Yogi sat apparently in meditation. "Old Man—or ought I to call you Holy One?"

"Like unto like," said the Yogi. "Call me what you feel like calling me, that I may know you better. What you see in me is a reflection of that part of you that you desire to hide from others; the remainder of me is, to you, invisible."

"Be generous then. Show me some of it."

"I can't," said the Yogi. "Can I educate you in a minute? It has taken me not less than a million lives on earth to learn the little that I know now. That little does not include the art of changing you instantly into a seer."

"I'm blue," said Joe. "I'm as blue as a hungry nigger. You seem to enjoy life. How do you do it?"

"If you can see that I enjoy it, that is something."

"Come on, take a peep into my future. I'm a bit desperate. I feel like putting a bullet into my brain. Nevertheless, I know I won't do that."

"Are you afraid to?"

"No. If I were afraid I'd do it, I'd despise myself for being afraid. I can't see anything ahead for me but more and more melancholy—more and more of a kind of existence I hate, with less and less chance to escape it. To put it bluntly I'm in hell."

"O man from Jupiter!"

"That's what you called me before. What do you mean exactly?"

"You would not understand if I told you. In part, I mean this: Jupiter–Gemini rising: a disturbing influence. You are in hell, to make you boil and put forth. You are a thunderbolt that might, indeed, be quenched amid a seething sea of trouble but no umbrella nor any information can withstand you. You are an influence that will burst into another's life. And you will raise that other to an equal height with yours, or you will struggle upward to that other's height, or you will strangle yourself and that other, like two camels caught in one rope."

"When?"

"You are at the threshold."

"I feel as if I had my back toward hope and ambition and were wandering off into a wilderness."

"You are an egg that is about to hatch. The tight shell yields."

"Yogi, I feel like Orestes. You know who he was? He slew his mother."

"That Greek legend is a symbolism and an allegory. Orestes destroyed a tyranny, not a woman; and the hounds of his conscience were changed into heralds of happiness."

"But Clytemnestra died," said Joe.

"As I might also, did I interfere with thunderbolts," the Yogi answered. "Listen to me: Darkness is the womb whence Light is born. No hope is the matrix out of which Hope burgeons. Discontent is a growing pain; it is the pangs of roots imprisoned in clefts of a rock that shall crush them or be burst asunder. Cowards cry out and shrink and their roots die under them. But strong souls reach into the Silence for more energy, though it brings more pain; they seek relief from pain by bursting that which hurts. It is they whose branches ultimately reach the sky and become a cool bower such as the birds of Wisdom love."

"Am I a coward?" Joe asked.

"You have been. What you are now is your own affair. And what you shall be is the outcome of what you do. You have my leave to go and leave me to my laughter at the simpleness of things."

FROM THE BOOK OF THE YOGI-ASTROLOGER
RAM-CHITTRA GUNGA SINGH

Some say there is no God. I agree with them, though I deplore the waste of even as little wisdom as is necessary to assent to a statement so silly and useless. There is surely no God of the sort they imagined and against whom their imagination, such as it is, now stirs them to obscenity less important than the chattering grimaces of a monkey at his own reflection in a mirror.

There is no God made in man's image; and if there were, it would be of paramount importance to rebel against him, and to conquer and enslave him, and to put him to work to undo all evil. It would be better to pray to a photograph than to a God in man's image.

I did not study history, philosophy and economics, I did not ponder anthropology and practise what the ignorant revile as magic, neither did I peer through telescopes at universes millions of light-years distant, to discover there is no such God as atheists assail with arguments that were ancient in Gautama's day. Nay, madmen and drunkards, the lame and the halt and the blind, or the asses and pigs could have told me.

It was not to learn the nothingness of nothing that I sought humility, which is a quality that few have, and that only they who have it understand. I knew that any God I could imagine must be something less than my imagination; even as machinery, although it raises cities and lays low mountains, must be less than the least of the men who set their necks beneath its yoke.

I have been a high priest. I have stood within the Womb of Wonders. Secrets have been revealed to me, of arts and sciences, whose time is not yet. I know of continents long vanished, and of continents yet to be. I know what man has been, and what he will be. And because I know, I view with tolerance the self-importance of those teachers who, as it were, dissect the corpse of an idea in a quest for the secret of life. I may smile when they say I am ignorant, though I take heed that my smile springs not from malice. Doubtless I was once as they are. Doubtless they will be as I am. I know truly what they only seek a way of knowing. I know nothing about God.

What then? I know this; it has been revealed to me: I am. And with the am-ness that I am I can, by constant effort, overcome the nothingness I am not. Can I then know God? Nay. But I can know what That Unimaginable knows concerning me. I know a little of it. Nevertheless, if I should try to tell you, you would try to kill me, if not with mockery then with malice, because of your ignorant faith in mechanical means to an end that is nothing, nowhere. That would be a sin that I seek not to stir you to do; though if I knew that you could learn the truth by killing me, I would at once insist that you should kill, because in Truth there is neither wrong, nor regret, nor unreality.

Truth is hard to seek. Verily it is hard to seek, and the road is long thereto, because ignorance hates it. Ignorant men are the slaves of ignorance, their owner, whom they idolise in fear lest disobedience bring punishment. And slaves themselves shall set themselves free first, before they can even dimly see and understand enough even to try to follow that thin line of thought that leads into the Freedom of the Universal Brotherhood of Man.

III

"Cut me off and set me free. I'll be so grateful."

The dusty moonlit road toward Cummings' bungalow led between slattern walls and ill-kempt gardens, through a grove of trees that had been blackened by the fires of vagrants and nibbled by goats into naked poverty—on past cheap, pretentious cottages of Eurasians—past shuttered shops and littered byways where the Christians did business and a Catholic chapel, neat and lean and hungry-looking, raised a crucifix above a white iron roof. Then past the park, so called, where a caged tiger lay dreaming of life with his paws through the bars and his white teeth agleam in a grin of despair made monstrous by the moonlight. On past the club and the tennis courts—the mean hotel "for Europeans only," in a compound in which white-clad servants slept like corpses under trees that cast mottled shadows.

Joe was conscious of being followed. He supposed that the man with the basket of snakes, and the ayah, were taking advantage of his company for the protection it might give them; they kept far enough behind him not to intrude, near enough to be heard if they should cry for help, walking one on each side of the road like ghosts who did not like each other but were wafted on the same slow wind. He glanced over his shoulder at them only once or twice, afraid that if he glanced too often they might take that for an invitation to draw nearer. It occurred to him once that they might be spying on him. He stopped to see if they would stop. But they came on, so he dismissed the thought and continued on his way, his shoes white with dust and his thoughts black with boredom.

He resented being bored, it seemed so stupid. He knew that with his tastes and spiritual equipment he should find life fascinating. He was offended because he did not—even more offended because he vaguely understood the reason, and whose fault it was.

"There's nobody to blame but me," he muttered. Nevertheless, he knew that to throw up everything and leave his mother to find some other vizier of her despotism, would solve nothing. Running away would merely substitute for his mother's tyranny an even more degrading one of laziness and fear. It was not business he dreaded. He well knew there is poetry in commerce, art in high finance and music in the melody and flow of manufacture; as a matter of actual fact and with only a few exceptions, he had found the conversation of artists even more platitudinous and dull than that of his business intimates.

"Bankers, bishops, band-wagon conductors—painters and musicians—doctors—scientists—politicians—writers —nearly all of 'em are paralyzed by public opinion. It kills 'em if they dare to stick their head out of the herd-thought and—got it, by God! I've got it! My mother is herd-thought individualized!"

He began to walk faster, with more resilience in his stride. He had begun to understand his enemy. "I've been tilting at windmills," he muttered. "No more windmills!" Once Joe Beddington had grasped the nature of a mistake he was not given to repeating it, although he would deliberately repeat one again and again until he understood it. He was built that way—so constituted. It was that that had made him suffer so beneath his mother's yoke. He had not understood her. He had sometimes thought she was a devil in a human skin. Not less frequently he had suspected himself of being one, since who else than a devil could hate his own mother? He had wasted breath and patience trying to argue with her. And he had feared her. "Might as well try to argue with the sea—be afraid of the sea."

"Public opinion? Wow! The thing to do with that stuff is to make it—mold it—navigate it. Look out for the tides and storms and currents. I can do it. Damn, I understand her now—I've been a blind superstitious idiot!"

He walked faster, leaving Chandri Lal and the ayah far behind him. He had forgotten the temple ceremony and the Yogi. He had forgotten Hawkes.

"She's public opinion. She's it, idealized. Greedy—fat—cunning—tyrannical—cruel—jealous—envious—intolerant—a hypocrite—a coward—opportunist—liar. She is all that—and yet she isn't. I've got to separate 'em in my mind. How come? That needs puzzling out."

He was excited. He had forgotten boredom. He had forgotten the dull inertia that usually crept into some corner of his brain when he thought of his mother. He had seen, as it were, a crack between her and her despotism, into which he could drive, he believed, his new-found wedge. It did not occur to him that he was using arguments familiar to king's sons, to rebels against the divine right of kings, and to all the arch-iconoclasts of history. It seemed to him he was the first discoverer of something new.

"Mother," he said to himself, "is a victim. It isn't she who uses power. Power uses her."

In a flash, as a man sees in a dream cause and effect and process simultaneously, he discerned the tactics and the strategy that he must use.

"Separate her from the power in my own mind. She's my mother. *It* isn't. It isn't a disease exactly, but call it one for the sake of clarity. It causes a disease. She's as good as mad this minute—mad with a cold intelligence that outwits anything human, her own humanity included. It's as merciless to her as to anyone else; it makes her ridiculous as well as greedy—makes her stupid in her hour of triumph. Good God! How stupid *I've* been. The thing for me to do, from now on, is to attack *it*, not her—and not to attack it like a damned fool and be overwhelmed. Guile—subtlety. . ."

Absorbed in thought he walked beyond the lane between the bougainvilleas, where the signboard bearing Cummings, the district collector's name, was clearly legible in the moonlight.

"God, but I'll need to be subtle!" He noticed he had walked too far, and turned back. "She's on *its* side. It's her God and her glory. Give her half a hint that I'm awake at last, and she'll kill me as she killed Dad. He was half-awake before the end. I think he knew she killed him. She broke his will. That broke his health. She made him sign that trust deed and then put him on his back and hired three nurses." He laughed a little. "Funny I never thought of that before. How many doctors—five?—six? And they couldn't agree what to call the disease. I can name it for them. Octopus-itis! She strangled his will. He simply quit and left her victrix on a bloodless battlefield. Bloodless? He hadn't a drop of blood left in him. I wonder if he loved her. I don't. But I don't hate her any longer. And I won't quit. I'll be damned if I'll quit."

He turned up the lane between the bougainvilleas—a narrow curved lane rising steeply to the garden surrounding Cummings' bungalow. The gate was open; he made scarcely a sound as he entered because the dust lay deep on the tiles of the garden path. The bungalow faced eastward and the garden gate was to the south, so that he had to approach one end of the long verandah where there was a screen of painted reeds to provide privacy; that and the shadows combined to make him invisible from the verandah or from the windows in front of the house. He had no intention of eavesdropping, but his mother's voice was too distinct not to be recognized; and to that he had been forced to listen since he was a child. It was a habit.

"What would life be without our illusions? And who knows that the illusions are not more genuine than what we think is real?"

Then the voice of Cummings: "Stark reality—stark reality—sordid grim reality—that is the life of a Government official, Mrs. Beddington. If I had one illusion left, I would not know what to do with it."

His mother: "When I was a little girl my dolls provided the illusion. I had a boy-doll that was the inspiration for most of my dreams. I have that doll even to-day, tucked away in a drawer. Sawdust, I suppose you will say—a Little Lord Fauntleroy suit—a yellow wig—a wax face, with the paint gone where I kissed it—diamond buckles made of cheap glass—one eye missing. But around that doll I built my dreams of a prince charming who should come into my life and make it romantic."

"Did he?"

"Not yet. I am like Queen Elizabeth, still hoping. Money, yes. Mr. Beddington possessed the gift of making money. He could think of nothing else. We were not romantic."

"Money, to me," said Cummings, "is the most romantic theme on earth. Money—the blood of nations—the key to independence—the essence of power. They tell you money can't buy happiness. I say it can."

Sharply: "Is that you, Joe?"

Joe mounted the steps. He merely nodded to Cummings—understood him, and lacked enough hypocrisy to pretend to feel more than tolerantly civil. But he stared at his mother. She was full in moonlight, all two hundred pounds of her, in a dress that he knew had made a modiste nearly frantic; she invariably wore out anyone who waited on her; her gowns were trophies wrung from defeated artistes whose profit was gone in time and overtime, and whose bills were paid when Mrs. Beddington saw fit. Such ingrates sometimes even sued her.

She looked magnificent. Joe knew she had saved that dress for an "occasion." Her conversation, too, was the sort that she reserved for disarming strangers when she had drastic ends in view. He wondered what design she had on Cummings. He could see at a glance that she had pumped him to a point where she knew the exact limits of his imagination and could foresee to a fraction how he would react to any given impulse. She would presently provide the impulse—not that that made any difference, or was of the slightest interest to her son; but he could not help wondering why she should waste her arts on such a futile person.

"Ready to go to the hotel, Mother? Shall I call for the rickshaw?"

"Not yet. I was telling Mr. Cummings—"

"Sit down, Beddington. Sit down and have a whisky with us. What's your hurry? You Americans are always on the run, and what on earth do you gain by it? I understand you even hurry to your funerals in a motor-hearse. I think that comical. If you hurried off to bed now, you would probably only lie awake inventing a way of doing twice as much in half the time tomorrow."

"Probably," said Joe. "The mistake, of course, that we made was to insist on independence. We ought to have kissed King George on both cheeks. Then we'd have been taught, like India, how to behave."

He was sorry at once that he had said it. Cummings was too futile to be worth snubbing and too dull to enjoy an argument with, but an argument now was inevitable; he had invited one; and, what made it worse, he could see that he had played into his mother's hand in some way. Desperately he sought to switch the conversation to another subject:

"Tell me about the nautch girls at that temple."

Cummings jumped at that. He was the type that loves to display familiarity with subjects on which he can't be checked up very easily. It opened the way too, for a retort.

"Don't try making love to them. Be advised by me and control your curiosity and instincts, both, as long as you stay here."

Joe let that pass. Cummings looked pleased with himself and exchanged a glance with Joe's mother. Middle-aged, fat bachelor he might be, but he knew how to give a younger man the right cue at the proper moment. He desired her to appreciate it, and apparently she did; she could disguise her feelings from almost anyone except her son, who looked the other way. Joe yawned and Cummings cleared his throat:

"Those are very unusual nautch girls. There are none other like them in India. Generally speaking, I regret to say, the Indian nautch girls are a blot on the country's reputation. They're a problem very difficult for us to deal with. They're a social evil so protected by religious custom and priestly privilege that no government can do anything about it. They belong to the temple. They're married to trees or to graven images. Their morals generally speaking—judged, that is, by our standards—are—well—they haven't any."

"How are they recruited?" Joe asked.

"All sorts of ways. Many of them are the daughters of nautch girls. Some are the daughters of well-to-do, high-caste Indians who dedicate them to the temple, usually along with an endowment. Some of them—the less privileged ones—are child-widows, who are given that means of escape from the otherwise deadly existence of the Hindu widow, who became the slave of her husband's parents. A few of them are the daughters of wealthy public prostitutes. As a rule they are all intensively trained, extremely highly educated in the legendary mysticism of the cult to which they are attached, good-looking—and more wicked than you could readily make yourself believe."

"Those girls I saw tonight," said Joe, "were marvelous. I've seen convent children in the States who looked much less spiritual. Loose women don't look as they did—at least, not any that I ever saw."

Cummings suppressed the interruption with a fatly important hand:

"I was coming to that. This temple is unique. It is very ancient and was formerly Buddhist. A century or so ago its Hindu priests were partly reconverted to the Buddhist teaching. Blending one traditional philosophy with another, as I understand it, they were able to discard the grosser forms of superstition and retain the essence of both teachings, with the result that something new and very remarkably good grew out of it. They retained the secrecy, but not the exclusiveness—to some extent the theory of caste, but not its system. I am told they sent some very highly educated priests to Europe to study the better known types of Christianity, from which they learned a great deal. To this day they are astonishingly tolerant of Christian missionaries. They own all the land hereabouts and could have made it next to impossible for Christian missionaries to obtain a foothold; but what they actually did was to let them have land for schools and so on at a rent so nominal that it amounted to a gift. They're funny. I believe they're trying to convert the missionaries. But they won't let any outsider inside their temple, and they're rather touchy about strangers witnessing their temple rites. They're on very good terms, by the way, with the Catholic priest, who has established a hospital, to which they contribute very liberally from the temple funds."

Mrs. Beddington purred. She almost looked like a well fed cat when there was a mouse to be coaxed within reach of her paws. Her bulk seemed all softly luxurious comfort. She exuded invitation and appreciation. Her son might recognize, even by lamplight, a certain hard glint in her eyes; but a mouse, such as Cummings, saw nothing but generous instincts oozing from a rather handsome widow.

"Oh, how fascinating, Mr. Cummings! What a wonderful life you must lead, with all this opportunity to study life's drama! Most of us waste our lives, don't we? You should write a book—truly you should."

"Ah!" remarked Cummings, but he deceived no one, not even himself. He was much too lazy mentally to write anything except a cut-and-dried report. However, he enjoyed the flattery. Joe wondered again why his mother possibly could wish to ensnare such a futile person—and again, from habit, not from sympathy, he straightway played into her hand.

"My mother loves to look into the guts of things," he volunteered.

Cummings blinked; he thought the expression coarse; he was already unconsciously taking the side of the mother against the son. "Your mother strikes me as a very able woman, if I may say so without offense.

It's rare to find intelligence and great wealth under the same hat, so to speak. If I had had such a mother as yours, I think I would have had more of a career." The imputation that Joe Beddington was a loafer in his estimation was only vaguely veiled.

Joe glanced at his mother and smiled to himself. He changed the subject, abruptly:

"I'd like to see the inside of that temple."

"Impossible, my dear man, so it's no use wishing. But why see it? Gloom—dirt—images of gods on ancient walls—obscene—monstrous—stupid. There are lots of other places where you can see it all, price two rupees, and a picture postcard thrown in."

"You know, I suppose."

"I can guess. One doesn't live in India for twenty-five years without knowing what temples are like. Archeology, in my humble opinion, is an over-rated subject. It's like art in general, which got the Greeks nowhere—got China, Egypt, India nowhere. Art, I take it, is a sign of decadence. As soon as a nation takes up art it goes to pieces and gets conquered."

It was aimed, of course, at Joe. Joe's mother understood, and relished it.

"Joe, I think, would rather be an artist than a business man," she remarked. "He paints really quite beautifully when he has the time."

It was a favorite trick of hers to tempt confidence and sympathy by hinting that her only son was a disappointing person. She was equally ready at any moment to advertise him as the greatest genius alive. It all depended on the circumstances and the viewpoint of her victim. Joe wondered again what she could see worth conquering in Cummings; he knew that her perception was uncanny and her sense for intrigue and strategy Bismarckian; but why pick such a specimen as Cummings? Why waste genius? He gave it up.

"Let's go home to bed," he suggested, yawning. "Shall I shout for the rickshaw?"

Mrs. Beddington decided she would walk. Perhaps she wished to intimate to Cummings that she *could* walk in spite of her weight. Joe knew that she hated to have dust invade her shoes. However, it was only a short way to the hotel; if she should turn bad-tempered he could endure it during those few minutes. He nodded to Cummings—shook hands, since Cummings seemed to wish that—and waited at the foot of the verandah steps, signing to the sleepy rickshaw coolies to go along home. His mother was in no haste.

"A delightful evening. What a time we two had until that gloomy person interrupted us! Imagine my telling you all about my dolls! It must have been the magic of the moonlight and your hospitality. Some day you must tell me all about the princess you have cherished in your dreams—I believe you're as romantic as I am under that proconsular mask of yours."

Cummings almost writhed with pleasure at being likened to a grim proconsul. He had missed promotion. He was a little lucky if the truth were known, not to have been sent home last year on his half-pay.

"Romantic?" he answered. He would be anything to please her, but it was hard to think of phrases on the spur of the moment. "Ah, but I have never dared to speak of it."

"You shall tell me," said Mrs. Beddington. "Confess—you owe me that revenge. Besides, it will do you good to talk of it. Romance dies, if it is not shared with some one. And romance is good for all of us. Good night."

On the way home Joe kept silence until his mother paused to kick the dust out of her shoes, holding his shoulder to balance herself. "Joe," she remarked suddenly, "I wish you could be more polite to people. You were positively rude to that man. It was disgraceful. Why, you couldn't even shake hands without scowling."

"He's such an ass," Joe answered.

"He's nothing of the kind. I like him."

"Mother, you know he's an ass. What are you planning? To make him find that purely hypothetical cholera baby? I'll bet he bungles it. Probably he'll foist a sweeper's daughter on you—or perhaps a half-caste brat with rickets and a chi-chi accent. Then what?"

Mrs. Beddington removed her other shoe, shook out its contents, replaced it and then waited for her son to kneel and fasten up the strap.

"I have all along intended *you* should find that child," she answered. "It will give you a chance to use those wits you are so proud of. When I have a hunch I am never far wrong. I know the child lives. I know it, I know it. So you look for her, and use all your ingenuity. Meanwhile, I will cultivate Mr. Cummings, so that in case you have to overstep the boundaries a bit there will be some one to stand between you and the lawyers."

That was one of her pet expressions. It made Joe

shudder, since it always meant that she was contemplating treachery of some kind that she would not even hint at until it would be too late to prevent her. He answered grimly: "I have taken steps already."

"You speak as if I had asked you to cut your throat. Listen, Joe. I won't have you being sulky with me. I won't stand it for a minute. If there's one thing I will not endure, it's disloyalty. Your father knew you all right when he had that deed drawn. He knew what he was doing when he put that clause in giving me the right to cut you off by a stroke of a pen without a nickel. One would think, to see your long face, that you were jealous of a child you'd never seen."

Joe laughed. "Come on, Mother," he said, "there's pen and ink at the hotel. Cut me off and set me free. I'll be so grateful that—"

She interrupted him. "Joe, I'm nervous. Can't you see I need comforting? Are you so mean you won't oblige me during the few years I have to live? Isn't it soon enough to be independent when I'm dead and gone? Do you wish me dead?"

He yielded—put his arm around her. She was as well as he was, and he knew it. She was insincere; he knew that also. But whenever she ceased threatening and coaxed him, there always stole over him that feeling of helplessness that was so like the effect of a drug that it made him feel worthless—even wicked. He had to take an antidote for it; when his mother had gone to bed he carried out a chair into the compound and made charcoal sketches of servants sleeping in the shadows under gaunt wind-twisted trees.

FROM THE BOOK OF THE YOGI-ASTROLOGER RAM-CHITTRA GUNGA SINGH

Ye sit at my feet learning, and I teach. But I sit at the feet of others, whom ye know not, neither can ye see nor understand them. But as THEY teach me, so I teach you. It is as water that flows into pool after pool, until it becomes at last a mighty river. Does the sea know where the springs are, whence the river came? It is enough that the river flows into the sea and the brine is freshened.

It is true, too, that the river has its banks and the sea its boundaries; these serve their purpose, failing only when they stand too stubbornly. Are not they the best banks that having gathered water, guide it so that it flows free and unobstructed? Are they not bad banks that withstand the water and confine it, producing a swamp and a marsh wherein the mist breeds and the pestilence abides?

It is so with mothers. He who will be born into the world must seek a womb as water seeks a channel. As a pool is his mother; she gathers him until he flows forth into the pond of infancy, and thence again into the sun lit lake of youth; thence onward into the river of life. And if she lets him flow, she does well; lo, she sends him on his way rejoicing and herself is filled again—filled full until she overflows with spiritual prana that shall follow along the way her son went. These be the mothers who love their sons. In love is wisdom.

But there are women who are fools, whose womb is as a cavern in the clay that chokes and smothers. It is these who send their sons forth loaded with their own filth to defile all waters that they meet. They confine their sons. They strangle them. They lead them in sloth into swamps where inertia breeds and foul ideas lay eggs to hatch forth monstrous sin.

IV

"You wish to question me?"

Joe sat at breakfast on the hotel verandah, prodding export bacon with an import fork and wondering why God had gone to all the trouble to create the universe. His mother had sent for him to her bedroom and had made him sign some documents of no particular importance except to nine unfortunates in New York, whose jobs had now ceased to exist. "Just like her. It's murder, as I sit here—long-distance murder by mail. They weren't rowing their weight. But is she? And am I? Are dividends the one criterion? If one of those poor devils—Weismuller—doesn't commit suicide, I'll take my hat off to him—sick wife—seven kids—a mortgage—probably car and piano half paid for. Dad never did that kind of dirt. He flogged old horses, but he didn't turn them out to starve. It was the last nail in the old man's coffin when he learned about her firing all the old-timers. She has more than quadrupled the money Dad left. He never gave a cent to charity, and she has given away more than he earned in his whole lifetime. Nevertheless, he was human. And she isn't. Damn! I hate her."

Gone was last night's resolution. He looked around him at the white-clad servants standing along the verandah rail in abject adoration of his mother's millions. There were far too many of them; she had insisted on traveling like a circus, as he phrased it, with a private car on the railway and a private crew of rickshaw coolies, to say nothing of interpreters, bearers, a cook, two cook's assistants, and a boy.

Beyond them, beneath the compound trees were unnumbered job-hunters, cheek by jowl with beggars, conjurers, acrobats and "guides." Among them he noticed Chandri Lal with his basket of cobras; and, not very far from Chandri Lal, the ayah. They added in some vague way to his annoyance. It was ridiculous to think they might be spying on him. For whom could they be spying? But why else were they here? Why did they keep on staring at him?

On the verandah was a horde of peddlers, opening their boxes if he as much as glanced in their direction, meanwhile arranging trash for his inspection—arranging the stuff so that he could hardly step off the verandah without treading on some of it. Pariah dogs were sniffing around the compound. Nine unpleasant-looking crows, with bright eyes on the breakfast food and obscene voices making probably appropriate remarks, were perched on the rail at the far end. The proprietor, smugly subservient, stood with his back to the doorway where he could watch the merchants and keep account of his rake-off from the price of anything they might succeed in selling. There were no other guests in the hotel; there was that much relief.

However, presently came Hawkes, slapping his leg with a swagger-cane and much too perky to harmonize with Joe's mood.

"I suppose he wants more money."

Joe decided not to give him any. He turned his back; resumed dissection of the embalmed remains of a Chicago pig, fried to a boracic cinder—prodding at it. But he could not carry on; two pale eggs, like the eyes of indigestion, stared up from the plate and put him out of countenance. The grease had grown cold; a fat fly struggled in it, toast, weak marmalade and strong tea. Hawkes invaded the verandah, perfectly aware of the annoyance he was causing; soldiering equips a man with a brass face for irritability to grind itself against. No snubbing Hawkes.

"Good morning, sir. I've news."

"Sit down then. Light your pipe. Tea's rotten. Have some."

"Thanks, sir, I've had breakfast. And if I'd tell the news myself you might think I was lying."

"There would be nothing abnormal about that. I'm quite used to disbelieving people."

"Yes, sir. And I want my thousand pounds. I'd like to take you straight to the source where I got my information."

"What information?"

"The identity and present whereabouts of that young woman that you spoke of last night."

Habit froze Joe's face at once. He had learned from his mother. Show her, black on white, a soundly reasoned statement and she would pitilessly and without shame rend it until no one but herself believe it even worth another moment's thought. "Remember this, Joe: if it's good, it won't be worse for being doubted. The more you can make others doubt it, the cheaper it's yours in the long run. So don't believe anyone—anything, until you've seen all sides of it. Make others sick of hanging on. That's business." He had learned in the end to doubt her also. A mere stranger such as Hawkes had no chance to get under his guard.

"I have letters to write. Sorry."

Hawkes, a trifle overeager to persuade him, made a wrong move: "Sir, you saw me punch a man last night. His gang is after that young woman."

"Sounds bad. As I told you, if she's fallen too far down the social scale my mother would not be interested."

Hawkes saw his mistake. He decided to show his own quality and see what came of it.

"All right, sir. I've done my part. Here's that three hundred you gave me for expenses. I don't need it."

He laid the money on the table. Joe let it stay, with the corner of one eye watching Hawkes; it might be Hawkes' way of suggesting a tip. But Hawkes stepped away from the table.

"Send for me, sir, any time you wish. I'll tell your servant where to find me."

"Why not tell your news?" Joe asked him.

"No, sir. If you'll take it straight as man to man—it may sound fishy, but it's fact—I wouldn't take a thousand pounds to be called a liar by you or anyone."

Joe had seen senators sell their souls for that price. He had bought the souls, and found them not worth buying.

"I will pay you ten pounds for your news," he answered.

"Keep it, sir. As one man to another, you agreed to pay a thousand pounds if I find the girl."

"All right. Bring her to me."

"Not so easy. If I fetched her, supposing she'd come, who's to prove she's it? No, sir, proof first—that's fair. Then when you set eyes on her I get my thousand and no argument."

Joe still suspected him. However, he heard his mother's voice. She was getting up, and finding fault. He knew that mood. He leaped at anything to escape her.

"All right, I'll go with you." He caught the proprietor's eye. "Two horses!"

"*Ek* particularly dum!" Hawkes added. "Make it sudden."

That Hindu had noticed the interrelation of speed and profit when providing for Americans. With the tail of his turban flying, scandalized crows on the wing, and the pariah dogs in flight in front of him, he scooted across the compound to the stable, where a needy relative-contractor kept starved horses and well fed flies. Long before Mrs. Beddington's voice announced through an open window that her shoes were no place for cockroaches, two unenthusiastic horses drooped in front of the verandah. Joe was swift; in another moment he and Hawkes, at a comfortless trot in the dust outside the compound wall, could hear her doing her worst to make the universe all wretched. Joe shuddered.

"Always that way when she has done dirt. Justifies herself by torturing some other helpless human. Then she'll feed the pariah dogs on buttered toast and gyp the peddlers out of half their junk. By the time I return she'll feel pious and want me to take her to call on missionaries."

He hardly noticed where Hawkes was leading him.

He remembered passing a squadron of native cavalry out exercising horses—might not have remembered it except that he was glad their officers did not halt to talk to him—as likely as not damned decent fellows who would invite him to call on the mess. He could enjoy meeting them if it weren't for his mother; she would insist on their being introduced to her. She would probably make their mess a gift of some useless ornament picked up in Kashmir. She would ask the Colonel's confidential advice about him, Joe's, character. He understood her game from *a* to *izzard*—understood, yet could not defeat it. She was his mother, worse luck. There are limits to what conscience will let a man do to his mother, even if he hates her, for accumulated reasons.

Knowing resentment would give him a headache he tried to interest himself in the streets and the early traffic. They had reached the heart of the native city almost before he realized it. He remembered now that there were things to see in this place. There were said to be architectural wonders—freaks that had set the antiquarians at loggerheads with thousands of years of differences between their estimated dates. He began to notice some of them—amazing carvings on patched walls at the end of mean streets, old and new all fitted into one another as if an earthquake, or perhaps a dozen earthquakes, had flattened the city and, after each cataclysm, men had rebuilt with the old material. One image that he saw was upside down—a dozen tons of it incorporated in a wall whose greater part was almost modern brick—perhaps a thousand-year-old brick, or even more recent than that.

It was a hodge-podge city. Corrugated iron side by side with ancient masonry and carved teak blackened by the course of centuries. Trees in which monkeys sported. Sacred trees a-flutter with scraps of rag and colored paper to remind some godlet of a bribe paid and a promise taken, in return, for granted. Walls without windows. Shops all unglazed window, with a wall behind them. Thatch, tile, rotting canvas—and a roof here and there whose ponderous calm suggested destiny perceived and understood by conjurers in stone. A Moslem mosque, chaste and pearl-gray in the shadows of high trees, frowned at from a hundred feet away by the obscene divinities carved on the gloom of a Hindu temple. Stinks—and then a breath of Oriental perfume—spices, dry dung and the horizonless scent of piles of gunny-sacks. An elephant or two—incessant streams of laden asses—bullock-carts—innumerable sweating porters, threading their way through a crowd whose black umbrellas cheapened sunlight. Vivid colors splashed on shadow—dark holes—dinginess drowned in golden light where clouds of parakeets as green as emeralds shot screaming from tree to tree. Veiled women—unveiled girls with white teeth dipping brass jars at a fountain—Ford cars—insolent policemen swinging yellow clubs. And then, when they paused at a trough that was a godlet's lap, to let the horses drink, none else than Chandri Lal, his flat, round basketful of cobras on his head. The ayah, draped in dingy black, was less than half a street behind him.

"How in hell did those two follow, at the speed we've come?"

"The same as rats, sir. They know scores of shortcuts where a horse can't get through."

"What are they spying on me for?"

"They're not spying. It's the jackal system. Follow a tiger long enough and something happens. It's like that piece in the Bible, sir, about the woman and her importunity—except that those two don't know what they want. What turns up can't be worse than what they've got, that's all."

Joe doubted it. He half suspected Hawkes of having told those two to follow, and he was still in a mood to be quarrelsome. He had an acrid comment hesitating on his teeth, when a *bhisti* went by swishing water from his goatskin *mussuk*. Just as no man can slay even himself in the presence of one of Leonardo's paintings, so none can harbor hatred with the smell in his nostrils of freshly sprinkled dry earth. Perfectly unconscious of the cause, Joe let his natural tolerance creep up like sap and he decided that to be a circus for whoever chose to stare at him was better fun than doing nothing. He, too, was a spectator, growing curious.

"Let's go."

Hawkes led through byways to a sunlit court, whose paving stones were masonry from ancient walls. Grass grew here and there between the cracks. In places, faintly visible, were carvings worn smooth by the tread of centuries. The buildings were all ancient, except one, a little lower than the rest, that occupied a corner and was white, in contrast to the gray-green dinginess of all the others. It had awnings, striped red and yellow, and the two-story wall that faced the street was pierced with as many windows as a colonial house in Salem. The windows had muslin curtains, clean and trim. The flat roof was entirely tented over and hung with a line of paper Chinese lanterns.

"Here we are," said Hawkes. He hitched the horses to a big hook near the front door. "Can you guess what that is, sir? That's a hook off a siege-gun carriage that was drawn by elephants at Plassy. There's a story to it; but maybe she'll tell you herself."

He used his swagger-cane to beat a tattoo on the brassbound teak front door. Then he lifted the latch and the top half opened. "Anybody home?"

A parrot answered—"Cup o' caw-fee—Polly want a cup o' caw-fee?" Then footsteps on a tiled floor. Suddenly a smell of lavender, and some one in larkspur-light-blue linen stood framed in the door like a painting, with dimness behind her.

"Hawkesey! Well, come in. My house is a mess; you must excuse it—but you soldiers notice everything."

She had snow white hair brushed well back from her forehead and pinned in an old-fashioned knot. Her eyes were almost baby-blue; they mocked the thin line of a mouth that seemed to disapprove of such amusement as those eyes insisted on enjoying. She had the calm chin of a fighter who fights seldom, having also diplomatic skill and self-restraint besides unconquerable courage. She wore a gold chain and a locket. The sleeves at each wrist were pinned with old cameo brooches. Wrinkled, used but well-kept, very slightly built—sixty years of age or thereabouts, but upright as an arrow and, beyond words, beautiful. She drew the lower latch and glanced at Hawkes' boots as she swung the half-door open. Hawkes kicked the wall and flicked the dust off with his handkerchief.

"Mr. Beddington—Miss Annie Weems."

She bowed, appraising Joe, then suddenly shook hands, as if the blue eyes had discovered something that the lips refused to tell. They were a wee mite stern, those lips—a bit convinced, perhaps, of masculine infidelity, deplorable but comprehensible and not beyond forgiveness.

"My school," she said, turning to lead the way in. She turned as neatly as they used to in the days of quadrilles and crinolines. "Today's a holiday. No pupils to tidy up. You mustn't look."

They followed her across a red-tiled floor that was as clean as the floor of a dairy. There were benches of scrubbed wood, mats folded and piled in a corner, a blackboard, a desk and a chair and rows of bookshelves. There was not even dust in the beams of sunlight slanting through the windows. Nothing seemed soiled or out of place, and nothing even faded except the flowers; those were yesterday's—the only hint of Asia; all the rest was neat New England, even to the ribboned cat that came and rubbed against Joe's trouser legs.

"There, Kitty likes you. I have never known her to make a mistake."

She led past a grandfather clock in a passage that contained a dresser made of maplewood, its shelves loaded with Derby chinaware, into a room that might have been a parlor in a Massachusetts village, except that there were no stuffed birds in glass cases and no samplers. There was a piano built not less than half a century ago and varnished to match the maple chairs and gateleg table. Flowers everywhere—framed paintings of New England landscapes—a parrot perch with seed and watercups at either end. Rag rugs on a polished teak floor. Nothing lacking but a fireplace—and in place of that a white stone altar carved with long-stemmed lotus flowers, built into the strong foundations of the house by pious Hindus, and now used by the cat as a snoozing place between two long-stemmed Copenhagen vases.

"You wish to question me?"

She chose the armchair near the window and sat facing Joe and Hawkes, hands in her lap. Joe hesitated. Since she put it that way he felt he had no right to question her. Hawkes intervened:

"Miss Weems has run a private school here since—how long is it, Miss?"

"Twenty-seven years."

"Anyhow," said Hawkes, "for seventeen years or more I believe she has known the girl you're looking for."

Miss Weems sat silent, mouth firm, eyes alight with interest and something else that might have been excitement. Joe crossed his legs and began calmly:

"One and twenty years ago—about—I don't remember dates—Carrie Morgan, who was my mother's youngest bridesmaid, married a young professor of botany named Owen Wilburforce and came to this part of India. We were informed she gave birth to a daughter; she is supposed to have written to that effect to an aunt in Charleston, but the letter has been lost. She and her husband are supposed to have died of cholera not long afterward, and their effects were said to have been burned in a raid by dacoits, who set fire to the house they lived in. But there was a plausible, undocumented story that an ayah—said to have been a wet-nurse—carried away the baby and concealed it. The girl should now be twenty years old, more or less. Hawkes appears to believe that you know a young woman who might be that one. And that you even have what you consider proof of her identity. Is that so?"

Annie Weems looked straight at him and blinked. She produced a plain white hemstitched handkerchief and touched her lips. She glanced at the cat—at the parrot—and back at Joe. Her eyes were steady now; a catch in her throat; she swallowed before answering:

"It may be."

ANTIDOTE

Take a fact or two for granted. It is possible to think,
Though pundits may not like it, that perhaps the
        angels wink
When sundry psychoanalysts adept at splitting hairs
Trace causes of coincidence to hypothetic lairs
Wherein, said savants, asservate, repressions of a force
(That other savants angrily repudiate, of course)
Through multiplying nothing by the square of
        nothing more
Alchemise a complex where a conscience was before.
It saves a lot of argument, it keeps yourself in hand
To swap the pap of publicists for Paternosters—and
Take Providence for granted, when the
        Weisenheimers rant
Freudian psychology and psychopathic cant.

V

> *"Amrita is a sort of Joan of Arc."*

It felt like Sunday. From without there were only a few sounds; someone, probably a servant, moved about a courtyard. A crow cawed on a nearby roof. Annie Weems picked up her reading spectacles from beside the book on the table, tried them on, and put them down again.

"About the proof, Miss?" Hawkes suggested.

"Judas Iscariot once sold Jesus," she retorted. Slapped down, as it were, Hawkes prodded his boot with his swagger-cane. Joe felt curiously pleased, but cautious.

"Hawkes," he said, "will be paid a stipulated sum if the girl is produced along with proof of her identity. That was the agreement. But it might not be wise to let her know who she is, unless she knows already; nor who is looking for her—you see, my mother has no actual obligation. Do you get my meaning?"

"No, sir." Annie Weems understood perfectly. Joe knew she did. However she was entitled to insist on clarity.

"I mean," he said, "she may be better off in India. Having been brought up in this country among colored people, she may be like a fish out of water in the United States. If she should happen to learn she is being looked for, she might jump to false conclusions. She has no legal claim on us—none whatever."

"You would like to look her over, so to speak, without her knowing why?"

"That's it," said Joe.

"You would need to be far more clever than I have any right to suppose you are," Annie Weems answered. "She is neither deaf, dumb, blind nor unintelligent. I have had her in this school, at intervals, for nearly sixteen years. I have not yet learned how to deceive her, or to keep her uninformed about anything that has stirred her interest. However, you can try."

"Does she talk English?" Joe asked nervously. "I mean—"

"You are afraid of a chi-chi accent? If she has one I can't detect it. Of course, my ear may be ruined by long association with Indian children. But I taught her to sing at this piano. She has recited, and acted, most of the female parts from Shakespeare, in this room. She has also read such parts of the Bible as are fit for decent folk. I can't detect a trace of accent."

"How long have you known she was not an Indian child?" Joe asked her.

"From the beginning."

"Did no one else know?"

"Others did. Some temple priests, for instance. She has been partly brought up in the temple. The priests have been very kind to her."

"Couldn't you have saved her from that?" Joe asked. He kept the note of horror from his voice, but it found means to express itself—vibration, probably.

"You would have had me turn her over to the Government?"

"I suppose, something of the sort."

"They would have sent her to one of the Government schools, or to a mission orphanage," said Annie Weems.

"Are those so terrible?"

"Prisons." She pursed her lips. "They are sometimes sanitary. They are places where children are taught to be hypocrites—cowardly thinkers, thoroughly mistrusting anything that has spiritual value. I tried to save her from that fate—so have the priests."

"Is she a Christian?"

"I know no way of answering that. You must wait until you get an opportunity to ask God, that is to say, if it is any of your business."

Annie Weems was becoming belligerent; the blue eyes glistened with enjoyment of the pugnacity at the corners of her mouth. Joe declined combat. He had tact enough to retire gracefully, and sense of strategy enough to leave that kind of conversation to his mother.

"She sounds interesting," he said. "I don't doubt she is a credit to your care and teaching. I would like to see her at your convenience. Meanwhile, Hawkes said something about proofs of her identity."

Anne Weems glanced at Hawkes, who nodded and stood up, hesitated and then started for the front door.

"See that she cleans her feet, and don't admit that person with the cobras. I will not have them or him in my house."

"Yes, Miss."

Hawkes strode out. His clean white uniform looked somehow dirty in that spotless room. But that, perhaps, was produced by suggestion; if one could judge by his eye and the set of his mouth, the reference to Judas Iscariot had bitten more than skin-deep.

Joe thought swiftly. "You are sending for the ayah? Does this explain why she was spying on me? Does she know the girl? How does she know I am interested?"

"Sergeant Hawkes has told me that you saw the temple ceremony last night. There is a Yogi there—I think you had some conversation with him. It was he to whom the ayah took the child the moment it was weaned, and it was he who gave it to the temple's priests. She suspects any white man who talks to that Yogi; she is afraid her priestess-princess may be taken from her."

"What is the girl's name, by the way?"

"Amrita."

Hawkes returned, the ayah following in time to hear the name Amrita. The yellowish whites of her eyes and her wrinkled face betrayed alarm, although she plainly did not fear Miss Weems, whom she salaamed with respectful familiarity. It was from Joe that she shrugged herself, wrapping her dingy black cotton stuff around her as if that might serve as shield against his iron-gray eyes. Joe noticed that she kept her fingers crossed and made curious furtive gestures with her right hand.

Hawkes sat down again. The ayah remained standing. There was silence for a moment, interrupted only by the parrot who appeared to know the ayah.

"Amal!" the bird cried. "Amal! Polly want a cracker!"

The ayah smiled and fell again on the defensive, scared of Joe and none too confident of Hawkes whom she seemed to suspect of telling tales. With a gesture of her arms within the long black garment she enwrapped herself in silence.

Annie Weems knew how to manage her. "Amal, I want you to tell this sahib why you followed him."

The ayah seemed to understand, but she had the excuse as yet that English was not her language. Itching to answer, she sulked. Annie Weems translated into the vernacular, and waited. Suddenly the ayah's pent up misery escaped—first two tears, like drops of water seeping through cracks in weakening masonry—then floods of tears—and then the dam went down in a torrent of words that tumbled over one another, galloping and plunging, ends of sobbing sentences surging to swamp their beginnings and two streams of argument fighting for room in the gap of one muttering throat. She ceased at last for the lack of tears and lack of breath to begin the tale over again.

"She says," said Annie Weems, "that that Yogi is her Yogi and she will not have you asking him questions and learning her business. She says she, not you, has fed and combed the Yogi all these years, and cleaned his cell, and cared for him, and asked for nothing in return except a little comfort now and then. Amrita, she says, is her child, not yours. And she says she knows what the Yogi told you yesterday: he said you are a man from Jupiter, and Jupiter is a royal planet, so she does not doubt you are a king. She says you are to go away and be a king where you belong, wherever that is. You are not to come into Amrita's life and cause war inside her, which is what she heard the Yogi say you will do."

"Why does she call Amrita her child?" Joe asked.

No need to interpret. Amal caught the meaning of that question instantly. She burst into another torrent of invective in her own tongue, flinging aside her *sari* now and going through the motions of nursing a baby, shielding it, loving it—suddenly denouncing Joe with out-flung arm and calling Annie Weems to witness— down on her knees then and surrendering the child to someone—hugging at her heart as if it tortured her and beating at her old dry breasts with knotted fists. On her feet again—glaring—breathless.

"Perfect pantomime," said Joe. "I'm sorry for her. What's it all about?"

"Her answer to your question. She says the baby's parents died of cholera, and bad men came—she means dacoits. So she took the child and hid it—she was its wet-nurse—who else should have taken it? But she was young in those days and desirable; she was afraid that the dacoits would catch her and carry her off. And she had no money, so she hid by day and ran by night And then someone accused her of stealing the child and threatened blackmail; she became afraid that if she took the child to anyone in authority she would be thrown in prison on a false charge. She was not so afraid of the prison, but she knew they would take the child away from her, and she loved it—could not bear to part with it. So she hid, starving, stealing scraps of food and fearful that her flow of milk would cease—as it began to do. At last, in despair, she took the baby to the Yogi. And he gave it to the temple priests, who have never allowed Amal within the temple precincts but have been kind about letting her see the child from time to time, outside the temple.

"So Amal borrowed a little money from the priests, and paid it back. She bought a loom, and lived near by, and made a living for herself. And she has watched that child grow. She has sat with her at the Yogi's feet by night and listened to the lessons that he gave her. And it was Amal who told me about Amrita, in secret, exacting my promise to keep the secret—as indeed I have done, on condition that the child should come here daily to be taught in my school. It was a little difficult at first to get the priests to agree to that, but the Yogi helped us. He cast her horoscope." Annie Weems chuckled. "I am told he understands that nonsense. Certainly they think he does. I have my own opinion. I know if I wanted to have my way, I could cast a thoroughly convincing horoscope for anyone who puts faith in such fancies—though I don't say, mind you, that there's nothing in it—I have seen some strange coincidences, of whom you are one. At any rate, they let the child come here to my school, and they have even let me visit her within the temple, so I have no personal quarrel with astrology."

"It's like politics—the bunk, with brass tacks here and there," Joe answered. "Did the ayah ever mention the name of the child's parents?"

"Wilburforce."

"Any birth certificate available?"

"No. The birth had been registered in the office of

the Collector of the district, but the office and all the records were burned by the dacoits."

"Pretty hard to prove then?" Joe glanced at Hawkes for amusement's sake. Hawkes shifted his feet; he had no notion of the pitfalls hidden in a partly proven title, but he began to feel uneasy. That thousand pounds seemed less material—more like an unkind dream of affluence with only disappointment in its wake.

"Maybe, sir, you might recognize the family likeness if you saw her," he suggested.

"Mother might."

"She is the child you are looking for," said Annie Weems.

"Not a doubt of it." Hawkes nodded eagerly.

"And it might even be possible to prove her identity legally," Miss Weems went on. "If there were money coming to her—"

"Not a cent," Joe interrupted.

"I was about to say: if there were money coming to her, even so I don't think she would wish to give up the life she is leading. She is one of the happiest girls I have ever known—I think *the* happiest."

"I've heard it said one can be happy in the U.S.A.," Joe answered.

"Ship me somewheres west of Ireland, where the money grows on trees!" said Hawkes. "I'm with you there, sir. Me for Hollywood. My name goes on the quota on the same day I get my discharge. I've heard they make you swear an oath to fight King George the Third. They may throw in Henry the Eighth and Cardinal Wolsey—I'll fight all three of 'em."

"Can I see her?" Joe asked.

"Why not?"

"When?"

"She will be here the day after tomorrow."

Miss Weems' effect on Joe was just the opposite of that of Hawkes. Hawkes' eagerness had made him hang back. Her coolness urged him forward. He felt genuine interest—almost excitement. He began to think of reasons other than his boredom why a wait of two days might be inadvisable.

"Hawkes said something about a Maharajah sending some of his gang to waylay her and carry her off," he remembered. "Is there any danger?"

"There is always danger in the world," said Annie Weems. "I have been facing danger here for more than twenty years. It is good for us. When danger gets too dangerous, we die and render our account; it will look better to God without cowardice stamped all over it."

"But there are risks a decent girl should not run," Joe objected.

"There is a risk that none of us should run—the risk of being false to our ideal," said Annie Weems. "Amrita is a sort of Joan of Arc. That girl has character. And she has good friends, who protect her. I suppose she is the only woman that ever lived who upset all the customs and traditions of a Hindu temple from the inside—mind you, from the inside. Nevertheless, I sometimes think the priests would die for her if necessary; and I know that a number of Indian soldiers would. Of course she is in danger. She has beauty, talent, intellect—dangerous gifts, Mr. Beddington. She has also courage."

"You've 'sold' me. I can't wait to see her," said Joe.

Hawkes leaned forward. "Mr. Beddington, if you should care to come with me tonight, I'll show her to you. I know her goings and comings—some of 'em—I know some. Shall I call for you?"

"You're on. What time?"

"About a half-hour after dinner."

"I'll be ready for you. Can you get two decent horses? Bring 'em."

Joe offered the ayah ten rupees. She refused the money, biting her lip, turning her head the other way, with both hands clenched and her bare toes kneading at the clean New England rug.

FROM THE BOOK OF THE YOGI-ASTROLOGER
RAM-CHITTRA GUNGA SINGH

I am a Yogi, I sit at the feet of Wisdom. That means not that I am wise, but that I value Wisdom more than all else. Neither does it mean that you are ignorant of Wisdom. Who is? Worms have Wisdom in their own degree, and is a worm not measurably less than you? But you, who prate of Wisdom as an infant cackles about stuff to eat, stand up and answer me: What is it?

Rain pours on a mountain. A thousand miles away, a river meets the sea. And you say: These are cause and effect. But did you see the rain become the river? Did you follow the drops of rain from sky to sea? You followed not one. Nevertheless, you have Wisdom enough to understand that every drop of rain obeys one law that guides rain, river and sea also, not one drop escaping from the scope of it. Some take one course, some another; though a drop should go down to the fathomless bed of the sea, and beyond that, into caverns beneath the sea, that drop shall none-the-less return and once more wet a hilltop, though eternities may intervene between one cycle and another. You perceive: there is a law that governs drops of rain.

But shall that law not govern you? Are you its master? Can you say to it: Cease? Or can you make one drop of water disobey law, you whose elements are nine-tenths water and whose soul is something you can neither see nor understand? Nay, you have Wisdom enough to answer that the same law governs you, sea, rain and river. There is that much Wisdom in you.

Nevertheless, you tell me: I departed thence, and I went thither. I met such an one by chance; by chance we loved; or, possibly, by chance we hated. Nay, say you, there was no law that governed me and her; it was a windfall, as the wind might blow an apple. But I answer; Law can govern apples also. I am a Yogi, I sit at the feet of Wisdom.

VI

"What's the odds? She's harmless."

Joe always had hated to dine with his mother alone. Fortunately there was a bottle of not-so-bad Madeira. Joe's mother drank two-thirds of it. Joe kept filling her glass; she sometimes became good-tempered when she drank too much—she even let pass opportunities to poison hope with cynicism. So he kept on pouring and did not even mention Annie Weems. There was a sort of silent laughter deep within him. He was so absorbed by his own line of thought that he had to jerk himself out of it to listen to his mother. It was never safe not to listen to her.

"Mr. Cummings told me, by the way, that it's useless to try to find the Wilburforce's child. If she's alive, which he doubts, she'd be beyond any hope of redemption—probably Mahommedan or Hindu, with three or four half-caste children of her own already and an inferiority complex like a stray cat's. He says white children raised by natives in this climate lose all sense of honesty and moral stamina. She'd be too old to be educated and too familiar with vice to be safe with anybody's children. I can't see myself taking that sort of young person back to the States with us, even if the immigration people would permit it. I believe we'd better leave her to the gods, as Mr. Cummings phrased it. What do you propose to do tonight?"

"Moonlight sketches."

He said that through his teeth, with eyelids lowered. He cracked nuts swiftly, finding one at last that he could pass to her: "Here you are—all the way from Brazil—but don't ask why." He knew her capable, because she knew he loved sketching, of inventing something else for him to do—for instance, find a doctor for imaginary, agonizing ailments. He had hard work not to betray relief when she seemed hardly to notice his answer—although he knew she weighed it and passed judgment on it before almost casually saying what, in turn, she wished him to believe.

"I'm so tired—I suppose I ought to go to bed. However, Mr. Cummings wants to show me photos of the Delhi Durbar, taken years ago. I think I'll take the rickshaw and submit to being shown."

Joe knew she was lying, although he had no doubt that Cummings wished to show his photographs. A creepy feeling down his spine warned him that she meant to make her own inquiries about the Wilburforce child and to set in motion means of legally disproving in advance the girl's identity, in case she should turn up and prove embarrassing. Thoroughly, through and through, he understood his mother's vanity and cruelty. The unfamiliar new laughter he had found within himself mocked the very nervousness that caused it.

He summoned the rickshaw, helped his mother into it and even delayed her by making her look at the violet mystery of shadows under the trees and on the compound wall. "I'd give a year's salary to be able to get that color right with oil or pastel."

"You will be a fool with money to your dying day,"

she retorted. "Don't disturb me if you're out late. I expect to return early and go straight to bed. Come to my room after breakfast in the morning."

And then Hawkes came, astride a waler mare that he had borrowed, leading an Arab gelding. He was smoking his short pipe and there was about him an air of genial recklessness that was probably due to thoughts about the thousand pounds, but it suggested adventure and Joe's mood grew luxuriously free from responsibility. He told himself he did not give a damn what happened that night. He ordered two whiskies and spilled his own in the dust while Hawkes drank.

The Arab gelding moved with silk smoothness and the night was aswim with impalpable dust made luminous by starlight. There were soft sounds at uncertain intervals, but for the most part a mystic silence enveloped everything. It was another universe, in which anything might happen except the rational and real. It seemed comfortingly familiar, and his own voice sounded, friendly fashion, like the voice of someone else—some fellow full of confident amusement.

He asked Hawkes the familiar question, that, from Greenwich Village to Darjiling, always crops up on a dark night amid strange surroundings.

"Did you ever come to a place where you knew you had never been before, yet the place was perfectly familiar and you recognized every detail of it?"

"Sure, sir, lots o' times. Once when I went with a girl near Woking and we came to a clump o' deodars. I hadn't never been in India in those days. But I saw those deodars, and smelt 'em, and I felt it was a place

I'd seen. I knew what was around the corner, so to speak, and where there was a waterfall—and mountains 'way away beyond it. Funny, 'cause there ain't a waterfall near Woking and the only thing that even hints at mountains is the Surrey Downs, about eight hundred feet high. Pretty soon I forgot it. She was a girl who made a man forget things—scrumptious, but too expensive for a soldier's income. And besides, I had to be back in barracks before midnight. Anyhow, I forgot them deodars. Forgot myself, too."

"Well, what of it?" Joe rather resented sharing mystic interludes with Hawkes. He was half afraid the man would bring him back to earth with inane explanations.

"This, sir: three years later I was in India, and I was always a one for getting myself transferred to places I'm curious to see. That's quite a trick. I'm not a soldier, I'm a tourist with a liking to have my expenses paid by Government. So, 'fore long, me and Simla makes acquaintance. Presently, ten days' leave; and I go pony riding, acting nursemaid to a subaltern who wants to see the sights. The subaltern goes sick with collywobbles in his tummy along o' being careless. Them hills, as they call 'em, are tough on amateurs unless they watch their stummicks. Camp—and I've time on my hands. A full moon—deodars—and I go walking. There she is! The very sight I'd seen that night at Woking, waterfall, mountains, mist in a valley, everything. And mind you, I say, everything. There was a woman there, the very spitting image of the girl I'd loved in Woking, only this one wasn't white and couldn't speak a word of any language *I* knew. But she knew me as sudden as I knew her, and we stood there grinning at each other until a savage with a long knife came and took her away, she looking back at me over her shoulder. How do you account for that, sir?"

"Can't. There's no accounting for lots of things that happen. What's the noise behind us?"

"Nothing but your bodyguard, I reckon."

Joe drew rein. A moment later the sound of pattering footsteps ceased. He turned back, legged his horse into a shadow, stopped again to listen—heard labored breathing. Hawkes, drawing rein beside him, chuckled and lifted a heel to knock the ashes from his pipe.

"Come on out o' there, Amal, nobody won't hurt you."

There was a moment's pause and then the ayah stepped out from the darkness, followed after a moment by Chandri Lal. Hawkes turned a pocket flashlight on the woman; her breast was heaving and her nostrils trembled.

"Ask what in the hell does she follow me for?"

Hawkes spoke to her, but she merely looked dumbly determined, nervous grin and sulky defiance alternating. There was something about her that was irritating but nevertheless respectable. Joe felt toward her as he might toward an uninvited lost dog that had adopted him.

"She won't let up, sir. Some people might try whipping her, but I'm not that kind and I don't think you are. We might gallop a bit, but we'd only make her suffer. She'd track us. She'd catch up. What's the odds? She's harmless."

Joe tried English: "What do you want, Amal?"

Silence. Joe's hand, feeling for support as he leaned back in the saddle to ease himself, discovered that the numnah was an over-size one that protruded about a foot behind the polo saddle. It suggested a rather amusing notion.

"Tell her, if she's so set on following, I'll save her all the trouble. She may climb up behind if she isn't afraid."

"She, sir—she's afraid o' nothing that'd scare you and me. Her kind keep a whole seraglio of fears that couldn't scare us in a month o' Sundays. How about it, Mother?" He translated Joe's invitation.

The ayah hesitated. Chandri Lal whispered—pushed her. The whites of the ayah's eyes were like green glass in the glare of the flashlight. She struck Chandri Lal with her elbow to silence him, grinned—stepped up to Joe's stirrup. Chandri Lal lent her the use of his shoulder. She was up behind Joe in a moment, gripping with strong legs that made the Arab restless, and with a hand under Joe's armpit that lay like a threat on his heart; he could feel his heart beating beneath it

"Who said anything about you, you devil?" Hawkes legged the waler mare away from Chandri Lal.

"Can't you take him up behind you?"

"He's got them blasted cobras with him in a basket. I don't know which gives me the creeps most, he or they. Besides, he don't belong to her. He's like a leech or a louse. He's a blooming parasite, that's what he is. He's like one o' them whimpering jackals that follow a tiger."

"Ask her if she wants him."

Hawkes asked. Joe could feel the ayah's laughter; it was soundless but there was plenty of it. She spoke, though, with what sounded like anger.

"She says he's none o' her business."

"Let's go."

They began to trot, Chandri Lal following with the end of a cloth in his teeth and one hand balancing the big flat basket on his turban. Ten minutes later, when they passed a pool of light that flowed from the open door of a Eurasian's bungalow, he was still following, his bare feet padding silently in deep dust and the basket bobbing up and down like a piece of machinery.

The warmth of the ayah's body against Joe's back excited him in a way that his brain could not analyze. She kept that left hand on his heart and her right hand on his shoulder. It was as if a current flowed between them—not of electricity—a current of thought. Partly, perhaps, because his mother, not he, possessed all the family wealth, he had often told himself that possessions do not constitute importance; and as the arbiter of the destiny of hundreds of employees from vice-president downward he had very often in his own mind minimized his own importance, in order to avoid the stings of conscience on account of arbitrary cruelties that his mother had compelled him to inflict. He was only a cog in a huge machine. In theory he could readily agree with the doctrine that no individual is more important than another. Nevertheless, if he had occasion to pass judgment and act on it, he would have considered himself as a matter of fact a great deal more important than the ayah. He was now uncomfortably conscious of importance which, apparently, she had and he had not. He could not have explained it. He was merely aware of a condition.

Small groups of Eurasian loafers and Hindus gathered in doorways or around flickering firelight; their mocking, obscene laughter yelped at the sight of a sahib carrying a native woman behind him. It was much too dark for anyone to guess that she was old and undesirable; her figure was young; as a silhouette observed against crimson bonfire-light, her bare legs dimly outlined on the horse's flank and her right arm on his shoulder, she probably looked bacchanalian—beautiful—suggestive. However, he was defiant; he rather hoped he might be seen by some one of his own race, on whom his scorn would not be wasted. All the same, the ayah's vibrant warmth and the pressure of her hand on his heart made him feel disturbed and unpleasantly creepy; and for that reason, not because of onlookers, he wished he had told her to mount behind Hawkes.

They skirted the small city, passing a slaughterhouse where foul birds roosted restlessly along the ridge of a nearby roof. Then they turned to the right through mean streets, where men and women slept in sheeted rows on pallets on the sidewalk to avoid the infernal heat of the unventilated rooms. Just as the moon was rising a street widened, became near-respectable and flowed like a spreading estuary into a paved square that had flower beds in the midst, and a fountain, and a few well-tended trees. Along the far side was a high stone wall and a sentry box to one side of an iron-bossed wooden gate that had spikes at the top. There was a roof behind the wall—a neat, plug-ugly thing of corrugated iron, painted white. In moonlight it looked like the corpse of a roof.

"What's that place?"

"The jail," Hawkes answered. He slowed to a walking pace, and the ayah vaulted to the ground, as active as an ape; Joe tried to see which way she went, but she vanished into shadow; it was several seconds before he saw her running toward a group of people who appeared to be holding an argument within the shadow of the wall, beside the sentry box. A small door in the wide gate opened and a man stepped out who seemed to be an officer. He shut the gate behind him.

TO H.P.B.

Beaches of Eternities, whereon in rhythmic order
Plunging as the rollers come that thunder on the reef
Æon follows æon—and no sounding and no border
Binds them as our shallows bind our tides of unbelief;

Beaches of Eternities, whereon with sullen thunder
Threnodies of empires—Babylon and Rome—
Blend into the death-wail of Atlantic, and the plunder
Is as drift upon the sand dunes, is as sand amid the foam;

Beaches of Eternities, whereon the souls of nations
Flung forth from the hurricane of birth and death and time
Glimpse the new Eternities—the courses and the stations
Kept by more Manvantaras awaiting cosmic slime

Wherefrom, anew, new universes lighted by new splendor,
Measured by the time-taught Master-builders shall arise;
Beaches of Eternities, whereon we strong surrender
To the Law—Is Cosmos trackless? Are there pilots of the skies?

VII

> *"So you sing to them, eh?"*

Now, by quite imperceptible stages, Joe changed—as a chrysalis does, only much more swiftly. He emerged out of a state of consciousness into another one, in which values were not the same, and he was not the same Joe Beddington. The strangest part of that was, that he could not tell how it happened.

It began by the moon coming over the wall of the jail. Then Hawkes took both the horses and tied their bridles to a god's leg on the fountain in the center of the square, so that they could drink all they pleased and make confession afterward, if they should happen to feel sinful. Hawkes made a more or less obvious and rather bawdy joke about that. The joke hardly penetrated Joe's thought; however, he laughed politely and set foot across the square in something of a hurry, trying to conceal his haste. He felt curious and queerly excited.

There were seven or eight native Indian soldiers—tall bearded shadows, standing around some sort of Eurasian official, who was insisting on talking English to establish his importance; further to establish it, he was wearing his white sun helmet in the moonlight. The man who belonged in the sentry box was standing, looking nervous, with his back to the small open door in the big shut gate, through which the undersized Eurasian had come.

Joe's first thought was that he was witnessing a jailbreak or perhaps an abortive attempt at one. But before he had come close enough to hear what anyone was saying—even the annoyed Eurasian was speaking in undertones—he heard a girl's voice. She was singing. She was somewhere in the jail yard, out of sight. Joe had heard all the imported voices and knew enough music to confess to himself that he might be fooled a little by the mellow moonlight and by the weird state of his nerves, but he knew that what he heard had quality. He had to stand still and listen—so intently that he did not notice whether the Indian soldiers and the Eurasian went on arguing or not; and he became oblivious of Hawkes.

The song was in some Indian language, of which he knew no word. But he could recognize tone when he heard it. He himself had perfect pitch. He might have followed music, if his mother had not had too much money. He told himself that he had never heard quite such quality in any other woman's voice in all his life. He stood still, spellbound, something happening within him that he could neither analyze nor measure.

It was a mystic moment—the sort when bankers make their big mistakes and men of destiny march toward Waterloo. There was a winelike inspiration of the kind that goes to Kaisers' heads and makes nursemaids yield themselves to soldiers in psychic ecstasy that the soldier mistakes for worship of himself. The mellow moonlight and the pastel-shaded shadows were the sort that make a Swinburne write odes to Revolution, or a Tennyson write idylls to the King. Joe felt, for the first time in his whole experience, a mood that some men can only attain by getting drunk—a mood that drink destroys in other men. To use his own phrase, he felt like old man Abraham on camelback, aloof from earth, conscious of incomprehensible destiny, borne forward, he knew not whither.

Meanwhile, his feet rang solidly on paving stones. Seven soldiers and a scared Eurasian, mistaking him for a British officer on a tour of inspection, faced him, saluted and stood at attention. Even when he drew near and it was seen he was not in uniform the tenseness was not relaxed, there being no accounting in the native mind for the peculiarities of British method, that seems to consist so often in having no method at all. He might be a new arrival with mysterious authority, snooping like Haroun al Rasehid in mufti in quest of embarrassing facts for the morning's session of the court. He might be that most awful of enormities, an officer on secret service. The man with his back to the open door presented arms with a rattle of carbine swivels.

Joe waited for revelation. And it came, of course, from the Eurasian, who saw Hawkes' uniform approaching and was sure now that Joe was an official personage.

"She sings, sir."

"So I notice."

"Sir, Mr. Cummings gave strict orders there should be no visitors at night. Nevertheless, she comes. She sings. What can I do?"

"Why does she sing, and about what?" Joe asked.

"Sir, she makes song to the prisoners. Mr. Cummings gave such strict orders I am afraid now there will be an inquiry and we shall all be punished. Sir, will you not speak to her and—"

"Hello!"

It was hardly a startling voice. It was too exactly in the middle of F major and too bell-like to have anything unpleasant about it, but it produced silence in the way the backstage gong does when the curtain goes up on the drama. Joe only had to turn his head a little to the left and he did almost stealthily, as if he were trespassing and hoped to see unseen. He was not scared. He could not have explained his attitude. He saw the black-robed ayah, like a shadow, glide past him and be swallowed in the darkness by the corner of the sentry box.

Framed in the gap in the gate, with moonlight on the white wall of the jail behind her causing a sort of luminescent aura, stood a girl with a chaplet of flower-buds, binding dark-brown hair. Beneath some sort of silken cloak that was thrown back carelessly she wore a low-necked garment of cloth-of-gold. There was a girdle at her waist that appeared to be made of gold wire woven into the form of a serpent with jeweled eyes. She had bracelets that clashed, and something gleamed on her ankle. Her bare feet looked like living marble. One hand resting on the edge of the doorway, she stood with the grace of a water carrier, one foot on the door-sill.

"Hello, Hawkesey."

The Eurasian interrupted: "Miss, please tell this gentleman I did my utmost—yes, indeed, my utmost to prevent your going in."

"Should he know? Do you wish him to think you cruel?"

"Miss, my job to me is not a joke, it is my daily bread. And my honor—"

Hawkes interrupted. "Miss Amrita, this is Mr. Beddington." She bowed, almost imperceptibly, the motion making the moonlight on her hair wave slightly as it does on water. She seemed able to leap to swift conclusions. She walked straight up to Joe and shook hands with him. Her hand was the most magnetic thing he had ever touched and she seemed in no haste to withdraw it. The sensation was of being touched by someone in a dream. She moved like someone in a dream. She was gentle, faintly scented with some mysterious eastern stuff that smelled dew o' the morning clean. Joe let her lead him out into the moonlight, where he really saw her for the first time as she turned her head to speak abruptly to the ayah. She had the marvelous rhythmic movement of an animal, such as even the most perfect dancers have only rarely, and as she turned her head the moonlight made a silver line along her neck that was almost maddening, it was so beautiful. The ayah slunk again into a shadow.

"You are not here by accident. Why did you come to see me?" she asked.

"How do you know I am not here by accident?"

"Hawkesey brought you. And you are pleased to see me. Why?"

He answered lamely. "Why were you singing in there?"

"Why not?"

"If I heard correctly, it's against the rules."

"Whose rules? Yours? God's?" Indignation, whether

it was true or simulated, made her lovelier than ever. Joe's impulse was to sketch her, with her shadow willowing beyond her on the mouse-gray paving-stone; but his left fist, obeying instinct, remained clenched behind his back, expressing disbelief in beauty as a mark of virtue, viewed from the banker's angle. He was conscious of Hawkes. He had a business man's distaste for being compromised by a woman before witnesses. Habit, instinct, training told him to go away before trouble began.

"Why should you sing at night?" he asked her.

Her voice changed to the soft, persuasive, reasonable note one uses to a child who can't grasp principles:

"Were you ever in prison? Were you ever in hospital? Do you know what the sleepless hours are like to men born in the open, who have lived with sky room for their thoughts? They wall them in. They roof them in. They shut out the wonderful wind of the night that whispers of friendly familiar scenes. They shut out moonlight, starlight—and they say to them, 'Be honest men, such as we are, who have stolen all God's goodness from you because you stole some devil's trash from us!'"

"So you sing to reduce their agony?"

She nodded. "And a spiritless official who, I dare say, thinks that toothache is worse than a broken spirit, says I may not sing!"

"And you defy him? I can sympathize. But aren't you defying Bumbledom in general? The man is backed up by society. He has to be obeyed."

"Has he? If he forbade me to give alms—or to smile—

or to bless all earth with every breath I breathe, should I obey him then?"

"But he's responsible for the prisoners."

"True! And the Lords of Life will hold the fool responsible! They will demand of him those prisoners' hearts that are breaking. But they shall not accuse me of neglecting to sing. In that prison are thieves, murderers, quarrelsome men, debtors, weaklings who have taken others' blame, and some who are in no way guilty of the charge against them. By day they have a little work to do that keeps their hearts from bursting. But at night, in the dark, and no stars? I come and I let the starlight melt me, I flow along my voice into their poor dumb hearts, so that for at least a little while they think of love instead of hatred. Do you think I would dare to obey that fool when he says I shall not? Will he dare to attempt to prevent me? If he does dare, let him answer for it to the Lords of Life, who have less patience with stupidity than with sin."

That was over Joe's head. He had sent cigarettes to an ex-vice-president of a bank in prison for defalcation, and had thought rather well of himself for doing it, but he had never even pondered whether Shakespeare meant what he was saying about music having charm. When he had thought of it at all, which was hardly ever, he thought that a prison should be as nearly hell as human ingenuity could make it—short, of course, of actual savagery or neglect. People should keep out of prison.

"How did you come by your name?" he asked her.

"I took it. Out of all the names there are, in all the languages I know, I liked that name best. So I took it—

just the way a crow steals anything it wants. It probably belonged to some one else, but there it was. I took it."

"What does the name mean?"

"Daybreak."

"Dawn?"

"Daybreak — break — break — breaking through — until it bursts my heart unless I become—do—act—instead of sitting still."

"I like that."

"Do you? You won't like it when your own break through begins! I mean, when it really begins. You have been incubating quite a long time. Which hen sat on you?"

Joe smiled. "Do I seem such a desperate chicken as that?"

"Eaglet," she answered.

"Flatterer!"

"You don't know me. And you won't like it when you feel your feathers quilling out. Ask Hawkesey. He got incubated, and he didn't like it either. Hawkesey got drunk and then tried to get sent to a war where hillmen rub the ends off bullets to make sure of killing. You may talk of killing yourself, to yourself; but you will think like dynamite; and when you go off, some one—who is it, I wonder?—will have to get out of the way. I should say you have Jupiter, Mars and Saturn all in Gemini."

"You're right. But isn't astrology rather piffle?"

"Yes, but so would mathematics be if they taught you twice five are eleven. Calling things piffle won't take the Jupiter influence out of your life."

Joe did not care to argue about astrology. "Who taught you such good English?" he asked.

"I never learned any bad English until I talked to an Englishman. There was almost a war between Hawkesey and me to see which could corrupt the other. It was funny. I liked the swear words, and that shocked him, because Hawkesey is a Puritan underneath the surface. He began to try to talk like an officer with a hot potato in his mouth and half his syllables missing. So I swore each time he mispronounced a word, and I had to swear so often that he went away all alone and practised how to speak, in order to save my soul from hell. Hawkesey should have been a bishop."

"Do you consider yourself an Indian?"

"Funny. Hawkesey asked that question the first day he met me. Is a bird in an oven a cake? Because I am caged in India, am I Indian? My friends are Indian, if you mean by that that they were born here. But so was I. I have the kindest friends that were ever patient with a strange bird in their high nest. It was so high in the treetops that I used to be afraid of falling out, particularly when the wind blew. But they taught me to fly. And I have flown. And I have brought back food for them."

"Do you know who your father and mother were?"

"Yes. Amal told me. It was sweet of them to bring me to be born in India. They must have been lovely people; so I suppose the Lords of Life let them go as soon as I was born. They may have had trouble enough, and perhaps they weren't yet wise enough to have let destiny take its course. They might have tried to struggle against destiny; and I think they weren't the kind of people who deserve such torture. So they were let die very swiftly. And I dare say the darlings thought dying was dreadful, until they found themselves out of their bodies."

"Do you believe in an after-life?"

She chuckled. "Who wants to believe in anything? I insist on knowing. Don't you?"

"Don't let's talk philosophy."

"You couldn't. You don't know any—yet. That shocks you, doesn't it! You have read Bergson, I suppose, and Kant, and Spencer, and William James—a little Aristotle—babies, all of them!"

"How do you know?"

"I, too, have read them. How else should I know? They are babies arguing in three dimensions, although if they would stop for a minute to think, they would know that of all the infinite number of dimensions they are pretty conscious of at least five. However, philosophers don't think; it is not respectable. Some day one of the gods will throw an apple at them, as was done at Newton. Then they will wake up, one by one."

"Where are you going?" Joe asked.

"Home."

"May I see you home?"

"No, it would offend my escort. They are gentlemen who have foregone sleep after a long day's soldiering merely because it pleases them to protect my dignity, as they express it. I must snub you rather than offend them. Life is a matter of choosing between predicaments."

"May I see you again?"

"How can you avoid that, if that is destined?"

"You believe in destiny?"

"It makes no difference to destiny whether we believe or not. But you don't believe? Then why not try going away? There are trains, camels, horses, motor-cars—there are even airplanes. Take one. Then you will soon know whether destiny has other intentions."

"You advise that?"

"Why not? It won't hurt you. Good night."

He thought her parting smile was wistful, although he was not sure. She and sadness seemed to have no bond in common, and yet—perhaps it was his own lack of pleasure in life that made him see her through a sad lense. Or perhaps it was moonlight. He could feel his heart thumping and it made him angry; he was a master of men and millions, not a silly emotional ass to be stirred out of his proper orbit by a girl's smile. He wondered what color her eyes were. How little and light she looked; how tall and graceful when the ayah followed and touched her *sari* that she wore like a Roman toga; how small when the seven-man escort formed up two by two and tramped behind her, one man grunting gruff commands and giving them the tempo, *sotto voce*—left—left—left! Probably a thousand pounds or so of bearded bone and muscle, fit to fight its weight in anything that breathed. Tamed by a girl who walked like something flowing in the moonlight.

"Guess I'm going crazy!"

Joe turned about, and found Hawkes facing him. The jail door was shut and the sentry was pacing his beat with shouldered carbine. Chandri Lal, sweating and breathing heavily, drew near and squatted with his basket in front of Joe.

"How do you like her?" Hawkes asked.

"She's surprising. What does that fool want now?"

"Nothing—I mean anything. Shall I kick him?"

"No. Tell him to go to the devil."

Joe strode to where the horses waited with their reins tied to a grinning god's leg by the fountain. In the shadow beneath the waler's belly the ayah crouched, shrugging herself.

"Damn you," he told her, "you stink and you're too much contrast. You offend my sense of harmony. Go home. Do you hear me? Beat it!" But the ayah watched dumbly until he swung himself into the saddle; and when he rode away she followed like a good dog padding, uncomplaining, in the dust.

FROM THE BOOK OF THE YOGI-ASTROLOGER
RAM-CHITTRA GUNGA SINGH

You imprison one another. You do it sometimes to protect the things you think you need, from others, who also think they need them and are not respectful of your ownership. You do it sometimes to avoid the trouble of changing cruel and impudent laws, since thought is tedious and change distasteful; furthermore, the men who make your laws are no less cruel, impudent and stupid than yourselves. You sometimes do it to prevent from thinking, men whose thought is less obedient than yours to what you choose to say are God's commandments. You have other motives also—envy—malice—jealousy—revenge—and a desire to justify yourselves, since you know that you terribly need to be justified. It suits you to say that these are prisoners, and those are free.

However, I say you are all in prison—to your own stupidity. That is a stronger and more cruel prison than those of steel and stone that you have built for one another. There is no escape from it by pardon, nor yet by violence, nor by passage of time; and least of all is there escape from it by death, as anyone may see who is not proud of his stupidity. For, is this world not finite? And is the life beyond death not infinite? I tell you, in proportion as the infinite is greater than the finite, so is the stupidity beyond death worse than that of this world; therefore to die stupid is to be reborn infinitely stupid, in a prison infinitely worse than this one.

You are here in this prison to learn to escape, and you are stupid because you wish to be. When you cease to enjoy stupidity you will soon see fall these prison walls that you have built around yourselves. There is no reason, other than your own stupidity, why you must learn by suffering. You suffer because suffering increases vanity, which you call humility and value as the brightest jewel in a martyr's crown, whereas in truth it is a Jack o' lantern.

VIII

"Do I get my money?"

Joe's first reaction took the form of anger against Hawkes and Annie Weems. To have allowed a white girl to be brought up by Indian priests seemed to him criminal. To have contributed toward her education without denouncing the arrangement was conspiracy. Money-hunger, no doubt. Educate the girl to have contempt for money; then, when she comes of age and gets some, make her sign it all away before she wakes up. Old game. That's the way religious institutions grow rich. Disappointment—no money after all—all right—beautiful, isn't she?—marry her off to some fat scoundrel who will pay a stiff price.

"Are you satisfied, sir?"

Hawkes, riding alongside, eyed him almost wistfully. The moonlight, full in Hawkes' face was like a Broadway spotlight advertising the price at which a commodity is practically given away—a thousand pounds—dirt cheap—and convenient easy payments if preferred. Commodity, however, rather evasively guaranteed.

"Satisfied of what?"

"Of her identity. Do I get my money?"

The sleepy Arab stumbled on a loose stone hidden in the dust, causing Joe to bite off the first few syllables of his answer: "—see mother about it"

"All right, sir."

Joe began to wonder what he should say to his

mother. If he had had a thousand pounds of his own money he would probably have paid Hawkes there and then. But his mother's habit was to make Joe pay the expenses out of his quite moderate income and to take her time before she reimbursed him—a system thoroughly characteristic of her. It enabled her to know what he did with his income; when he needed money he had to explain to her why he wanted it and to submit to lectures on extravagance. Of course, he had a big letter of credit with him, but if he drew against that his mother would know in no time. He might give Hawkes a check on a New York bank and write a letter asking the bankers to pay the check on presentation. But Hawkes would probably not know how to handle such a check and would almost certainly take it either to a native banker or to one of his officers, either of whom would start gossip circulating.

Lees of Joe's many suppressions were boiling up and their fumes half-blinded him. The midnight of his discontent was worse than its moonless gloom had been. He had seen a new moon—come to think of it, the new moon was a suggestive symbol of her—beautiful—emerging suddenly out of obscurity after nights of darkness. And the glimpse had only made him feel more miserable. When they reached the hotel he was curt and something less than decently polite; he threw the reins to Hawkes and, hardly pausing to thank him, hurried to his room.

"See you some time tomorrow."

He had a cot on the verandah on the side of the hotel that faced a line of low hills; there was nothing very alluring about them by full moonlight; they suggested to Joe's mind dry bones of monsters that died of weariness. He turned his back to them and lay facing the wall, cursing the stuffy mosquito net that smelled of sour dust; sleep repudiated him. He lay thinking, and his thought was broken into installments by the gusts of native servants' snoring and the irritating, hysterical barks of a jackal fossicking for filth. He wished he had stayed in New York—wished he had done anything but come to India.

He began to hate his mother, not because he thought the effort worth while but because it kept a more important thought veiled in the background; and he understood perfectly, too, that hatred of his mother was merely a form of self-contempt in a particularly ugly mask. He told himself, for at least the hundredth time that year, that if he were a man he would have cut adrift from his mother long ago; a man who would endure what he did for a pittance of fifteen thousand a year and the prospect of inheriting control of millions was not a real man, he was a coward—a spineless nincompoop. Nevertheless, although he writhed at his own accusation while he let its lash bite inward, he knew, but refused to admit, its gross unfairness. No son of his mother, tutored and dragooned from infancy by her, could escape from her toils without violence. She was a Clytemnestra, only to be overcome by being slain. Nero did it. Joe was no Nero, and he had no desire to be one.

Moonlight helped him to imagine endless ramifications of that theme, including theories of poetic justice, easier to contemplate than to believe really possible.

At three in the morning, by the alarm clock of the man who had to take the mail-bag to the so-called midnight train, he sat up in a long-armed chair to face the problem of Amrita and his own reaction to that strange encounter near the prison gate. Even indignation of his mother failed to blot Amrita's image from his mind. The color of her eyes still baffled him. The instant he let his thought have rein she sprang to life in his imagination, color, line and gesture. He had the artist's faculty of summoning from vacancy a thing once seen. He could have drawn her there and then. His long strong fingers itched to do it, as they had never itched for money or for anything else he could remember.

It was rather a shock to discover what an inroad she had made into his consciousness. Perhaps surprise accounted for it; she was so totally different from anyone he had supposed she might resemble. He yielded only very gradually, thought by thought, until he admitted to himself at last that she had made an impression on him far too deep to be accounted for by logical analysis. He liked her. He liked her strangely. He liked her far more than he had ever, in all his life liked anyone at first sight. He liked her so much that it made him angry to include her in the same thought with his mother.

What, he wondered, would his mother do with her—if—if—if his mother ever learned of her existence. Instantly, he knew his mother would begin to sharpen strategy. His mother had imagined someone of the "orphan-Annie" type, who might be broken to her will and added to the list of sycophants. She would no more tolerate her as a high-spirited, intelligent and independent protégée than an old she-wolf will tolerate a new young female in the lair; her fangs might be better concealed than a wolf's and not so sudden, but they would be much more cruel.

Well, it was none of his business. But that thought made him restless. He could make it his business, couldn't he? Should he permit his mother to ruin that bright young girl, simply because she had dared to meet her son by moonlight and was possessed of attractive manners, charm and good looks? Here was once when his mother could be outmanœuvered. But how?

Why tell her? Why not pull out on the afternoon train? Why not leave Amrita to the gods, as Cummings had suggested—futile fool! He hated to adopt that tame cat's flatulent suggestion, but it seemed the best one after all. Joe had seen too many people ruined by his mother's malice. He had rescued a few, although he had to do it treacherously, dropping warning hints that always were interpreted as glimpses of his own infernal cunning. It was no wonder the people he saved never liked him afterward—no wonder he had so few friends—such a host of discreet acquaintances.

Well, this could be one time when his mother need not know a thing about his strategy. Neither need the potential victim know. He would run no risks. He would never see the girl again and she should never guess who he was or how close she had come to the claws of an ogress.

"Ogress?" he said to himself. "Ogress? By God, I believe that's what mother actually is. Catherine of Russia—Catherine de Medici—those two were gentle sheep compared to Kitty Beddington."

He would write Hawkes a draft for a thousand pounds—say for five thousand dollars, payable on presentation in New York. He would hand it to him, to hold his tongue. He would get Hawkes' written promise, ever more to hold his tongue. Hawkes would be afraid to talk until the draft was paid; payment might be stopped by cablegram unless the stipulation about silence was fulfilled. Meanwhile he would send a cablegram in code to New York and get the office to summon him home. His mother would have to go home too.

He liked the program, and the thought of home was pleasant in his psychic nostrils; so that when morning came he shaved with some contentment, whistled in his bath, dressed without as much as noticing the yellow-eyed servant who got in his way, packed his own trunk with methodical deliberation, and ate breakfast without swearing at the waiter. Then he went for a ride on a hotel hack to kill time until the ogress should be up and on the warpath. The word ogress amused him. Funny that he had not thought of her before in that light. The word unaccountably clipped her sting—clipped off the worst of it; he feared her far less as an ogress than as a natural human being. There was something even comical about the word.

It rather annoyed him to see the ayah, lean and tireless but a little sulky-looking, climb to high ground whence, he supposed, she intended to watch him. It annoyed him more to notice Chandri Lal with a basket of snakes on his head come trotting behind him in the dust. He afforded Chandri Lal some exercise by cantering the raw-boned hack for several miles and returning to the hotel by a different route, remembering legends about Indians hounding people to their death by merely following them—following—saying nothing.

As he neared the hotel he began to consider how to get in touch with Hawkes in order to complete the business with him before train time. He had a proper speech all set for Hawkes; what with that, and the quiet conceit that he was planning the most gentlemanly action of his life—he was feeling in fine humor.

So it rather dashed his spirits to see Chandri Lal and the ayah sitting side by side, a yard or two apart, beneath a tree in the hotel compound; they appeared to be laughing—perhaps at the snake-charmer's knowledge of shortcuts across country, or perhaps at that other unpleasantly ominous sight that greeted him. Hawkes on a good-looking horse with a pipe in his mouth was riding away from the hotel; Joe's mother was up and having breakfast on the verandah instead of in her room. There were three crows on the verandah railing.

Joe's instantly assumed air of nonchalance did not deceive his mother for a moment, any more than her wave of the hand and invitation to what she called coffee deceived him. It was some sort of coffee substitute, as much like the real thing as his greeting and hers. There was war between them, for the thousandth time, and both knew it, although both concealed it, as he sat down to sip at the Borgian brew that his mother mixed for him with her own bejeweled fingers.

"Did you enjoy your ride, my boy?"

"No, Mother."

He forgot he had enjoyed it. Even had he not forgotten, he would probably have lied. He was half-panicky. Rebellion had come. He, Joe Beddington, had raised his standard, secretly as yet, but with a determination that seemed, even to him, out of all proportion to the issue; and he hardly knew yet what the issue was.

"Did you make nice sketches last night?"

"No. Mother, why stay on in this infernal hole? Let's go. I've packed my trunk. Let's take the afternoon train."

He hit something and she almost blinked; but she was as skillful as a Mongol empress at hiding astonishment. Her answering voice was pitched a half-note lower than the normal, with its harshness in abeyance.

"Joe, dear, I have made all sorts of plans to photograph the caverns near here. I have even wired for an electric-light plant."

"Wire and cancel it then. Here—I'll send for a blank—I'll write it for you."

"No, Joe. Mr. Cummings has arranged for coolies and all kinds of assistance. He has even set men exploring to find passages that may have been forgotten for centuries. Even if I didn't wish to make the photographs, I can't be rude to Mr. Cummings."

"I've known you rude enough when it suited you to be. Mother—why waste time on this damned wilderness when India is chock-a-block with things worth seeing? Order your electric-light plant shipped to Benares. There's a place worth photographing."

"No, Joe, every one has done Benares. Here I've a

chance to get something unique. Who knows? I might find a sort of Tut-ankh-Amen's tomb! At least I'll have photos that no one else can duplicate."

Neither of them even hinted at what was uppermost in both minds. Each knew that the other was masking the real objective. Habit lay strong on Joe; in the face of firm finality, as usual, he blustered to cover his search to discover an opening on the flank of the position—tactics taught him by his mother, and that she understood and read as swiftly as if he personally had explained them to her.

"Look here, Mater." It was always mater, not mother, when Joe was angry. "I came on this idiotic tour to oblige you. I've put up with all the boredom of it, and I've done my best to see that you got all the enjoyment possible. Now it's no more than fair that you should move on to oblige me. I hate this place. It's on my nerves. I can't sleep. Lay awake all last night. There isn't a decent horse or a decent meal to be had, and there isn't a decent man to talk to."

Skilfully she heaped a little fuel on his fire. "Joe, dear, Mr. Cummings is very interesting." She knew exactly what he thought of Cummings.

"That ass!"

She incited him a little further; he was checkmate now in one move:

"If you weren't so self-opinionated you could improve your mind and learn a great deal by studying Mr. Cummings' methods of administration. There is always something to be learned, everywhere. And with Mr. Cummings so obliging and willing to—"

Joe exploded. "Damn Cummings! The very sight of him upsets me. Pompous imbecile! If he were anyone, at his age he wouldn't be relegated to obscurity in a jerk-water hole like this. See here: there's a limit to what I'll endure, and I tell you, I'm through with this place. I'm going. I've packed my trunk. You'd better pack yours too and plan to take the afternoon train. Kiss Cummings on both cheeks and promise to send him some picture postcards."

"Very well, Joe. You take the afternoon train and amuse yourself somewhere else. I'll stay on here and take my photographs. I think you're right. You're suffering from boredom. You go. I'll stay."

Check-mate! He knew now, Hawkes had told her about Amrita. He had been willing to leave the girl in the lap of the gods, as Cummings phrased it; but to his mother's machinations—not exactly! Under his mother's calmly observant eyes he instantly manœuvered to recover lost ground:

"Nonsense, Mater! How can I go and leave you here?"

"I am not exactly helpless, Joe. I even managed nicely before you were born. It wasn't you who taught me how many beans make five."

"I suppose you would like to be able to throw in my teeth for ever afterward that I left you on your own resources and at Cummings' tender mercy?"

"Mr. Cummings is at least a gentleman. I think you had much better take the afternoon train, and not let Mr. Cummings hear you talk to me like that. Where do you propose to go from here?"

Joe ignored the question. Exasperated, he launched

another—a shot at random: "Been talking to Cummings about me, have you? I suppose he told you I should have gone to an English public school."

"Is there anything more natural than that I should talk about you?" she retorted.

"I don't discuss you with strangers." He knew he often did; and she, too, knew it.

"Why not? Are you ashamed of your mother?"

He recognized defeat. He accepted it there and then by reaching for his hat and stalking off to chew the cud of solitary discontent. Defeat pro tem, at all events.

And not one word, by either of them, about Amrita who was uppermost in both their minds.

FROM THE BOOK OF THE YOGI-ASTROLOGER
RAM-CHITTRA GUNGA SINGH

I have traveled and seen wonders. This I saw: a watch no wider than an orange and no thicker than my thumb. Upon its face were tenths of seconds, seconds, minutes, hours, days, weeks, months; even phases of the moon. Its owner boasted it was accurate within three seconds and a tenth in four-and-twenty hours, and I agreed with him: a master-workman made it. Nevertheless, said I: There is a greater marvel; for the sun, moon, earth, and stars keep time exactly and need no winding. Whereupon we found ourselves no longer in agreement, since he saw no marvel in the timing of the heavens, which, said he, is accident.

He showed me how the wheels within his watch revolve, each in its own orbit at the proper speed, until a hidden mechanism moves the hands, each in relation to each; he told of having saved a fortune by a hair's breadth once when he knew the time within a fraction of a second. But when I spoke to him in one breath of the twelve signs and their degrees on the face of the watch, and of the twelve signs of the Zodiac, he mocked me, saying: That is superstition, there is neither mechanism in the sky nor can there be.

I asked: Did not a mind conceive that watch? Did it make itself? And did it make the law whereby it works? And is it not a symbol of the mechanism of our destiny? He laughed. And when I said: The Great Stars and the Constellations and the Planets in their courses are the mechanism whereby the Almighty Mind directs our evolution and the progress of events, he thought me mad. But what to think concerning him, I knew not—him with his watch in his hand, and the stars in the sky above him.

IX

> *"Read thou thine own book."*

Joe was usually most unhappy when his mother was most in her element. What amused her made him miserable. He could endure her, even if he did not like her, when she was frankly predatory, taking what she could because the law was too ill-served to interfere. But when she talked high altruism while she did damned cruelty, he hated her. His brain groped blindly for the opposite of what she would expect him to do—some move that she would not understand. He thought of and found he could not dismiss from his mind the Yogi by the temple wall. Calling himself an idiot for his pains, he hired a horse and cantered to the temple, knowing it was out of bounds without a permit or an official escort; but at that, he supposed he had escort enough; the ayah and Chandri Lal pursued him, dodging through traffic, taking short-cuts, stealing rides on motor-wagons; whenever he glanced backward one or the other was not very far behind him.

He found the Yogi seated in his beehive hut. The old man's eyes shone in the darkness, though his shape was hardly visible; his nose looked beaklike and his beard was the shape of a gray owl's body. Wondering how to open up a conversation Joe fetched a stone and sat on it before the hut door, so that he could peer upward and seem not too disrespectful. For a long time then he waited for the Yogi to say something, but the silence only deepened as the minutes marched.

"Old man," he began at last in his friendliest voice, "I am sorry I was rude to you the other night."

"Rudeness is a consequence of ignorance. Of what are you afraid?"

"How do you know I'm afraid?"

"Are you a special sort of book that none may read?"

"If you can read so well, then turn a page or two and tell me what you see," Joe suggested. There was silence again for so long that, if he had not seen the eyes in the gloom within the hut he would have thought the old man was asleep. He was about to repeat the question when the answer came:

"What did I call you? And what did I tell you?"

"You called me a man from Jupiter. And you told me I stand on a threshold."

"Should I say it again?"

"You might explain it."

Another silence. Then at last: "If I explain, will you believe? Not so. Three thoughts will seize on your imagination: that I am mad—that I have designs on your purse, perhaps by subtle byways of intrigue—that I flatter my own vanity by claiming understanding that I have not. Thereafter your credulity will fluctuate between those three thoughts, accepting first the one and then the other. But the truth will escape you altogether."

Joe pondered what to say to that; the ancient offered no suggestions. It was true, he was not a believer in forecasts. But on the other hand, he felt intensely curious.

"Suppose I agree not to doubt your honesty," he suggested.

"Are you a master of doubt? Can you order its goings and comings? How shall you agree to what you know not how to fulfil?"

"All right. Suppose I say this then: I will use my best judgment and try to believe you."

"Would that be good judgment? It is written on your face as plain as writing in a book, that you have been taught to disbelieve all that is told you."

"Taught—yes. But I have never fully learned it. For instance, I don't doubt your honesty."

"You are a fool then. Great liars are they who claim they are honest. Honorable, yes, a man may be—but honest, not yet—not for a few thousand million eternities, and not then without striving. Worse liars—mean, immodest dogs are they who yelp their scorn at the mistakes of others seeking to be honest. It is better to make mistakes than not to make them."

"How so? I'm a banker, for instance, among other things."

"And have the bankers learned by making no mistakes? Do you know the history of banking? Is there one thing that they knew and fully understood in the beginning? Is there one thing they have learned by any other means than by mistakes? I tell you, no man learns by any other means. And by that means I learned silence when young fools come to me for readings of their plainly written destiny. Read thou thine own book."

"Naturally, if I could I'd do it."

"Learn! It is excellent knowledge."

"Are you subtly kidding me, I wonder? You look like Diogenes under a barrel, and you've come near selling me a line of goods I never thought I'd fall for in a thousand years. Dammit, I'll bite! I'll trust you."

"If I wish not to be trusted—what then?"

"If I trust a man, I trust him."

"That is the excellent way to make mistakes, since trust adds keenness to the later disillusion. Not the wisest man knows very much, and he who volunteers advice knows very little. Nevertheless the biggest fool is he who blames another whose advice he took."

Joe grew determined. "Do you refuse advice when you are asked for it?"

"What is your security? Does your bank lend money to each would-be borrower? If I should give advice, as you call it, then I am lending knowledge. Can you guarantee to spend that knowledge wisely? And if not, what then? When the Examiner examines my account, how shall I answer his accusation that I loaned good knowledge for an unwise purpose? He will hold me answerable."

"Can you profit by keeping all your wisdom to yourself?" Joe retorted. "What's the good of it, if you don't share it with someone?"

The Yogi chuckled again. "Are there not rules for the lending of money? I tell you, there are far more certain rules for the employment of wisdom, and a mistake is much more costly."

"Maybe. But you said just now that it's better to make mistakes than not to make them."

"True. You are a man from Jupiter. There is no refusing you. Very well, I will make a mistake. I will answer one question. What is it you wish to know?"

Joe hesitated. He knew what he wanted to ask, but he was doubtful how to phrase it. He suspected the Yogi would evade him with vague generalities unless he cut the issue fine, with diamond distinctness. On the other hand, his intuition warned him not to be too personal, since it was after all a point of principle that troubled him, and once a principle is grasped it is no great problem to apply it.

"One question and one answer." said the Yogi.

"Yes, but how many words? I want to make sure you understand me."

"Use ten words."

"It can't be done. I doubt that I could state it in a hundred words. It's so complicated."

"Nothing is complicated, except folly. I know the question."

"Impossible. How can you know it?"

"You wish to know whether that threshold, whereupon I told you that you stand, if crossed will lead to freedom. Is that it?"

"That's only part of it."

"That is the whole of it. But the answer will seem to have three parts, though they are one in essence.

"Go on. I'm listening."

"It will lead to strife with one. It will cause you to put warfare in another's heart. It will lead to greater freedom than you ever dreamed of if—I say if you have manhood enough and march forward."

"You're too vague. I want to understand you clearly. Is the strife with my mother?"

"Why not? Can you break her hold otherwise?"

"I'd give a lot to know how you read my history. However, all right, that's that. Does the warfare that you say I shall cause in another person's heart concern that girl Amrita?"

"Why not? When the ayah asked, did I not speak of it?"

"I think I understand what you mean by the threshold. I have reached the stage where I can't stand being owned and used. But what if I refuse to cross the threshold? It isn't too late to turn back?"

"Cowardice seems comforting to some—until it bears its fruit."

"Would I not be justified in refusing to turn against my mother?"

"If you wish, you may continue to contribute to her sin until the sin destroys you both. In the end, what would she or you gain by it?"

"I've reasoned that way sometimes; but you put it more clearly than I did. All right, I can face that issue; there'll be hell to pay, but I guess it's the only manly thing to do. I'll cross that bridge and burn the blasted thing behind me."

"That is for you to decide."

"I've made up my mind. But how about making trouble for that girl Amrita? She never harmed me. What right have I to interfere with her?"

"Can you avoid it? Can one man's prayers for a longer night prevent the sun from rising?"

"That sounds like fatalism."

"To a fool's ears! Idiot! When a promissory note is due, is it not due and payable? Is it not timed? And does the interest not accumulate, with added penalties? Shall the creditor not collect it or else throw the debtor into bankruptcy? And though the debtor forgets the note, can he deny he signed it? Stands his signature not written? Shall he call that fatalism and repudiate it? Are your ears deaf and your eyes blind?"

"I don't get the drift of your argument."

"Ass! You sleep and wake; you wake and sleep; you see day follow night, and night the day; you have seen old men die, and young ones born. Is it not clear to you then that we die and live, and live and die? I tell you we are reborn millions of times. And what we owe to one life we shall repay, either in that life or another. Each deed done is nothing but a promissory note to meet its consequences. When it falls due, call it destiny and meet it with determination to pay it and set new, sweeter consequences forming; or call it fate and fall beneath it and be rolled on. Each one's destiny is his own, to make or unmake as he pleases."

"Do you mean you think I owe that girl a debt?"

"Or she you. Or you owe each other. Destiny will make you both pay—as it will make me pay for wasting wisdom on a blind fool! You have asked. I have answered. I have more profitable thoughts to think, and there are only a few eternities in which to think them. Go. You may spare your pride. You need not bow to the earth or call me Holy One."

FROM THE BOOK OF THE YOGI-ASTROLOGER RAM-CHITTRA GUNGA SINGH

You speak of fatalism as if that were the same as confidence in Destiny, O inconsistent asker of innumerable riddles, the answer to every single one of which is so simple that your conceit rejects it. You demand of me difficult answers, but I give you easy ones; wherefore you turn aside and say my wisdom is nothing and not worth hearing. Nevertheless, it is no concern of mine how impudent you are, nor how sincerely you love ignorance nor with how much insincerity you seek the truth. So I will answer this one also, though you take my answer and make sport of it in taverns, and though your fashionable pundits mock me from the doorways when I pass.

A fatalist is like a man who steals and gambles with another's money. He is lazy, a thief and a fool. Fate overtakes him in the end. He has no destiny, since he created none. The destiny of others crowds him to the wall, and he says: What must be, must be.

Not so he who trusts in Destiny, which is the working of a Law that gives to each one his immediate deserts, no more, no less. He is too busy creating destiny to pause and wonder what the past may bring forth; he will meet that when he must, and make the utmost of it, rising thus to a nobler destiny. It is now noon, and he knows that Destiny decrees there shall be another noon tomorrow. Waits, he therefore, meekly for tomorrow's noon? Or does he smite the drum of this one till it echoes down the corridors of this eternal NOW, that he may smite tomorrow with a stronger blow made shrewd by exercise?

In former lives and this one you have earned exactly what you now have. That is fate, if you like the word, and it is inescapable. Your destiny depends on what you do with what you have. It depends on how hard you hit fate on the nose. And neither my knowledge nor your ignorance can change one fragment of it.

X

> *"India would be all right if it weren't for rajahs."*

Joe spent the remainder of the day searching after a fashion for Hawkes, but nobody seemed to know where Hawkes was. He inquired at the officers' mess of an Indian cavalry regiment; Captain Bruce, who received him, sent an orderly to make inquiries, but the orderly came back none the wiser.

"Are you in a hurry?" Bruce asked. "Then why not ride the rounds with me? We'll run across him somewhere." The aroma of many millions of dollars is a curiously catholic sort of key to hospitality. "If you'd care to ride back here afterward and have lunch with me—perhaps I'd better tell the butler now—we don't have many visitors—the rogue might have to open tinned atrocities unless I warn him in advance."

The subject of Hawkes served well enough as an open wedge into conversation.

"Hawkes been making himself useful to you? That's his specialty. Hawkes is probably unique in all the armies of the world. He could drive a herd of sheep through a gap in the King's Regulations that a practised lawyer couldn't see, and he can make himself so useful that nobody ever calls him a loafer and sends him back to his regiment. I think his regiment has probably forgotten him. If we should be ordered to Tibet I'd expect to find Hawkes ahead of us in Lhassa with a document of some sort proving he had the right to be there and draw extra pay for doing things that aren't provided for in the Regulations."

"I suppose," said Joe, "the fact is that he's in the secret service?"

"No, I think not. You see, a secret service man goes where he's sent, but Hawkes goes where he pleases. He's a genius, and something of a joke. A good part of his secret is that the natives like him. He has a gift that isn't tact exactly, it's a sort of fluid understanding crossed on to a lack of prejudice and a rare quick trick of learning a language while another man waits for a textbook. In addition to that the man's a mine of information. Ask Hawkes if you want to know anything. And by the way, he's a magician when it comes to skin wounds. Nobody knows how he does it, but he can stitch a wound and leave no scar whatever. Who is that woman, I wonder, and why is she following?"

Chandri Lal, too, was less than fifty yards away but Joe said nothing. He was vaguely disturbed by that remark about Hawkes being a mine of information, although there seemed to be no particular reason why it should disturb him. What if Hawkes had told about Amrita? Why should he not tell, and what harm could come of it? At any rate, it ought to be easy to discover whether he had or had not told.

"Has any European ever been into that enormous temple?" he asked.

"I imagine not. We let temples severely alone. In other words, we let 'em run their own idolatries to suit 'emselves."

"No inspection of any kind?"

"None that I ever heard of."

"I saw the procession the other night. Worth seeing. But I've wondered once or twice since then whether there was anything in my impression that there might be a white girl or two among those nautch girls."

"Oh, no. Some of 'em may look white, but—"

"Some of them look like well bred European women."

"Illusion—moonlight—lantern-light—shadows. No, no European women. Their caste laws and traditions are too strict. And besides—it isn't generally recognized outside India—but the Indians are extraordinarily decent about our women. Even in the Mutiny of '57 there wasn't one instance of rape, although scores of our women fell into their hands. Our troops, I am sorry to say, were gingered up with propaganda about rape and there was some dirty work done on the strength of it. But there was a rigid inquiry afterward and not one single instance, or even a suspicion of an instance of rape was discovered. Murder, yes, lots of it. Rape, no. There isn't another country in the world that you can say that for."

"How about the Rajah's harems?"

"Oh, I've heard that two or three of 'em have white wives, and they're almost all polygamists, but that's different. If a woman wants to sell herself in that way, Government can't stop her. They can bring pressure to bear on the Rajah in all kinds of ways, but they can't legally prevent that kind of thing. It happens very seldom."

"How about the Christian missionaries? Is there any check on them?"

"I think so—in fact, I'm sure there is—mainly, of course, to prevent their falling foul of native prejudice. One fanatic might start a riot that'd take an army corps to squelch. However, there's nothing o' that sort hereabouts. The local missionaries, so far as I know, have been more than usually tactful and the local Hindus seem to be a particularly broadminded lot. We've no rioting or any rot like that."

"Lots of missionaries?"

"Lots of 'em. Presbyterians—Methodists—Baptists—Catholics—all sorts."

"They would be likely to know, I suppose, if there were a white girl living in an Indian temple."

"They certainly would. And they'd soon raise hell about it."

"Do you know Miss Annie Weems?"

"I should say I do. We all do. She's the only woman who was ever made an honorary member of our mess. There's your information bureau—if you're curious about girls in Indian temples or rajahs' harems, ask Annie Weems. She actually rents her mission from the trustees, or whatever they call 'emselves, of the Hindu temple. She and the high priest are on such good terms that we joke her about it. There's a story that she's allowed inside the temple once a month, but that's probably untrue and, anyhow, she denies it."

"What's her mission for? What does she do, I mean—proselytize?"

"No—doesn't believe in it. Education, pure and simple. Runs a day-school for Indian children. I've often ragged her about being more a Hindu than the Hindus are themselves, but of course that's an exaggeration. She's a sane old lady with some very admirable prejudices."

Full stop. Joe did not care to pursue that subject any further. It was clear enough that Annie Weems had somehow contrived to keep a secret, and it was certainly not Joe's business to expose it—yet, at any rate. The mystery of Hawkes' disappearance was easier solved; a squadron farrier, who knew nothing about the breech-lock mechanism of a modern sporting rifle explained that the Maharajah of Poonch-Terai had asked for some one who was expert in such occultism and that Hawkes had volunteered to go and doctor the potentate's expensive weapons.

"That," said Bruce, "is Hawkes all over. By the time he returns, he'll not only have repaired a broken gun or two; he'll have learned nine-tenths of the Rajah's business. However, he won't talk about it—until the time comes to let a cat peep from the bag in order to serve some other object he may have in view. If you don't believe that, try to pump him."

"I have tried. He's expensive," Joe answered.

"Yes, and saves his money. Greed is probably the secret of his genius for doing odd jobs. However, he does 'em, that's the main thing."

Bruce, too, seemed to be a lonely sort of fellow, and there is just as much affinity in loneliness as in any other state or condition. Hardly realizing that they liked each other they talked like a pair of old gossips as they rode the short tour of inspection, Bruce explaining things that interested Joe for no other reason than that he liked the other's confidences. By the time they were ready for lunch Bruce had even offered the loan of a horse, and Joe had reciprocated by asking Bruce to take care of a magnificent sporting rifle "in case I should ever return to India and care to use it." They were sowing seeds of friendship, hardly realizing it.

There were very few officers there to lunch and most of those dropped in and bolted out again after a hurried meal and perfunctory remarks. There was something or other mysterious in the background that was keeping every one on a strain that they tried to conceal; Bruce made no reference to it, but while the others were there he seemed as conscious of it as they were. There was no indication of what its nature might be; it was certainly not personal ill-feeling; they appeared to be a hard-working outfit who got along well together. The only possible clue that occurred to Joe was the abruptness with which they changed the subject when he asked a casual question about the Maharajah of Poonch-Terai; however, he doubted that that was an accurate guess.

Luncheon over, Bruce took him to his quarters and they lolled in long-armed chairs, Joe asking nothing better than escape from the hotel and from his mother's neighborhood. True, she had probably gone to the caverns ten or fifteen miles away, but even that was too near, she might return at any minute. When Bruce invited him to spend the night he leaped at the suggestion.

"We've a bit of a tent-club near here—nothing to boast about, of course, but not bad. I thought of riding out there this evening and turning in early, so as to be ready for pig soon after daybreak. Did you ever stick pig? I can promise you something worth your trouble. Take your pick of my spears; they've all been sharpened. I'll lend you a Kathiawari mare that stands right up to 'em—she's savage—all you have to watch is that she doesn't spin around and try to use her heels. You have to give her lots of spur—she spun me off once—if she hadn't stayed there savaging the boar I'd have been a dead man."

Joe sent a note to the hotel informing his mother and warning her not to expect him until the following afternoon. The invitation made him thoroughly cheerful; it enabled him to avoid her until after keeping his appointment at the mission, and gave him meanwhile something wholesomely barbarous to do and to think and talk about. It was characteristic of him that he was not even tempted to discuss his personal affairs with Bruce, although Bruce became more and more intimate as they rode together toward the tent-club in the cool of the afternoon. Bruce even talked of his mother, but Joe was silent about his.

Perhaps Joe in that mood was a companionable audience; he was sympathetic, making no demands on the other's patience, inviting confidence by simply not inviting it. At any rate, Bruce soon began to verge on telling secrets, and then finally to tell them—nothing serious, of course, but regimental intimacies normally not discussed with strangers, such as the Colonel's wife's flirtations and the sinful rate of interest charged by the local moneylender. Then, within sight of the tents, peeped forth the fundamental worry that had made the mess a sort of morgue at lunch-time. Joe's shrewd guess had been right after all.

"India would be all right if it weren't for rajahs. Thank God, we've got this tent-club to ourselves—Poonch-Terai won't spoil things for us this time."

"What's the matter with him?"

"He's a cad, for one thing. Sends out shikarris to hamstring the best boars, so that he can ride 'em down easier. Can you beat that?"

"Can't you interfere?"

"We did. But we're supposed to keep on decent terms with him. He's the principal landlord hereabouts and he has extraordinary influence. He even has some kind of subtle authority over the temple. He's said to have the right, among other things to choose a concubine a year from among the nautch girls. It's a right, like the European *droit du seigneur,* that has lapsed from disuse, but they say he's trying to revive it, having set his cap at some young woman. The trouble is, that some of our troopers and non-coms got wind of it and took steps to protect the girl—no one knows why—they won't talk, except to one another and, I suppose, to the priests. We got called down for snubbing Poonch-Terai not long ago; they sent an officer from H.Q. to give us hell about it—something about his influence in the House of Princes that the Government happens to need at the moment. So we're forced to be civil, and Poonch-Terai takes full advantage of it—riding for a fall, of course, but meanwhile we're in difficulties."

"The military usually are," said Joe, "when they run into politics."

"*And* religion. Don't forget religion. Some one—and we're pretty sure it's Poonch-Terai—has got at a lot of our troopers—set them by the ears against the others. Some of our men are Hindus, some Mohammedans; they're snarling, and the Colonel has the wind up, which makes it ghastly for the rest of us. We can't put the temple entirely out of bounds because of the religious edge to things. We can't picket the temple for protections unless the priests request that; we can't even offer to do it until they ask, and they won't ask. If they did ask, they jolly well know that Poonch-Terai would put the screws on—politics and one thing and another; I've been told he could cut off more than half their revenues at one stroke of a pen. I wish they'd let him have the girl; she'd probably prefer even that to a life of belly-shaking in the moonlight."

"What sort of girl is she?" Joe asked, wondering why the goose-flesh rose all over him. He told himself there was absolutely no reason why he should be disturbed on Amrita's account, even supposing he knew for certain that Amrita was the girl in question. And, wondering what the color of her eyes was, he felt more disturbed than ever. He could imagine his mother as a fat spider; never having seen the Maharajah of Poonch-Terai it was easy to imagine him as something much worse—a sort of combination hornet-scorpion, with whiskers like a mogul on a ketchup bottle.

"Damned if I know. All those women look alike to me," Bruce answered. "I've been told that they're beastly immoral and inhumanly mischievous. Let's hope we have better than goat for supper. I told the cook I'd kill him if he serves me goat again. The fat rogue knows I won't, he's too important. Time before last he tried to fool me by calling it Viceroy Stew."

However, it was "curried venison" this time, and though the goat was more than usually tough it was so embalmed in curry powder that the benefit of reasonable doubt was on the cook's side, so his life was saved, but not Joe's digestion; when they turned in, early, he wooed sleep in vain; and when at last he did sleep he had a nightmare. A monster came out of the temple pursuing Amrita; and another monster came out of a cavern pursuing himself. He struggled to overtake Amrita. But Hawkes, who seemed in no hurry at all, kept demanding his thousand pounds and saying: "Then you'll see the color of her eyes, and what about it?" Every now and then Hawkes changed into the Yogi with a pipe in his mouth, but even so he said the same thing. One of the monsters, when he dared to look at it, had bristling black whiskers and was male; but the other was female. Both of them looked like spiders, and that futile ass Cummings wanted him to catch flies for them. At last one monster pounced on him and he began to fight desperately; but it turned out to be Captain Bruce waking him for the tea and toast that are the bread and wine of Englishmen's religion.

FROM THE BOOK OF THE YOGI-ASTROLOGER RAM-CHITTRA GUNGA SINGH

I am old. I have traveled in more lands than any of you have seen, and in some that you have hardly heard of, seeking Wisdom from the Wiseman. But I found none–only knowledge, of which, indeed, there was plenty; but as knowledge is to Wisdom, so is the husk to the kernel, and so is the kernel compared to THAT which made it grow. It was only among the ignorant that I found a little Wisdom. Having my own belly full of ignorance and neither need nor hunger to increase that, I returned hither, where I sit at the feet of Wisdom, learning, if it may be, how to think.

The men whom ye think wise are they who think least; what they think is thought, is observation of phenomena; and what they think is depth, is surface. Lo, they work like bees; like ants they labour; like the beavers they employ their talents; but to what end? I have studied what they say is their philosophy, for which fools pay them reverence; but I find the fools are wiser, since at least they feel their ignorance. I have learned much from the ignorant; but from the men who are said to be wise I have learned nothing that the insects do not know. They prate of Wisdom, but they know not what it is.

They invent, they discover, they build. But they are as savages compared to the Atlanteans. And where is Atlantis with all its wonders? Can ye do what the Atlanteans did? Atlantis and its sciences have vanished so completely that your pundits say it never was, and only fools believe in it; but fools are sometimes wiser than the wise. Atlantis has gone, and its wonders. But the sun shines; and I sit here in its vibrance, even as the Atlanteans did.

They invent, they discover, they build; and why not, since the ants do also? But the ants build better. And do they go to the ants for Wisdom? Lo, with what determination and what labour they learn to fly? But the bees flew better before they thought of it. The goose flies farther, with less trouble; yet among them goose is but a synonym for fool. They can kill the goose and cook and eat it. But they kill each other also; earth and its elements cook them; worms eat them; are they wiser than the goose?

They invent, they discover, they build. They measure what they think is light. They measure what they think is thought. And they imagine marvels, saying always that they seek the great good of the greatest number. Lo, they write innumerable books, each contradicting each. But they ignore one book, wherein the whole of it is written in a dozen words: Seek ye therefore the Kingdom of God and all these shall be added unto you. Truth, but they ignore it. Wisdom, but they say it is not so. They say: There is no God, can that which is not have a kingdom? And they argue: Jesus never lived, because we have no proof of it; and if he did live, he was only saying what the poets said a thousand years before his day. They said it ten, and a hundred thousand years before his day. But they believe a poet is a fool with long hair.

They invent, they discover, they build. They invent needs; they discover laws; they build new temples to necessity. They say: This is water; lo, how wise we are, we observe it obeys a law of gravity; its parts are oxygen and hydrogen. But do they know what water is? Or do they understand the saying: Ye shall be reborn by water and the spirit? Do they know what spirit is? And is there one, among all your scientists, philosophers and pundits, who can answer: What is gravity?

I am a Yogi. I sit at the feet of Wisdom, and I look for it not in the springs of ignorance. I seek it not from Aristotle, nor from Karl Marx—blind fools blowing on a surface, saying: lo, how deep we look!

XI

"Are you drunk, Joe?"

Joe's horsemanship was good enough but nothing wonderful. The Kathiawari mare lived up to the reputation Bruce had given her; she had to be blindfolded before Joe could mount her, and when the blindfold was removed she wished with all her savage heart to kill the unoffending sais, who ran for cover. Joe was enjoying himself; he liked that kind of fight; it brought his dogged patience uppermost, and the mare learned presently that she had some one on her back who owned a stronger will than hers. However, she tried all ways of testing him and she was going backward toward the rising sun, and Joe was consequently facing Bruce when he heard Bruce swear and saw his face set like flint before it thawed again into the deliberate smile that the English imagine makes them pleasant to approach. Joe did not understand what was happening until he veered the mare around. Then he knew without Bruce telling.

Gone was the glory of Indian morning. None save Joshua has ever made the sun stand still, but there are men whose uninvited presence can rob sunlight of its charm; and of such men Poonch-Terai was chief, at any rate that morning. He exuded a dry diabolism; each of his handsome features seemed an accent of the underlying guile; his suavity was insolence, his seat on horseback arrogant, and the horse had cost him fifteen thousand rupees. Well aware that his presence was unwelcome he rode forward showing his white teeth in a smile that set every fiber of Joe's being tingling with resentment. It was a case of instant hatred as unreasoned and sudden as the war between fire and water. Even Bruce detected it, and Bruce had malice of his own to keep him busy.

The Maharajah drew rein fifteen paces from them, spinning his spear before he let it lie across his saddlebow. He was a sartorial dream; from crimson turban to the spurs on his beautiful boots he was the last exquisite word of elegance. His black mustache was waxed, his black beard oiled and curled, his dark eyes underlined with pigment like a woman's. His lithe body, only a little coarsened by debauch, sat like a centaur's. He was a challenge; Joe itched to couch a spear at him and actually eyed the point between his ribs where he would drive the blade home, smiling at his own absurdity—a smile that Poonch-Terai interpreted as a salute to his rank. Bruce introduced them. Joe nodded. The Maharajah displayed his teeth in another radiant smile, his dark-ivory skin so slightly changing color that Bruce did not notice it, but Joe did.

"I have heard of you," said Poonch-Terai. "Are you not the man from Jupiter?"

That brought the Yogi to Joe's mind, and the temple—the nautch girls—the man whose jaw Hawkes punched so unexpectedly—the story that the Maharajah sought new fuel for his harem fires. Was this the man who desired Amrita? Joe had never felt so venomously jealous in his life; it almost frightened him; from force of habit he tried to smother the emotion and answer civilly.

"Why do you ask that?"

"I was told you were named that by a man who makes very few mistakes."

"You mean the Yogi at the temple? I think he had probably heard the name of a business corporation in which I have some interest."

It was an unfortunate answer; it opened the way for a sneer of the sort that Americans abroad are learning to expect but not to suffer gladly.

"Wise old Yogi. But I wonder, don't you, how he realized that an American and his business can't be separated, even on a temple threshold?"

"He's the sole one of your countrymen I've met who wasn't hungrier for dollars than for decency," Joe answered.

Poonch-Terai subsided for the moment, half-pretending not to have caught the meaning of that counterthrust, but he threw Joe one glance sideways that meant war as surely as the shot at Sarajevo did. He began to talk to Bruce about the wild boars. He had spoiled all Bruce's quietly made arrangements.

"I'm camped five miles away. My men reported your men beating in this direction, so I ordered mine to join yours. We'll get pig, don't doubt it. Can your friend ride?"

"We only want one apiece," Bruce answered. "Have to be back at mess in time for tiffin."

"I'll bet you my men will show you fifteen boars worth killing."

"Any of 'em lame?" Bruce asked him, but Poonch-Terai affected not to hear that; he stood up in the stirrups, shielding his eyes with his hand.

"That's my headman signaling. They've a sounder of pig in the scrub beyond that clump of trees. Shall we ride on?"

He began to canter, Bruce and Joe following three horses' lengths behind him, Bruce trying to signal to Joe his disappointment and apologies for the unwelcome intrusion; his lips moved, but he said no word aloud because Poonch-Terai's perfectly modeled ears with the little gold earrings in their lobes were notoriously keen.

They took cover beside the clump of trees and Poonch-Terai gave orders to his head man, who directed scores of almost naked beaters. Armed with tin cans, tom-toms and dissonant trumpets, they had surrounded a sounder of pig in a maze of waist-high undergrowth some acres in extent. It was a perfect place for pig—impossible for horses and by no means easy for the beaters. At a nod from the Maharajah the head man manœuvered the beaters all to one side of the copse, and then the tin can chorus started as the scythe-shaped mob of beaters invaded the cover to drive the pig into the open. It occurred then to Poonch-Terai that he was possibly usurping precedence.

He turned to Bruce: "You'd better give the word." Bruce nodded, his quiet eyes watching the billowing undergrowth, his rein-hand restraining an excited horse. There was more than one sounder within that small area; the Maharajah's men had swept down in a huge semicircle like a dragnet; there were pigs of all ages in there milling, grunting, squealing and the surface of the undergrowth suggested a section of sea in which huge shoals of fish have been surrounded.

There were collisions in there—fights—until suddenly one whole sounder more than a hundred strong turned and charged back through a gap in the line of beaters. Poonch-Terai swore excitedly:

"That's your men's fault! You ought to thrash your headman—I believe he left that gap on purpose. He'll try to blame it on my man—"

But there was no time for an argument. The other sounder, following a huge gray boar, broke cover in the opposite direction, the gray boar well in the lead of his tremendous family and turning between spurts for a glimpse of what the danger might be.

"Ride!" said Bruce.

The target was that gray grandfather-boar. He saw them, and he knew it. Never a gray boar breathed that was not more than willing to take on fifty times his weight in any kind of enemy whatever. No need to explain the situation to him. He grunted and the obedient sounder turned back into cover, leaving him free of responsibility and unimpeded to choose his own battleground.

First blood is the objective. Whoever can first show crimson on his spear-point is the winner of the race. The fight with the boar, as a rule, does not begin until the race for his tushes is over. Poonch-Terai on his expensive thoroughbred got away with a lead of a length, Bruce following and Joe last. The boar took a straight line away from the sun, to put plenty of distance between himself and his family before giving battle. He went like the wind. With a judgment worthy of a fox he chose a line of country that would strain the horses to the utmost but without overtaxing his own strength.

Boulder, sheet-rock, dry watercourses, scrambled under-growth, he took them all; and not until he judged the horses were well winded and the foam was frothing on his own jaws did he turn in a wide semicircle with his savage little red eye studying his pursuers to discover which could be taken at worst advantage.

That "jink," as they call it, cost Poonch-Terai the lead. It left him far out on the left flank, fifty yards from Bruce, who lost sight of the boar for the moment and checked to save his horse unnecessary labor in a wrong direction. Joe was alone on the right, with the gray boar waiting for him in a narrow pass between two boulders; and the Kathiawari mare as eager as the boar to get to business. No spur needed. Joe couched his spear and charged. The Kathiawari slipped on a loose stone, stumbled and recovered, giving Poonch-Terai the fraction of a moment's opportunity; he came on, passing Bruce and spurring to overtake Joe, who saw him through the corner of an eye and accepted an unspoken challenge.

It was all over in thirty seconds, and Joe the winner. But a man can be reborn in thirty seconds. His whole life's history can review itself, with the essentials selected and the unimportant, so-called major crises faded into the background. All his acquired characteristics can slough off in less than that time and the underlying man, the unknown man who has been learning from experience behind the baffling mask, can break through—never again entirely to return to hiding.

Joe had never suspected himself of chivalry. As he rode at that boar, with Poonch-Terai spurring to overtake him, he was conscious of another set of values than had ever dawned on his imagination. The excitement, the reckless speed, the delirious sense of danger, were all relative to an idea, and the idea was within him. Poonch-Terai was the devil. Paradoxically, too, the boar was Poonch-Terai. A woman's eyes, whose color he could not see, were watching him; he was not fighting to protect her but for approval, on which he knew perfectly well that his own opinion of himself must depend henceforward. Should he fail, she would suffer; he knew that, but he knew, too, that she would ignore the suffering; nothing at all could grieve her but a lack of grace within himself, and grace was wordless—something to be lived, not argued. He would know within a brace of seconds whether or not he had it. He rode like a plumed adventurer, to find out.

The boar turned tail suddenly, but that was a ruse to throw his adversary off guard and to get room to build impetus. He faced about again as suddenly and charged downhill with every concentrated ounce of speed and courage there was in him, timing his effort perfectly to meet his enemy on the narrow ground between two hillocks, where only one at a time could meet him and there was no avoiding his froth-wet tushes or the shock of his furious onslaught. It was death for him or for his adversary, and long odds on the boar, but Joe's spear took him straight and strong between the shoulder blades as he rose to slash at the mare with his murderous little ivory daggers. Speed, weight, strength of horse and boar and man combined to skewer him dead to the earth as the spear-haft snapped in Joe's hand. He was Joe's first boar—first and last blood.

It was neither the boar nor the Kathiawari mare's attempt to turn and use her heels on a fallen foe that sent Joe sprawling on the hard earth. Poonch-Terai came crashing into him, whirling his spear, indignant to have missed by half a dozen strides and hurling into the collision every ounce of venom he could muster. His thoroughbred's shoulder caught the mare in flank, as she turned with one hoof on the ground, and sent her rolling. Luckily she threw Joe three times his length as she fell, and though he skinned his face and forearms on the rock-hard earth and he was rather badly bruised, he was not stunned and no bones were broken.

He was rather less badly hurt than Poonch-Terai. The thoroughbred tripped on the Kathiawari's scrambling legs and fell in a heap a yard or two beyond her, spraining both the Maharajah's wrists as he extended his hands to protect his head. It was Joe who raised the Maharajah to his feet; Bruce drew rein beside them and, seeing there was no great harm done, began edging his horse toward the other two in order to catch them before they could bolt home.

"Good spear!" he said laughing, but Joe and the Maharajah hardly heard him. They were face to face, toe to toe, glaring, Joe's nose dripping blood on to his shirt and the blood from his forehead trickling past his eyes; but even the blood did not make him uglier than Poonch-Terai, whose glowering eyes and out-thrust under-lip told of more than pain in his sprained wrists. There was hatred there—racial, temperamental and intuitive, increased, set flaring, but not caused by rivalry. Beneath it there was the deadlier enmity of one ideal for another.

"Damn you, what do you think this game is—polo?" Joe demanded.

Poonch-Terai backed away from him, nursing his wrists, glancing over his shoulder to make sure Bruce was out of earshot.

"Your pig," he said, "But go back to America and stick them in the slaughter-yards. That's something you understand."

"When your wrists are in shape to protect yourself I will thrash you for that," Joe answered.

Poonch-Terai grinned savagely. "You? You will thrash me? Go back to America before you learn what I can do to you! And meanwhile, stay away from temples!"

Bruce came with the horses and dismounted to help Poonch-Terai into the saddle, interrupting that low-voiced conversation, which had left Joe strangely cool but with a queer sensation up his spine. They rode slowly campward until they met the Maharajah's men, who fussed over his wrists and swarmed around him to escort him to his own camp. Bruce waited until some of his own *shikarris* came, and when he had sent them to cut out the dead boar's tushes he and Joe cantered toward the club tents for a bath, rough bandages and breakfast.

"I can get the dirt out for you. It may hurt a bit, but I'm a dabster at getting a cut clean. However, don't forget to let Hawkes go over you afterward. The man's a wizard. If you asked me, I'd say it's magic that he learned from some Yogi or other. I was telling him only the other day, he's a fool not to buy his discharge and go home and open up a beauty parlor—make his fortune!"

Tent-club operations are not pleasant to endure, nor

were Bruce's bandages artistic; an hour's work made Joe fairly comfortable, but he was still bleeding a little and it was fortunate for more than his vanity that he did not catch sight of his face in a mirror; had he known how unpresentable he looked he might have postponed calling on Annie Weems. However, Bruce encouraged him to call on her:

"It may be she who taught Hawkes how to titivate a cut skin. Let her look at it; she'll be no worse than a military sawbones, and she's sure to improve on what I've done to you. And by the way, thank you for keeping your hands off Poonch-Terai. You had a perfect right to kick him. But if you had—I don't know what might happen."

Joe had read the murder in the Maharajah's eyes. He knew that the brief exchange of insults only hinted at such hatred as could never have been caused by rough-stuff in the hunting field.

There was a woman—a girl whom he had talked with only once, the color of whose eyes he did not know. She was at the bottom of it. He knew that, though he could not understand it. Not for a moment did he think of himself as in love with her, since that would be ridiculous. He could not be. Beyond the fact that she was possibly the daughter of his mother's bridesmaid, she meant nothing whatever to him. With his trained, deliberate mind he knew he was the last man likely to fall in love with a young girl met by moonlight near a prison wall. She had reached to him. She had mocked him. She had made him feel like ten cents. She was in some mysterious way involved in a religious cult with which he had no sympathy. He would be likelier to fall in love with a Salvation Army lassie in Union Square, New York, tambourine and all. If he did, it would startle his friends less, though it might offend his mother more; she would prefer to be able to make up lies, perhaps, about an Indian princess and get them printed in the papers and in *Who's Who.*

He could hardly talk to Bruce, for thinking of Amrita. Strange name, it stuck in his memory; he could not normally recall a girl's name fifteen minutes after he had met her. Meeting girls never excited him—never had. But he was excited about meeting this one again. He put part of that down to the shock of being thrown from a horse. But he knew there was more than that to it. He wished he could remember what color her eyes were—ass!

But he told himself he had a right to be curious. Curiosity amused him; that was it, he was amused. In Joe's life there had been precious little genuine amusement. Always his mother there to embitter the juice of things. He had a right to taste amusement while he could. And he would take care this time that his mother should have no finger in the pie until he had his fill of it. It even occurred to him to take Amrita for his mistress for a while, but the thought was colorless and insincere. He could say that to himself; the words came easily enough; but he could not quite imagine it; it gave him no thrill.

"Well, why should it? If I were in love with her it might be different. I wonder how it feels to be in love. I'd like to try it. But I suppose I'd play the damned ass, just like all the others."

In a sort of day-dream he dismounted at the front door of the mess and waited inside for the dog-cart that Bruce offered to lend him. Bruce ascribed his silence to shock from the accident and made no attempt to force conversation.

"You'll be all right in a day or two. Keep quiet and stay off liquor. Show your cuts to Annie Weems, and let Hawkes see them, but avoid the doctor like the devil unless something serious sets in—which it won't if you keep good-tempered. Here's the dog-cart. So long. Enjoyed your company no end. I'll send those tushes to you. When you're through with the dog-cart tell the sais to come straight home. Come and see me again when you're well enough—or if you're not, send for me and I'll come and see you. So long."

Joe liked him. But he was glad to leave. He let the sais drive. It suited him to sit still and imagine what the next hour might bring forth, and to think of steps he might take to prevent that blackguard Poonch-Terai from having his will of Amrita, as he had no doubt whatever now was his intention. He always did despise a man who employed agents to bag women for him. Also he despised women who fell for that kind of negotiation—not that it made them worse than other women—they were merely lacking in dignity. The whole world was a whoresome mess of guile and blackmail. Might as well stick to dignity as long as possible—it can be done—costs nothing—pays not bad dividends, in self-esteem, which may be silly but feels good.

He grew more and more excited as he neared the mission—more and more pleased with the thought that he was stealing a march on his mother—more and more confident that he would manage the whole business of Amrita and her future without even consulting his mother. He would tell the old termagant what he had done. She could like it or lump it. All one to himself. The day had dawned at last when her authority was broken. He would not stand by and see his mother bind this young girl captive to her chariot as she had bound so many other men and women. But it would be easier to manage if he kept his discovery secret from her for a while.

As they entered the quiet square and the horse's hoofs rang on ancient pavement he heard Annie Weems' piano going—strangely brilliant sound amid that quiet setting. Then he heard song—recognized Amrita's voice—but the words were unintelligible, in a language he did not know. He climbed down and stood by the mission door listening; the upper half was ajar on a long brass hook. The song ceased. He heard a girl's laughter and then voices in conversation, but there was a curtain in the passage and the only voice he could recognize was Amrita's—clear as a bell, yet not unpleasantly assertive.

"Why, yes. I have written all my songs in English. Annie insists on it. Would you like to hear this one?"

She began to sing in English—something about stars that wonder at men's inconsistency. As she sang the curtain parted and Hawkes strode through into the outer room. He saw Joe—beckoned to him—tiptoed to the door and led the way in. In the passage he turned to speak behind his hand:

"I took you at your word, sir—"

But Joe was listening to the song. Hawkes led the

way—parted the curtain. Facing the door, at the piano, sat Amrita, singing, with the soft light through slatted shutters making an aureole around her. Annie Weems sat in an armchair wearing spectacles, seeming to be studying some one else who sat in a corner near the door. That some one was invisible to Joe until he strode into the room.

"You said for me—"

Joe strode in, aware of something damnable and resolute to meet it, but not yet guessing what it might be. Amrita stopped singing and stared at the blood on Joe's bandages. Annie Weems sprang to her feet. Joe turned toward the corner near the door—and faced his mother.

"You? Oh, hello."

"You said for me to see your mother, sir, about that thousand pounds, and—"

"And I have told him it's too much. I won't pay it," said Mrs. Beddington. "If you make promises like that, Joe, you may keep them yourself. Possibly you think you can afford it. Why did you keep this secret from me?"

Joe kept silence.

"Have you been brawling? What have you done to your face?"

"Are you drunk, Joe?"

"Stone-cold sober—for the first time in my life, I dare say. How do, Miss Weems. How do, Amrita."

He was glad he had no pistol in his hand. He knew, for just one fraction of a second, something that no jury ever understood—exactly how some sorts of seemingly motiveless murder happen.

THE STARS ARE WONDERING

Look you how the starlight rains
Into earth's day-weary veins,
Pouring through the purple night
Overflow of liquid light—
Drenching, dripping, healing streams!
Light is loyal! Why are dreams
What we set our courses by?
The stars are wondering, wondering why.

Refrain: A prefix put to a maiden's name,
This much money and that much fame,
This little hat, that little coat,
This little habit, that little vote,
This little home in a different street—
Makes us strangers when we meet,
Dumbly, drearily passing by.
The stars are wondering, wondering why.

Hark you! Music of the spheres—
Harmony for inward ears—
Melody of melting day
Mellowing the years away—
Music of emerging soul!
Why is dissonance the pole
That we set our courses by?
The stars are wondering, wondering why.

Refrain.

XII

> *" 'Taters à la Kaiser Bill."*

"Miss Weems, can you get a doctor for him? Joe is my only son. If anything should happen—"

"I'm all right, Mother—scratched, that's all." However, he sat down, glad to do it. Annie Weems came over to him and undid the bandages. Swift, silent, sure of herself, she only glanced—then led Joe to a bathroom, where Hawkes pushed up a chair behind him and Amrita produced medicated cotton and a basin, pushing Hawkes out of the way. Joe let go—leaned back—hardly knew that his head was resting on Amrita's bosom; but he felt a relief that was almost like sleep as her fingers touched his temples and passed through his hair. His mother ceased to have any importance in the scheme of things. Amrita was essential. And the strangest part was, that he seemed always to have known Amrita—always to have trusted Annie Weems—always to have liked Hawkes. He neither belonged to his mother, nor she to him.

He heard Hawkes whistle in the way a man does who is estimating damage. The next thing he really knew he was lying on a couch not far from the piano and Amrita was singing softly to a tune that Hawkes was strumming, while Annie Weems talked to his mother. At last Amrita stopped, and then he knew the song was nonsense because she said so:

"Hawkesey, won't you understand that if a song isn't beautiful it isn't worth singing?"

"There's ugly things worth mention," he objected.

"True, but it's the contrast between ugliness and beauty that is interesting. This isn't a comic song."

"It is," said Hawkes. "I laughed while I was writing it."

"You laughed at you!"

"Am I beautiful?"

"You're comic. There is beauty in your effort to do what I said you could if you would only try. But you must try harder."

"I sang it to some of the men and they laughed like anything."

"At you. They would laugh at the song if you put some humor in it. I've seen corpses that were funny, but the corpses in your song are only nasty. They're dead, whereas they ought to be masks and garments that the actors left behind them. You can't make death funny if you don't remember there is no such thing as death. Do you know why audiences sometimes laugh when they see a man slain on the stage? It is because they know intuitively, without knowing that they know, that actual death is just like that; they know the actor only takes his costume off and goes home. You go home and write that song again."

"Teaching's a trade," said Hawkes. "It's like drilling rookies. You have to praise a fellow now and then."

"Don't I take pains with you?"

"Yes, but–"

"Isn't that the kindest sort of praise?"

"Maybe, but–"

"Bring me something good. I'll praise it, Hawkesey."

Joe stirred. His mother crossed the room, resentment bristling through her well spread smile.

"Are you feeling better, Joe?"

He knew he was hardly well enough to fight her just yet. He tried to postpone the issue.

"Feel rotten."

"Never mind, I'll take you to the hotel and get you a doctor."

He sat up. "No," he answered. "Hawkes, would you be kind enough to see my mother back to the hotel?" He caught Miss Weems' eye. "May I stay a while?"

Hawkes offered himself. Mrs. Beddington was no terror to him; he had acted orderly to a general with dyspepsia; he had been drilled by a sergeant-major who desired to keep him from promotion; there was nothing Hawkes did not know about enduring insult without letting it sink under his skin. She ignored him, but he did not mind that either.

"It isn't polite, Joe, to inflict yourself on Miss Weems."

"I came to talk to her," said Joe. But he glanced at Amrita. His mother, too, glanced at Amrita. "Joe, I wish you to come home and talk to me first."

"What about?" he demanded.

She compressed her lips into a thin line with a trained smile at either corner, meant to seem inscrutable. Her eyes now deliberately avoided Amrita. "About personal matters," she answered.

"See you later, Mother. I'll be back in time for dinner."

War—war—war at last; he had declared it and she understood him. Joe felt all the hot exhilaration that accompanies a challenge, but he masked it, not wishing to seem ridiculous, since none but he, he supposed, knew what ferocity and resources he would have to combat. He was not given to mock heroics. He invited no one's sympathy. He meant to fight this to a finish with his own resources, yet not more than guessing what those might be. He was not fooled by his mother's instant change of tactics.

"May he stay with you a little while longer, Miss Weems? He seems to be worse shaken than he realizes."

Annie Weems' smile masked nothing. "He may stay here as long as he pleases," she answered, plainly intimating he should stay until Annie Weems saw fit to let him go. Mrs. Beddington realized it—bridled—accepted the challenge:

"I will send the doctor to him here."

"Dr. Karter Singh would very likely come if you should ask him."

"A native?"

"A Sikh."

"Great heavens, is there no white doctor?"

"There's an army doctor, who is usually busy, and a civilian who is nearly always drunk."

"For God's sake send the drunkard," Joe interrupted. "Tank him up before you send him. I can manage drunkards."

"Joe!"

"See you later, Mother."

Mrs. Beddington fussed her way out of the place, ignoring Hawkes deliberately and apparently forgetting to notice Amrita. She kept Annie Weems standing at the front door for several minutes, asking her barbed questions about the mission school but saying nothing that could be interpreted as actual insolence. Amrita, straight faced, strummed at the piano.

"Don't you love to know the worst?" she wondered. "Man from Jupiter, why didn't you tell her about me?"

"And my thousand pounds," Hawkes added.

"And why are you pretending to be worse hurt than you are?"

"Can't you see for yourself?" Joe asked her.

"See, yes. I can read your aura. Smoky crimson. Where was Mars in your horoscope? Are you afraid of her?"

"Too many questions."

"Answer one then."

"No, I'm no longer afraid."

"You will be soon—unless I'm seeing you and her all crooked. Can't you read auras? No? You're psychic, you could learn. Hers is dingy indigo and sulphur, with lurid smoky-green tonguelets like the petals of a sunflower. When you see it that color, you perhaps don't know you see it, but it scares you all the same. It would scare me, if she were my mother. Do you hate her? You shouldn't. When you hate her, you establish a vibration along which she can get you as a spider gets a fly. If you were sentimental about her, she could get you that way too. She is dreadfully strong. I'd hate her if I dared."

Her fingers strummed on the piano keys a sort of obbligato to her conversation — strange experiments with chords that seemed to illustrate the color of her thought. It was perhaps not music but it was humorous, like a Greek chorus mocking the speaker. Joe felt intimate, as if she and he had known each other all their lives.

"Why did you keep me secret?" she repeated suddenly. "You have a way of doing that. You boil and sulk inside yourself. It poisons you. That isn't like a man from Jupiter. Your forte is direct action. It would be good for you to dance and sing—scream—yell—swear—do anything to boil off."

Joe grinned. He had a sudden mental picture of himself cavorting like a temperamental Frenchman.

"Laugh!" she urged. "That grin is a habit of being solemn. Do you know what solemnity is? It's the gloom with which asses disguise their ignorance. Why imitate them?"

"It was quite unconscious," Joe answered humbly.

"That doesn't make it harmless. If your head didn't ache I would make you dance with me. Hawkesey used to go everywhere looking like a sermon on the predamnation of unbaptized infants. But I made him dance every time he saw me. When I had corrupted him enough, so that he even began to like himself a little, I made him promise to dance whenever he thought of me. Now see him. Hawkesey is almost human."

"Cost me money. I wore out a pair of boots," said Hawkes. "It nearly got me out of the army. I was sat on by a medical committee—two fat doctors and a thin one—claimed I was crazy. I didn't deny it. I told 'em I dance to try and feel as happy as a nigger. So they gave me a month's sick leave and I went to Mount Abu, where a heathen taught me how to dance like Krishna with a flute."

"He means," explained Amrita, "that a venerable Yogi taught him."

"He wasn't pious," Hawkes objected.

"Venerable people never are," she answered, fingering the keys. She struck chords like Stravinsky's—several in quick succession to a startling tempo. "Venerable people laugh with God instead of making faces at Him. That Yogi who taught you, Hawkesey—"

"Swag-bellied old corner-man, as full of repartee as a big drum's full o' thunder."

"—is an ex-subadar-major of Bengal cavalry. They say he can talk with tigers and that wild birds come when he calls them."

"Do you believe that?" Joe asked.

"Why not? It isn't difficult. But it's bad for the birds and tigers. They learn to trust people. Do you trust people?"

Annie Weems returned into the room, a wee mite ruffled, mastering indignation.

"Scream," Amrita suggested. But she suddenly left the piano and sat on the arm of Annie Weems' chair. "Was she as cruel as all that?"

"She accused me of raising you for blackmail purposes."

Joe flushed with shame. "Did she use those words?" he asked.

"No. She merely said that she is blackmail-proof but that if I care to talk with her attorneys she will give me their address."

Joe swore under his breath.

"Explode!" Amrita urged. "You man from Jupiter, one of these days you will kill some one, or else some one will kill you. You vibrate like hell with the lid shut, as Hawkesey would say."

"Hell?" said Hawkes. "My dreams of affluence—ten centuries—a thousand quid—"

He eyed Joe sideways. Joe observed him without comment. Amrita observed both of them.

"Are you a mean man?" she asked suddenly. "You don't look it."

Joe stared at her. "Damned if I know," he answered. He continued to stare. She returned it. He perfectly understood that she was in some way reading his character. He did not mind. He felt no impulse to deceive her as a man normally does when a woman tries to understand him. He could see the color of her eyes at last—deep blue with a hint of violet. He wondered whether she was really beautiful or whether he was prejudiced and perhaps not seeing accurately.

"I would like to paint your portrait," he said abruptly.

"Why? If you are really skilful you can only paint your own opinion of me."

"Are you afraid of my opinion?"

"I'm afraid you might produce a lie and hate that. Next, you'd hate me. Painters become enamored of their models, but they end by kicking them out-of-doors."

"Are you afraid of my falling in love with you?"

"One can only fall out of love, not into it. One might as well talk of falling on to horseback or falling up a mountain. Love? Climb and find it! Wings—you need wings and speed and courage to come within a million miles of love. That's closer than most folk come. Most of them catch their mates with traps or quick-lime and then cage them and say Sing! Those fall hard, and it hurts them. Didn't you fall hard enough this morning?"

"Who taught you to be cynical?"

She laughed. Hawkes almost jeered. Annie Weems glanced at the clock and excused herself, saying she had a new cook who needed attention. She paused in the door of the passage that led to the kitchen:

"Rita cynical?"

"Cynical?" Hawkes echoed. "Shall I show the cook potatoes à la Kaiser Bill?" He followed Annie Weems into the kitchen.

"So it offends them to hear you called cynical?"

"They think it's funny."

She settled down into the armchair. Joe decided she was genuinely beautiful. She reminded him of some one—some actress—he couldn't remember who.

"Are you a fatalist?" he asked her suddenly.

"That is like asking me, am I a fool. Destiny is—whether or not we believe it. Fate is what overtakes fatheads!"

Joe winced. He did not like her to use Hawkes' phrases. Was he jealous of Hawkes? He wondered. It might not be a bad idea to pay Hawkes that thousand pounds—he might quit the army—leave India. But—

"Do you know Maharajah Poonch-Terai?" he asked.

"Indeed I do. Fate."

"Your fate?"

"Trying to masquerade as destiny."

"I can't see any difference."

"There isn't much. It's like the difference between day and night, that's all. Opposite sides of one idea."

"We are slaves of destiny?"

She laughed. "We are slaves of fate, if we don't rebel against it. I'm a rebel. Aren't you?"

Joe did not wish to think about his mother just then.

"Was I destined to fall from a horse this morning?"

"Fated. Destiny is our servant. We create destiny. Fate is created for us by the things we do or don't do."

"I don't get you."

"Fate did! And destiny saved you. Something you did to some one else, in this life or another one, produced its exactly measured consequences and—"

"It was Poonch-Terai who bunted into me—on purpose."

"That makes no difference, except to him. He set new consequences cycling on their course; he will have to meet them whenever the clock strikes, and it is sure to strike at an inconvenient moment. Possibly you injured him some time."

"I never met the man before."

"How do you know? Can you prove you didn't? What were you, and where were you, before you were born, say, thirty years ago? However, possibly you didn't injure him. You did wrong to some one, or you wouldn't have had wrong done to you this morning. On the other hand, you had built up destiny. Fine things—splendid, noble, magnanimous things you did in former lives, or possibly in this one, built up forces that saved you. Probably you call it accident, but it makes no difference what you call it. Names don't alter cases. What does make a difference, is, how you behaved when it happened. If you had turned on Poonch-Terai and beaten him, you would have set new consequences cycling for yourself. That is what was meant by 'turn the other cheek'; you not only learn self-control and build up character but you also pay forgotten debts and create new destiny with which to meet fate when it happens. It's like the difference between having money in the bank, at compound interest, and incurring debts at compound interest. Every time you pay a debt you make a friend, and the quicker you pay the less it costs you."

Joe smiled. "Rather a complicated scheme of things."

"So is astronomy, complicated. So are biology–chemistry–law. And yet it's all divinely simple. Reread history and see whether it doesn't fit what you call the complicated scheme of things. Try to make it not fit; you can't without distorting all the facts."

"Do you mean, for instance, that I've met you in a former life?"

"Of course you have. Lots of times, in lots of former lives."

"And my mother?"

"Certainly. You can't create an intimate relation such as that by accident. It must have taken millions of incidents to bring you two to a point where you could help each other best in just that way."

"Help each other? Lord God! Wait until you know her!"

"Let me think of an illustration. Don't you think it helped the English to be bullied by the Tudors and the Stuarts? Didn't it make them wake up? What but pressure made the colonies win their independence? Do you know what pressure does to certain sorts of seed? You were born your mother's child because you were ready to stand just that test. There is no injustice—nowhere in all the universe—not for a moment."

Joe laughed outright. "If you'd ever run a bank, or a business, or fought a lawsuit; or if you'd ever seen my mother sack a raft of her employees; or if you know how laws are forced through legislatures—"

"Justice—every atom of it including all the injustice! No one escapes his exact deserts or lacks his opportunity to learn. Those on whom what seems to be injustice is inflicted would do, if not the same thing, something like it—its equivalent—if they had the power and the temptation. They are learning the feel of the sting of injustice—learning not to inflict it. The first shall be the last and the last shall be first. The unjust judge is reborn to a life in prison on a false charge. The usurer spends a life or two in debt. The cheat gets cheated. The cruel man suffers cruelty. Each to the fate his deeds have caused—and each one to the destiny that he himself has earned."

"But what's the purpose of it?"

"Character. We seem unable to learn except by experience."

"And the end of it all?"

"Nobody knows. But even the materialists, who are blinded by matter—probably to make them hopeless, so that they will be forced in the end to wake up and to tear away the bandage from their own eyes—even they assure us that nothing in all nature is wasted. It is logical to deduce that we ourselves are not wasted."

"Nothing is finally wasted," Joe agreed. "I know that. When we're dead we decompose and are reabsorbed into nature. That's law. Law itself must have a cause. I can grasp that much. Most of us call the cause God. It happens I believe in God; the arguments against the omnipresence of a First Cause seem to me ridiculous. Finite calculations can't measure infinity and we can prove, for instance, that infinity squared is equal to the square root of infinity plus or minus anything you please—which knocks the props from under logic, with which, nevertheless, we prove the existence of a calculus that transcends logic. So I'm wide open to believe anything—except that some super-intelligence doesn't direct the Universe. All the same, if what you say is true, or even half true—and I admit it sounds plausible—there ought to be something that at least looks like proof of it. How can you prove, or pretend to prove, that you, for instance, have lived more than one life in this world?"

"I can prove it as easily as you can prove that you are sitting here, or that the sun shines," she answered.

"I'd be interested."

"Possibly your time has come to wake up. If it has, there isn't a force in all the universe that can prevent you. If it hasn't, I could pile proof on proof and you could no more understand it than Pilate could understand Jesus. Did you ever try to teach a blind man about color? Or a tone-deaf person about music? Or a dog about poetry? It's sometimes easiest to teach the dog. Or did you ever try to teach a criminal the principles of ethics? It can't be done, until experience ripens us. Then we can't help learning, because that kind of intelligence evolves within us."

"Lunch," said Annie Weems, appearing in the door. "We don't call it tiffin. It's plain New England lunch."

"And 'taters à la Kaiser Bill." Hawkes peered over her shoulder. "You pull 'em from the pot before they're cooked, then chill 'em. Subsequent you treat 'em handsome on a hot grid. Then add applesauce and condiments to suit, with Dutch cheese—grated. Yum-yum!"

FROM THE BOOK OF THE YOGI-ASTROLOGER
RAM-CHITTRA GUNGA SINGH

The arrogant vanity of the incredulous is a mystery more difficult to penetrate than life and death. Experience and wisdom are alike incomprehensible to the incredulous, to whom their senses are their guides and their bellies their impudent gods. They despise imagination; though with what else they imagine themselves superior to the Unseen, the Unknown and the Unsuspected, they irascibly refuse to tell.

Such fools speak of themselves as critical, though no true critic is incredulous or could be. Knowing, because he is a critic, that hunger for the unknown truth and hatred of false appearances is the two-fold state of consciousness from which true criticism springs; and knowing, because he is a critic, that what he actually knows is no more than the shallow rind of knowledge and as relative to truth as space is to infinity or as an organ is to the music that inspires its player, he is eager to believe what he does not know and only watchful against the snares of rash conclusion. He is like a mariner exploring unknown seas. He is watchful for rocks and shoals; but had he been incredulous he would never have gone exploring.

Great critics are the great creators. He who has created nothing is incapable of judgment. He who boasts of incredulity and sneers at what his senses cannot crucify, not only knows nothing but is a liar misleading the ignorant; calling himself critical, he trades on their credulity the while he mocks it.

Genius is ability to perceive the hitherto unknown and to adapt it to a purpose. All things, all qualities have their opposites. The opposite of genius is incredulity. The opposite of judgment is the weird delusion that the truth is governed by, or is contingent on a man's opinion.

XIII

> *"I am not in the world to learn cowardice, but courage."*

Lunch was astonishing. It felt like the first real family meal in which Joe had ever taken part. Hawkes, at the end of the table, making jokes about the food and telling anecdotes from far-off barracks about brass hats' lapses from dignity, seemed part of it. It was impossible to realize that Rita, in a Sears-Roebuck summer frock and with her hair looking as if Pan had run his fingers through it, was the same girl who had sung to prisoners by moonlight. The light was different in the dining-room; it made her eyes look mischievous and her lips luscious. Joe wondered why Hawkes had not tried to seduce her. He felt a sudden pang of jealousy. Then something that he supposed was racial pride distressed him as he wondered how so beautiful a girl could possibly have been raised in an Indian temple and remain a virgin. He pondered that a long time, taking privilege of silence on account of his headache. He studied Annie Weems. It seemed to him she was a woman who knew secrets—and could keep them.

He hoped Amrita was a virgin, but supposed it didn't matter; nobody nowadays troubled about that trifle. Nevertheless, he already felt so much like one of the family that he almost had a right to know. He wondered whether she would tell the truth if he should ask her. He smiled at himself. Being human, he would believe a confession of guilt; a claim to virginity would leave him incredulous. Better not ask. Might embarrass her. All the same, he would give a lot to know what went on in an Indian temple.

The hell of it was that his mother would make insinuations difficult to disprove. She would pound away at it, perpetually harping on the same string. He supposed, if his mother had been first to find the girl, it might be different; she would almost certainly have tried, in that case, to subdue and enslave her, tempting her first with a glimpse of what money can do, then gradually imposing insolence on insolence until the victim surrendered—he had seen her kill a girl in that way; the doctors had called it anemia, which it probably was, but Joe knew what had caused it.

She would kill this girl too, if she as much as suspected he thought well of her. And, what was more, she already did suspect. She would stop at nothing—at nothing—no limit. How could he take the girl's part without first arriving at an understanding with her? Should he quit before the fight began and let his mother wreak her savagery unimpeded? He smiled at the thought of it—smiled with his eyes too, as he recognized suddenly how swift and absolute his own revolt against his mother had been, and how determined he was to protect Amrita. Was he in love with her? He wondered.

"What amuses you?" asked Annie Weems.

"Something I want to ask you afterward."

That was the right idea. He had not meant to say it; it had slipped out; but he was glad he had said it. Annie Weems was the kind of woman you could talk to intimately without risk of betrayal. She might not say much, but she would listen; and what she did say would be something a man might bet on. Damn that fellow Hawkes; he could make his wisecracks, couldn't he, without leaning so close to Amrita's chair? To offset Hawkes' impertinence Joe started telling stories of his own, and he could do that admirably when he made the effort. His stories were a mite too heavy on their feet, he knew that, but they were interesting; he had worked hard at the accomplishment, to help overcome the prejudice against himself as his mother's son. He could talk Hawkes out of the limelight. He did.

As they left the dining-table Annie Weems, low-voiced, invited him to join her in the schoolroom. However, he had to postpone that tête-à-tête. The doctor came—Tobias Fetherstonehaugh Muldoon M.D.—a trifle husky from his morning quart of Scotch, but steady on his feet and primed with virtue. Annie Weems was civil but he snubbed her.

"I will see the patient alone," he said abruptly.

Annie Weems opened the door of a small room furnished with a couch and two chairs. Joe walked in. Muldoon closed the door behind him—paused—opened it again suddenly—then slammed it.

"Never know who's listening in a place like this."

Joe made no comment. He studied the man's dishonest nose.

"Your mother was so insistent that I put off another patient. May I see your tongue a moment? Pulse, please. Temperature—under the tongue and keep the lips shut." Silence, during which antagonism grew. Then: "Thank you. Nothing much the matter. You've had a dam' bad shaking up, but you're young and strong. Just take things easy for a few days. Mild cathartic. I will send you something from the dispensary."

Joe awaited his mother's message. He could not imagine her sending this man to him without putting words in his mouth. At her best she was as subtle as a howitzer. The two men stared until the silence grew awkward and Muldoon screwed up courage:

"I'd get out of here, if I were you. You might find yourself badly compromised. Chi-chis—know what I mean?"

Joe did, but he pretended ignorance.

"Eurasians—touch o' the tar-brush—strange people—dam' dishonest as a rule—no character—inherit the vice of black and white, with the virtues of neither."

"What about it?"

"She's Eurasian. Thought you ought to know it."

"Who? Miss Weems?"

"No. Can't accuse Miss Weems of that exactly. I mean the Rita person. Dam' good-looking wench with dark hair, dark eyes—and dark intentions, you may take my word for it. Nod as good as a wink to a blind horse—be on your guard—blackmail—very plausible, I don't doubt—conspiracy—h'sss!—don't say a word."

Joe said none—waited. There was an awkward pause before Muldoon renewed the assault:

"This is confidential, of course. Keep it to yourself. That pretty little Rita person is the daughter of a British Tommy and a half-breed whore in the bazaar, who died of cholera."

"You've proof of that?" Joe asked. His voice had

changed perceptibly. He was leading his witness, thawing toward him slightly on the surface, tempting him to deeper indiscretion.

"Never can prove a thing when you want to in this dam' country. She's a psychic—know what that is? It's a form of psychosis not uncommon among Chi-chis. Fortune-tellers call it second sight. Old as the hills—old as the Delphic Oracle—nothing more nor less than an over-developed and vaguely spiritualized sex-instinct overbalancing a character weakened by superstition and a craving to be important."

"Have you examined her?"

"Can't say I have. Don't care to. Can't be bothered. Dam' stuff's too familiar. But why are we standing? You should relax yourself at every opportunity for the next few days. That's better—sit slack. Privately, between you and me, it might do you no harm to get a bit drunk tonight, but don't tell your mother I recommended it. Come around to my bungalow and we'll pull a cork together."

"Good of you, I'm sure."

Another pause. "Why, no, I've not examined her, but the girl's notorious. Too bad we haven't an institution where she could be properly looked after, but the government can't afford that kind of luxury. The case might yield to careful treatment, though I doubt it—there's a religious complex there—sings mystical hymns in the jail-yard at midnight."

Joe nodded but looked incredulous. He wished to hear the full indictment. His mother he knew could pump a man like Muldoon dry in fifteen minutes, and corrupt him utterly in five. If he could hold his own tongue this fool would betray her. Muldoon mistook silence for proof of his own astuteness, so he blundered on:

"You know, Annie Weems isn't socially recognized. There's nothing regular about her. Luckily for her she keeps out of politics, or we'd have closed her mission long ago. She has some sort of understanding with the Hindu priests—nobody knows exactly what's the basis of it, but you know the proverb: 'Love of money is the root of all evil.' Love o' money—superstition—blackmail—black arts—clairvoyance—mixed blood—you can't make head nor tails of that mess or separate one ingredient from another. The best thing is to let it alone. There was a rich young Englishman who got caught in a mess like that. Persuaded him to finance a new religion. He took the girl to London. He not only lost social caste but half his fortune with it. Ended by his being blackmailed half out of his senses. And at that, the girl was only a poor half-wit who handed over the cash to a few conspirators behind the scenes!"

"Has Miss Weems ever blackmailed anyone?"

"I can't say. But nobody knows where she gets the money to run the mission. All we know is she gets it. I've worked for years on police court cases. It's one of the commonest occurrences to find criminals, or potential criminals, using a clairvoyant or a trance medium to guide them in a conspiracy. They think they can get information from another world. What often gets them into trouble before any serious harm is done is the neurotic sex-psychosis of the mediums—loose morals—jealousy—vanity—vengeance—and the cat's out of the bag. That Rita girl is a good-looker, of course. I can easily understand your wanting her. But beware of those Eurasians—they're too promiscuous.

That fellow Hawkes, for instance—you know what soldiers are. Besides, she's in some way mixed up with the orgies that go on in a Hindu temple. As a medical man with more than a little experience of this country, I advise you to keep clear of her. Good God, I've seen scores of fine young fellows sent home ruined—physically, morally, mentally. Cured? Yes, after a fashion—cured of happiness and manhood for the rest of their natural lives. Would you like me to look at those cuts on your face? They're beautifully bandaged—seems a shame to disturb such a neat job—Annie Weems do it? She and Hawkes, eh? Well—that fellow Hawkes is something of a wizard. Let's let it rest. We'll have a look at it tomorrow."

Another pause—a long one—Joe as conscious of his mother as if she were there in the room. Quick work! And what luck she always had in discovering creatures like Muldoon to do her bidding at a moment's notice.

Muldoon broke the silence. "My Ford is outside. Let me drive you to the hotel."

"No, thanks."

"Well, young man, I've warned you."

"Good of you, I'm sure. Will you send me your bill? I've no checkbook with me."

"That's all right. Your mother—"

"All right, send the bill to her."

"I think I'd better see you in the morning. Those cuts may need attention."

"Just as you like." Joe had opened the door. There was nothing for Muldoon to do but walk out. To preserve his dignity he blustered, snubbing Annie Weems again, ignoring her as he swaggered to the front door where he turned for a final word to Joe:

"Tomorrow then. Meanwhile I'll have my assistant mix you something—send it to the hotel. Good day."

Annie Weems stood in the door of the living room. Joe faced her. Suddenly Rita's gay laugh broke the silence.

"Can you see his aura, Annie?"

"Hush, child! Do you still wish to see me alone, Mr. Beddington?"

"Yes, more than ever."

Rita put both her arms around Annie Weems from behind. In that light it looked almost like two heads on one pair of shoulders—one gray but eternally young, the other young but humorously wise. There was something ageless about Rita—something, too, that made a fellow's heart jump when he saw her suddenly. Her eyes seemed to see beyond surfaces.

"Me too—talk in front of me," she urged him. "She would tell me afterward—and besides, I know what you are going to say."

"All right." Joe accepted the challenge. He followed them into the living room, where Rita again sat on the arm of Annie Weems' chair. "Where's Hawkes?" he asked. He did not want Hawkes to listen in.

"Hawkesey is on the roof, mending the valve of the water-tank."

She had the light behind her, through the slats of the window-shade. It streamed in layers on her dark hair, edging it with gold. One stream of it poured on her hand; she was pressing the tips of her fingers, perhaps excitedly, on the book that lay on the table beside the chair; Joe noticed that the half-moons of her nails showed no trace of tell-tale color.

Annie Weems folded her hands in her lap. "Well?"

"No," said Joe, "Let Rita say it. She said she knows what I'm going to say. Let's see if she's bluffing."

"I know part of it and I can guess part of it," said Rita. "You're curious, and yet you know the answer to what you're chiefly curious about; but when you think about it with your brain you're not so sure you know. And what you're quite sure that you know is where you're wholly wrong."

"Say it in plain English," Joe retorted.

"Last first. You think you know a Hindu temple is an awful place, where there are orgies. So there are, in some temples, but only in some of them. You think my mind, and probably my soul has been corrupted. And you wonder about my body. You wonder whether I'm loose, as you would call it."

"Right," said Joe.

"But you are wrong," she answered. "If it is your business to know that, you know it without my telling you. If it is not your business, nothing I could tell you would make the slightest difference. You would form your own opinion, and if it differed from my statement, you would think me a liar. But that would not alter the truth."

"Frankly, I'm deeply interested."

"In me? What else do you wish to know? Do you wish me to tell that, too. Very well. You wonder why Annie let me continue in a Hindu temple instead of sending me to the United States as soon as she discovered who I was. Is there a color line in the United States?"

"There is," said Joe.

"Do you know why I pressed my fingers on this book? I have no Indian or Eurasian blood, but who can prove it?"

Joe hesitated. All the arguments that occurred to him seemed trite before he turned them on his tongue.

"Civilization—" he began.

"Am I a savage?"

"I should say you have had experiences that you should have been spared from."

"For what are we in the world, except for experiences? Could I do more good in the United States than I can here? Could I learn more? Tell me something you know that I don't."

Again Joe hesitated. "Cultural surroundings are important," he said awkwardly. "There's an indefinable something that a college education gives—"

"I lack it?"

She did not wait for him to answer. She came over to him, stood beside his chair, speaking in a voice that thrilled him so strangely that he felt as he did when listening to organ music stealing by a stair of overtones toward infinity.

"Joe—I don't want to humiliate you. If we talk to each other like this we'll both be sorry, because it's something you don't understand. It's something you will have to find out for yourself, since nobody can tell you—not even the wisest person—although you can have help—I can try to help you."

Puzzled more than ever, trying to resent what he felt

was a slur on his dignity, Joe looked up at her. But that is not an attitude from which a man can easily assert his superior manhood. He found himself smiling. The smell of her body was sweeter than honey and wine in his nostrils.

"Funny," he said. "*I* came here to help *you*."

"It was funny, wasn't it? Something like helping a plant by pulling it out by the roots!"

He almost ached to put his hands on her. The artist half of him danced to the sweep of the line of her figure; she was one of Botticelli's springtime mistresses, more maddening because nature seemed so in love with her that she was guarded by something impassable—something that checked impulse. The part of him that had been trained to make cold appraisal and to view ironically anything that named its price or did not name it, recognized a challenge. The opposing force locked him in a sort of vise in which speech died unspoken.

It was Hawkes who broke the silence, entering the room with the deliberate calm of a bearer of exciting news. He walked over to Annie Weems as if to whisper to her, changed his mind and broke his news aloud:

"I've fixed the valve, Miss Annie. You can have the tank filled now. Did you know you can see down four streets from the bricks the tank rests on? There's a closed carriage and two good horses waiting about a hundred yards away. Two men on the box. Two footmen. Four tough customers on foot, lurking near, one of 'em speaking now and then through the slats to someone in the carriage—probably a woman. They're Poonch-Terai's men."

"Can you get help?" Annie Weems asked.

"Yes, Miss. I'll go and attend to it." He walked out as nonchalantly as he probably would have done if they had told him that the empire was in ruins.

"Amal must have told them where I am," said Rita laughing. She appeared afraid of nothing. "Poor Amal—she has set her heart on high places for me. She thinks if I were once inside Poonch-Terai's palace all the world would lie at my feet to be petted and blessed."

Annie Weems rose from her chair. "That ayah!" She put on her spectacles—stared at Rita, then at Joe. Joe stood up; she stepped toward him. "I will tell you something."

"No, no, Annie!"

"I am determined. Mr. Beddington, that ayah—who saved Rita when she was a baby—who has served and watched her ever since—who worships her beyond all reason, as it isn't right that any human should worship another—Amal, her name is Amal—is the principal reason why I have never sent Rita home to the United States."

"The other reason is that I would not have gone," said Rita.

"You would have gone, child, if I had seen my way to send you without doing you a worse injustice than was done by keeping you in India. Mr. Beddington—that ayah is the only person in the world who actually knows who Rita's parents were. I say I know, but I have no proof. Amal is a brave, loyal, obstinate, fanatical, devoted woman, with far more intelligence than appears on the surface. Her whole heart and soul is wrapped up in Amrita. She told me the truth, but she has never once told it in the presence of witnesses. She even lied to Rita about there being black blood in her veins, in order to make her dislike the idea of calling herself white."

"But Rita knows she's not Eurasian," Joe objected.

"Yes, I told her. So did Ram-Chittra Gunga. So did the temple priests, who have their own means of judging. But then Amal spread the tale through the bazaar. She spread it so cunningly that it became what the courts would call common knowledge. After that she threatened to go before a judge and swear Amrita is Eurasian if anyone should make any kind of move to take the child away. And she got witnesses, of whom one is a snake-charmer; and he found others. I don't know how Amal found enough money to bribe them, but she did, and she bound them later on into a sort of secret religious cult, based on prophecies about Amrita's future. You would think Amal is stupid, to look at her. She is as cunning as she is determined."

Joe smiled, sympathetic but ironical. "An attorney, Miss Weems, could have solved the problem for you."

"So I thought. I tried one. There are only Indian attorneys here. I chose the best of them, but Amal learned of it. She ran to Maharajah Poonch-Terai. Tell Poonch-Terai about a new young girl and he would cross the Himalayas on foot to take a look at her. Once tempted, he would rather die than let the girl escape him. He saw Rita—Amal told him my attorney's name. He interviewed the attorney. The following day the attorney washed his hands of the case, saying he had convinced himself that Rita is Eurasian. We were alone—in this room. I accused him of dishonesty, and of taking pay from Poonch-Terai. He denied it, but he laughed nervously and threatened to accuse me of trying to procure false evidence, and of conspiracy."

"Conspiracy to do what?"

"Conspiracy to blackmail the relatives of Rita's alleged parents, in the United States. He declared he would charge me with it, and would produce witnesses, if I made one move to take her out of India. He meant, out of Poonch-Terai's reach. In this country, a dishonest person can buy witnesses for any purpose."

"In other lands," said Joe, "it's sometimes easier to buy a juryman—or to send a judge's wife and daughter for a fine vacation on the continent. A mistrial is more expensive, but it's safer than perjured evidence."

"None of that really matters," said Rita. "It isn't the real reason why I stayed in India."

"Hush, child, I was speaking. There was another reason, and a very strong one. Rita has gifts of a kind that could not have developed amid harsh surroundings or in a critical atmosphere. She is strong now and perfectly balanced; but it would have been not far short of murder to have sent her to a public institution, where other children would have treated her like chickens picking on a lame one. I don't mean she could not have survived physically—she is as healthy as a young horse—always has been. But her spiritual nature would have died, like something exotic shrinking from chill wind. Misunderstood, she would either have rebelled against routine, or perhaps have gone mad from suppression. I was not ill-pleased to keep her here. I have given her the very best there is in me, and I have never left this mission even for a short vacation in all these years, for fear of neglecting her for a single minute or of being absent when she might need my help."

"Did it never occur to you to adopt her?" Joe asked.

"It did. But there were legal difficulties. I have had to protect her as best I could with the aid of those good Hindu priests. But now I can't protect her any longer. Poonch-Terai is too powerful—too cunning—he has too many agents and too much money for me to be able to resist him, even with native Indian cavalrymen and Sergeant Hawkes to help. Rita must go to the United States."

"Why do you confide in me?" Joe asked her. The side of him that was trained to examine motives and to disbelieve all unproven statements, doubted her. The other side knew she was telling the truth. "Why me?"

"That is something Rita must tell you," she answered.

He faced Rita, curiously pleased. So he had been discussed already—passed on—in a sense accepted? It gave him an indescribable feeling of cosmic importance, that had no logical basis whatever, but was none the less pleasant. But he was vaguely disturbed by Rita's eyes that seemed to have lost their quiet humor. They were not hard now, but there was fire behind them. It dawned on him for the first time, and suddenly, that she was a person of terrific strength of character.

"Do you care to tell me?" he asked.

"No. You won't believe. Annie has told you surfaces. Perhaps she thinks you can't see deeper than a surface. Few can."

Rita faced him like a huntress using waves of thought for weapons—hunting for something hidden—something to be caught, not killed. He felt an impulse to help her find it.

"All those reasons Annie gave are surface reasons," she repeated. "They are fate reasons, provided to protect my destiny. I don't leave India because my place is here, and I know it is here. Why else was I born here? Here is my opportunity, and Annie knows that."

"Do you think we are always all in our proper place?" Joe asked her.

"Of course we are. And you know we are. Are the stars not in their proper places? Are you or I more powerful than the stars that we can pull ourselves out of our orbit?"

"Do you consider it your place to be taken and raped by Poonch-Terai?"

"How do I know? I may have to learn that lesson. May there not be—within his palace—something to be done that I alone can do? If so, does my convenience matter? If not, then he gives me an opportunity to learn how to defeat dark forces, such as he thinks are omnipotent. He may possibly learn from defeat. I am not in the world to learn cowardice but courage. I have faculties and talents; I will use them where I stand. Joe—did you ever conquer by running away?"

"Conquer what? I've conquered very little, come to think of it."

"Could you conquer your mother by running away?"

"I never thought of running. I was born her son. I accepted the implied obligation; and I have stuck to my job, hoping for illumination that would show me how to tame her without doing murder."

"I, too, have stuck to my job. I was born in India. And here I stay, until my work is finished."

"You'll find plenty to do," he suggested. "To me it looks like a distressful country."

"I said, my work—not everybody's work. When mine is finished I shall find myself picked up and planted elsewhere. Or perhaps I shall die. Are you afraid of death?"

"Not specially." He laughed. "You think I'm in my proper place, in India, this minute—not in New York."

She nodded. "You can prove it easily. You can try to go away before your work is done. Fate—that is to say, the sum-total of your liabilities translated into action—may be strong enough to cheat you of your destiny for the time being. But it won't change destiny. Destiny—which is nothing else than earned character—will make you fight fate sooner or later. The sooner you stand and fight, the simpler will the fight be. No one can escape by running away."

"You suggest I should go home?"

"Try. If you like, I will help you try. You have my leave to go, as the Indians say. I don't ask your help. I will try not to see you again. See—I wash my hands of you." She went through the motions. "Much good that will do you, if you are the man I think you are, and if you have the character I think you have. But try it."

Something that Joe knew was filthy—a whiff of the complaisance with which he had too often viewed his mother's cruelties—stole over him.

"All right," he said. "I'll take you at your word. I'll try it."

Hawkes entered the room, grinning. "All right, ladies. I found a messenger. Some o' the Indian troopers'll be down in half a jiffy to lick the stuffing out of Poonch-Terai's detail."

FROM THE BOOK OF THE YOGI-ASTROLOGER RAM-CHITTRA GUNGA SINGH

In the West, where I travelled far in search of Wisdom, I found much courtesy and kindness, which, indeed, are essences of Wisdom. But I found that certain other essences were lacking, though there was great energy, an admirable scorn of the impossible, and what looked like efficiency until its skeleton appeared.

I met high scientists of such intelligence that they can do by complicated means what insects manage simply and what Nature does without an effort. Some I met who are so diligent that they commence to rediscover by devious means the truths the Lord Gautama Buddha taught, and that others taught earlier, thousands of years even before his day. Nevertheless, those spoke of the Lord Buddha as an ignorant person having certain intuitions, but no wisdom, and no knowledge.

Claiming to base judgment solely on verified observation, several such men assured me, with the condescension of the learned toward the ignorant, that Gautama was right in saying we evolve from nothing into nothing. Nevertheless, He never taught that; though He did teach that this material, self-seeking self must cease before the true Self may appear. I told them so. I proved it to them. But they answered: There is no self other than this personality that dies and then disintegrates; else, if there were we could observe it, verifying observation, keeping check on one another.

So I asked: Wherewith would you observe that Inner Self? To which they answered: With our brains, which are the seat of our intelligence.

So I asked: Of what are brains made? And they showed me water in a jar, some carbon, iron, salt and a few small quantities of other elements. They said: Of such stuff we are wonderfully made—nerves, brains, ears, eyes, bodies. We evolve from that stuff. We return to it. It consists of atoms, aggregated. And the atoms possibly are nothing in the last analysis. All this, said they, is capable of proof.

I answered: Surely they are nothing, as the Lord Gautama

Buddha and a great and mighty Teacher of your own assured you long ago. But with what, then, do you perceive these atoms and these aggregates of atoms? With your brains? Can water, iron, salt and so on think? Or can they cause thought? Must thought cease when those disintegrate?

They said: When those are gone, there is nothing left of us to think with. Who has seen a corpse display intelligence? Whereat they laughed.

I answered: You identify yourselves with nothing. Nevertheless, if one of you identifies himself with a wheel or a horse, you call him mad and lock him up. He has to eat the fruit of madness. You must eat the fruit of nothing until iron, water, salt and so on cease to hypnotise you in that mirror in which you see yourselves so learnedly.

Whereat they smiled; and they were very courteous, perceiving that I needed sympathy. But in the course of time they caused their government to pass a law concerning such as me, excluding us and our doubts of the validity of their verified observations leading out of nothing into nothing.

I am a Yogi. I sit at the feet of Wisdom, willing to be taught by any circumstances that can teach.

XIV

"Better watch my step!"

Hawkes went in search of a native *gharri* but it was a long time before he found one. Meanwhile, Joe went to the roof to look for what Hawkes had called the Maharajah's "detail." He saw a shuttered carriage standing by the corner of a side-street, its two fine horses stamping fretfully; there were two men on the box, two footmen lolling on the platform at the rear, and several men who looked like loafers near at hand. He had not watched long when a Ford car stopped two streets away and disgorged five Indian troopers, one of whom strolled casually to the intersection of the streets, hardly glancing at the two-horsed carriage, and returned to his friends who hitched themselves a little but appeared to hold no conference, although they stood in an idle-looking group. There might be something wrong with the ramshackle car; with an air of boredom they watched the native driver peer beneath the hood.

Presently a one-horsed, two-wheeled vehicle known as an ekka arrived with four more troopers, who joined the first party, straightening their tunics but not seeming to have anything to say. The driver of the ekka left his sweating horse to peer, too, under the hood of the motor. Presently, one more man came on a motorcycle, the echo of its exhaust spattering off blind housewalls like the noise of gunfire. He leaned his cycle against the stone pillar to which the ekka horse was hitched and joined the others. Still there was no conference; they appeared to act now like automatons guided by one impulse. They formed up two and two and marched with jingling spurs toward the sidestreet where the two-horsed carriage and its attendant loafers waited.

The ensuing development was sudden. The driver whipped his horses savagely. He departed thence like a field-gun going into action, starting with such a jerk that he left the platform-footmen sprawling in the gutter, where they were pounced on by four of the troopers and kicked until no more consciousness was left than enough to drag them, bruised and bleeding, out of sight. Meanwhile, the loafers sought safety in flight, but fortune appeared not to favor them and strategy was lacking. They all ran in one direction in pursuit of the two-horsed carriage; but eight more troopers, hitherto invisible to Joe, came marching down that street toward them, so they turned back—headlong into the arms of the original ten.

It was hardly a fight that followed, and it was not exactly massacre, since nobody was slain. It was premeditated mayhem and as close to being murder as was safe considering the awkward nature of the evidence of dead men's bodies. Not one of the troopers used a weapon of any sort except his hands and feet, but those were swift and horribly efficient. Their victims made the gross mistake of drawing knives, thus loosing lawful indignation.

Then Hawkes arrived at the intersection, seated on the back seat of the *gharri* he had hired. He stopped as if to interfere in some way, but suddenly ordered the driver to whip up his horses and vanished out of Joe's sight. After about sixty seconds, the Maharajah of Poonch-Terai arrived on horseback with two mounted attendants; he drew rein and watched, until the beaten and tortured corner loafers recognized him and cried to him for help. He turned his back and cantered out of sight then. The troopers laughed but left off punishing their victims—let them limp away—even stopped a passing bullock-cart and made its driver carry away the worst injured. Then they straightened their tunics, returned to their own vehicles and departed by the way they first came. The whole proceeding had occupied, perhaps, ten minutes.

Joe turned toward the wooden stairhead, not wishing to keep Hawkes and the hired *gharri* waiting. He found himself almost face to face with Amal, who had apparently been watching from the other side of some bed linen hung on a clothesline. He noticed that her dingy black *sari* was made of excellent material and that, though she used the outward gestures of respect, her stare was defiant. There was nothing timid or obsequious about her. Recalling Annie Weems' account, he thought her eyes looked more than normally intelligent; but there was a suggestion in them of the baffled anger of a savage. He decided to speak to her:

"Why do you follow me wherever I go?"

No answer. She raised a corner of her *sari* and hid the lower half of her face with it.

"I know you can speak English. I won't hurt you. Why do you follow me?"

But she acted as if she could not understand a word of English.

"Well," he said, "I've heard of your kind being hanged."

He wondered why he had said that. Something in the woman's expression, or mood, he supposed had suggested it to him. Had he seen her aura, as Rita would call it? What did that mean? Vaguely, and yet in a way distinctly, he was conscious of a murky red sensation; but when he stared again at Amal there was not a trace of red anywhere about her.

No use talking to the fool since she refused to answer. He turned away. It was dark in the upper stairway, although not too dark to see the steps; all the way down to the upper floor he saw that same dull murky red; but the peculiar part of that was that he also saw the steps and the stairway walls in their proper color. There was no red anywhere; the woodwork was black with age and the stairs were covered with a strip of dark-blue carpet. He was seeing in some way double—one way with his eyes, entirely normally—another way that seemed entirely independent of his eyes. Perhaps he had hurt his head that morning more than he supposed. But he felt all right; he had not even a trace of a headache now.

At the foot of that flight of stairs he turned and looked back. At the top stood Amal staring down at him, dingy as ever, sharply outlined against the sky behind her, but too far within the stairhead casement to be bathed in sunlight. He saw her as she was, but also as he had never seen another human being in his life. She was outlined in that murky red, although the outline was no part of her and he could see her proper outline, too, etched by the sunlight. The dull-red waxed and waned like the light of embers blown on by an intermittent draught. He shut his eyes, to test them, and found that with them closed he could still see dull-red, although it began at once to take different shapes, condensing into long lines that were barbed where they pointed toward him.

"Better have Muldoon examine my eyes," he remarked to himself. But the thought of Doctor Muldoon brought to mind his mother, who undoubtedly had suborned him to destroy two women's reputation. Suddenly the ayah laughed. She pointed at him mockingly, then checked herself and turned toward the roof.

"Is she seeing things, too?" Joe wondered.

He descended to the lower floor, where Hawkes was already waiting. He heard him say to Annie Weems: "That's probably the end of that, Miss. Next time he'll try some other strategy. Look out he doesn't burn the mission and catch Rita as she pops out one fine afternoon."

Nice state of affairs. Two more or less helpless women up against a nineteen-gun Maharajah. What had Government to say about it? Joe decided there and then to find out. He would mention it to Cummings. The effete fool might resent it, but he would mention it nevertheless. He looked for Rita, but she had vanished.

"She went," said Annie Weems, "back to the temple two minutes ago."

"She'd make a slap-up shock-troop brigadier," said

Hawkes. "Poonch-Terai's men took a licking in the street ten minutes back. I saw some of it. I came and told her. Rita popped through the hole in the line like General Byng at Vimy—through and gone before the enemy can think up a new idea."

"Alone?" Joe asked.

"She's safer alone than with a platoon," said Hawkes.

"She would not admit she is alone," said Annie Weems.

Joe objected. "Hawkes, you'd better follow her. I saw that rough stuff from the roof. I should say she's as safe as a canary in a cage full of cats."

"I'd follow her," said Hawkes, "but she said not to. Sir, it may sound comical to you, but there's more than two or three of us who obey her absolute."

"All right," said Joe, "I'll go myself." He thought that Annie Weems' eyes smiled a little as he said that, but there was no accounting for the moods of women. Possibly she was grateful and not amused at all; he had begun to doubt his own eyes since he saw the ayah's aura—if it was an aura—he was not all sure what an aura is. "You found a *gharri*? I suppose the driver can't understand a word of English? Come out and tell him for me where I want to be driven—to the temple. Make him understand, if you can, that I want to follow Amrita to the temple."

Hawkes interpreted, although what he said to the *gharri* driver was beyond Joe's comprehension. The man had no nose; he looked like a caricature of death, his whip a scythe, his dismal horses skeletons; he thrashed them mercilessly and the wheels began to rumble over paving stones that were cut from the dèbris of ancient splendor. Joe sat back and wondered what possessed him that he should feel so disturbed about a girl who had no logical claim on him whatever.

"Am I in love?" he asked himself. "I don't believe it." Nevertheless, he had begun to believe it.

He glanced backward and saw Amal following at the patient dog-trot that would have made her resemble a man—almost—if it were not for her garments.

"Can't see her aura now," he reflected, screwing up his eyes to study her. "Must have been the toss I took this morning—may have busted a blood-vessel." But his eyes were painless and he noticed he was seeing now as well as ever. "Damn the fool, I'll have this out with her."

He stopped the carriage—waited for the ayah—beckoned to her—ordered her to get in and sit on the dickey-seat facing him. She obeyed without any noticeable hesitation. *"Cheloh!"* he commanded, and sat back to stare at the woman as the iron-tired wheels resumed their jolting to the clicking obbligato of a loose shoe. He could see no aura, but he sensed antagonism.

"Dammit, she knows English. How shall I make her talk? Money?" He recalled her strange indifference to money when he had given her some in the Yogi's presence. "Threats?" She would know he had no real intention of carrying them out. Anyhow, she looked like the sort who would take a whipping in stoic silence. And besides, he rather liked her—admired her determination.

"You know which way Rita has gone," he said at last. "Tell the driver. Tell him to overtake her."

No answer. She did not even trouble herself to grin uncomprehendingly. She met his eyes unflinching.

"Where's the man with the snakes?" he demanded.

Again no answer, and no trace of embarrassment. He turned his head to see whether Chandri Lal was following, but there was no sign of him. He turned again swiftly, intuition warning him of danger; but the ayah had not moved—or, at any rate, he did not see her move. He could have sworn he almost felt a knife-point touch him. It made his skin creep.

"Do as I tell you," he said, "or out you get. Tell that *gharri-wallah* where to find Amrita."

She sat still for a moment, then decided suddenly to understand him—faced about, knelt on the seat and spoke to the driver hurriedly in low tones, apparently repeating some direction again and again. Joe noticed the shape of what might be a long knife underneath her *sari*. At last the driver made a gesture with his whip as if he understood, and the ayah resumed her former position, staring at Joe as if he were some kind of curiosity.

"What's the knife for?" he demanded; but she seemed not to hear, or at any rate not to understand him.

They began to drive through criss-cross streets, in which there was scarcely room to pass another vehicle and wheel-hubs scraped the wall on one side while the driver screamed obscenities at calm indifferent owners of bullock-carts, who leisurely twisted the tails of more leisurely oxen. They threaded a tortuous course between tented street booths and piles of smelly merchandise. They crossed an ancient bridge, beneath which was no water but a most amazing smell. Joe, watching the crowds and the narrow side-streets for a glimpse of Rita, presently lost sense of direction; but when they passed the jail he recognized it, and it seemed to him then that the driver almost exactly reversed his course as they turned again into the city, straight toward the declining sun. He glanced at his watch and was surprised to discover how late it was.

He noticed presently that their course intersected a street down which they had come three-quarters of an hour ago. He understood then.

"I get you," he said, laughing at himself. "Your turn now to get me. Out with you—and walk home, damn you!" He laughed again; it was the first time in his life that he had ever taken a woman for a drive and made her walk back. He supposed he should kick her out into the street, but he felt strangely unresentful—amused at his own stupidity and rather admiring the ayah for getting away with the trick. "Here, wait a minute—tell that *gharri-wallah* to drive me straight to the hotel."

It was too late to go to the temple if he hoped to be back in time to dress for dinner. Rita must have reached the temple long ago, if that was where she had really gone, and if she had not been kidnapped on the way there. Somehow or other, the thought of Poonch-Terai acquiring Rita for his harem or seraglio, or whatever the scoundrel called his collection of women, made Joe hotter under the skin than even his mother's tyrannies had ever made him.

One thought merged into another. He imagined himself riding to Rita's rescue—plain Joe Beddington on horseback, making D'Artagnan look like ten cents.

"Guess I'm younger than I thought!" He had a sense of humor anyhow; he could laugh at himself. He could even laugh at the totally strange emotion that surged in him when he thought of Rita. "Am I a stage-door Johnny? What's come over me? Would I care to marry her?" He pondered that a long time as the comfortless *gharri* bounced and rumbled toward the outskirts of the city. He decided he didn't know. It was a serious business to marry a woman.

He might make her his mistress. That was what sensible men did—he could think of scores of them. If a woman hasn't social position, make her your mistress and consult your lawyer at the same time. Have to look out for the Mann Act and the immigration laws. A few awkward situations now and then, no doubt, too, but what the hell—life's full of awkward situations. Not so good for credit, either. A lot of snooping hypocrites, with rented pews in church and their souls in their pocketbooks, soon pass the word around if a man with a reputation worth attacking keeps a woman on the quiet. Swine, he'd seen 'em at it—had had the word passed to him dozens of times—had seen what happened to the offender's credit.

"If I'd sense I'd not see her again. Get out of India. She doesn't want to see me; if she did, she'd have had word with me again before she left the mission. Interesting girl, though—never yet liked any woman half as much. Innocent? I wonder. She spoke without shuddering at the thought of being kidnaped for a harem.

Better pull out—leave her to Annie Weems and her own devices—save her from mother's teeth and claws by clearing out and taking mother with me."

But he was afraid of his mother. He knew it and laughed at himself. As he neared the hotel he ordered the driver to stop, overpaid him recklessly because he did not know what the proper fare was, and walked, to avoid being seen by his mother. He wanted to get to his room and lie down for a while before dressing for dinner. Dinner at eight or eight-thirty—time for a bath and forty winks or so. However, his mother saw him—called to him through her window. He would rather interview the devil just then. But there was no avoiding her.

"Joe, that doctor says there's nothing much the matter. Can't you take that bandage off? It looks awful. Won't court-plaster do?"

"Who cares what it looks like?"

"That's not the proper way to speak to your mother. I care. I've ordered a special dinner in honor of Mr. Cummings; he will be here at eight o'clock. If you're so selfish that you can't make yourself look presentable—"

"Mother, I don't feel up to facing dinner with Cummings. I can't endure the ass; besides, my head aches."

"You're a cry-baby, bemoaning a scratched face—and with no more sense of obligation to your mother than a dog has."

"You yell loud enough when the least thing goes wrong."

"I'm a woman. And besides, I put up, without a mur-

mur, with more insolence from you than would drive some mothers into their graves. I won't have you running out on me like that. The idea. Maharajah Poonch-Terai is coming too. I need you to help entertain him."

"Oh, my God."

"If you'd swear a little less about your God, and think a little more about your mother, you might be a man, Joe."

"Poonch-Terai, eh?"

"Yes, but be careful to call him Maharajah Poonch-Terai. His title is older than the King of England's. He's—"

"I'll be down in time for dinner."

He was not afraid, at any rate, of Poonch-Terai.

FROM THE BOOK OF THE YOGI-ASTROLOGER RAM-CHITTRA GUNGA SINGH

I have heard this talk and that concerning free will, aye indeed, much talk concerning it. I was freely willing to listen to a lot of petulant and childish nonsense from the lips of learned men, of whom some were liars laying claim to wisdom that they had not, and to chastity of purpose that they had not, and to love of the truth they had not, fearfully avoiding it with proud words. But some were noblemen, to whom it was my privilege to listen.

We are free, said this one, to obey or disobey the laws of Nature. Nevertheless, that which can be disobeyed is no law. Who can disobey the law of gravity?

We are free, said another, to choose between good and evil. That one was a prelate who wore finery to indicate he was a guide to less laudable folk; nevertheless, he grew angry when I quoted to him the words of his own teacher. For that which I do I allow not: for what I would, that do I not; but what I hate, that do I. He sent me forth without his blessing, but I think he obeyed his anger, not his free will.

Therefore I sought a prelate less enslaved by anger; and he said also, We are free to choose between good and evil. Of him I asked, Is God omnipotent? He answered, Yes. I asked him, How can the Omnipotent be disobeyed? He answered me, You trespass into a forbidden mystery. But I said, If I trespass, is it not Omnipotence, whom none can disobey, that causes me to trespass? Whereat he spoke in circles as a jackal runs, seeking to throw hunters off its scent. However, he gave me his blessing.

So I sought another prelate, of whom again I asked, Is God omnipotent? He said, Yes. I loved him for the yea-ness of his yea; and whom we love we pester, so I asked him, Is Omnipotence not free? He nodded. He began to doubt my good intention. Nevertheless, perceiving that he doubted me, I asked, Is freedom good or bad? He said, Continue: I will answer when you ask the question that is behind your question. So I asked, Is Omnipotence not omnipresent? And again he nodded, on his guard against me. Speak on, he said, and I will try to answer you. He did not flinch. I loved him, even though I knew I had him on the horns of a dilemma and that his love for me would assume disguises when I thrust with either point.

I asked him, If Omnipotence is omnipresent, then what other presence can there be; and who or what are you and I? Then I loved him more than ever, for he said, I know not, it is beyond my understanding. Had he said he knew, I would have turned away, because I knew he did not know. I said, It may be beyond my understanding also; nevertheless, it seems to me Omnipotence must be omniscient as well as omnipresent; where then is this ignorance that we imagine for ourselves, and with what do we imagine it? And once more, Who are we?

He answered, We are blinded by our sins. But I asked, Is sin not also part of the Omnipotent? And if Omnipotence is free, Is free will not within THAT also? Is it not written, Seek and ye shall find? And where shall we search if not within the Omnipresent? Are we not the presence of the Omnipresent? What else is it possible to be? Should we not, therefore, search for this Omniscience within ourselves? And are we not like fish who swim in search of water, hoping to find it anywhere but where it is, around us and within us?

He answered, If you look within you, you will find corruption and the seeds of sin. And he believed that. Nevertheless, I think he was, in part at least, mistaken.

XV

> *"Walls have ears in India."*

Joe stared at himself in the pinchbeck bathroom mirror. He was doing his best to shave around the bandages. He was standing naked. Except for a bruise or two his body was in the pink of condition, with the glow of health all over his skin, well muscled—beautiful might be the right word, although it would have offended him, had he thought of it. He had a thoroughly masculine contempt for the idea of beauty in his own person. Nevertheless, he knew his naked body would have thrilled a sculptor, especially when the muscles rippled under the skin. But his eyes were—

"No, not ghastly. What the devil is it?"

There was fear in them, he thought, but also something else that underlay the fear. He remembered a bedside at which he had sat watching an acquaintance die—not exactly a friend, although he should have been. Damned decent fellow, Edmondson—uninsured—a wife and kids—racked by the pain of his broken bones—refused morphia—knew he was dying—horrified by the thought of poverty awaiting his dependents—and yet—

"Confident—that was it, confident. I knew he could see something that I couldn't see. My eyes now—look like his did then. Exactly like 'em. What does that mean?"

He went on shaving, tubbed himself and dressed in the clothes that the servant had laid on the bed. He felt a ridiculous impulse to stick an automatic pistol in his back pants pocket.

"Must be going crazy."

He locked the pistol away in a suitcase, took a last tug at his tie before the bathroom mirror and started downstairs. As he left the bedroom he was conscious of a series of extremely clear mental pictures—Rita—Annie Weems—Hawkes—the ayah—last of all, but equally vivid, the Old Yogi down by the temple wall.

"What's that ayah's game, I wonder."

One second she appeared as if his brain had photographed her perfectly; the next she was a soot-black specter edged by tiny tongues of dull-red flame, rather resembling one of those dark *dugpas*° painted on Tibetan banners. He wanted to prepare himself to meet Poonch-Terai and be properly nonchalant, but he could not conjure up a mental picture of the man—nor of Cummings either.

"Fatuous ass. I like him like a boil on the back of my neck. Of the two, I'd choose Poonch-Terai as a boon companion. Poonch-Terai isn't a sheep with false teeth and a hypocrite's hair on his back. Cummings should be selling socks in a department store."

He wondered why he hated Cummings—no earthly reason for it—no sense in hating him—he wasn't worth hating. He decided to be extra civil—to try to draw him out in conversation—to look for something admirable in the man.

He glanced into the dining-room and saw flowers on the table—extravagant cutlery, too; his mother had evi-

---

° A *dugpa* is an evil force or person in Tibetan folklore.

dently dug out the silver-gilt Kashmiri knives and forks that she bought in a store in Srinagar.

"If she knew what the pattern on those knives and forks was all about, she'd maybe hide 'em," he reflected. He had taken the trouble to ask the antique dealer for an interpretation, and it had shocked even himself. He was no sickly-minded moralist, but he was shocked all the same. He rather liked the notion now of shocking Cummings, who could probably read the pattern's meaning. Poonch-Terai, of course, would understand it perfectly. The Maharajah's malignant amusement and Cummings' hypocritical embarrassment ought to be worth watching. He strolled out on to the verandah, where his mother waited in a creaking wicker chair.

"Joe, do you feel better?"

"Feel like ten cents."

"Nonsense. Come over here and let me fix your tie for you, it's coming undone."

He submitted patiently, hating a bow-knot the way she tied it, tight in the middle; he turned away from her and loosened it surreptitiously as soon as something else attracted her attention.

Then the night shut down with Indian suddenness and Cummings came, important in a brand-new rickshaw with nickel-plated lamps and pneumatic tires. The contraption looked vaguely familiar; suddenly Joe remembered where he had seen it on exhibition. Had his mother wired for it and given it to Cummings? He whistled softly to himself.

"Wonderful!" said Cummings, advancing up the steps with an air of subdued pomposity. "Upon my soul, dear lady, I never enjoyed such luxury in all my life. A long day in the office, but then this—why, thanks to you I'm young again!"

So-ho! So she had given him the rickshaw. Why not a perambulator? Little the fat fool guessed what sort of strings were attached to a gift from Kitty Beddington! But what could she see in such a specimen worth tying strings to?

"Oh, good evening, Joe. How are you? Hurt yourself? Not anything serious, I hope?"

"No, nothing serious."

Joe, if you please! He wondered what Cummings' first name was. Probably Percy or Archibald. Or possibly Harold—Joe anticipated an awful kick out of calling him Harold, a name for which, for no earthly reason, he had a fathomless contempt.

"Will he call her Kate or Kitty? Or are they already at the pet-name stage?"

No. It was still Mr. Cummings and dear Mrs. Beddington. Just as dangerous for him, but not so compromising for her. What the devil was in the wind? The Maharajah, of course, was late—probably seeing a priest about spiritual prophylaxis against contamination from a white man's table. Rotten manners, all the same, to come late to dinner, priest or no priest, religion or no religion. Caste? All hokum—simply a scheme for putting money into Brahmins' pockets and to keep the under-dogs from becoming upper-dogs. Joe had read up caste in the encyclopedia—knew all about it. Mess of idiotic nonsense.

Poonch-Terai was twenty minutes late; there was plenty of time for Joe to observe the new development. He went into the dining room to mix cocktails, standing near the open window while he shook the mixture. Cummings and his mother sat in wicker chairs under the hanging oil lamp on the verandah, in a circular golden pool surrounded by velvet darkness—"Oh, you Harold, watch your step! Oh, Albert—so his name was Albert. Born in lower Tooting. Hmn—telling her something about himself—he'll tell her too much after three or four of these—gets sentimental when he's drunk, I'll bet a dollar. Two of them will make her as hard as chrome-steel in a rubber glove. And champagne afterward—I'd pity him if he weren't such a fatuous jackass. I wonder what her scheme is. He's swallowing hook, line, sinker—and the gaff, too."

Poonch-Terai at last, in a landau behind jingling thoroughbreds, with two men on the box and a brace of footmen up behind him—wearing a diamond aigrette in his turban—

"Handsome devil—walks like Mephistopheles," thought Joe, delivering the cocktail shaker to a hotel servant. "Are the glasses clean, you heathen? Let me see them. All right—watch, and as soon as anybody's glass is empty, fill it—all except mine—you understand me?"

Poonch-Terai was courtesy incarnate—cordiality in cream and gold-embroidered crimson. Joe almost liked him; the fellow knew how to wear his finery, no doubt of that—nothing of the Knight of Pythias or Shriner parading himself in strange towns to escape from repressions at home. Good manners, too—knew how to carry off a rather awkward situation.

"Mr. Beddington, I can't tell you how glad I am to see you on your feet. For a moment this morning I feared my clumsiness had almost killed a fine horseman. If I had not been almost stunned myself I would have insisted on seeing you home."

Confounded liar—he had not been stunned at all, but it was a courteous alibi, and his smile would have thawed an ice-berg. Good sense, too; he did not offer to shake hands; Joe had been ready not to notice his hand, had he extended it.

"Good job it wasn't worse," said Joe. "We might have both been badly damaged."

"Good pig," said the Maharajah.

"Pig was all right."

"Nice fellow, Bruce."

"Yes, dam' nice fellow."

Joe watched the servant pour the cocktails. "Hope you'll all like this one—it's my private recipe—the Rocket—it has a stick to it that no one notices till after the explosion." He looked over the rim of his glass into the maharajah's eyes. "Here's looking at you."

Poonch-Terai sipped at his drink, then finished it in one long draught.

"I'm like you," he remarked. "I like things strong. Strong men — strong drink — strong language — strong prejudices. Yes, that was good, I would like another."

He looked ugly and handsome alternately, depending on the light. It was easy to tell when a shaft was coming from his spleen; he smiled for a second, half closing his eyes as if enjoying it in advance.

"The United States will be known for its cocktails long after its statesmen are forgotten."

Cummings objected instantly. "Come, come, Poonch-

Terai, is that polite before your hostess? She's American, you know."

Joe's comment was inaudible. "You futile idiot!" But he answered Poonch-Terai aloud:

"What will they remember India for, d'you think?"

"Oh, our nautch girls, I suppose. I hear you're interested in them."

"So? Who told you?"

"Walls have ears in India." It was pointed. There was a barb at the back of the point. The Maharajah's face was lit with malice and there was fire in his tigerish eyes, but his smile was suave and his voice almost caressing. Joe realized he had been warned and it made him feel hot at the back of the neck; a warning from that dark devil was as good as a challenge. He was about to answer, but his mother interrupted:

"Dinner—I do hope you're all hungry. No music—nothing to do but eat, and drink."

"And tell secrets," suggested Poonch-Terai. "I want a secret out of Mr. Cummings. Give him lots of champagne."

They had the dining room all to themselves and Poonch-Terai had sent on two of his own servants in advance, who took charge unostentatiously, so that the service was almost good, although there were whispers and muttered oaths behind the big screen near the pantry door—scuffling—even the sound of blows.

"It's a beautiful world," said Poonch-Terai, observing the iridescent bubbles in his second glass of champagne. The overhead oil lamps stank like fumigators, but the fish was from Fortnum and Mason, its original chaste insipidity perverted into a sophisticated mess by pepper and a rather vinegary white wine. "Why are we in it? I wonder. If there were any such gods as the priests pretend, it might be comprehensible—ridiculously arbitrary gods inflicting ironical penalties. But no sensible person believes in gods—I don't believe even the priests do—in fact, I'm positive they don't. The gods are as out of the running as crinolines. So why are we here?"

" 'Cæsar, *morituri*—' " Cummings quoted. He knew several more quotations, good ones, but he was always careful not to use up more than one an hour. "I'm here obedient to orders." He ceased in suggestive silence, remembering that Poonch-Terai had said something about probing for secrets. District Collectors don't know any, but that was no reason why he should not cultivate appearances.

"Yes," said Poonch-Terai, "they sacrifice you like a piece of old furniture, and when you're all worn out they'll send you home to Cheltenham to die of abscess of the liver. Serves you right, too; you should never have chosen a career in India."

"Why are you here?" Joe retorted.

The Maharajah accepted more champagne and smiled as he turned the glass stem slowly in his fingers.

"For the sins of my ancestors, doubtless. The laws of Moses seem to function in India also—thou shalt not covet thy neighbor's landmark, or thy days shall be long in the land that the Lord thy God hath given thee and thy descendants shall rack-rent their tenants unto the thirtieth and fortieth generation. My ancestors on the whole were covetous. My tenants pay for it. I am here to compel them to pay. But why you?" He looked at Joe over the rim of his wine-glass. "It isn't healthy for you."

Mrs. Beddington stormed in to Joe's rescue—an annoying habit that robbed him of many an adroit retort.

"Joe is as healthy as a horse; he takes after his mother in that respect." She glanced at Cummings, who didn't notice it, but Joe did. Why should her health interest Cummings? "We're here to photograph the caverns. They're marvelous, and almost unknown. You know, in the United States we have no ancient culture of our own—no mysteriously occult symbolism."

Poonch-Terai toyed with the handle of a silver-gilt Kashmiri table-knife. "You should visit my corner of Poonch," he suggested. "Symbolism? I have a palace there that simply reeks with it." He glanced at the knife, then at Joe. "I keep the place in more or less repair, though no one lives in it. If you care to go there you can study symbolism to your heart's content."

"But I don't care to go there," said Joe before his mother could get a word in. Cummings looked a little restless and attacked his snipe on toast as if hoping to get the others, too, absorbed in more polite distractions.

"What wouldn't they give for snipe like this in New York," he suggested.

"We have everything in New York," Mrs. Beddington corrected. She could not resist letting the eagle scream.

"Including charming women," said Poonch-Terai. He glanced at Joe again. "India may be rich in symbolism of a sort. But when it comes to living women who may be approached without danger"—he watched the waiter refill his wine glass—"London—Paris—Vienna—Berlin—

New York—even New York—I suggest New York as safer and less expensive in the long run."

"Try it," Joe suggested. "The authorities would let you stay for six months if your passport was in order."

Cummings tried to turn the edge of that retort by discussing passports:

"Very necessary evils, and a great convenience at times. All immigration laws, of course, are—"

"Don't let's talk of them," said Mrs. Beddington. "They make me sick. We can't get servants in the States, and we're letting in so-called intellectuals who undermine our laws and the constitution. Even to think of it spoils my appetite."

Poonch-Terai accepted the amendment—possibly remembered he was dealing with unoriental obtuseness that prefers its hints hit home and clinched with riveting machines.

"I enjoy," he said, accepting more champagne, "coincidences. They amuse me with the opportunity they give to priests and similar charlatans—astrologers, for instance—to prove, as they would call it, their ridiculous ideas. I understand you are the president or something of the Jupiter Chemical Works."

"Or something," Joe answered, "is nearer the mark." But he almost held his breath, anticipating that the next shot would shiver the bull's eye. Cummings began to talk to Mrs. Beddington, raising his voice, hoping to prevent her, and perhaps himself too, from hearing the thrust and riposte that a blind fool could have guessed was coming.

"Curious, is it not," said Poonch-Terai, "that someone should have called you man from Jupiter?"

"I find it much more curious," said Joe, "that anyone should go to so much trouble to learn what an old man called me."

Poonch-Terai carefully opened the skull of a snipe and spread the brains on a scrap of toast. "No trouble—no trouble at all," he answered. "I mind my own business, in quite a number of ways. I have servants, too, who mind it for me."

"Did one of them get punched?" Joe asked him.

"Yes. Did it amuse you?"

"And did some of them get licked this afternoon?"

"There was a fracas—so I'm told. If I had been there—"

"But you were," said Joe; "I saw you."

The Maharajah darkened but his smile was skilful and did not look forced. He had perfect control of his voice; he changed to a tone of good-natured raillery and answered, almost without hesitation:

"You Americans are what the French call *enfants terribles*. Did you never hear, for instance, that if a Frenchman of any social distinction is seen in Paris during July or August, he is incognito? Nobody notices—nobody speaks of it. I, too, when I ride through sidestreets, like to be considered incognito."

"You should wear a symbol," Joe suggested. "Something phallic. Or an armlet with 'Cherchez la femme' inscribed on it."

The Maharajah's lips smiled but his eyes were tigerish: "A woman solves so many riddles, doesn't she?" he answered. It was a threat. Joe saw the edge of it. So did his mother.

FROM THE BOOK OF THE YOGI-ASTROLOGER RAM-CHITTRA GUNGA SINGH

You find me ridiculous, and I you; somewhere along that line of mutual agreement there should be a place where we can understand each other. Let us seek it.

You say, It may be possible to read the stars, but who can? Even to this or that great scientist they are as a sealed book, though he knows of what stuff the stars are made. You say, Let us believe in theories susceptible of proof. I say that also. There appears to be agreement.

Nevertheless, if I, who observe the stars as you, it may be, observe sign posts on the road, inform you that tomorrow this or that will happen and it happens—you say it is accident. But is it accident when you, who read the road-signs in a language that perhaps I cannot read, inform me that in an hour we shall come to this or that place—and we come there? Nay, say you, that is knowledge won by understanding from experience. We are again in agreement, but without consistency; your one and one make two, you say, but mine do not.

And when I say you have lived at least a hundred thousand lives in this world, you answer, How then can I not remember some of them? To which I say, Take pen and paper; write down all that you remember of your doings day by day in this present life; can you recall a tenth part, or a hundredth? Nay. Then how shall you remember former lives? But you answer, I have a diary; I can read that and remember.

You have a better diary, wherein is written all your history; and not of this life only, but of all your lives. It is you yourself. And I, who know a little of that language, read, in that book that you are, a few humiliating reasons why you cannot read it.

XVI

"Funny—I don't feel scared a dam' bit."

Conversation after that descended into trivialities. Cummings assumed pinchbeck dignity and talked insufferable platitudes after the manner of "safe" men all the wide world over.

Mrs. Beddington, trying to be chummily intimate, boasted about her "little place in the country."

"Sounds like a wonderful place," said Cummings with a meditative hunger in his eyes that Joe began to understand. He switched opponents for a moment—devastating—almost shocked his mother's breath out of her body; she had never known Joe to defy her in front of other people.

"No," he said, "it's just a pig-farm out in Putnam County—frame house—hired man's laundry on the line—a lot of unsprayed apple trees—and nine swaybacked horses."

Poonch-Terai's eyes glittered with amusement. By niceties of subtlety he made it understood that he had endured the dinner merely for the sake of warning Joe against trespass. He even yawned, taking such pains to disguise the yawn that the others could not avoid seeing it. By the time dinner was over there was not a remaining vestige of even mock-conviviality, and Joe was fuming. Coffee was to be served on the verandah but the Maharajah took his leave at once without the formality of excuses. Joe walked with him to the *porte-*

cochère where his carriage waited, and under the hanging oil lamp they took a last envenomed stab at each other:

"Good-by. You will be leaving India soon?"

"No sooner than it suits me," Joe retorted.

"Ah! A bad climate and bad people—I might say mad people, Mr. Beddington. The women are particularly mad. The men are crafty and vindictive. It is no land for the inexperienced to attempt dangerous amusements in. Do you ever hit below the belt by any chance?"

"Not if I know it, I don't. Why? Have I said something that frightened you?"

"No. I was asking from curiosity. I always hit below the belt. So happy to have met you and your charming mother—a delightful dinner—good night."

And Rita's name not once mentioned! Joe watched the carriage whirl away, its lights bewildering countless bats that had chosen the course of the drive as their hunting ground. A black thing, vastly bigger than a bat came flitting out of shadow and was cut off from view by the horses that were reined in staggering and plunging, kicking up clouds of dust that obscured the dark specter, although Joe got one more glimpse of it—and it was followed by Chandri Lal the unmistakable, with his basket of snakes on his head. There was a pause long enough for the exchange of fifty words; then the carriage drove on and Joe was almost sure he recognized the ayah vanishing in shadow.

"Joe!"

That tone of voice would normally have made him nervous. True, in a sense he was on the defensive now—on guard, at any rate; but he was guarding a new resolution, not dreading the outcome but rather coolly looking forward to it. The coffee had already been set on a small table under a hanging lamp. There were four wicker chairs. He sat down facing Cummings, intuitively choosing the antagonist who, at the moment, most needed watching.

"Fat fool," he reflected.

"Joe," said his mother, "you make me ashamed."

"You've told me that so often," he retorted, "that I feel I was born for just that purpose."

"Must you insult me in front of Mr. Cummings?"

"No. Shall I leave you alone with him?"

"Have you had too much champagne?"

"Probably." He had had two glasses and left two-thirds of the second one.

Cummings waddled to his rescue. "No, no, Mrs. Beddington. In fact, I noticed—I couldn't help noticing all through dinner how abstemious he was. If you or I had been thrown from a horse—"

Joe finished the sentence mentally: "—you'd have broken your fat neck, you ridiculous duck—you poodle's poppa."

"I hope he didn't hurt himself more badly than the doctor seems to think," said his mother.

"They're in cahoots already," Joe reflected. "I'd better open the can for them and let the gas out or they'll blow up." Aloud, he retorted: "The doctor was drunk—and too busy lying about Amrita and Miss Weems to know which end of me was my head. I told him, by the way, to send in his bill to you, Mother—just as I told

Hawkes not to; but Hawkes seems to have misunderstood." To himself again: "There, that ought to start the bung and let things ooze a bit."

It did. "Now, Joe, you listen. If you're going to be rude to Mr. Cummings, as you were to Maharajah Poonch-Terai, and to me just now, I'll have you know beforehand I won't stand for it. You've embarrassed Mr. Cummings badly—for political reasons—by insulting the Maharajah; and you've embarrassed me more than I can tell you by getting yourself mixed up with that illegitimate Eurasian girl that Miss Weems is trying to foist on decent people."

"Illegitimate—Eurasian—foist?" said Joe. He could feel his face flushing with anger. "Naturally, and of course, I don't care whether she's illegitimate or not. But whoever says she is Eurasian is a liar; he may have that in his teeth. As for foisting, I'd like proof of it."

"Official information," Cummings began, "confidential, of course—"

Joe interrupted him. "Head waiter at the Waldorf— soles à la meunière very good today sir. Confidential information means that the kitchen is overstocked with something nasty."

"Joe, go to bed. I insist. I will get the doctor for you."

"Thanks, no, I'm all right," he answered. "By the way, pay Muldoon and tell him to go to hell. I'll pay Hawkes."

"Where will you get a thousand pounds? You fool, Joe! I've learned all about that girl from Mr. Cummings. Sergeant Hawkes is her lover. The whole story of Amrita is a trick to get your money—can't you see that?

215

You'll be blackmailed and all New York will know it. Annie Weems is—"

"I don't agree with you," Joe interrupted. "However—" He had a sudden inspiration. He remembered Rita's speech, and his own promise to try not to see her again. Test destiny and his mother at the same time. He had more than a suspicion of her attitude toward Cummings—none whatever of Cummings' toward her—piteous little tradesman—sell himself—marry her—live for the rest of his life like someone's poodle.

"Tell you what, let's take tomorrow's train for Bombay, and the next boat for New York. In fact, I've decided to do that."

"Joe, do you mean, you would think of going off and leaving me here?"

"Come, too." His eyes were watching Cummings. Fat ass. Like a poor relation, scared he'll miss a tip at Christmas. Steal my heritage? I guess not. "Come home with me, Mother. India's a hell of a country, anyhow."

Cummings couldn't keep still. "Your mother has made very definite arrangements to remain here until she has photographed every square foot of the caverns. Men engaged. Paraphernalia wired for and on the way. Expensive, definite arrangements."

"She can change 'em."

"Joe, I won't hear of it. It's not only myself I have to think of. Mr. Cummings has gone to tremendous trouble. I couldn't be so rude as to let him do all that and then leave him flat for the sake of your bad temper."

"All right. You stay. I'll go."

"Certainly not. I won't be left here without my escort. You will stay because I wish to stay."

Joe saw his chance:

"All right then. You pay Hawkes. Otherwise I go straight home and raise the money."

"Joe, have you gone crazy? I never heard anything like it. To think a son of mine would walk into such a trap with his eyes wide open, and then—what did Doctor Muldoon say to you?"

"What you paid him to say, I don't doubt."

"Joe Beddington!"

"I'm satisfied that Hawkes produced the goods. He drove a smart bargain, but I promised. So he gets his money now or I go home to get it for him."

"Have you dated this girl? Are you in love with her?"

Joe knew what she was capable of saying next. She saw him flinch.

"Fallen for her, have you? Well—you've made your bed—you lie on it. If you can't take good advice from Mr. Cummings—"

Cummings, leaning back, observant, hands folded on his stomach, took his cue and sat upright:

"Joe, let me tell you something. Did you hear the Maharajah, shortly before dinner, say he wanted to coax a secret from me? He pretended he was joking, but he was not. He wanted to know how much I know about his schemes to get that girl Amrita from the temple into his own seraglio. I happen to know he offered money to Miss Weems, although I don't know how much. I understand Hawkes paid him a visit yesterday, on the pretense of mending a rifle. Hawkes is the girl's lover—

you needn't doubt that for a moment; the two of them, with Miss Weems aiding, are simply using you as an argument to make the Maharajah raise his bid; and any money Hawkes can get from you will be just that much added. Believe me, my boy, you are being duped."

"Played for a sucker," said Mrs. Beddington. "Your father would turn in his grave if he knew it."

It was Cummings' turn to flinch at that remark; it shocked him to hear such expressions from a lady. Perhaps the shock stiffened him for a moment; or the flinty indignation in Joe's eyes may have found in him a trace of iron. He leaned forward and laid a fat hand on the edge of the table:

"I will ask the police to work on this. If they can prove conspiracy—that's always rather difficult to prove, but—"

Joe interrupted him: "In a land where witnesses are bought and sold, I imagine almost anything can be proved, especially by a Government official."

It was almost a pity to waste such an insult on Cummings, but the fat hypocrite had to be made to understand that any move he might make would be scrutinized. Joe's mother set her face like flint. Joe recognized the symptoms—eyes—mouth—knew he must give her her head and let her crash or conquer; neither he nor any other man could stop her now.

"Joe, go and get my checkbook."

It was on the tip of his tongue to ask her what she paid her Indian servant for. The lazy rogue was sitting at the end of the verandah, doing nothing. However, he restrained that impulse—went and fetched the checkbook and a fountain pen. It gave him time to consider his own next move, he knew exactly what was coming.

"What are Hawkes' initials?" she demanded.

Cummings told her. She wrote out a check for a thousand rupees.

"There, give that check to Sergeant Hawkes. Tell him it's on account; and get him to write a receipt for what the money's for." She turned to Cummings. "If there's a criminal law in India—"

He nodded.

Joe pocketed the check and glanced at Cummings with an added feeling of contempt. Mean little swine. Sell his soul for a meal-ticket. God, what an alderman he'd make—what a piker he'd be—how he'd nibble at graft—how he'd squeal when the big boys passed the buck to him.

"All right, I'll go and look for Hawkes. Good night, I may be back late."

He strolled off, both fists in his pockets—found his servant—told the man to bring a lantern—then walked down the drive in the dust, not turning once to look at Cummings and his mother in a pool of lamplight on the hotel verandah. What was the use of looking? He knew. Telling that futile nincompoop how she has trained her Joe with sympathetic firmness—always gets him to obey her, though he may seem obstinate at times—terrible problem, only son—terrible responsibility—and some boys never seem to grow up. Hell, yes; and she'll tell him all about that trust deed—how it gives her full control of all the money. Won't he wriggle—won't he eat out of her hand—and won't he whimper when he wakes up!

"Will she marry him? I wouldn't put it past her. She can't live without someone to bully. She could introduce him at home as a prominent Anglo-Indian official—the man who taught Viceroys how to behave. She'd do it to spite me, if she thought I'd discovered my soul is my own. Well—all right—let her. She's smart, but he isn't; she can only use him for a poodle. She can't run the business without me. Gee, they'd rob her to a frazzle. Give her her head. Let's see what happens."

He had no idea where to look for Hawkes—no real intention of any kind except to get away from his mother for a while and think things out. Think what out? He would certainly not try to trap Hawkes; he would give the man the money and a letter with it—payment on account for services rendered satisfactorily to the undersigned—something brief that lawyers couldn't twist into what it didn't mean. Lawyers are pretty much like doctors—half a dozen good ones to the hundred thousand. The client pays; the prison or the undertaker buries the mistakes, and what price glory?

Chandri Lal emerged out of a shadow—disappeared into another one.

"Here, you!" A chink of silver. "Get me a *gharri*. Wait a minute—where's Hawkes? Know where to find Hawkes — Sergeant Hawkes — you understand who Hawkes is?"

"Oh, ah, Hawkessee. Yes, sahib. Yes, sah—you come along, you follow."

"Bring a *gharri*. I'll walk along—you overtake me."

There was no need any longer for the lantern so he dismissed his servant. He walked along the dusty road that lay like a river in silver moonlight. He had walked about a mile before the *gharri* overtook him—one horse and a loose shoe—click-clack—click-clack. Chandri Lal was on the box beside the driver, snakes and all, the driver extremely nervous of the snakes and cursing their owner in fervent undertones.

They drove straight toward the temple—a long drive, skirting the city—the longest way undoubtedly. Joe knew where they were going—knew intuitively—wondered where an intuition came from; understood, too, that Chandri Lal had bargained with the driver for a percentage of the fare. Better do something to stop 'em driving around all night long—

"Here, you—five rupees for you if you find Hawkes in fifteen minutes."

First turn to the right instanter, and the shortest kind of shortcuts—alleys barred even to one-way traffic, where the hubs scraped door posts. A sleepy constable blew his whistle and ran after them but Joe gave him some money and that was that. The constable seemed interested in the rear end of the *gharri* and asked incomprehensible questions. Joe supposed a license plate was missing, or perhaps there ought to be a rear light—some such triviality. He gave the man another rupee and ordered the driver to get a move on. Damned disgusting smell of dead air in the narrow streets; he almost wished he had let them take the longer way around.

What was he doing anyhow? Crazy business, driving all over an Indian city in search of—Hawkes? To hell with Hawkes. Did he give one continental damn whether he ever saw Hawkes again? He did not. Rita! Why lie to myself about it? Looking for her like a mad man hunting Jesus on the town dump. Fat chance of seeing her that time of night. Probably get slugged on the head for his trouble. Not even a revolver in his pocket—nothing—not much money either—lean pickings—some satisfaction in that—no fun in financing thugs. Taken for a ride, eh?—bumped off like a rabbit—well, it wouldn't pay 'em. Turn back? Over my dead body. See this through or never look at my face in a mirror again. Foolishness? Sure. But who's wise?

The *gharri* came to a standstill at the edge of the grove of trees outside the temple wall—around the corner of the wall from where the Yogi's beehive hut was. Pretty dark place. Music and chanting beyond the wall—soft, dreamy stuff, but lots of volume—smother the sound of a hold-up—

"Funny, I don't feel scared. All the same, better keep both eyes lifting."

He left the *gharri* standing there and followed the wall toward the corner, glancing back to make sure that the driver had understood and was waiting. He saw the ayah step out from between the rear wheels. She was as black as night—a mere shadow—but there was no mistaking her. He lost sight of her in less than a second as she was swallowed by the deeper night within the grove of trees.

"That's what troubled the cop, eh? Stealing a ride on the axle. Can you beat that? And I paid him a rupee extra for her fare!"

Turning his head again he found Chandri Lal within

a yard of him, his wide flat basket balanced on his flattened turban and his whole being apparently a-quiver with fear or excitement. But that might have been the effect of moonlight streaming through the branches, some of which reached almost to the temple wall.

"Where's Hawkes? Go on—find him."

Chandri Lal gestured toward the corner but appeared unwilling to lead the way. The singing swelled, as if there were a procession drawing nearer on the far side of the wall, within the temple area. Chandri Lal seemed to be trying to explain in pantomime that the music was the reason why he dared not trespass any farther.

"You can speak English. Say what you mean."

But the man had grown suddenly dumb. Joe shrugged his shoulders. He walked forward, both fists in his pockets—just a mite more nervous than he had been—trying to disguise it, even for himself. He kept wide of the wall, heading for the bright moonlight beyond the deep shadow cast by the wall where it turned at nearly a right angle. The sound of the stringed instruments and singing made him feel as if he were taking part in a procession.

"Feel like a guy on the way to the gallows. Out o' bounds, I guess. Well, who cares?"

"Hull-ut-uh— Who comes—thurr-r-r?"

He nearly jumped out of his skin. An Indian trooper turbaned — bearded — armed with a club apparently— came looming out of utter darkness near the corner wall. He looked enormous.

"So's your old man," Joe assured him. He had the white man's gift of mocking his own terror and of at least appearing indifferent to climax. "One seat," he said, "on the aisle, down front, for anything that's doing."

The trooper, holding out the club or whatever it was to bar further progress, spoke over-shoulder rapidly—a streak of gutturals with T's and K's exploding out of it like sparks. Footsteps, rapidly approaching. Hawkes, with a pipe in his mouth.

"Hell's hinges! You, sir? All right—good boy, Magadh—pass and all's well. Step this way, sir."

Hawkes led through the darkness at the foot of the wall toward where moonlight was just touching the top of the Yogi's dwelling, but he stopped near the narrow high door in the wall and kicked a stool into place for Joe to sit down. There was breathing all around him, and the occasional sound of shifting feet, but nothing visible except Hawkes' shadowy shape, standing upright with his hands on his hips, and the glow in the bowl of the pipe in Hawkes' mouth.

"Good job you came when you did and not later," Hawkes said.

"Why? What's happening?"

"Nothing so far. Lucky for you it was Magadh at the corner; any of the others might have hit you first and challenged afterward."

"What's the trouble?"

"There ain't going to be no trouble. But there might be a broken head or two. There's liable to be a broken head or two—or maybe three or four—the more the merrier—no knowing."

Hawkes' pipe glowed contentedly. It glowed in time to chanting and the tom-tom beat of temple music.

"Rita?" Joe asked.

"Bet your boots it's Rita. That dam Maharajah won't rest happy till he's raped her out o' here. He's all set for a surprise party tonight, but it was tipped off. I'd never ha' guessed he'd have the guts to try this stratajum. He offered me money yesterday, God-dammim. Probably he only did it to make me think he's that kind of a louse. I wish I'd took his money and then double-crossed him. But I've no common sense in crises; I get that hot under the collar that I can't act sensible for thinking up a snooty repartee."

"Do you expect Rita through this door?"

"Pretty soon now—the whole dam' shooting-match in single file—singin' a hymn to the Bride of Siva—song about death being all my eye and Betty Martineau. It's a cheerful theory but takes a heap o' proving. Do you see that well-head yonder in the moonlight? That's where somebody got killed about a million years ago—forget his name—some kind of nice old bishop, I don't doubt, fond o' teaching piety to folks like you and me who don't know what it is. If I remember right, the story goes he raised a dead man that the king o' those days had ordered executed; so the king sent soldiers who ambuscaded him near the well. They cut him to bits and chucked the pieces down the well. Since then nobody has used it, but they keep it in repair, and every anniversary they have a procession—at night, 'cause they say he was killed at night—through this gate, 'cause they say it's the last gate he used—singing a special hymn that they say he taught 'em. Over near the well, on the far side, they have a small crowd of laymen waiting who are supposed to represent the soldiers who did the murder—or maybe they're descendants of the soldiers, I don't know; anyhow, they act solemn and sorry, and they all wear hoods o' some kind, same as them in the procession. Do you see what an opportunity that is?"

"You mean, for the Maharajah to wait near the well and—"

"Hell, no. He's inside the temple. Can't be kept out. He has the right to be there, and to be in the procession because, a million years ago—or maybe a thousand, it don't make much difference—the one of his ancestors who happened to be staying in the temple to get cured o' some disease or other weren't a bad sort of a begum's bastard and took sides with 'em against the King. That's what they say. There's generally some truth in legends. And they say, too, that if you drink the water in that well, or even wash in it, you're dead—as dead as mutton before the nex' day's sun goes down."

"But I have drunk, and I have washed in it for fifty years," said a voice beside them.

It was the old Yogi-astrologer. The moonlight, that had already bathed his beehive hut, touched the crown of his head with silver and made his eyes shine, but the rest of him was no more than a shadow, only a little less invisible than Hawkes was. There was a coppery outline of him, that was all. He appeared to be leaning on a long staff, but the staff was within the shadow.

"O man from Jupiter!" he said, and looked at Joe as if he could see clear through him.

Joe bridled at what he thought was mockery behind

words. "Riddles again?" he objected. "Why not say what you mean?"

The old man ignored the protest. Dim moonlight, suffusing his entire face now, seemed to have filled his wrinkles. It made him ageless and magnificent. He stood astonishingly upright and his naked shoulders were those of an athlete.

"You are at the threshold," he said, "at the threshold," he repeated. "Will you cross?" he demanded.

A sort of excitement seized Joe. "Do you mean they will let me enter this door?"

"He who passes pays the price."

"How much?"

"How much have you?" asked the Yogi. He turned away and walked a dozen paces, out into the moonlight—stood there leaning on his staff, then stared for a moment in Joe's direction and came back, as if he had forgotten something.

"It is not too late to turn," he said. "You may turn back if you wish to. But you will pay the price nevertheless, because it is an old debt and the time has come to pay it."

Hawkes took umbrage at the old man's air of omniscience. He took a stride forward, squared up to him and spoke belligerently, raising his voice because the temple music was swelling in volume.

"You," he said, "why don't you stop all this? You can. You're the one man they'd all listen to. You spill the beans—and even that swab Poonch-Terai'd say, 'Please, teacher, mayn't I leave the room?' He'd eat out o' your hand. You're the only man he's scared of; and you know it. What's the use talking riddles, when God Almighty knows, you've only got to come on out with a word or two o' straight talk and they'll do what you tell 'em."

"Does not God Almighty also speak in riddles?"

"Maybe. But you're not God Almighty."

"That is true, my son. But it is also true that the fool who tries to stop the wheels of destiny fulfils his destiny by being crushed beneath them."

"Hell! See here," said Hawkes, "that bloody scoundrel Poonch-Terai has got a gang of his dependents ambuscaded out there by the well-head letting on they're innocent spectators o' this here ceremony. What they're there for is to snatch Amrita, and you know it. Damn your eyes, if you know anything, you know that. And a word from you 'ud stop it."

"You, my son, are you not here to stop it? Should I do your dharma? Should I rob you and your friends of merit for a deed done generously?"

"Damn," said Hawkes, "there's less than twenty of us. Not enough to scare 'em. If there's a fight, I warn you now, there'll be some cracked heads—and you to blame, because you might have stopped it."

"Should it be my privilege to stop that, I will doubtless do so," said the Yogi. "I will be there. Let us do our dharma without anger at one another. You, my son"—he was speaking to Joe now; he dismissed Hawkes as if he brushed a fly away—"you man from Jupiter, remember this: though each of us must pay old karmic debts before he crosses each new threshold of another phase of his eternal life, a debt paid is a clean key in a washed hand; and a death or two—an agony or two—is nothing much; it is less than a speck of sand in all that ocean of eternity. Disaster is opportunity. Remember that."

He turned away and left Joe with a creepy feeling up his spine, though that was no doubt partly due to the chant within the temple precincts. It had drawn near. It was ominous. There was a pulsing underbeat of tom-toms that accentuated dread, although with a hint again, behind that, of an exaltation that should conquer dread and change it. It was weird. It had a rhythm that made Joe's breath keep time to it while the goose-flesh tingled on his skin. Hawkes stuffed his pipe into his pocket.

"Now they're coming, sir. Stand back, please—back into the shadow. Do me a favor—please stand right here and don't move until I come for you."

There was a sudden clash of cymbals. The music and the chanting changed to a rhythm of triumph. The narrow door opened slowly. One by one, from almost utter darkness, came forth hooded celebrants whose long robes masked even their sex. There were no signs of rank. Voices, and a subtler grace of movement, distinguished the women from the men, but they were robed alike and they walked alike, with a stride that was part of a ritual and as much an element of the hymn they sang as the moonlight was that streamed over the temple wall like amber liquid and squandered itself amid shoals of gray and violet shadow. They were shadows walking amid hues of mauve and honey—shadows that sang like angels. And though Joe strained his eyes he could not guess which one of them was Rita, though he thought he spotted Poonch-Terai—the one tall figure walking with less grace than the others. He was walking behind about a dozen women, any one of whom might be Rita. Doubtless he was ready to give the signal and to indicate her to his ambushed men. Joe cursed him fervently and wondered what to do.

The old Yogi led them all, magnificently naked, with his staff held high, the moonlight gleaming on his long white hair and beard. He was tall; Joe hadn't suspected how tall he was. His voice—a bell-like baritone—was as clear and strong as the youngest man's in all that company. He was incredible—something almost more than human.

To the right and left, nine men on either flank, at a respectful distance, walked the Indian troopers who had come to guard the procession. They stole out from the darkness one by one at intervals of twenty paces, and Joe noticed the man who he thought was Poonch-Terai stare at them as if disconcerted. Fifty or sixty paces away on the right flank, like a dog in command of the flock of sheep, Hawkes strode alone—no part of it.

"Hello—Joe from Jupiter!"

He turned slowly. He was too excited not to govern himself with a rein like iron. He had doubted his ears. He believed his eyes. She—Rita—stood there in the doorway, luminous because she had thrown back a monkish hood and cloak and some trickery of reflected moonlight made her white dress glisten and her face and hands look humorous—mischievous—vital. Then he knew he loved her; and because he knew it and burned with the knowledge he forced forth ordinary phrases that might give her no inkling.

"You startled me. Thought you were in the procession."

"No, I was warned."

"Who warned you?"

"The old astrologer. He warned me about you also—talked of Cæsar and the Ides of March—of Mars in your house in the heaven in trine to Saturn . . ."

Suddenly she screamed. Joe felt a flash like fire between his shoulder-blades—spun on his heel with all the stars of heaven whirling before his eyes through a veil of lurid crimson—saw through the same veil Amal, the ayah—teeth—eyes—then the rest of her, all black and blood-red—white-hot eggs of eyes with crimson pupils, at the end of streaks of angry crimson flame that seemed to flash forth from the ayah's skull. Then darkness and a dreadful roaring in his ears. Then silence—nothing—and not even consciousness of nothing.

HYMN TO THE BRIDE OF SIVA

Life! Whither wilt thou lead us!
Whither after death hath freed us
From the Wheel Desire decreed us?
Life's sombre sands are shifting,
Wendless, endless, mendless, drifting;
Death's dreadful gates are lifting—
Dreadful to the eyes discerning
Only burial and burning,
Bodies into ashes turning.
Lonely! Loneliness is weeping!
Time, toward thy curtain creeping,
Sleepless karmic record keeping,
Cries, "Oh lie, while ye have leisure!
Buy, oh buy, ye Maya's measure,
Maya's multiplying treasure!"
Maya—Death! Thy gates appalling
Now are falling! Now are falling!
And the deathless gods are calling—
The all-knowing, the all-seeing—
From the splendour of all-being
And we hear the rhythmic thunder
As Mayavic fetters sunder
And in gratitude and wonder
                                      Lo, we come

XVII

> *"A fool is a person who lives in his senses and likes it."*

Moments of dim lucidity, shot through with something that was either color—or frozen light—or white-hot pain. Eternities of darkness, haunted by twilight just beyond reach. Consciousness of concrete nothing, in which the ayah's face leered at someone who was not Joe but the Joe whom Joe knew—mixed up with the New York office, the Chicago office and the San Francisco office, picked up with all their clerks on a vellum trust deed and poured into India down rays of amber moonlight—only the amber was yellow-green and blood-red, and not amber at all, except that the Yogi called it amber. Cymbal-sounds within a skull that was where his head should be; but he knew where his head was, it was in his hands, so that was someone else's skull and the pain was someone else's pain. Darkness again, in which no light could be, or ever was. He recognized it; it was the darkness of his mother's black skirt. It rustled. He was a small boy, hiding from her. And the Maharajah said it was a good pig; but the pig was Rita; and his mother went after the pig with a knife that stabbed between the shoulder-blades, so that Joe felt white-hot fire go through him. He knew it was Joe who felt that, and he was sorry for Joe in a way, although he knew he should not be.

There was a man from Jupiter who looked on, and

who was Rita's friend, or so the Yogi said. He was jealous and took the knife to ride him down on horseback; but he could not see him when he tried to kill him. Muldoon threw a whisky bottle at him, so the horse fell and the spear went in between his shoulders with an agonizing stab that made somebody scream; he knew it was someone else who screamed, because he heard it. Silence, blood-red; but the red was really black and mauve, and he was lying in an oven being burned to death. He and the pig were being burned together, and the pig was thirsty.

Hawkes' face then, and he had to pay Hawkes all the money in the world because the Yogi said so, and if not the man from Jupiter would run away with Rita. Out of Hawkes' face grew his mother's; and out of hers Cummings'; and out of both of them the maharajah's—until all three turned into the ayah, who had a snake's body that came out of Chandri Lal's basket and was cut in pieces by a long knife but grew together again. Voices—fifty million miles away, inside his head; and someone's caressing fingers in his hair that stroked and stroked and would not let him lie down and be rolled on by Cummings' brand-new rickshaw with the nickel-plated lamps that were really the ayah's eyes.

Pain, at last, vivid and comprehensible, that came as almost a relief and stung him until his eyes saw daylight and he felt his lips and nostrils being moistened with a wet cloth. He appeared to be in prison. He could see a bare wall with what looked like iron slots that let the light through. When he dared to move his eyes a little he could see a door that had slots in it too. Looking upward he saw a vaulted ceiling and he knew where that was; it was the room you waited in at college while some fool took your name in to the president. Only it was too damned hot. Was he back home? Well then, how did he get there? He felt dreadfully weak, and when he tried to call out to inquire where he was a stab of pain shot through him that turned everything electric-blue and muddy green and indigo and saffron. Someone said "S-s-ssh!" but simply wasted breath. Joe fainted.

After a while he knew he was the man from Jupiter. He sat—or was he standing? It didn't matter—and watched Joe being tortured by two humans. He couldn't see them very well but he thought they were women. He could see Joe perfectly and rather liked him, though the man didn't deserve much sympathy. He looked as if he wanted to die, but the women worked hard and wouldn't let him. Why not? As a man from Jupiter he felt undignified and foolish waiting for that damned fool Joe to get through with breathing; yet he couldn't get away until he left off breathing, and there was nothing he could do to stop him—not while those women kept on pulling at him.

He could feel them pulling. It annoyed him. They were pulling him back into Joe and he dreaded it—hated it. Some mistake. He wasn't Joe at all and he tried to make them realize it, but they couldn't hear or else didn't understand. The funny thing was that he felt it every time they wetted Joe's lips with a cloth and sponged him down from head to foot. He didn't wish to feel it; he wished to be done with it all and go away, but when he wondered where he would go to he had no idea. And anyhow, he couldn't go because they kept on pulling. He suddenly lost consciousness.

When he recovered it he knew he was Joe, and in great pain. The man from Jupiter was someone he had dreamed about and he was glad that the dream was over. He felt something drip on his face, so he opened his eyes and looked straight into the face of Annie Weems, but it was upside down and she was crying. It was some time before he realized that she was standing at the head of the cot and leaning over him. Then, when he tried to speak, she touched her fingers to his lips and he heard what she said so distinctly that it was almost a shock:

"You mustn't speak. You must lie still. Rita, come and see him. I believe we win."

He recognized Rita's voice instantly: "Of course we win. I never doubted that. But does he win, too?"

"Rita, come and see him."

"Annie, I have been seeing him whole and well so long and so persistently that I'll crack if I see him any other way just now. I do wish I'd been born a savage."

"Why, child?"

"Savages hate and despise their enemies without being afraid to do it. I want to hate like Hawkesey's hell for an hour or two."

"Why, Rita!"

"And then go to sleep and not wake up again."

"I don't wonder you're tired. However, before you sleep you'd better talk to the Yogi, or—"

"I did, two or three hours ago. I told him his teaching makes me sick."

"What did he say?"

"He said, 'Of course it does.' He quoted your Bible about honey that made the belly bitter. So I told him it didn't even taste good. And he said, 'Of course it doesn't.' So I told him about Joe's mother and what a hypocrite I am not to spit at her."

"Didn't he scold you?"

"No, he laughed. He said, 'Spit if you wish; it is better to spit than to stew in it.' I could see I wasn't even scratching the face of his calmness. And I had to scratch something or die. So I told him God and all the gods are liars and cruel devils; and I wished all the lies and cruelty might turn back on God who invented them and bore like worms into his big fat belly and turn his heaven into hell."

"Rita!"

"He said he wondered I hadn't thought of that before. So I told him I'd thought of it plenty of times."

Long silence. Annie Weems again: "Well, I suppose that was better than stabbing yourself with doubts. But I confess, you shock me, Rita. Didn't you shock him?"

"No. I knew it wasn't any use just asking him to help me; he would only tell me to do my own work. So I told him everything I'd ever heard from his lips was a lie. That gave him work to do."

"Rita!"

"He agreed with me. That's the best of Ram-Chittra Gunga. He has humor. He agreed that everything I ever heard with my ears, saw with my eyes, smelled with my nose, tasted with my tongue or felt with my senses was a scandalous lie and no good. He said: 'If you should listen to me with your ears and tell me afterward with your lips that I am truthful, I would turn you away and never again try to teach you anything. He said, I would let you go to the mission-school and learn that God is in heaven and all's well with the world; because that would be good enough for such a fool as you at any rate.'"

"So he called you a fool after teaching you all these years. That doesn't say much for his teaching, does it?"

"He said a fool is a person who lives in his senses and likes it. He knows I don't do that some of the time. He said, 'Now let us talk with our souls and listen to each other with our inward ears.' And while he talked, and I listened, I felt lots better. But I'm so tired, Annie, I can't hang on to what I know and I can only resent what I feel. You're tired, too. Between us, if we don't look out we'll let Joe slip."

"You go to sleep, child. I can hang on."

"No."

"You don't trust me?"

"Yes. But my trust isn't worth two annas—not just now it isn't. I'm going to ask Ram-Chittra Gunga to stand watch for a while and let both of us sleep."

"He won't come."

"Do you think not?"

"I am here," said a voice. Joe heard it very plainly, and understood it; but when he thought about it afterward he never could be quite sure whether the voice had spoken English or some other tongue. The next words that he heard were Rita's:

"Most reverend and holy teacher, I kiss feet."

He was sure those words were English because Annie Weems objected to them:

"Rita, I can't help wishing you wouldn't use those forms of speech. They are all right, I don't doubt, in their inner meaning, but in English they sound degenerate. Perhaps I don't mean that exactly. The Magdalene bathed the feet of Jesus with her tears, and Jesus washed the feet of his apostles; but there's something not quite dignified and womanly in ignoring racial distinctions as entirely as you do. I may think I understand it, but I resent it, and I feel sure other people always will."

"I'm tired, dear. Do you mind not arguing? Phrases don't mean much. Feet mean understanding, if you know how to follow the line of thought; and a kiss means opening your whole soul to be comforted. Lie down, dear. He came, that is the point. He will wake us at the proper time. Sweet dreams, Annie, darling–"

"Sweet dreams."

Joe, however, dropped into a dreamless sleep, from which he awakened at long intervals to find someone tending him, only to drop off to sleep again as soon as whoever it was would let him. Now and then he heard voices–Hawkes–Bruce–Cummings–Rita–Annie Weems–and others that he did not recognize. But they meant nothing, and if he heard their words, the words stirred no responding thought; he simply slept, and slept on, painless at last and untroubled.

FROM THE BOOK OF THE YOGI-ASTROLOGER
RAM-CHITTRA GUNGA SINGH

I am a Yogi. I prefer that Wisdom should give me knowledge, and not Knowledge wisdom; knowing that the two, like horse and cart, are necessary to each other, I have avoided much unnecessary trouble by refusing to put the cart before the horse.

And out of all the mysteries of Wisdom I was led to learn this first and wring the juice of it from much experience: That nothing is bought unpaid for. Pay now. Pay then. Payment is exacted to the last, least atom; and the easiest time to pay is always now, before the interest begins.

You wonder how I understand your difficulties, they being yours, not mine. How should I understand them, unless I solved them? I, too, before your day, sought short cuts through swamps of self-deception into perfect manhood. I, too, followed Jack-o'-lanterns, even as you will continue to do until Wisdom finds you fertile after many ploughings and descends to sow her seed within you.

Then you will learn what I learned: That there is no new credit until all old debts are done with. Then, even as I was, you will be rebellious and seek unseemly ways of cancelling accounts. But when rebellion has wounded you and starved you long enough, until you understand you fight against yourself, not God; then, even as I did, you will set to work to pay those debts; and you will pay ungrudgingly because you owe them to yourself, none other.

You will learn that there is more to pay than you anticipated. But you will also learn that one big payment wipes out many small debts when the heart is willing, and that debts present themselves in accurate proportion to your good will and ability to pay. Who tells you otherwise is a liar with debts of his own that he wishes to hide from himself beneath a screen of speciousness.

XVIII

"Ram-Chittra Gunga, come at once; I need you."

Joe was never able entirely to reconstruct in his memory the stages of recovering consciousness. Some dreams appeared more real than reality, and some reality was much more baffling than the dreams. It was not long before he realized he was in a room within the temple; on the other hand, it was a long time before he understood he had been knifed between the shoulders, and when he did understand it and tried to remember the details, he lost at once all semblance of understanding in a maze of mental pictures of the ayah's face, and Rita's, mixed up with the splashes of furious color.

He very soon recognized Rita, and Annie Weems, but they would not talk to him or let him talk to them. They cared for him as he never had been cared for, but they were as strict with him as if he were in training for a Simon Stylites Marathon—no speech—no movement, except when with their united strength they raised him to change the bed linen and so on.

"If you wish to be tied," said Annie Weems, "you may be."

"But it will be better for you," said Rita, "if you can control yourself by will power and lie quite still."

There was never a moment when one or the other of them was not watching him. A tall, ascetic-looking Hindu, who appeared to be a doctor, came at intervals and examined his wound, questioning the women in a language that sounded not unlike the melody of water in a tunnel; if he gave instruction, it sounded at any rate more like the recital of a mantra. He left no medicine; for which Joe was grateful. But he did leave behind him a feeling of confidence that it would have taken death itself to shatter.

There were birds, apparently in cages somewhere out of sight, that sang delightfully; and there was a musical sound of water splashing from a fountain in a courtyard. Once, when the door opened suddenly, Joe saw the courtyard bathed in sunlight that shone on gloxinias, amid ferns, surrounding a marble pond into which the water came tumbling from a huge jar held by a carved female figure; but he had no time to photograph the figure in his mind because the sunlight dazzled him and, when the door swung shut, it was a relief to be again in semi-darkness.

Better even than the music of the water and the birds was Rita's singing. There was never any knowing when she would sing. Between songs there were intervals of sometimes half a day, but they were always worth waiting for, although she sometimes sang in languages that had no meaning, for Joe, whatever. When she sang in English they were songs he had never heard before and there was always a mystic meaning in them that seemed to act like a salve for restlessness—so that Joe wondered whether he had become childish and able to be calmed like a baby with lullabies.

But when he thought about it he knew that the songs were not lullabies. They induced no sleep but, on the contrary, awakened in him skeins and cycles of thought of a kind that was totally unfamiliar to him, and yet, in another sense seemed so familiar that he welcomed it and almost leaped with his mind to meet it when it came. Her voice suggested to him glimmerings of daylight creeping amid shadows—gentle—natural—unassuming—and yet full of the strength and splendor of evolving day. To test an absolute of which he felt vaguely aware, he tried to imagine a world without Rita in it—and the world went dark again. He wondered what had happened to him. Not to his back; he knew that now. To his consciousness, or whatever psychologists call a fellow's inside being.

Then he thought of his mother at last; she seemed a stranger and a bit distasteful but a long way off. He remembered he used to hate her. What had happened? Why was she not here, fussing and making everybody wretched?

For a long time after that Joe wondered whether he was not dead. It might easily be. No scientist, no minister, no teacher had ever returned, so far as Joe knew, to tell what death is like. He, Rita and Annie Weems might all have died—he by a knife-wound—they from any cause whatever. There was no logical reason, that he could think of, why a man who died of a knife-wound should imagine himself healed and whole and well the moment death had seized his body. This thing, that now and then hurt so badly, might not be his earth-body. Weren't there theories about a man having an astral body—sort of inside the other one—invisible to most folk on the earth, but much less perishable than the thing that gets eaten by worms or burned up in a furnace when we die? This thing in the bed might be his astral body.

There was nothing, as far as Joe could see, in the least illogical about the idea that a man might wake up after death and find himself being taken care of by his friends. If there was, so much the worse for logic. Trot out a logician who can prove what life is, and he would listen to the man; but all they do is argue about the perceptions of senses that perish as soon as a black-jack or a thirty-two caliber bullet makes a contact with flesh and blood.

Friends—that was a bright thought. Which are a fellow's friends, he wondered; and what is friendship? Quid pro quo—to hell with it; he had done things for men, and for women too, and been done in the eye, done brown on both sides. He had done things for his mother; and if she was his friend he would eat—

"They've fed me regularly. Funny sort of food, but—probably they don't eat food in hell or heaven. Can't be dead then."

But he saw through that illogic. If a man could need hospital nursing after death he could need food also—maybe temporarily. He remembered having seen in Egypt food placed in the tombs of dead kings. Might be something in it. People who could build the Pyramid, and paint imperishable symbols in three colors on a dark wall, and calculate the orbits of planets that they couldn't see, weren't ignorant—might know more than modern scientists about a heap o' things, death and life included. Why not? Food in a tomb might be a symbol, just as paintings on the wall were. It might symbolize faith in Providence. Not a bad notion. Better than bla-bla marble figures or a mail-order Magdalene weeping on a slab over lines of bum poetry.

Friends—who are they? People you like, and you don't know how they get that way, and don't care. You like 'em and they like you. The less logical reason for it, the better you like 'em. Dogs, for instance. Why should a man like dogs? And yet the man who doesn't like 'em isn't fit to trust as far as you can kick him through a window. Trust him with money, perhaps, but not with your inmost thoughts or your reputation. What's money, anyhow? A mere commodity. Symbol of liberty? Hokum. Symbol of slavery. Necessary, yes; but so are sewers. Hope this is the next world and there's no money in it—and no trust deeds done on vellum.

But there were moments of something more like pragmatism, when he knew he was not dead, and wondered what the consequence would be of having fallen in love with Rita. For he knew he was in love with her. Emotion—unturbulent so far, because of his physical weakness—seemed to flow in him like a tide that followed her movements. It was physical, he supposed, in a sort; but not wholly physical. And it was pleasant. Was it mental? Partly; but there was something else there. Spiritual? Who knows what the word means?

What would Rita have to say about it when he told her? Maybe she knew already; women are intuitive; Rita seemed sometimes to be almost all intuition. Besides, he had undoubtedly been delirious; was it likely he had not raved about her? He had heard men raving in delirium; they almost always blab their inmost secrets. He knew of business deals that had been balled up that way. Probably she knew more about him than he knew himself—might know that easily—he did not know much.

Knew a good thing when he saw it, though. Knew he loved Rita. Damned fool, certainly, in a lot of ways, but wise enough to fall in love with Rita.

There were hours when he hardly thought at all but lay still watching her, wondering whether the curious lights he saw were real or something imagined and due to his injury. Punch a man's nose and he sees things. Men with the willies see spotted mice and pink snakes—imaginary? Why? Simply because other people can't see 'em? Hokum. Booze may open a man's psychic faculties until he sees things on a fourth–fifth–sixth dimension. Brain may be too sodden to interpret 'em, but that doesn't prove he sees nothing. Opium—same thing; poor chaps fall in love with what they see on other planes and want more of it, more of it. Must be plenty more than three dimensions; any fool could understand that if he'd only think a minute. Funny why so many scientific people don't think—suckers get all sogged up with facts—like getting drunk on dust—same way that bankers get drunk on statistics until banks go broke—biology class at college—studying frogs' corpses to learn what life is. Jesus!

And he wasn't seeing pink snakes. They were colored lights around Rita. Like bubbles, only much more beautiful. And they moved with a marvelous motion as if they had power inside 'em. Colors—awfully difficult to catch and name 'em. Rose predominant—like early morning rose with dew on it—blue—yellow—green—violet—the colors of the prism; only he had never seen such perfect color in a prism, or even in a rainbow—even in a garden in the early morning. And when he almost closed his eyes and watched her she seemed to have a rose-colored outline that faded away into daffodil-yellow and larkspur-light-blue as you see it through the mist on Monhegan Island.

The Hindu doctor who came in at intervals to stare at him and sometimes to examine his wound had a green outline—green and rich brown of the shade of oak leaves in the autumn. Practical looking fellow, Joe thought—practical, and maybe proud of it. He'd be good for a line of credit at the bank if he could show a statement that was even half presentable. Trust that bird; he wouldn't crack; he'd stick to it long after other men quit; you couldn't lick him; he'd have resources up his sleeve; he'd come through. On the other hand, there was a pink edge around the assistant who sometimes came in with him with a mysterious kit of implements on a silver tray. Lousy color, pink; Joe hated it. No guts—not one thing or the other; sentimental—silly— easily deceived—no vice in him, but no determination either.

"Hells's bells, how do I know it? Am I growing wise, or something? Or am I dead after all? I know I'm feeling as weak as a wet rag. But I don't feel actually sick any longer. And I don't feel stupid. Can't be dead. But if I'm not, where's mother—and what's happened anyhow?"

When he thought of his mother he saw a mental image of her that seemed very much alive; and it was colored, too; but the colors had mud in them. Cummings, on the other hand, was pink and not particularly muddy. He might have known that. Futile nincompoop—he hadn't guts enough to get mud in his eye; perhaps that was why his mother liked the pompous little specimen, he would never have guts enough to contradict her; he would go with her to Greenwich Village parties and feel devilish when female men and spider-women blasphemed everything they couldn't understand.

When Annie Weems came near him he could almost feel the mother-mood exuding from her, and he enjoyed it, because it was a new experience to have a mother who didn't bully-damn and hell-drive, and set traps, and disbelieve every decent motive. He liked Annie Weems a million times more than he had ever liked his own mother; and he knew, without exactly knowing how or why he knew it, that his mother would tear Annie Weems' character into fouled and dishonored shreds if she were given half a chance.

But what would Rita say to him? There seemed to be nothing remaining to say to Rita. He seemed to have said it all, long ago, only he knew he hadn't—unless he said it in delirium.

What in thunder should he say to Rita? Tell her he loved her? It was a safe bet that she knew that long ago. Tell her he wanted her? Like a guy going into a bank and asking for a loan without security. Fat prospect. What had he to offer? Money? More likely a lawsuit. His mother would claim her trust-deed privilege and try to disinherit him with one stroke of the pen. All right, he'd fight her. What for? Oh, because. Nobody but a damned idiot would want all those millions. But there were things to be done with the money—decent things she'd never dream of. If a man inherits money, he's a stinker if he doesn't use it, and a coward if he quits.

"Am I a coward? Don't know. We'll find out. What's to be said to Rita? Tell her that Mrs. Beddington—the famous—no, the infamous Mrs. Beddington, who—hardly to her son's knowledge, but to his very shrewd suspicion—had perhaps not murdered but had helped Tom Beddington to die when he had signed that trust deed—tell her that Mrs. Beddington would stop at no conceivable cruelty in order to punish her for daring to seduce her son? She'd call it that. And she'd stop at nothing. Nice enticing prospect to offer a sensitive girl!"

But take another view of it. There are things a man does, and things he doesn't do for any reason. Probably he might be able to bluff his mother into acquiescence. There were things he knew about her that she certainly would not want known; they were things he could prove. Nothing—not even torture—could make him tell them; he knew that; but his mother did not know it and was not even capable of believing that anyone, even her son, would be so loyal in the final showdown. He might threaten her, and she might credit the threats. She might go through all the motions of accepting Rita, spend an idiotic sum of money on the wedding and announce to the world that she was proud of her daughter-in-law. But her revenge would be something so damnably ruthless, and so intricately worked out, that it would almost rank as fine art. It might entail poison; it might not; prison was likelier.

He worked himself into a fever about it, until Annie Weems spotted the rising temperature and Rita began singing. But the song was too late. For a moment or two he felt quiet steal over him. But then everything went blood-red once more and he saw the ayah's face—soot-black—with eyes like eggs at the end of lobster-tentacles—glittering green rays emerging from them. Roaring in his ears again—waves of it, followed by tension like the fore-feel of a typhoon, in which he could hear Rita's voice like writing on a wall a long way off, and it seemed natural that he should hear what was written:

"Ram-Chittra Gunga, come at once; I need you. Ram-Chittra Gunga—"

Silence. He felt someone near him—and then lost consciousness.

AMRITA'S SONG

Open the heart in me, open and show
Lonelier leagues than Himalayan snow
Grey on the ledges and white to the sky?
Blue in the void where the lone eagles fly.
Oh, but the hollow wind moans and is cold,
Drear is the desert and ashen and old—
Tell me, O wilderness, heaven and hill,
Why is the heart in me lonelier still?

Gone is that darkness and gone is the night.
Morning and May renew,
Fountains and streams, spilling jewels of light.
Stir fragrance from the dew.
These do I love until my heart aches
For pain such marvels be—
O arrogant Giver, O veil these eyes
That unto anguish see!

XIX

> *"Cradled in the destinies of thousands lies the future of your soul and mine."*

"Yes," said Rita's voice, "I know it."

Joe's recovery was almost sudden when he turned upgrade at last and began climbing back to strength and health. But he learned of it indirectly first from Annie Weems, who told Rita, entering from the sunlit courtyard, what the doctor had told her in ten or twelve words in the vernacular only a few minutes ago.

"Then you speak to him first," said Annie Weems, and retired somewhere behind the head of the bed, where Joe could not see her. There was a screen there and he supposed she went behind it.

Rita came forward and stood by the bed. She was dressed in some sort of pale-rose cotton stuff that made her look almost Chinese, what with her dark hair and the Kwan-Yen curve of her figure. She was silent for a moment. Then:

"Hello, Joe from Jupiter. Have you forgotten how to speak?"

"Pretty nearly."

"Almost flew free, didn't you? But you're back in your cage and we've mended the hole. You're condemned to stay more or less dead for a number of years."

"You mean I'm crippled? Paralyzed?"

"Not you. You'll probably be stronger than you were, and more active. Perhaps I had better say you are back in school again, and no vacation for a long time."

"Quit kidding, Rita."

"Oh—you mean, talk your language? Why not learn mine? You almost escaped out of your body but we dragged you back, and now you will have to continue in it for a number of years. You haven't a genuine chance again to die like a steer in a slaughter-house until nineteen forty-two according to your horoscope. And within a week from now you will know so much that even if nineteen forty-two should catch you napping it won't really matter. Nothing matters when we understand it. Do you know who stabbed you?"

Joe knew. But something made him hesitate before he answered. There was a double impulse—to answer, and not to. He compromised; he shook his head. He knew then instantly that there were two good reasons for not telling, or at least reasons that seemed good to him. The ayah had been Rita's wet-nurse to begin with, and her faithful watch-dog during all the ensuing years; it would hurt Rita to be told the truth, whether or not she already knew it—although it would be strange if she did not know it, since she was standing so close when the stabbing occurred. The second reason was the better one; he felt toward the ayah as he had once felt toward a friend's dog that had bitten him; the dog had acted simply from mistaken loyalty and he had insisted on sparing the dog's life, although the bite was serious.

Rita stood watching his eyes while he remembered details.

"They will try to force you to tell who stabbed you," she said.

"Who? Why?"

"Mr. Cummings — your mother — the public prosecutor — Hawkesey — Maharajah Poonch-Terai — and the priests—and some newspaper men. And why not me, too? They have accused me of having stabbed you."

"Asses! Why weren't you arrested?"

"No evidence. They have also accused Hawkesey, who has been confined to barracks. And they have accused several Indian troopers, who are supposed to have resented your being near the temple."

"Why accuse Hawkes?"

"Your mother said he did it for revenge, because she had refused to pay him a thousand pounds."

"Easy," said Joe. "I will swear on a Grand Central Stationful of Bibles that Hawkes had nothing at all to do with it."

"But who did?"

"What does it matter?"

"Amal—my ayah—is missing. Might not she have done it?"

Joe detected some sort of ulterior motive behind the question—felt as if he, not the ayah, was being impugned—wondered whether anyone other than Annie Weems was listening behind the screen. He shook his head.

"What motive could the ayah have? I have given her a little money once or twice. No other dealings. She had no grievance."

"Are you sure?" She took his hand in both hers. "Are you so sure that Amal had no grievance?"

"The point is," said Joe, "that I haven't any. I feel I paid, perhaps a high price, but not too high, for a tremendous privilege. Has it occurred to you—"

"That you are talking too much? Yes," she said, and drew her hand away and left him.

Annie Weems came in again and bossed him off to sleep. She seemed to possess the knack of shooing thoughts away over horizons, until nothing was left but the drone of a fly, that she slew with a slap of a flystick. And then nothing, except dreams of contenting meadows from which he did not wish to wake up, but which he only half remembered when he stirred, and which he forgot entirely as soon as he was fully awake again.

And when he awoke it was morning. Attendants stood beside his bed—half-naked fellows as bronze as statues with immaculate white linen on their loins. Without a word to him they picked up the bed, moving like automatons, and raised it shoulder-high. No one gave any command. He felt himself borne out into the courtyard, and the sunlight dazzled him so that he had to close his eyes until they set the bed down in shadow beneath a cloister. There, on the bedsheet, they lifted him into a chair that he instantly recognized—a thing that he had fervently cursed at least a dozen times and wished at the bottom of every harbor they entered. His mother had hardly ever used it, but she would no more travel without it than without her checkbook. It had cost twice its original price already in extra tips and excess freight, to say nothing of fuss and annoyance. He had grown so to hate the thing that he resented being lifted into it. However, it was comfortable. They raised the back so that he could sit almost upright. He was alone then; there was no sound but the splash of water and singing of birds. He saw the birds at last—at least a hundred of them, of a dozen different varieties, in an aviary in a corner of the court between two bright-green trees. A servant came and helped him into an embroidered jacket that looked as if it might be Chinese, it was such a gorgeous yellow; but the red and blue embroidered patterns were such as he had never seen before. The servant left him; the man apparently was dumb; he said nothing.

Joe tried to think about his mother, wondering where she was, but though he lay in her chair he could not form a picture of her in his mind. It was as if even the memory of her had no right to trespass in that sanctuary.

"Why think of her? She'll be here in the flesh all too soon."

He wondered whether that thought was unfilial but he found he had grown contentingly frank with himself. He was curious about the ayah, not in the least curious about his mother—although he wondered why and by what means she had been kept away from him all this time; she was not an easy person to keep away from places. He began to study his surroundings.

Beyond a high wall he could see temple roofs, trees, pagodas—acres of them. The wall appeared to segregate the section where he found himself, as if it were a lay enclave surrounded on three sides by the temple buildings but not belonging to them. The pool, shaped like an egg split lengthwise, occupied almost a third of the space exposed to sunlight. It was brim full, and immeasurably tiny driblets, hardly more than moisture, slipped over the brink to feed gloxinias and ferns that grew around the pool in riotous profusion. There was evidently a hidden drain that carried away nine-tenths of the overflow.

He saw now that the statue of the woman who held the jar from which the water spilled into the pool was more than life-size and peculiarly un-Indian in conception. It was almost Junoesque, and the face was not like any Indian face that he had ever seen. Nor was it Greek—or Chinese. It resembled, if anything, the Polynesian type of female beauty. It was as pagan as the purple shadows on the wall beside it and as gracious as the flowers at its feet. Its marble was not the dead stuff many sculptors have to use; time had not robbed it of life, it had stolen time's secret and stood gracious at the door of the eternal Now.

The courtyard was paved and worn smooth with the tread of centuries; the gray stone was so in harmony with the hues of vivid flowers that it was difficult to tell where sight began and sound left off. New York was a forgotten dream; a month might be a million years; even Cummings, and the hotel, and his mother were a legend. But Rita was real; he could half close his eyes and imagine her walking beside that fountain.

Reverie was broken almost immediately. He was aware of a man beside him, and then of several men who approached in single file, in silence, dressed in white robes but with turbans of various colors. He vaguely recognized the man beside him but was puzzled by his clothing, although the beard and the long hair looked familiar; mighty of shoulder and taller than the others, he alone wore splendor, and he wore it like a high priest of the ages—a robe of peacock-color, lined with crimson and edged with gold embroidery on silver braid, time-mellowed but not faded. Of them all, he was the only one unturbaned. Probably a minute passed before Joe recognized him as the Yogi of the beehive hut—the Yogi Ram-Chittra Gunga, who had led the line, stark-naked, on the night when someone's knife had made a target of his lungs. He refused to name the ayah as the culprit, even in his own thought.

"Glad to see you," he said weakly.

"Be at ease, my son."

Attendants brought flat stools with gilded legs and set them in a semicircle facing Joe's chair—seven stools, the largest in the midst. Six men, none of whom looked less than seventy or eighty years old, sat cross-legged on the stools to right and left and fell into meditation, like graven images, each man's posture so exactly like the others' that the same hand might have carved them. The old Yogi gestured as if including them within the orbit of his blessing. His lips moved, but his blessing seemed to need no aid of noise.

"My son," he said, when he had stood in silence for the space of ten long breaths, "we men of experience ask indulgence from you. We come seeking your leave to ask questions, in the hope that our experience may guide us in interpreting your answers, so that we may act with wisdom."

"I will answer as well as I can." said Joe.

"But you are not obliged to answer—now—to us men. There is no deed done that can avoid its consequences. But the effects of cause may be tempered by the element of mercy; and all forces, of whatever violence, may be transmuted one into another. One word at the proper moment may affect the destinies of thousands; cradled in the destinies of thousands lies the future of your soul and mine. Answer or not, as you will, my son. But if you answer, do so truly. And if you are silent, be so in the knowledge that your silence shall bring forth consequences, because silence is the very womb of words and deeds."

"All right," said Joe. He felt awed, but he tried to hide the feeling, not exactly ashamed of being awed, but ashamed of showing it.

The ancient of days took his seat on the seventh stool.

"My son, you received a hurt at our threshold," he said after a long silence.

"It was not your fault," Joe answered. "And if it were, you owe me nothing. In fact, the obligation is the other way. You have been almost incredibly kind."

The Yogi bowed his head until the grey beard widened on his breast. He stroked it straight again, using his right hand.

"Nevertheless," he said, "although a man may bear no malice, may he stop what once is set in motion? The finger that touches the trigger may stand forgiven. But does the bullet cease from its course, or does it strike less surely? Who, my son, struck at your back with a knife?"

"I don't know," Joe answered.

"Do you mean by that, you did not see who struck you?"

"How could I see? My back was turned."

"My son, I did not ask you how you saw. I asked you, did you see? We are men of experience, we seven, who have seen more than our eyes have shown to us."

"Sorry. I'm afraid I can't interpret visions."

"Do you know who struck you?"

"Put it this way: I respectfully decline to say who struck me."

"That is different."

A long pause. No interchange of signals, or of speech; but a sensation, on Joe's part, that the seven were by some means reaching an agreement. They sat stock still, except that the ancient of days in the midst kept on twitching sections of his skin, as a horse does in fly-time; it appeared that the unaccustomed clothing did not feel good. Joe had the peculiar experience of seeing him in imagination naked, as he usually sat by his beehive hut outside the temple—naked and yet, at the same time, robed in the more than royal garments of a high priest. The imagined picture was almost as real as the other; they coalesced—coincided—coexisted; there seemed to be no word in Joe's vocabulary that could be made to fit the circumstance exactly. Not that it mattered; he was having a good time—liked the seven solemnities—liked him in the midst particularly well.

Presently: "My son, I warn you, there are two ways—and the hour has passed when you might stand still. Backward you may turn and take the way of vengeance, not intending that, nor able to avoid it. Forward you may go and take the way of severance, not willing that, nor able to avoid that either—severance of your ties and another's—aye, and of many others. Good and evil—do one with your right hand, and you will do the other with your left, whichever way you take. But there are the upper and the lower choice; and it is yours to choose."

"Sorry," said Joe. "I am doing my best, but I can't understand you."

"There is the way of intuition that transcends prudence; and the way of prudence that postpones crisis to a more convenient occasion."

"I still don't understand you."

"It would be prudent in you to go hence and to name the assailant who struck you."

"I won't do that."

"Nevertheless, my son, it would be prudent; because they will accuse those who are not guilty."

"How can they convict anyone without my evidence?"

"But they can suspect, and they can bring calamities to pass. There are more ways, man from Jupiter, of punishing the suspected than by legal process."

None knew that better than Joe did. Business had taught him what can happen to suspected men whose guilt is not demonstrable. His mother had too often shown him what self-righteous malice can inflict on underlings. He had no doubt that Hawkes, for instance, could be transferred to a barracks and demoted on circumstantial charges; even the maharajah could be wrecked politically; Annie Weems' mission-school could be wiped out with a stroke of an official pen; possibly the priests could be accused of political offenses. Rita—he grew hot at the thought of what slander might do to Rita in a land where evidence is bought and sold. And all because he chose to protect the ayah from the consequences of her savagery.

"It is my opinion," he said, after a long pause, "that I brought this stabbing on myself. So, if anyone is guilty I am. Whoever actually struck the blow was a mere automaton acting on impulse supplied by someone else."

"And does it not occur to you, my son, that if you should name the assailant he—or she—might serve justice by revealing the source of the impulse? Might you not thus bring your enemy to book?"

"I might. But—it may sound strange—perhaps I'm crazy or something—anyhow, I don't feel even a trace of resentment against the individual who used the knife."

"But you think you know the instigator? Against the instigator, whoever that is, you feel resentment?"

"No. He probably regards me as an intruder; and from his point of view I imagine I am. I will forget him, once I get what I'm after. If I win, he loses, that's all; he may cook in whatever emotions he cares to cultivate."

"And if—that you may gain your object—you must bring down upon others much perplexity—perhaps calamity?"

"Too vague," Joe answered. "What I can't see, I can't decide on. My objective might seem unimportant to you. If I told, you might see fit to work against me. It is something I don't wish to tell about—not at the moment."

"It may be something that we do not know, my son. Understanding is not to be judged by the speech of the lips." The ancient of days rose, leaning on the staff he carried; they on either side of him rose also, exchanging neither word nor glance. "We men of experience thank you for your answers, courteously made to questions that to you may have seemed impertinent." He turned to the left, then to the right, reading the eyes of the men on either side of him. Then again he faced Joe. "We are guardians of a threshold."

"Sorry," said Joe, "I guess I'm stupid. I still don't understand you."

"My son, it is the guardians, not the wayfarer who know what they are guarding. If you knew, you would already be within and there would be no need to enter. They, who from without, attempt to judge what is within, are fools whose voice betrays the multitude into the maze of many opinions, of which each least byway leads into the swamp of disillusionment. We bless you. Be your footfall guided. Be your courage steadfast, and your lack of courage no more than the cup that courage fills. Be faithful to the fire within you. Be a light amid the darkness. Be at war without—at peace within—and be your way straight."

They were gone before Joe realized it. The weight and strength of the old Yogi's blessing almost dazed him. He lay wondering what it all meant, trying to refit himself into the mold of thought that had so pinched him formerly. He could not do it. Old realities had grown absurd. New values dawned that once seemed ridiculous. He did not understand them yet, but he knew that

Rita could help him to understand them. He wished he might talk with her, alone, uninterrupted.

And there she stood—smiling a little wistfully, he thought, but sweeter to the sense than any saint of legend. Jonquil-yellow was the color of her cotton dress; the sunlight edged it with a sheen of brilliant gold, and the skin of her bare arms and of her sandaled feet seemed like the substance of which flowers were woven in the looms of love.

"I wanted you," he said.

"I knew you did."

"How did you know?"

"You make your wants known—Joe from Jupiter. Perhaps you don't know how you do it, but you make them very clearly known."

FROM THE BOOK OF THE YOGI-ASTROLOGER RAM-CHITTRA GUNGA SINGH

Incomparably more amazing than madmen's deeds, or than the ignorance of savages, is the credulity of critics. They believe in their own importance and in their own ability to draw true inferences. They assert their scientific unbelief in all that is not proven; nevertheless, they believe in their own enlightenment, which is as the darkness of the dugpas howling in a wilderness of doubt. They believe the evidence of senses that discriminating and discerning men have long since demonstrated to be unreliable. Like harpies they descend on newborn knowledge and destroy it with tongues and pens and with the ordure of their insolence. I know that, because I myself have been a critic.

That is why men of science, of whom there are few in the world, though there are hosts of claimants to the name, keep hidden what they do until the thing is done. They loose it on the critics like a man in armour able to resist all interference and to tread thieves underfoot. It is the same with the men of art, of whom there are equally few, though there are hosts of aspirants; they keep their young idea hidden, as the she-wolves hide their cubs in dens within the earth.

Boasting their own righteousness, the critics say: Let only that idea stand that can resist our incredulity, for we are the important people and the only wise ones; thus no false idea shall find lodgement in the public mind. Like oxen are they, treading with cloven hoofs on tender seedlings.

Lo, like pigs they are that root up reputations for their own big bellies' sake; they drop their ordure in the fountains. And they deceive the credulous, who are deceived enough already without the need of being mocked by fools who know less than the credulous themselves.

XX

> *"Imagination is the window through which the soul looks at reality."*

"Rita, can you drag up a chair and sit beside me?"

"You are only a convalescent yet, Joe. You have talked too much already."

"This will rest me, Rita."

"How do you know?" She came closer to him, arranging the sheet that lay over his knees. "You men who have Jupiter's sign so burned on your foreheads all burn yourselves up, if we let you."

"Do you know how to prevent us?"

She was now so near that he could take her hand in both his. And he was not so weak as he had been. He felt life leap in him, and her aware of it.

"I love you."

"Did you think I don't know that?"

"And the answer?"

"Joe, there is only one possible answer, if I tell the truth."

"You couldn't lie."

"Oh, yes, I could."

"I would know you were lying."

"Joe, be generous and don't ask."

"You want time to consider it?"

She smiled; and not even a glimpse of flowers sunlit through a morning mist can compare with the smile of a woman in whom wisdom is at war with natural desire amid perplexity of impulse. It lighted her whole being—as if it were the color of her soul emerging through a dread of consequences. But a man can't read a woman when the love-surge rises in him; he can only see—hear—feel—and try not to be too impulsive. "Do you want a little time? I'll hold my horses."

"Joe, do you imagine time has anything to do with it? Love is now, and for ever—or never."

"Then tell me the truth."

"No."

"Rita—see here: I don't know what love is—I've never experienced it before. I've had a sort of dull regard for things and people, and I suppose I've loved my mother in the stupid way an animal loves habit. But I've never loved, or been loved, that I know of—until I met you. Do you doubt me?"

"Not for a moment, Joe."

"I wonder why not." He was doubly puzzled—by the fact that she believed him, and by her reticence. She looked straight in his eyes without flinching, but her hand trembled and he knew her heart was beating like a bird's.

"Why should I doubt you? I know. I can see." Then, after a long pause: "Joe, can you not see?"

"See?" he answered. "I can see you; and you look more beautiful to me than morning. What did you say your name means, Rita?"

"It means Morning."

" 'Yonder mountain in the morning is the symbol of my soul;' " he quoted. "Rita, I'm a damned ungraceful novice, but I love you. Do you love me?"

"Joe, I must not answer."

"Must not?" He rebelled at that word. Iron crept into his gray eyes. But she no more feared the iron in him than she did his eloquence. Her own eyes laughed an answer to the challenge.

"Joe, the truth is sometimes deadly."

"All right. Turn it loose and let's see who dies."

"There are some things worse than death, Joe."

"As for instance—?"

He thrilled as her right hand touched his shoulder—then his head. She had done that dozens of times while he lay between death and life with four walls crowding him, when nothing but her touch could keep the over-brooding life from leaving the tortured body. It had calmed him. Now it fired him.

"Rita, I won't accept an evasive answer from you, and I won't wait. Yes or no—and now! I love you; and, as you told me, time hasn't a thing to do with it. Damn the consequences. You're *the* woman, not *a* woman. I don't care who you are, or how you came here. You're the only creature I have ever met with whom I can share full confidence and not regret it. I feel I know you, and you me. I'm offering you, without reserve of any kind, the utmost that a man can give. I'm willing to stand or fall by it—to live or die by it. And I'm entitled to an answer. Do you love me?"

He knew then that he had known it long ago. But how shall a man know what he knows until knowledge leaps like light in him? And shall less than an answering beacon satisfy him?

"Say it, Rita."

"Joe, I love you."

Naked honesty—a craving to be honest—a contempt for sham of any sort—that underlay all Joe's motives broke through now and challenged her—himself, too.

"I'm making no concessions to temple vows or any other kind of limitation. Do you understand that, Rita? I'm not even a Christian. I don't know anything about Platonic, or sexless, or what the puritans call pure love. When I say I love you, I mean with all my heart and every faculty I have."

"Aren't you funny! Do you think I could love you, Joe, be afraid of you, and rob you, at the same time? Or do you think I'd rob me? I have loved you more than all the other people in the world all put together, since the night I saw you by the jail gate. And I loved you before that—before you saw me. I knew you were coming."

"Kiss me, Rita. For God's sake—I can't get up and—"

For a second he felt like a fool because he had no strength to take her in his arms and make her feel his manhood with every vein and nerve of her body. But she overwhelmed that self-consciousness; he lost it in the perfume of her breath and in the rhythm of her heartbeat as she crept into his arms and it was she, not he who yielded. Lip to lip, heart to heart, her arms around him, she let the vibrance of her being flow into his senses. And he knew then it was true that he had never loved or been loved before he met her—knew he had never known what love is or what its vibrance does to the springs of the deep of man's inmost consciousness. He discovered he had senses, super-physical and secret from him until now, that mocked all limits and all habit—that denied both strength and weakness, since they seemed to be a law unto themselves—senses that opened flood-gates and released in torrents that were color, light and music, cosmic consciousness and cosmic rhythm. For sixty seconds he knew that ecstasy is unconditioned, absolute, and no more to be reached by material means than the Pole-star or the source of music—something to be tuned into and to become aware of, not to be imprisoned, limited or made.

"Do you believe me now, Joe?"

"God, yes. You believe me?"

"I never doubted you."

"I suppose I'm easy to believe. You're difficult. You're almost too good to be true."

Rita sat on the arm of the chair and let him hold her hands against his breast and press them to his lips. She had governed the very gates of nature and her restraint now was as rhythmically potent as the flood-tide had been. Her calm made Joe feel as if he had been half drowned in the thunder of organ music and was listening now to melody like sunshine after rain. There was almost a scent of sprinkled earth.

"Joe, dear, learn my language. Too good to be untrue. Why not? Why pay homage to the gods of chaos? They only take advantage of it to inflict more cruelty. The only truly true things in the universe are so good that we almost daren't imagine them. And because they're true they're everlasting. Too bad to be true might make sense. But we all dishonor truth, and honor lies, so readily that unless we carefully guard our speech we get lost in a plausible swamp of untruth. We need phrases to remind ourselves to take the high view and the long view."

"I'll be good, dear, but you'll have to educate me. Tell me: why did you refuse to answer when I first asked you?"

"Joe, I'm ashamed. I made no fight at all. I didn't even try to fight."

"Fight what, dear? For God's sake—me?"

"Yes, you—or me—or destiny—or something. Joe, I knew about you nearly a year before you came. I even saw you."

"You mean, you knew what I looked like?"

She nodded. "You came to me at the worst time—at the terrible time, when Poonch-Terai had begun to try to get me. I went at night to Ram-Chittra Gunga, and I told him Poonch-Terai had spoken to me. Poonch-Terai had spoken to the priests, too, and I told him that, although he knew it; he is really the high priest here and knows everything, although he sits outside there like a hermit and pretends to know nothing. That is because he has grown beyond rite and ritual, although he knows the need of it in others. It was Ram-Chittra Gunga who accepted me into the temple when Amal first carried me here."

"Good luck to him. I wish I understood the old bird."

"He is too wise to be entirely understood. He says I understand him best, and that must be true, because he never flatters anyone. It was he who let me go to Annie Weems' school. He taught me psychic things, while she taught me Latin and Greek and poetry and western music—history—mathematics—"

"Come closer. You were talking about Poonch-Terai."

"Poonch-Terai has power here, although he may not go below the temple floor. He can't get by the guardians. They test him, and he can't pass. But he has hereditary rights. Almost two-thirds of the temple revenue is derived from his estate in the form of endowment, which he has the right to cancel if the rituals are discontinued or changed, or if unauthorized people are admitted into the temple on any grounds whatever."

"Me, for instance?"

"This is no real part of the temple. This place is a guest-house where distinguished visitors are entertained. But me. He was direct at first and tried to tempt me, but he saw at once that I could see right into him and read his aura. You would think that would make him hesitate; he must know that his aura isn't a tempting thing to look at, it's all murky cobra-color and a sort of sour green with shots of muddy indigo."

"What color is mine, Rita?"

"Just now? Blazing blood-red."

"And yours?"

"Look and see."

"I don't know how. You look most awful sweet to me. Is that your aura? Go on, tell me about Poonch-Terai. Am I hurting?"

"You? I wouldn't mind if you did. Poonch-Terai asked questions, and he soon learned I am what I think the West calls psychic. That means, I have certain faculties that most people haven't developed. He learned that the priests were admitting me into the crypt, and that I am favored, and free, not in virtual bondage like the nautch girls, although I have been trained in all their ritual. He has the right, by ancient privilege, to select a nautch girl every six months for his own use. He selected me. So the priests explained to him that I am not a nautch girl; and they told him I am psychic, and that they use me in the mysteries. He knows what those are, though he has never seen them."

"Hasn't he tried to see them?"

"Oh, no. He knew he could never do that. He knows it is impossible to begin, let alone finish them, with one unauthorized person present, even if the person is in hiding. A spy got in once—an Englishman who knows a great deal about occult things, but not enough to know the uselessness of the attempt; he only delayed things a short time. He was like dirt in the wheels of a watch. So nothing happened, until Ram-Chittra Gunga poked him with his staff and made him come forth out of hiding. He was very frightened, but Ram-Chittra Gunga only scolded him and said: 'My son, before you try again to unlock mysteries, seek first the key to them within your own soul, and when you have found that you will need no hiding-place.' He went out trembling and Ram-Chittra Gunga sent him to the city in an ox-cart."

"You say, Poonch-Terai understands all this?"

"In a sense, all Indians understand it. That is why they don't try to intrude. But Poonch-Terai is as famished for occult knowledge as a wolf for warm blood, and he holds mysteries of his own in his palace. All India has heard of them. They say he does terrible things in the dark. So he thought, if I am useful in these mysteries, I may be useful in his dark ones also; and he began to use schemes and threats to get me into his possession."

"Tried force, too, didn't he?"

"Yes, but Hawkesey and some of Hawkesey's friends prevented that. The schemes were cruel and the threats were no joke. To prevent any British officials from becoming too much interested in me, he spread rumors about my being a half-breed, and about my being loose with soldiers. Then he threatened the priests that unless they turned me over to him as a nautch girl, chosen in accordance with his privilege, he would stop their revenue on the grounds of their having admitted a white woman into the temple. The ancient deed of endowment says nothing at all about color, but it does say that strangers may never enter. The question is, who is a stranger? Am I one? Ram-Chittra Gunga answers, no. But it is very easy for Poonch-Terai to bribe the Brahmin council who decide such matters."

"Can't two play at that game?"

"Probably. But it's not a good game, and Poonch-Terai's purpose is much the deeper—to say nothing about Brahmin jealousy that would tip the scale against Ram-Chittra Gunga in any event. He has never paid bribes from the temple treasury and I believe he would rather die than do it; it would be robbing charity to pay thieves. And the worst of it is that a decision in favor of Poonch-Terai would entitle him, at least in theory, to recover all the money paid to the temple from his estate since the day I was first admitted. Poonch-Terai sent someone who told Amal all this, and Amal told me."

"Amal favors Poonch-Terai?"

"She thinks that my greatest conceivable destiny is to become a maharajah's favorite."

"How much would all this money amount to?"

"I don't know. Millions of rupees."

Joe remembered that he had been unable, so far, even to pay Hawkes a thousand pounds. In his present mood, if he had had the cash, it would have amused him to outbid Poonch-Terai, or at least to finance a protracted lawsuit that would provide time in which to discover weak points in the maharajah's personal affairs. He had seen even Wall Street magnates wrecked in that way. But he knew he knew nothing about Indian internecine struggles for financial control.

"I went to Ram-Chittra Gunga by moonlight," said Rita, "and I asked him to instruct me what to do. He refused to instruct me. He said: 'You have been taught all I can teach you. It is now time to use your own judgment. What have you? If it is gratitude, use it. If it is wisdom, use it. If it is ambition, use it. You, who have been taught the law that in the end each pays his own bill, put that teaching into practice. As for me, I have finished my part.' He refused to add another word to that; he can be as silent as a stone wall when he pleases."

"Dear, we'll work this out together," Joe assured her. There was a wistful sadness in her eyes, that saddened him too. "You and I together deal with destiny from now on."

"Joe, you don't know yet. Do you know the Sanskrit saying, that of all the unmerciful forces of nature, the least yielding and the most torturing is love?"

"Sounds like hokum."

"What is hokum?"

"Blatherum, Hokum and Blaa, sweetheart, are the three great gods whom Lizzie of Hohokus worships. Lizzie of Hohokus is a synonym for Sweet Adeline, who is the Queen of the United States. She inspires our Sunday sermons and she censors art and the motion pictures. Incidentally, she educates our legislators and she dictates what is known as justice in the courts. She is blind, sentimental, conceited, good-looking, and owns the Marines, who are sent to impose respectability on backward races. Love shocks her; she intends to pass a law that children shall be born in tin cans, certified in New York by the Rabbi, and in the United States by properly elected bishops nominated by the D.A.R. and confirmed by Rotary. Altogether she has upward of seven million laws, about a million of which define and govern love in one form or another, and most of the laws are cruel. Nearly all of them are ignored, except for blackmail purposes or when the cop needs practise with a night stick. Lincoln to the contrary, she fools all of the people all of the time, myself included. But she can't fool me any longer about love. I'm having some. I love you; and sweet Lizzie of Hohokus may go slap to hell, along with her spectacles, bustle, inhibitions, proverbs, superstition, politics, pure meat and certified plumbing. I'm in love from now on. So are you. Let's see Lizzie try to kink that with her Hokum."

Rita smiled because she knew he expected it, but there was trouble brooding on her forehead and behind her eyes. "Everything would be so easy," she said, "if we might only remain ignorant—and selfish. You and I might run away together—"

"Excellent," said Joe, "I'm game, as soon as I can stand on two feet. Let's do that."

"And leave Ram-Chittra Gunga and all my other generous friends and teachers to pay the price and take the consequences?" She shook her head. "Leave Annie Weems, too, at the mercy of Poonch-Terai?"

"What could he do to her?" Joe felt serious at last. In theory he could sympathize with Hindu priests; in practise his own kind countrywoman's danger stirred him instantly, whereas theirs left him philosophically unexcited.

"He has already closed her school. The building is temple property, and he has the right to forbid that for the use of foreigners. He has threatened to sue her for twenty years' rent, on the ground that the property should have reverted to him the moment it was used for anything but temple purposes, and that she has therefore really been his tenant all these years."

"But she paid rent to the temple, didn't she? Let him sue them."

"No. She paid only a nominal rent. Ram-Chittra Gunga let her have the building for a rupee a month, but he gave her no contract in writing because he lacked authority to do that; and besides, he despises written contracts, which, he says are usually efforts to keep God from having His own way."

"God and grown sons! I could tell him something about trust deeds," Joe reflected.

"What should I do? After I had asked Ram-Chittra Gunga and he refused to give me any advice, I went back into the temple to try to decide what to do. I have a room away up in a tower, and there is a balcony where I can sleep under the stars or lie and watch what looks like a whole world bathed in moonlight. I prayed, and I prayed, and I prayed that I might have wisdom to take the right course, whatever that might be, and however difficult it might be. I could see Ram-Chittra Gunga sitting motionless in the moonlight, and I loved the old man. Joe, you have no idea how deeply one comes sooner or later to love a genuine teacher who isn't afraid to show you your own soul—and his. I decided to go to Poonch-Terai, if he would withdraw all claims against the temple. I decided I would let him use me, if he could, in his black art mysteries, if that would save my friends."

"Do you mean that your friends would have let you go?"

"They will let me do whatever I wish, if they know that I truly wish to do it. They love me and I love them. They are not such incompetent guides or such ignorant fools as to think they can do my duty for me, or change my destiny, or regulate the fire in which my soul is privileged to burn away its dross. They are good friends, to whom the lesser of two evils is the next step forward. I decided that night I would go to Poonch-Terai. But then you came."

"How do you mean, dear—I came?"

"You—none other. You were probably asleep in New York. I mean, your body probably was sleeping; in fact, it must have been, because you don't know how to leave it otherwise. You came and stood there on the parapet, with the planet Jupiter so exactly behind you and over you that it looked like a flame on the crown of your head."

"You've a wonderful imagination," said Joe.

"I know I have. Imagination is the window through which the soul looks at reality. Without imagination men are blinder than the pigs. There is neither music, mystery nor mirth without imagination. Who said, 'Where there is no vision, the people perish'? He knew. They die like rats and so-called scientists and scholars, in a frozen wilderness of adamantine fact, forgetting, if they ever knew it, that a fact is no more than a symbol of a truth unseen by the physical eye. I saw you, Joe. I recognized you, too. And you knew me."

"And yet I was asleep in New York?"

"Your clothes were asleep in New York. I mean your body was—your brain was. But your brain is only phosphorus and salt and water. Never mind—you will understand that one of these days. You came to me that night. I saw you and I knew you. And you knew me. You said: 'If others wish to push the stars out of their courses, why not let them?' And I understood that to mean that I should not make haste, because destiny is working unseen and it is foolish to try to hasten destiny, but wise to rise and meet it when it comes. I answered: 'Come soon.' And you said: 'I will come exactly at the right time, because I also must deal with destiny, and if I come too soon it must all be done over again.' Then I knew I should not go to Poonch-Terai until every last expedient has been exhausted. And I knew that you would come in time, if not to save me, at least to lend me courage."

"Hell, I'll lend you courage," Joe said grimly. "Something lend me half a lick o' luck and Poonch-Terai shall learn exactly where he gets off. Feed me meat and get my strength back, that's all. How did I return to New York? In an airplane—or on a ray of the moon?"

"Now you talk like Hawkesey or Mr. Cummings. You know better than that Joe. In one sense, of course, you never left New York at all; your body lay there fast asleep. But is your soul in your body—ever? Did anyone ever find a soul inside a body?"

"You mean, it was my soul that came to you?"

"You are your soul. What else are you? It was your soul that sent your image to me, because I was too bewildered and dense and scared to understand you otherwise. We get bewildered, Joe, and think our bodies are ourselves, in the same way that a man with a new suit thinks he has changed his nature; and we get even more bewildered when we remember only glimpses of the truth, because the one offsets the other, so that people think we are mad because we seem illogical and can't explain ourselves. That is why people like Beethoven and Rodin and Queen Elizabeth and Joan of Arc are thought mad and the critics can see nothing but their inconsistencies. How can a great soul talk to a critic who thinks his brain and body are himself?"

Joe smiled; he was feeling weak again; strong excitement had carried him so far, but he was almost aching to be back in bed between four walls, where he could wait for life to come and strengthen him.

"It all sounds reasonable, darling, when you say it. But I'd like to see a bum check met along those lines. Isn't a fact a fact?"

"Of course it is. And we're all here in the world to deal with facts and overcome them. That is how our souls grow. I don't know what a bum check is. Is it a mistake of some sort?"

"Oftener than not a pretty serious mistake."

"Then it's something nobody would make if he remembered always what he is."

"You mean, if he remembered his balance."

"Yes, his balance."

"I mean his balance at the bank."

"He would remember that, too, if he knew who he is."

"All right, dear. I can't argue it; it's too mysterious for me. But answer me two riddles, will you? Plain questions and plain answers that a chap can understand without getting swamped in infinity."

"If I can."

"Where's my mother? What's she doing? And how has anybody kept her away from me or prevented her from taking me to a hospital?"

Rita chuckled. "Your mother is having what she calls a love affair with Mr. Cummings. She intends to marry him, and they say he has already written home to have his pedigree traced back to Charlemagne or someone. He imagines himself a *beau sabreur* or a *preux chevalier*. He neglects his work to trot around with her to caverns; and I think they both hope you won't get well too soon."

"But didn't she raise Cain when I was stabbed?"

"She tried to. In fact, she did. But you couldn't be moved or disturbed. And neither she nor Cummings knew that this is not really a part of the temple to which nobody can be admitted without esoteric tests. She wanted to send in Doctor Muldoon. The priests saw fit not to admit her, or Muldoon either. They agreed to let a Hindu doctor come in once a day to report that you are receiving proper treatment. And they agreed to let her enter just once, to observe you through the open window, on condition that she kept silence and went straight out again. However, because she was good and did keep silence, they rewarded her by letting her walk out through one of the ancient passages; so she is bragging now about being the only white woman who has ever been into the temple and she is posing as rather an authority on Hindu gods."

"Aren't you a white woman?"

"Not according to her. And she says Annie isn't either. Someone has told her—probably Poonch-Terai—that Weems is a contraction from Waheem-issa, which might be the Moslem name of a half-caste ancestor. She says that is why Annie gets along so well with natives; and Cummings, of course, echoes everything she says. The Hindu doctor came in daily for a while, although he apologized for coming, because if there's anything in India that's notorious it is the skill of our Yogi-physician; and after a while he left off coming because he said there was no excuse for it, and Annie sent a daily bulletin instead. But your mother is breathing fire and brimstone against whoever it was who stabbed you; and she has even threatened to try to have the temple raided unless the culprit is forthcoming. She sends flowers for you every day, but they are not nice flowers, they are charged with malice, so we throw them on the rubbish heap. We have plenty of flowers charged with good vibrations, and of the right color, not too strongly scented."

"That explains that. Now the other question. Why did old Ram-Chittra Gunga, dressed up like a peacock, come here with six other near-Methuselahs and ask me questions that had neither head nor tail to 'em? What was he driving at?"

"You."

"Plain words, dear. You promised."

"Joe, Ram-Chittra Gunga has no need to question you or anybody else to discover your character. He can read you as you and I read books, only he reads with more intelligence. But the law says seven men must hear the answers of whoever sounds the challenge."

"I've challenged no one."

"Do you think not? You might as well say that I challenged no one when I came here in Amal's arms. Is a man with a knife in his back not a challenge?"

"I don't get you."

"Joe, dear, anyone in all the world has a full right to enter the crypt of this temple and to be born into the Mystery, as the phrase is, if he cares to challenge and can pass the scrutiny."

"But I didn't challenge. I'm not at all sure that I care to be born, as you call it. Rita, darling, I'm a dam' bad joiner. I'm not even a Mason or a grand-juryman or a lord high hocus-pocus of the order of the Tin Can. All I want is you, out of this nest of mystery—you, and a chance to repay your Yogi and his friends for all their kindness."

"Joe, dear, nobody can make you enter. Nobody can even urge you. You must make your own decision."

"Let's decide it now, then. I'll remain outside—grateful

for the compliment and all that sort of thing, but too fond of facts to wish to lose myself in a maze of esoteric symbolism. It's beyond my mental grasp. I can't rise to it."

He suddenly felt sadness almost drown him, it was so intense. He set that down to weakness after too much conversation.

"Joe, it's time to return to your room," she remarked; and he thought her voice seemed strangely far away and listless.

"All right. I guess I'm tired out. Come closer. Won't you put your arms around me once again and kiss me, before the bearers come?"

"No, Joe, dear."

"Why not?" He felt so gloomy all at once that he could almost weep, if weeping had been worth the effort.

"Joe, don't ask me. I can't answer—not now."

"Sweetheart, what in hell's the matter?"

"What in hell? Just hell, that's all. Here come the bearers."

"Kiss me."

"No, Joe."

Strong men came and carried him into the familiar room, where Annie Weems made his pillow comfortable, leaning over him to look into his eyes through horn-rimmed spectacles.

"If you should fail," she began, then changed her mind. Instead, she closed the shutters, so that dimness might send him to sleep.

He wondered what she meant. Fail? Didn't he love Rita? Hadn't Rita said—

He dozed off. Or perhaps he swooned. No difference.

FROM THE BOOK OF THE YOGI-ASTROLOGER
RAM-CHITTRA GUNGA SINGH

My son, it is not this world that is illusion, but the thoughts of fools concerning it, that are; not even the most learned fool can have illusions or delusions about nothing. There are seven aspects of the universe, each subdivided into seven times seven, and each is right or wrong according to the rightness or the wrongness of the percipient; but each is transitory, because not one of them all is infinite. And he who prates about infinity, but knows not finite measures first, is less wise than the finite fool who owns, at least, the gift of being honest with himself, which leads to honesty with others.

I have heard men, saying they are occultists, maintain that human love is as deplorable as that of beasts. But wherein is the love of beasts deplorable? I have heard men say that it is lust, not love, if man and woman yearn towards each other. Yet I tell you, if they yearn not, they are of less worth than the weeds that yearn towards each other as the dew does to the thirsty earth. I have heard men, mouthing blasphemy, maintain that love is universal and never personal. Nevertheless, are they themselves not persons? Are not persons members of the universe? Could love be universal that did not love persons also?

Nay, I tell you, neither man nor woman can receive a spark of consciousness of universal love and love impersonally, which is infinitely, if he have not first loved some one more than all else. They who say they can are liars and deluded fools, obeying pride and following preferment, knowing not what pride is nor the way preferment takes; they are in love with nothing, in a wilderness of nothing, and of such fools there are many—to whom I would say; Get ye hence and consider the geese.

I am a Yogi. I sit at the feet of Wisdom, which is an attribute of Love. I came not to this glimpse of Truth without first yearning to a woman with the whole strength that was in me. As I gave I have received; she also. If I love now with a wider wisdom, that is because like induces like and multiplies it, until it overflows its limits. I have first loved one with all my might before I dared to trespass in the dust before the feet of Wisdom. Had I said that I loved many, who could not love one, I doubt not Wisdom would have left me lying in my wilderness to learn the bitter misery of self-love, than which there is nothing less worth effort spent, in all this universe.

XXI

> *"There's dirty work—dam' dirty work!"*

Joe awoke in the night with a feeling of crisis impending. He felt like a man in a death-cell awaiting the summons. The feeling that he was destined never again to see that room was so strong that he began to stare about him, peering through the shadows cast by the dim night-light. But even so, it was a long time before he noticed the old Yogi-astrologer, Ram-Chittra Gunga. The ancient of days was so motionless that he was hardly separable from the shadows, and even though Joe moved to attract his attention he made no response; he was like the shadow of an image seen in an ink-pool. The silence was almost terrifying.

"I'm awake, " Joe said at last. "I'd like to talk to you." But his own voice startled him so that he almost wished he had not spoken. He experienced the weird sensation of having shattered, by speaking, an actual structure of silence that the Yogi had built up. The sensation was heightened by the old man's movement; he appeared to look around him with a kind of patient disapproval at the shattered remnants.

"Since you need speech, have it," he answered after a long pause.

Joe felt he should apologize. "If I could read your thought—"

The Yogi interrupted him. "My son, if you could do that, you would not have needed this experience. Your soul has set you here, as some men's souls set them in battle—because the soul needs education. It is the law, to which there never has been one exception, that as the soul asks it is given. Why not? Is infinity exhaustible? Is there not plenty for all?"

"Do you mean I'm a marionette that struts and dances when my ignorant soul pulls unseen strings?"

"You are your soul, my son. The rest of you is mere environment. But you identify yourself with flesh and bones, so you experience the suffering of flesh and bones."

"From which my soul learns what?"

"Responsibility. I will explain it to you. There was a rich man who had two sons with whom he offered to divide his business. But the elder said, 'It will be time enough when death shall overtake you; and may that be a long time hence, since you are kind and give me all I need without my troubling.' And the elder went his way enjoying substance that he had not earned. But the younger said, 'I am not yet wise enough to share so great a business; let me therefore learn it.' So his father set him down among his meanest men, and gave him all the tiresome tasks, and found fault, and instructed him, until he won his way by merit to the highest post and was his father's right hand.

"And then death came, and the two sons divided the heritage; and because the elder had first choice he took that portion that required least management; but the shares were equal; each was the employer of a thousand men. Then, presently, came tidal waves in the affairs of commerce that demanded skill and vast experience. The elder failed; a thousand men, their wives and their children justly blamed him that they had no bread and no employment. But the younger did not lack experience; and because he had labored with the lowest he knew well their need. He knew himself responsible. He toiled, he invented, he guided; he gave of his knowledge and skill, having plenty to give. So he saved that day; a thousand men, their wives and their children justly praised him that they had bread and honorable work to do.

"Now answer me: when death shall overtake those two men, so that they recognize themselves as two immortals who have shed their mortal limitations, which shall be the greater? He who saved that day, or he who lost it? He who knew himself responsible, or he who thought a thousand and their wives and children were responsible to him?"

"It's no riddle," Joe answered. "The younger obviously is the better man."

"There is only one riddle that is hard to answer," said the Yogi. "It is, why will men not understand that they receive exactly what they ask? Who is there who demands not proof, with every breath he breathes, that he is fitted for better than that which he has, be it health or knowledge, power or possessions? But how few are they who stand up to the proving and make no complaint! Nevertheless, I tell you, they who fail in this life must return to it, like bad steel tossed again into the furnace. Shall the Lords of Life entrust such souls with tasks they have not proved that they can do?"

"So you think I'm being tested?"

"Does it occur to you to think otherwise?"

"Who is testing me?"

"You are testing yourself."

"That sounds absurd. Did I choose my mother?"

"Who else chose her? Did she not provide for you the very chains you had to learn to break? If you are strong enough, then break them; but if not, then be born again and again until at last you learn."

"I can't help wondering why your interest in me."

"You challenged. You lay at my gate with a knife in your lungs; and who am I that I should dare to let that challenge pass?"

"I think I understand that. Well, you've treated me with absolutely priceless courtesy and kindness. I'm beginning to think I can best repay you by going away as soon as possible, to save you from further trouble on my account."

There was a long pause while the Yogi turned that over in his mind. Their voices had awakened Annie Weems, who came in to see what the matter might be.

"This is my watch, and you have my leave to sleep," the Yogi told her, rather rudely Joe thought, so she retired again, saying nothing. "There is no such fool," the Yogi added, "as a half-wise woman. She would have bidden you be silent in your hour when sun and moon and Jupiter all pull together for you."

"It's incomprehensible to me," said Joe, "that a man of your philosophical bent and high intelligence should take any stock in astrology. I don't believe a word of it."

"It makes no difference to astrology what you believe or disbelieve, my son. Nor does it matter if a million fools are cheated by a thousand rogues in astrology's name. Would you go to a defeated litigant to learn law, or to an infidel to learn religion? Nevertheless, you learn astrology from cheap-jacks who could not foretell tomorrow's weather; and you cackle the conceited unbelief of scientists who never studied it. Now is your hour. I am a pilot telling you the tide flows with you and the wind is fair."

"Will you answer questions?"

"If they are such as concern the pilot."

"All right. Tell me then why Rita suddenly grew sad this afternoon and left me as if she and I are doomed never to see each other?"

"Whence comes that thought? Have you tested it? May it not be a true thought?"

Joe raised himself up on his elbow. He spoke with cold restraint that sounded ten times more convincing than emphasis:

"If it is true, I will make truth work to prove itself. I love Rita and I have told her so. She has said she loves me, and I believe her. I will not be easy to be rid of."

"Very easy. Nothing else is possible unless you change your course. For she goes one way, you another."

"Do you believe I would go to New York and leave her at the mercy of Poonch-Terai?"

"He is not incompetent, that maharajah. Neither is your mother incompetent. Nor is Cummings without resources. They three together have Amrita in one trap and you in another. And there is no escape from either trap by any way that you know."

"Do you mean, you know a way?"

"I said, I am a pilot."

"All right, guide me. Do you mean, you know my mother's plans and Poonch-Terai's?"

"How else should I guide you?"

"Have you talked with them? How do you know their plans?"

"My son, have I for nothing endured this existence of flesh and bones and foolishness? Have I observed and seen and studied to no purpose? Do I not know all the ways of evil, which indeed are few and not original, though they are subdivided into millions of subtle methods? Have I not, in countless lives, done evil—that I might learn to avoid it? I tell you, no mouse can escape from a trap, and no tiger can burst from a net, by sheer strength. Neither can indignation help him. Pride avails him nothing. Malice makes him only as one weak force against many strong ones. Nay, nay; he must first learn cunning, that he may use their malice against themselves."

"Can you teach that?" Joe asked. He felt curious. He took no stock in Oriental cunning, but he felt strangely drawn toward the old man and unaccountably inclined to trust him.

"Have I not said twice, I am a pilot?"

"All right, teach me."

"None can teach. None can teach even arithmetic. None can do more than pilot forth that knowledge that awaits within. It awaits its opportunity to burst forth like the sap in springtime."

"Very well. I hoist the signal for a pilot. Step aboard."

"There is a fee for pilotage."

"Ah! I suspected it."

"There is nothing for nothing in all this universe. Each least vibration earns its recompense. If you accept my pilotage there is no escaping liability."

"How much?"

"I don't know."

"Money? Or some other kind of payment?"

"I don't know. Who am I that I should weigh such matters? And with what scales should I weigh them? I have lived long in this body, but I have yet to see such pilotage as mine repaid with money. Nor have I ever demanded payment for myself. Nor would I accept it for myself, because I have no need."

"I'm trying hard to understand you, but you seem to me to talk in circles. First I must pay. Then you won't accept payment. Frankly, I much prefer paying for what I receive."

"It is because I know that as well as certain other qualities you have that I am interested in you. But until you asked me of your own free will to guide you through the dangers I foresee I had no right to give you more than sympathy; not a finger might I raise to guide you one way or another. And until I warned you that you will have to pay the full fee for the guidance, I incurred the risk that I myself must pay it, and pay, it might be, double, because the pilot has double responsibility. Again I warn you: if you go your own way you will miss your goal because of ignorance, and you will pay for ignorance, which is expensive. But if you accept my guidance you will pay for knowledge—or the knowledge will consume you as the rust eats iron. When you lay wounded at my door you were a challenge that I did not dare overlook. I accepted it. Now it is my turn to challenge. Do you dare to accept my guidance? Think before you answer."

Then a strange thing happened. The Yogi made no movement that Joe could see, but the light went out as if an unseen hand had pinched the wick. For a while he could see nothing, although his skin tingled and he felt as if dozens of unseen eyes were staring at him. Then he saw purple where the Yogi sat, although it was not exactly light because it cast no shadow and illuminated no object. But as he watched it, it became the Yogi's outline, although he could not see the man himself, and the space within the outline slowly became suffused with colored light like tongues of flame, in a pattern that vaguely resembled plated armor or the scales of a gigantic fish. There was no sound.

And then Rita came, or so it seemed, although in a certain sense Joe knew she was not Rita. She appeared quite naturally, robed in white—quite simply—there was nothing strange or supernatural about her. But how she came and how Joe saw her was a mystery; she appeared to be standing about two feet above the floor; no light shone on her that Joe could see; none came from her; but he could see her plainly. Presently he noticed there were ropes around her. She appeared to be tied to a stake and there were hands that reached toward her, threatening. He knew one pair of hands were his mother's and another pair belonged to Poonch-Terai, although he did not know how he knew that. Over

Rita's head there hung a rock suspended by a cord. He saw the left hand of Poonch-Terai seize a sword and start to cut the cord strand after strand. For a moment he saw Poonch-Terai's face, grinning with malice; and his mother's. She nodded approval.

Joe almost shouted. Perhaps he did shout. He made a sound of some sort as he struggled to sit upright. But the moment he moved the vision vanished, and then the Yogi's voice said calmly:

"Answer me: was that a dream or the truth, or what was it?"

"I was awake," said Joe.

"You saw, reflected in infinity, an image of your own bewildered thought," said the Yogi. "But now answer: Do you dare to accept my guidance?"

"Tell me first what you saw," Joe retorted, and the Yogi laughed.

"I saw a man who would have slain his mother in his own mind, had the vision lasted. And the borderline is thin between the thought and the deed."

"You are right," said Joe, "although I don't know how you know it."

"Few men would have pleaded guilty to the thought. Nine hundred and ninety-nine out of any thousand would have sworn that no such idea crossed their minds. You are as ignorant as the men who let the world war happen; but you are as frank as a child. Do you see how simple it would be for someone skilled in malice to induce you to do murder and thus remove yourself from his path? The law would hang you, and the cause for which you slew would be a lost one. Can you understand that?"

"Darkly," Joe said, "I have glimpses. Do you mean that Poonch-Terai can hypnotize?"

"None can—not in the way that you have heard of it. And I say nothing about Poonch-Terai; him I am not instructing. But I tell you, there is darkness as well as light; and nine-tenths of the evil in the world, nay, more, is done by the ignorant who know not whence the impulse comes. Even as you, they grow bewildered. If they see the light it terrifies them. And the first thought then suggested to them, that they do. And what they do condemns them to the endless chain of hopes deferred and disappointed toil that fools call life on earth."

"Do you believe I can break that chain?"

"Not all the universe can break it until the last soul learns its lesson. But break free from it—you and she—each aiding each—you may go far. But you will need as much courage as she has."

"Do you think I have it?"

There came a startling hollow thunder on the teak door. The Yogi lighted the night-light. He was smiling. The thunder resumed. Annie Weems came hurrying from the inner room, her face haggard in the light of the lantern she held.

"We are about to find out," said the Yogi.

"Open!" a man's voice shouted. "Let me in!"

"Shall I?" Annie Weems controlled herself until even the lamp in her hands stood steady. "Who can it be, Ram-Chittra Gunga? Shall I open?"

"Open," said the Yogi. "Why not?"

She set the lamp down on the table, slid the bolt

and stepped back. The door swung violently. Hawkes swayed in, staggering. He slammed the door behind him—bolted it—and stood there bleeding, swaying on his feet.

"There's dirty work," he announced, "dam' black dirty work. I took a long count. I'll be all right in a minute. Poonch-Terai's got Rita! Now put on your thinking cap. Get busy quick and tell me what to do next. Damn the army! Damn all consequences! Tell me how to go about it and I'll fetch her back or bu'st!"

AMRITA'S MANTRAM

Open, like stars discerning, Eyes of my Soul,
Like strong suns burning up this night of gloom;
Burn me these thronging lies woven of dole,
Light me my destiny, show me its bloom
Bright with Thy purpose—gay—not this infernal
Grim, grey shroud shadowing.
Blow with Thy gusty breath,
Bring forth the sap of Thy spring-time, Eternal!
Life, art thou Lord over Death?

XXII

"You will keep still."

Hawkes sat down on Joe's bed. Annie Weems came closer to him to examine his injuries, but he objected:

"Miss, I'm all right. There's no killing a man till his time comes. My time ain't yet. Strike me pink, though, it weren't their fault I'm not all set for the undertaker. If I hadn't had the sense to sham dead I'd be faking a pass for the Pearly Gate this minute. As you were, Miss; I'm not sneering at religion. Jus' a bit upset, that's all. I feel as if I'd had a drink or two. I haven't."

Annie Weems went out in haste for a sponge and water. Suddenly Hawkes turned and faced the Yogi:

"Damn you, couldn't you foresee this?" he almost shouted. "You with your astrology and second sight and magic—couldn't you have warned me? She'd ha' done what you said. Couldn't you have told her to stay home tonight and not go singing in the prison yard? God-dammit, somebody—probably Cummings—got the acting commandant to order all troopers kept in barracks. Last minute order. Me, I was the only bodyguard she had and I'm no fighting man. I thought I was. I swung for the three of 'em—hand running—and I hit two—solid. One fell. Then they got me. Miss, I wish you wouldn't."

But Annie Weems was one of those women who deal with crises by doing promptly and efficiently the first job that presents itself. Hawkes had to hold his head the way she wanted it and to continue his remarks in jerks between the ministrations of the sponge. He talked to the world at large, but at the Yogi:

"Came a carriage and they popped her into it, all wrapped up in about a bale o' white cloth—smothered like as not, God-dammem! Not a scream from her. I let out a yell that anyone had thought would bring the prison roof off. But I didn't wake nobody. And then they got me. Couldn't recognize a mother's son of 'em; they all had cloths to hide their faces. But they were Poonch-Terai's men or I'll eat my tunic. Now what?"

He glared at the Yogi, raising his head so that water ran down in his eyes and he wiped them, all unconsciously, with the end of Annie Weems' kimono.

"He will wonder what we will do; and he will come to find out," said the Yogi. "Furthermore, he will wish to prove he knows nothing about it, and he will think that to come here will be the best possible proof. He will have a most ingenious excuse for coming. He will be here in a moment. He would have been here while the incident was taking place, but for the fact that men who deal with evil never are quite confident; so he watched from a point of vantage. Possibly he saw you come here."

There came a noise at the end of the passage. Voices. Footsteps. Then a knock on the door of the room.

"Right you are, here he is." Hawkes took the towel from Annie Weems and stood up. "Miss, I'm grateful. Thanks to you it don't hurt half as much as I wish it did. If I had my rights I'd be a dead man—me—to let that happen!" Fiercely he turned to the Yogi: "You—with all your second sight and what not else! If I'm a rotter to have let this happen—and I am, God-dammit!—what price you that could have warned us? No, don't open; I'm not through yet; keep that black swine waiting out there, alibi and all. See here—you let me handle this from now on."

"You will sit down," said the Yogi. "You will keep still."

"Will I?"

"Yes," said the Yogi. "You will remember your own promise. You are forgiven for forgetting for the moment what a man of your word you are. But now, remember it. And having done your best, improve on it by letting me do mine."

Annie Weems brought a chair and Hawkes sat in it, wiping his face, perhaps to hide embarrassment.

"Somebody open the door," said the Yogi and Annie Weems drew the bolt gingerly, stepping aside at once as if she feared contamination. She was ashen-gray-faced in the lamplight, evidently conquering hysteria by sheer will. If she should break down it would be from over-exercise of self-control, not lack of it. The Yogi observed her calmly.

In strode the maharajah, but the Yogi hardly seemed to notice him; he was booted and spurred, magnificent, and jeweled as if he had just come from a durbar; there was an emerald in his turban whose price would have fed his peasantry for a whole season. He affected to notice Hawkes first, but Joe detected his swift glance around the room and grudgingly admired the man's vitality. His self-assurance was superb.

"Brawling? Drunk again?" he asked, with the easy tolerance of a man who sympathized with soldiers. "You should drink like I do, systematically, then you'd carry it better and not get found out. Ah—Annie Weems sahiba—my respects, ma'am. Too bad that I had to close your mission, but even princes have to stick to principles, and religion, you know, is an exacting mistress; I shall go to a Christian hell most probably for having let you use that house so many years. I invite your prayers on my behalf. Will you pray for me? Yes?"

He was received with stony silence, which he seemed to enjoy.

"Ah—his reverence," he continued in English, raising both hands to his face with perfectly simulated respect. "I kiss feet. I beseech your blessing."

Sonorously, solemnly the Yogi blessed him, stressing vowel sounds and rounding out the olden phrases so that organ music seemed to come from nowhere and imblend itself. A man felt blessed, not merely noticed, when Ram-Chittra Gunga did it. Even Poonch-Terai lost something of his swagger. To revive it he turned on Joe:

"How is our invalid? Better? You look a great deal better."

"I will soon be able to attend to business," Joe answered, letting the words dwell on this teeth, his eyes narrowing.

Poonch-Terai misunderstood him adroitly: "Ah, you Americans! Always business! Well—you are well enough now to be moved to a more comfortable place. I have my carriage waiting."

"Is that an invitation?"

"A command! I am commanded by your more than regal mother to transport you to a guest house that I am privileged to place at her disposal. She awaits you in the carriage."

"I won't go," Joe said simply.

"She assured me you would say that. She instructed me that, should you say it, I am to exhort you. Will you consider yourself exhorted, or shall I—thank you, we will call that done then. Exhortation failing, I am privileged to intimate you will be forcibly removed. Permit me—"

With the sudden lithe speed of a leopard he thrust his hand under the pillow.

"No revolver? Wounded men are sometimes irritable. You will pardon the inquiry? Your annoyance is entirely offset by my satisfaction to know that you have no weapon. Are you ready? Shall I call my servants?"

"Bring my mother here," Joe answered grimly.

"Bring her? My dear man, she terrifies me!"

Hawkes sat silent. Annie Weems stood, staring at Poonch-Terai's back with an expression of frozen horror. The only really calm man in the room was the Yogi; Poonch-Terai was obviously masking either triumph or else nervousness; his insolence was skilful but too carefully deliberate; he was fencing. The Yogi looked interested, but merely as a dispassionate observer, his eyes moving but his body absolutely still as he considered first one individual, then the other. Joe, wondering what to say next, recalled the Yogi's conversation and it suddenly became very clear to him that Poonch-Terai was trying to goad him either into speech or action, either of which might be deadly dangerous. There was some sort of trap, although he could not imagine what it might be. Silence, at the moment at least, seemed the best alternative; and the moment he decided on that he thought he saw a thin smile of approval flicker at the corners of the Yogi's eyes. Poonch-Terai betrayed a trace of impatience.

"Shall I call my servants?" he repeated.

"You will suit yourself," Joe answered. "I have told you to bring in my mother. You will do anything else entirely on your own responsibility, and you will take the consequences."

Poonch-Terai smiled, showing marvelous, malicious teeth; it appeared that Joe had suggested to him something that he might not otherwise have thought of:

"Let me explain to you what the consequences will be if you offer resistance. The law is that only a Hindu may reside within these walls. Two-thirds of the revenues of this temple are dependent on strict observance of that law. One infringement known to and connived in by the temple authorities would oblige me, naturally much against my will, to discontinue payment of that money, which would revert to me for other uses. The Brahminical council that decides such matters probably would rule that reasonable sanctuary extended to a wounded man is legitimate; but when that wounded man is convalescent, and is requested to take that strain off hospitality, the case is different—particularly when other, more suitable and entirely free quarters are placed at your disposal. You doubtless get my point. But perhaps you would like to say good-by to someone?" He smiled with exquisitely acted condescension. "I don't, for instance, in the least mind waiting while you send for Miss Amrita. I am told that you and she have struck up quite a friendship."

Joe wished then that he did have a revolver. He could have shot the man without a trace of compunction. It was a moment before he could trust himself to speak calmly. Then he turned to the Yogi: "Is he telling the truth? Can he cut off the revenue as he says, and for that reason?"

Ram-Chittra Gunga nodded. "Malice usually uses as much truth as serves its purpose," he remarked. "And it is very true indeed that he would not mind waiting while you summon Miss Amrita. Am I right?" He looked suddenly, keenly at Poonch-Terai, who returned the stare with interest. Wills clashed, as it were, in mid-air, and the Yogi's by some means so enraged the maharajah that his eyes flashed and he clenched his fingers.

"Do you mock me? Do you dare mock me?" he demanded.

"Did I not say you are telling the truth? Is it true you are willing to wait?"

"True? Yes. I will wait ten minutes." He spoke with a curl of the lip and a sneer that made Annie Weems shrink toward the wall and stare astonished at Ram-Chittra Gunga, who seemed to be chiefly interested in Hawkes' emotions. Hawkes was knotting his fist and flexing his right-arm muscles in readiness for action. "Ten minutes gives you time enough for whatever nonsense you are contemplating."

"One suffices," said the Yogi. "I will summon her. She may come now." But he sat still, making no sign nor any further sound.

There was a minute's silence. Hawkes leaned forward ready for a sign from Joe, and Annie Weems shrank tight against the wall, for she could see that Poonch-Terai's hands, too, were ready for instant violence. Wondering what the Yogi's purpose possibly could be, Joe shook his head, hoping to make Hawkes calm himself; there was not a doubt in Joe's mind that Poonch-Terai wanted a fight. He probably had attendants outside the door, ready to break it down and rush in to his rescue. Hawkes was probably out of bounds and possibly absent without leave; a fight within the temple precincts could only end in disaster to him and it would do neither Joe nor Rita any good whatever. Poonch-Terai sucked at his teeth impatiently.

"Well?" he demanded at last. "Where is she?"

Then the door that led into the fountain-courtyard opened wide and Rita stood there framed against the starlight. She looked like a white ghost. She was draped in the swathing soft cloth Hawkes had seen wrapped around her near the prison gate, but it hung from her now like a shroud, with one end thrown over her head.

There was a whisper of wind in the courtyard; it moaned low in the cloisters and a shutter trembled against its bolt. If she herself made any sound at all those others smothered it. Her wide eyes gazed into the room as if she wondered at the importunity that summoned her from her eternal peace. She seemed come from a tomb, she who was singing an hour ago and was surely not yet buried. Poonch-Terai backed away from her and almost crushed Annie Weems against the wall; his left spur pricked her ankle before he controlled himself enough to step aside and borrow the wall's stiffness for his back. He was like to have backed clear through it had it been less solid. Joe's skin tingled from head to foot and a sweat broke out all over him. Hawkes sat gaping. Silence—subdivided into eons by the maharajah's almost strangled breathing.

Ram-Chittra Gunga's voice broke on the silence—cavernous—sonorous—seeming to come from almost anywhere but where he sat: "Is this true—or a lie—or a dream?"

Poonch-Terai spoke scurrilously in his own tongue, snarling, until he suddenly thought he might need witnesses and changed to English, picking his phrases and growing gradually bolder as the sound of his own voice heartened him:

"Trickery, such as any wayside fakir can do in the dark!—Treachery, intended to convict me! I know what is coming. Someone has hidden the girl away. I am to be accused—"

"Of having killed her," Joe said grimly. "I accuse you of having caused her death."

"But *is* she dead?" Ram-Chittra Gunga asked. He stared at Joe. "What need was there to accuse one who is self-accused?"

Joe gathered strength from somewhere and sat upright. He stared, remembering all kinds of stories, his heart in his teeth and his incredulity alert. But the light was baffling. Hawkes suddenly leaned backward in his chair and glanced at Annie Weems, trying to make some signal to her but her hands were before her face. The maharajah spoke again:

"You say self-accused. You lie, you outcast renegade! Unless you knew the girl were dead you couldn't produce her resemblance. I am not ignorant. I know something of the arts you practice. You propose to terrify me, and then by trumped up evidence to lay her death at my door. Come on, magician! Make your specter speak! Perhaps you can make her say who killed her!"

"Why should I not speak?" Rita asked. "And how shall I tell who killed me, seeing I am not yet dead?"

She stepped into the room—then hurried. Annie Weems was fainting. Rita and Hawkes together were in time to save her from collapsing. They set her in Hawkes' chair with her head against Rita's bosom and Rita's hands stroking her temples.

"Now what?" Hawkes asked, turning, facing Poonch-Terai. He was as truculent as the devil, and as eager to bring on a climax as if he could foresee the end of it. However—

"You will sit down," said the Yogi and the steam went out of Hawkes as suddenly as it had boiled up. He found himself a stool and sat on it with his back to the door through which Poonch-Terai had entered.

"Paddle your own canoe," he said. "I can wait for my turn."

Joe, still sitting upright, thought his own turn was about due. He was feeling weak again; reaction had set in; but he felt almost jealous of Annie Weems that she should monopolize Rita just then. He had not been as much as recognized.

"Rita, can you spare me just one minute?"

She was whispering. Annie Weems pushed her away. She crossed the floor to Joe's bedside and stood smiling at him until he raised his arms, and then she stooped and kissed him.

"Joe, you don't have to ask for minutes. Very soon now you and I have all eternity."

"Dead or alive?" he asked her, laughing. "Rita, Hawkes says Poonch-Terai's men—"

Poonch-Terai strode forward and interrupted. "Hawkes is a drunken liar! I can account for the movements of all my men. I know where every one of them has been. I knew some kind of plot against me was afoot, so I took precautions."

"I, too," Rita answered. "Hawkesey injured one of them—"

"Not one of my men!"

"All his front teeth are broken, and I don't know how to mend teeth. But I put some antiseptic on his gums and a dressing on his cut lips; they will need stitching when the swelling goes down. Hawkesey is an awful pile-driver of a man when he's angry. But none of the rest were hurt worth mentioning."

"I don't know what this all means," said the maharajah. But he was getting nervous. "What is supposed to have happened?"

"Not much, except that your carriage met me at the jail gate. Some of your men leaped out of it and wrapped me in this cloth, so that I couldn't scream or struggle. Then they carried me into the carriage, and threw the hurt man in, and followed."

"Not my carriage, I assure you. Not my men."

"No? Would you recognize the carriage?" It is in the temple compound."

"Bandits must have stolen it."

"Oh! Your followers are bandits? Would you recognize them? Should I bring them in? I have them with me." She turned and faced Ram-Chittra Gunga. "Shall I?"

Poonch-Terai cracked his heels together, making the spurs jingle.

"So the plot thickens," he said. "No, I would not be interested. I know where my men are. These are certainly impostors." And he strode toward the door, against which Hawkes sat with his chair on two legs.

"No," said Hawkes, "you stay here until me, and Rita, and Ram-Chittra Gunga"— that was an after thought— "has done with you and gives you leave to go."

Poonch-Terai whipped out an automatic pistol. Hawkes kicked his wrist, still tender from the injury when he creased Joe in the hunting field, and sent the pistol flying. It fell on Joe's bed. Joe broke it open and removed the shells.

"And now," said Hawkes, "we're man to man, conceding that you are one for the sake of argument. So you behave yourself. Go and sit down on the chair—that one. If you don't I'll smash you one that I've been saving for you longer than you'd guess."

FROM THE BOOK OF THE YOGI-ASTROLOGER RAM-CHITTRA GUNGA SINGH

My son, it is as true today as when the Master Jesus taught what He had heard in Tibet and what Tibet received from so-called Lost Atlantis: that out of the mouths of babes and sucklings cometh wisdom. Why? Because the babes and sucklings have imagination.

But the pedants and the proud have not; for they have slain it. They become enraged if they are told they do not understand. If offered proof of something not within their narrow view, they persecute. They call the poets fools, the prophets madmen, and the mystics they misname dreamers. They forget it was the mystics and the madmen and the fools who accepted Jesus; but the scientists of that day and the scholars, and the pedants, slew Him, as they will slay you also if you dare to demonstrate a trace of understanding of the lore of which Jesus knew more than men guess. They speak of physics, but I say they know no more of physics than a fish knows of the sea; they swim in physics, and the fish in water. If I ask such an one how he knows that weights fall downwards, he will answer: By experience. But if, in the words of the poet, I say: I know that my Redeemer liveth; and he asks me how I know that; and I answer: By experience, he thinks that I insult his intellect that tells him much concerning chemistry but nothing about Life—nay, nothing.

Lo, they look in books for Wisdom, and they search for the secret of Life in testing tubes, like apes that gape at their reflections in a mirror. They mistake their vanity for Wisdom. Arrogance they think is honesty, and incredulity they call sincerity. They believe that their fear for their reputations is integrity. They think conceit is pride, and they believe that jealousy is love of justice. Nevertheless, if they would take what they have learned and thereto add imagination—then—how wonderful they might be.

XXIII

"There's rather more in this than meets the eye."

Poonch-Terai preserved a fragment of his dignity if dignity there is in flouting one's inferior; all save that fragment was lost in the sneer of contempt with which he declined the chair, strode to the door that led into the courtyard, opened it and glanced out. Then, however, instantly his natural, his highly trained adroitness asserted itself. He saw a staggering array of evidence against him. Even in India, not even princes may set ambuscades and seize unwilling women without putting their thrones in peril; and though thrones have thorns that make their owners restless, men have foresworn faith to win them; and to preserve them many a prince has sent a hundred thousand citizens to death.

He stepped astride the threshold—scowled—looked terrible—and hurled abuse, in their own language, at some men from Poonch whom no one in the room could see but who evidently waited in the cloister. Joe reinserted the shells in the automatic and the Yogi watched him with mildly curious attention.

Poonch-Terai faced the room again, his hands on his hips and his legs astride, his stomach outthrust, as if he was a conqueror inspecting someone's harem. Plainly he was in no mood to ask anybody's mercy; nor would he grant it.

"Now what?" he demanded. "Get this nonsense over with."

Ram-Chittra Gunga snorted, as if a bad smell suddenly annoyed him.

"Yes," he said, "you have my leave to make an end of nonsense."

"Ingrate! I will end yours!" Poonch-Terai retorted. "Too long I have tolerated you. You and your abominable priests have grown too fat on revenues from my estates. You are an infidel and an imposter. You corrupt religion and profane the sacraments with your innovations. I accuse you in English, which you understand, because I wish these witnesses to know what I am saying. You have overstepped yourself at last by plotting against me and tampering with my men. I intend not to leave this place until I have had you thrown out,"—he glared at Joe, and Hawkes, and Annie Weems—"you and every trespasser whom you have encouraged."

"Bold words—very bold words," Ram-Chittra Gunga answered. "Let the coachman enter."

Strode in promptly, through the door that led to Annie Weems' room, two men from Poonch, erect and bearded, splendid in the maharajah's livery but looking scared. They saluted, but hardly knew whom to salute. They faced the Yogi. Their eyes were like leopards' that trusted nobody and doubted everything except death's fangs. Poonch-Terai glared again at Annie Weems and showed his wonderful white teeth in a grin of malicious triumph:

"So you, too, are in this conspiracy. I might have known it. I should have expected it when I closed your mission. But vengeance, madam, you will find is bitter when it is clumsy and fails! That is your apartment. You had those men hidden in there?"

"No," she said indignantly, "I did not."

"Let me see that room." He strode toward it, thrust the screen aside, kicked the door open and stared. At the end of the passage, with closed doors on either hand, a lamp shone on a big door bossed with iron nails that evidently led into the open air. He turned and sneered again at Annie Weems. "Who else is hidden in your room? That door at the end of the passage is locked."

A thin smile flickered on the Yogi's lips. "Are you sure it is locked?" he asked him.

"I will soon see."

Insolence had gained momentum. Poonch-Terai did not hesitate; he strode into the passage. Hawkes leaned forward and made eager signals like a boy in school who knows the answer to a question. The Yogi nodded. Swiftly, silently, Hawkes closed the door, locked it and set the screen in place; grinning, he stowed the huge key in his tunic pocket.

"What have you done? He will search my room!" Annie Weems objected, horrified. Her courage steamed up to the surface. No New England spinster likes to have her bedroom searched by a critical male.

"But he will find what?" asked the Yogi. "Presently he will go out through the end door, since he can not return through this one. Let the coachman tell his story."

But the coachman stood speechless. His companion whispered to him, obviously urging silence.

"Come on, out with it," said Hawkes. "No conferences. Speak quick, if you know what's good for you. You make 'em talk, Miss Rita; you could coax the truth out of the biggest liar unhung."

Suddenly Hawkes' jaw dropped. He was facing the door to the courtyard and he looked as if he saw the devil out beyond it in the shadows. Joe saw it next. Then Annie Weems. It was a ghost that swayed and shivered on a draught of dark air.

"Amal!" Rita was the first to recognize her.

Rusty—starved—scared—with her clothing all in rags—an embodied shadow of unhappiness, the ayah—if it was the ayah—swayed beyond the threshold in the baffling half-light from the open door. Her eyes were like holes through which pale star-light dimly peered.

"Amal!" That was Rita's voice again, but it might have been anyone's; it gave tongue to collective horror.

The vision crossed the threshold, as if thrust forward—someone's shadow. Even in the room, in lamp-light, she looked unsubstantial, until she threw herself at Rita's feet and lay fondling them, sobbing and murmuring such foolishness as ayahs use to children. Rita stood still, staring at the Yogi as if at a loss to know what to say or do, until the sobbing ceased and Amal lay still. Then, at last, Ram-Chittra Gunga spoke:

"Silence was the part of wisdom. And not a word of reproach; I praise that."

Annie Weems stiffened herself to face a new crisis. She came and knelt beside the ayah.

"Bring me a sheet quickly."

Rita snatched a sheet from Joe's bed; she and Annie Weems together spread it over Amal's body.

"Dead?" Joe asked. He would have said more but his throat was dry, and as the victim of Amal's knife he felt he had the right to appear calm, even if he was not.

"Dead?" said Hawkes. "Good God, what a hell of a night! What killed her?"

"Poison," said the Yogi.

Hawkes resented such swift omniscience. "How do you know?" he demanded. "If you're as wise as all that, say who gave it to her."

"She did. Who else? She is fortunate. Some people spend eternities before the creeping poison of their malice teaches them the lesson that they came into the world to learn. But she was a soul whose malice was as simple as her generosity. The poison of her malice acted swiftly, and—like unto like—some fool more reckless of his destiny than of his present need sensed what he thought was opportunity and gave that poor starved body what her soul knew it deserved. Is it not thus that the soul learns? How else? She did evil, and because she was faithful and simple, evil punished her thus soon that she might learn swiftly and not suffer too much. But he who killed—have you not heard the teaching that it needs must be that evil come, but woe unto him through whom it cometh?"

Rita went down on her knees beside Amal's body and covered her eyes with her hands; she appeared to be weeping. But Annie Weems stood up and faced Ram-Chittra Gunga. She look dreadful in that lamplight, with her white hair disarranged and all the hollows of her face in shadow; ancient sibyls may have looked as she did when the priests of other temples turned their oracles against them.

"How dare you! Are you a devil quoting Scripture? Sri Ram-Chittra Gunga, you shall not use Christ's words to support your dreadful teaching! I will not endure such blasphemy."

A dozen generations of New England heritage uprose and swamped her. But she was a swamped rock. Not even that moment could destroy her gentleness; it was as strong as granite.

"Words from an aching heart are as the stings of wasps. But whom do they sting? And does the heart ache less?" he answered.

"Yes, I spoke unkindly. I am sorry. But I denounce our bargain. This must be the end of it; I can't—I will not keep it any longer."

"Woman, who are you and I to speak of bargains? Was it we who laid down destiny and bounded it within the limits of our choosing? What you speak of as a bargain—"

"Was one," she interrupted. "God in His infinite wisdom must judge me for my share of it. He knows I meant well, as I know you did; you and I have too much mutual respect to doubt each other's motive."

"What then is it that you doubt?" he asked her.

"Oh, don't argue with me. When I took this child and agreed to share her education with you, I struggled against scruples that I should have known were warnings. We may not serve two masters. I have tried to serve mine and yours also; and here, at my feet, between us, is one part of God's judgment on that. The least and the last first. I might have saved poor Amal."

"Until she slew you? Yea, you might have saved her from small sinning until impulse waxed strong and she slew you and me also."

Annie Weems would not be comforted. She stirred the barb of self-contempt that made her heart ache. "I have done with self-deception. I am guilty, and the blame is mine, not yours. You knew no better. What you taught Rita, you believe is true; but what I have brought on her by letting her as much as hear your teachings, neither you nor I can guess, Ram-Chittra Gunga. And the dreadful part is, that the blame is mine but she must suffer for it."

"It is we, and only we ourselves, who cause ourselves to suffer," said the Yogi. "Nevertheless, we do well, because suffering loosens ignorance and lets in light."

But she shook her head; she would have none of his argument. "And I have wronged you, too, Ram-Chittra Gunga. I should not have let you wrong this child, whom you have loved as much as I did. You were loyal to your teachings, false though they are; and I was false to mine. Forgive me. I should not have yielded to your urging. It was not your voice that spoke then; it was Satan speaking through you. But you did not know that; and I should have known it. I sinned, and it is too late to undo it. But I declare our bargain ended. Rita must stay with you or come away with me. There can be no alternative."

"There is," said Joe, "there is a fine alternative."

But only Hawkes and Rita heard him. Hawkes drew his pipe from his tunic pocket, stared at it and thrust it away again. A thousand pounds was a fortune to a man in his shoes. He looked vexed, as if he understood that fortune is evasive. Joe read his thought as easily as if it were a printed page; but he could not read Rita's. Rita glanced once, swiftly; she was listening to Annie Weems, still kneeling but so disturbed that she hardly realized it. She stood up and embraced her, whispering and coaxing.

"No, child. No, I tell you."

"Annie, after all these years do you turn your back on me?"

Ram-Chittra Gunga interrupted. "Amal has turned a page of life's book. Let her body be laid in the cloister."

Wordlessly he intimated to the men from Poonch—the coachmen—that they should do that. They objected, not without speech, sullen and half defiant.

"What is their trouble?" Joe asked. He, though probably for other reasons, was as eager as the Yogi to get that corpse out of sight.

"They declare they are clean men but a corpse is unclean, so they will not touch it," said the Yogi.

Hawkes strode swiftly toward them, temper twitching in his right foot. They backed away. They almost stumbled over Amal's body. A long knife, whistling out of darkness, missed the coachman's throat by half an inch and struck point first into the wall above Joe's head, where it thrummed sharp like an off-key tuning fork. Joe fired three blind shots through the doorway. He could see nothing.

"Take that thing from him," said the Yogi.

Hawkes came to the bedside. "Pardon me, sir. That

can only get us into trouble. May I have it? Your nerves are a little upset." But Hawkes was sweating; he had nerves too. His hand had hardly closed around the pistol when he nearly jumped out of his skin.

"Who shot at me?" demanded Poonch-Terai's voice.

He stood full in the doorway, hands on hips again. Had he been master of the situation he could not have looked more truculent. Joe tried to snatch the pistol back but Hawkes was a shade too quick for him.

"You black murderer!" said Joe. "Who threw that knife?"

"How should I know? But I have two witnesses to the shooting," Poonch-Terai answered. He beckoned the two coachmen. They hesitated, but he seemed to hypnotize them. Hawkes interfered:

"You stay here, both of you. Come and stand over here by me."

But Hawkes' voice startled them. They almost ran toward their master, dreading him more than they did Hawkes and attracted, in their panic, toward the greater dread. Poonch-Terai stepped aside and let them pass him through the door-way. Then he faced Ram-Chittra Gunga and spoke with mocking malice:

"Father of miracles! Perhaps now—of your wisdom and your sanctity—you may be shrewd enough to tell these priests to open the temple gate."

"I perceive that you tried to climb the wall," the Yogi answered. "Why your great haste?"

Poonch-Terai swore as if stung, trying to look indifferent as he glanced down at the tell-tale marks on his breeches and riding-boots. "Either you let me out of here," he answered, "or I will force my way out."

"I do nothing," said the Yogi. "I am contented to let that be, which is. I am not destiny."

"You are a dog, whom I will kick into the dirt," said Poonch-Terai. He took a long stride forward and then suddenly stood still. There came a knock on the door through which he had first entered—one knock followed by impatient thunder.

"What now?" he demanded, thrusting his jaw forward. "What have you done?" He betrayed alarm by much too carefully disguising it. He overplayed the note of insolence.

Hawkes strode to the door, glanced toward the Yogi for permission and drew back the bolt. He saluted instantly, surprise making him as stiff as a raw recruit.

"Oh, hello, Hawkes, you here? Not trespassing, I hope?"

Bruce of the Lancers strode in, stared at Poonch-Terai and then saluted Annie Weems. He seemed annoyed to have to be there.

"Were you invited?" Poonch-Terai asked. Probably he himself could not have told why the sight of Bruce enraged him, but it seemed to Joe that mental flint and spiritual steel were striking sparks.

"Invited? Yes and no," Bruce answered. "I was passing. Mrs. Beddington is outside. Oh, hello, Beddington, how are you? Your mother seems worried—seems she has been waiting out there for you—wonders what has happened. She asked me to come in and help get you out to the carriage."

Rita, holding Annie Weems' hand, edged toward Joe.

It was a natural, self-betraying movement that made Poonch-Terai grin savagely. Joe took her hand and held it tight.

"Courage!" he said. "I need all yours and mine, too." Then, louder, to Bruce: "It's mighty good of you. I wonder if you'd mind asking my mother to come in."

"No need," said his mother's voice. Her foot was through the door, her weight against it. It flew open. Baffled temple servants choked the passageway behind her. "Joe, I must say I'm surprised that you should keep me waiting when the maharajah has been kind enough to go to all this trouble!"

Hawkes closed the door behind her. He sensed crisis.

"Have a chair, ma'am."

She glared at him—at Annie Weems—at Rita—at the Yogi—then again at Rita.

"Thank you, no," she said. "I came to bring my son away. Joe, are you ready?"

Instead of answering, Joe signed to Annie Weems and Rita to help to prop him up with pillows with his back against the wall. They draped a blanket over him.

"I am ready to talk," he said then. "Sit down, Mater. Take the chair Hawkes offered you." He glanced at Bruce and nodded to him: "Sit down, won't you, Bruce? There's rather more in this than meets the eye."

FROM THE BOOK OF THE YOGI-ASTROLOGER RAM-CHITTRA GUNGA SINGH

My son, I know no reason, none whatever, why your seekers after Wisdom should seek in the East what the West holds also. Lovers of long words and incomprehensible phrases that sound in your ears like passwords to admit you, but not others, to the company of angels, ye behave as fools and scoundrels, though ye wish to be both virtuous and wise. Ye are no more wise than scientists who plough the putrid marshes of disease in the search for the pellucid springs of health. Ye desire to be special people, using special words to denote your special knowledge of the special ways of God. Ye turn to Gautama and Sanskrit Vedas, because their speech was not your speech and ye may memorise and mouth their sayings but be unashamed by what they said.

Jesus, who said the same things, shames you too much because His words were simple. If ye understand not Jesus, ye will never know how wise is Wisdom. It is the fruit of the soul's experience. A man may have all knowledge, yet no wisdom. Better it is to be a wiseman with the fools than a fool with the worldly—wisemen, because character is all God cares about and none is great or wise without it, though His greatness may seem smallness and his wisdom may appear as folly to the fools who set false standards and claim authority, but whose vanity dies with them. Character is the only key to Wisdom; nay, there is none other.

Wisdom is neither here nor there, but in your own Soul. That is why the learned fools, who say that death ends all things, seek Life on the glass slides under microscopes; but foolish wisemen find it, because Wisdom finds them, and their own Souls show them marvels that the vain can neither see nor understand.

XXIV

> *"Let judgment answer!"*

Ram-Chittra Gunga fired the opening gun. He aimed it at nothing that anyone saw, yet every one knew he had hit the target.

"Light," he remarked, "cannot see, hear, feel or touch the darkness. There are many kinds of darkness. There is one light. And where the light is, darkness is not."

Joe's mother, for no evident reason, seemed to think her dignity was challenged. She accepted a chair because her shoes pinched. She was much too expensively dressed and perspiration was exuding through the mauve silk. She had on her heavy diamond necklace and its weight, in the heat, was irritating. Joe could recognize another symptom: she had eaten too much, and had not had too little champagne; he supposed she had dined with Albert Cummings.

"I did not come here to be preached at," she announced. "As I told you, I came for my son. His Highness"—she smirked at Poonch-Terai—"has very kindly offered us the guest-house at his summer palace. Joe, dear, how long will it take you to get ready?"

The Yogi answered her:

"It is wise to be ready. Destiny waits on no man's will. Man made it, but can he change it? The sum total of his merit is arrayed against the consequences of his sins, each at an end of the scale and himself the fulcrum. When? they all ask; when is the hour of the weighing? Tomorrow? But there was no yesterday. Tomorrow never shall be. Now is."

"A demented religionist. You must make allowances," Poonch-Terai remarked with impatience. "I will wait for you outside, Mrs. Beddington."

He beckoned his two men to follow him and strode toward the door. Hawkes' face would have made a landslide stop and think things over. Poonch-Terai saved shreds of dignity again by putting the problem up to Bruce:

"I suppose this sergeant will obey you? Be good enough to order him to stand aside."

Bruce hesitated for a second and Hawkes took full advantage of it. He locked the door, removed the enormous iron key, then crossed the room and dropped the key into the Yogi's lap. Bruce smiled polite contempt at Poonch-Terai.

"That solves it," he said, almost chuckling. "I have no authority in this place. I've no business to be here. To be frank with you, I don't know why they let me in."

"Then go out," Poonch-Terai suggested. "They won't dare to detain you."

"I'm under no restraint that I'm aware of," Bruce retorted. "Rotten manners—to protest before there's any excuse for it. What's *your* hurry?"

"Possibly you mean *my* hurry?" Mrs. Beddington suggested tartly. "Locked in? I never heard of such impudence. However, I have sent for Mr. Cummings. We will soon see. When the carriage servants tell him I am in here—"

Joe refused to tolerate her bombast. He interrupted,

finishing the sentence for her: "He will whistle *Rule Britannia,* light a Murad and come charging in on horseback to show us how St. George slew dragons."

Mrs. Beddington glared at him, speechless. She had not come prepared to fight in that place; she preferred her own ground. Poonch-Terai stepped close and whispered to her. Bruce, embarrassed almost beyond endurance by the prospect of a family squabble in which he had no concern, but in which Poonch-Terai appeared to be a confidant of one side, looked around him for an excuse to change the subject.

"What's this in the middle of the room?" he asked.

Annie Weems glanced at the Yogi. He nodded. She went to the sheet that covered Amal's corpse and raised one corner of it.

"Dead?" Bruce whistled softly to himself. "What did she die of?"

Annie Weems answered him. "Someone said poison."

Mrs. Beddington rose from her chair to look and Poonch-Terai tried to prevent her.

"Who is she?" Bruce asked.

Joe spoke. "Probably you remember. She was Rita's ayah—you recall that day when you and I went pig-sticking, and I told you about an old woman who kept shadowing me wherever I went. That's the one. She came in here and fell down dead."

Bruce stared at Joe. "Yes, I remember we talked—" Then, suddenly: "How did that knife get stuck into the wall above your head?"

"It was thrown through that door."

"At you? Did you see who threw it?"

"No. But I fired three shots into the darkness; and then Maharajah Poonch-Terai entered and accused me of shooting at him."

"Your pistol?"

"No, his."

"How did you happen to have his pistol?"

Hawkes stood forward at attention. "That was me, sir. His Highness drew at me, so I kicked his wrist, not wishing to have no unpleasantness. The pistol fell flop on the gentleman's bed. It was what you might call one o' them coincidences."

Bruce rubbed his chin thoughtfully, then stared at Poonch-Terai.

"What might be your version of it?" he demanded.

Poonch-Terai seemed on the edge of explaining, but thought better of it.

"You have no authority in here," he answered; "you just said so."

"Very well," said Bruce, "I'll send for the police."

Mrs. Beddington flared up. "Joe, you put some shoes on and I'll have you carried out this minute! This is a nice mess you've gotten yourself into. Here am I engaged this day to Mr. Cummings—my engagement day—you grasp that?—and here he must come and find my son mixed up with murders—and the police—and I don't know what else."

"My engagement day," said Joe, "was yesterday. No need to introduce Rita to you. You met her at Miss Weems'. I owe Hawkes fifteen thousand rupees."

"Do you! And doesn't he hope he may get it! Joe,

you listen to me. Under the terms of your father's will I can cut you off with nothing if you marry without my consent before you're forty. I know all about that girl. She's nothing but a cheap little Eurasian adventuress and I'm glad to have her hear me say it. She and Sergeant Hawkes are in cahoots to get your money. She set her cap at you the minute Hawkes told her you were looking for an American orphan born in India. It's a fraud that any fool could see through."

Hawkes stepped forward. "Are you accusing me, ma'am?"

"Yes," she answered, "and I hope you'll start a suit for slander. I'll soon show you." Scornfully she pointed at the sheet that covered Amal's body. "Do you mean to tell me that isn't murder, and that it isn't all part of your plot? Who is that? Wasn't she the ayah? Who else was there who could swear to this girl's parentage? I suppose you were afraid she'd tell the truth. Dead ones don't say much—do they? But they sometimes hang the live ones! Now I've said my say I'm going."

Joe felt strange strength stealing over him, not merely mental, it was physical as well. Some impulse made him glance toward Ram-Chittra Gunga and he saw him flame-colored. It was so distinct and so astonishing that he looked to see whether the others noticed it, but apparently they did not, unless—he was not sure whether Rita did; she, too, glanced toward the old man and ceased trembling directly afterward.

Joe reached out for her hand but she drew away from him as if she had resolved to fight her own battle.

She even pushed Annie Weems away from her. "Mrs. Beddington," she began.

"I refuse to speak to you. You may tell your tale to the police, young woman."

"Tell it now," Joe interrupted. "Go on, Rita, tell it. Sit down, Mater. Do you hear me? Sit down."

Her indignant retort was spoiled by Poonch-Terai. He took the wind out of her sails. It seemed he wanted none of Rita's revelations just then.

"No, no," he objected. Then he made an admirable effort to control himself; his voice grew suave, his attitude magnanimous and rather princely. "Nobody, I think, has actually sent for the police and meanwhile we are all losing our tempers. We are likely to create a scandal where there actually is none. Someone mentioned murder." He turned his back to Mrs. Beddington, with a hand behind his back, it seemed to Joe he signaled to her. "Let us see what that woman died of."

No one moved until Hawkes made a gesture to Bruce, who nodded. Then Hawkes raised the sheet that covered Amal's body. They all stared. They all saw. There was hardly room for doubt; a cobra kills within an hour of striking and leaves no question as to who slew.

"She must have been sitting or crouching," said Bruce, "when a cobra bit her. It got a good hold. It struck through her cotton clothing. How long had she been in here before she died?"

"About a minute." That was Rita's voice.

"I wonder you didn't notice what was wrong with her."

"I did," said Annie Weems.

"Then why the silence?"

But she grew silent again, only staring at Poonch-Terai as if it had been his fangs that had bitten Amal. He returned the stare with interest, then suddenly resumed his air of being the only unhysterical person in the room. "So you see after all, it is only a case for a doctor's death certificate," he remarked with a shrug of his shoulders. "Let us send for Muldoon."

"Muldoon—certainly—why, yes, of course," said Mrs. Beddington. She spoke from behind the maharajah's back and he looked vaguely annoyed, as if she had spoken out of turn.

Joe's memory of Muldoon had been bitten in with acid.

"How much have you paid Muldoon?" he asked his mother. "How much have you promised him? See here, it's as clear to me as daylight that every fair or foul means you can lay your hands on are to be used to destroy Rita's reputation and to separate her from me. This is conspiracy. Let's have it out here, now."

She approached him. "Are you talking to me, Joe?"

He could see her, too, in color. Sulky saffron, glowing sour-green, smoky crimson and, behind it all, inky indigo. He felt steal over him the old familiar sensation that had made school-days, and even punishments at school seem preferable to the life at home. Scores—hundreds of times, to avoid that feeling, he had yielded to her. He believed that his father had died of it.

"Joe, were you speaking to me—your mother?"

"Yes, I was. It's a fine line, isn't it, for a man to have to take with his own mother. I accuse you of conspiracy. And I intend to marry Rita. Come here, Rita; come and stand beside me."

"Very well, Joe. It must be perfectly clear to Captain Bruce and the maharajah that you have ruined yourself by falling into evil company. There's something filthy about it that has corrupted your brain. You are as good as drugged. I suppose next, you'll become a Hindu. I can only wash my hands of you. I won't be guilty of conniving at such self-disgrace as you contemplate. Marry that girl? That little Eurasian snippy who has been free with Hawkes and half the soldiers in the barracks? Not with my permission? I cut you off now, this minute, without a nickel. I repudiate you. I shall cable at once, and confirm it by letter, that I have removed you from every position you hold in every one of my companies. You needn't look to me for one more cent of money. You may go home third-class."

"I will go home if and when I please," Joe answered.

"You will go home the minute the Indian Government learns that you are destitute. You will be deported, and I will pay to the government not one cent more than enough for your third-class fare."

Mrs. Beddington turned, trembling like a battleship in action. She had fired all bow-guns. Now she swung to bring to bear stern turrets that should finish matters.

"As for that young person whom you say you mean to marry, she and Hawkes shall learn what the law has to say about trying to get money under false pretenses. I have sent to my bank for that check." She favored Hawkes with one withering glare that should have reduced him to panic. But the check she had written with Cummings' knowledge as a trap for Hawkes had never left Joe's jacket pocket. That shot missed. Hawkes looked abominably unafraid of her, and nothing is more disconcerting to a bully than an unexpected failure to impose fear. She glanced at the maharajah, who had been running fingers through his well kept beard, so that it no longer looked like a symbol of aristocratic *savoir faire.*

"You wish to go?" he asked her. "Certainly. I will escort you to my carriage." He offered his arm. "That door, please. Someone open it. Get the key from the Yogi."

"No," said Joe, "we'll wait for Cummings." He pointed an accusing forefinger at Poonch-Terai. "You'll wait here, whoever else goes."

The maharajah turned to Bruce. "I appeal to you. You are locked in. Command them to open that door."

"No," said Bruce. "As Mr. Cummings is expected I propose we all wait for him. In fact, I accept that much responsibility. I order that the door shall not be opened, and that nobody shall leave this room, until someone with authority arrives who can—er—ask such questions as he sees fit. I vote we all be seated."

Silence fell. Then suddenly a tremendous peal of thunder shook the very basement of the building. As if India's gods were entering the argument with nature's huge artillery, such darkness fell as seemed to dim the lantern-light. Forked lightning shook the darkness, and a din of rain seethed in the courtyard.

"Judgment!" boomed Ram-Chittra Gunga's voice

between the thunder-claps. "Ye have challenged destiny!"

Salvo after salvo shook the masonry, and now the wind shrieked, adding horror to the darkness. Terror, guised as lightning, lit and relit livid faces.

"He who summons to himself ten soldiers must control them or they overwhelm him. He who summons violence to do his bidding must control it, or it overwhelms him. He who summons to his aid dark forces must control those, or they overwhelm him. Set your strength into the balance against THAT WHICH IS. I challenge judgment. I demand it. I demand it **NOW**!"

Thunder again, cannonading amid rain-swept masonry. A night sky, seen across the courtyard, chaos—black with rolling storm cloud, split by stinging flame that crackled as it split into a thousand bayonets of light. And then, again, the Yogi's voice:

"Let her speak who has felt no malice and has said no blame. Stand forth, thou. Say thy say. Let judgment answer."

He commanded with his right hand. Rita stood forth beside Amal's body. Lightning through the open doorway showed her ghost-white, gentle, almost like a spirit summoned from an unseen world.

FROM THE BOOK OF THE YOGI-ASTROLOGER
RAM-CHITTRA GUNGA SINGH

My son, most people and the devil are concerned with quantity—how much is this or that, and how much of it. God is concerned with quality, whose dimensions are not measurable by any material standards whatsoever. The quality of music, of mercy, of chastity—can that be measured with a yard-stick? Nevertheless, is it unimportant? Can the vivisectionists dissect it, or the men who make laws change it, or the slanderers destroy it? The quality of a man is his soul, and that is also something that the masons cannot measure nor the grocers weigh: so much so, that there are many logicians and so-called scientists of great fame who deny the soul's existence—which is to say, that they deny their own quality, wherein they come far nearer to the truth than they suspect. Such men may measure fractions of the millionth of the millionth of an atom; they may bask in flattery and self-esteem as gluttons delight in quantities of rare food; they may dig amid the ruins of the past and say: Here were the Mysteries held, and here was this temple and that one, but the Mysteries have perished and the temples are the rain-washed skeletons of superstition; lo, how wise are we, in whom no superstition is. But I tell you, a singer, in debt for his meals and ignorant of the very names of so-called learned men, knows more than all of them combined if he can sing with the hundred-millionth of a skylark's passion.

Quality cannot be measured in terms of three, or even four dimensions, and none but the grossest ignorance of the nature of quality would presume so to measure it. The quality of knowledge is the Soul of Truth; and they who say they have no souls are blind fools buried in the substance they were sent to transmute; drunkards are they, drowned in sour wine of their own fermenting. How much better are they than the insects that can lay low forests and build islands in the sea? The insects also judge results by quantity; and what they do, they do well, without aid from books.

Remember this, my son: Science, philosophy, affluence, art—

all these are no more than a phase of ignorance, unless a man knows he is, he himself, his Soul in temporary occupation of a body. Then, however, if he understands that, all the realms of knowledge are his own dominion, wherein he shall neither stray nor waste one moment's effort. In his hand, then, is the Key of all the Mysteries. He can unlock the keeps of Disaster, unharmed. He can yoke the Bulls of Cataclysm to his plough. Because a Soul has wisdom. But a man who thinks he is an animal possessed of somewhat better brains than pigs have—what can he accomplish? Politician, priest, philosopher or chemist—he can only multiply the numbers of the things he does not understand.

XXV

> *"It is the wrong time of the year for storms."*

The violence of the storm increased. For several seconds Rita waited, perhaps listening for the quarter-tone on which to pitch her voice to make it audible. Mrs. Beddington spoke, but the elements dealt with her voice in the way that blotting-paper deals with ink; there was neither modesty nor music in her—each as necessary to the other, to be audible above the anvil-chorus of the gods. When Rita did speak, though her voice was level and not loud, it was as distinct as the thread of a melody inwoven amid drums, the brass of lightning and the wood-winds of the splendid orchestra.

"I love Joe. That is no one's business but his and mine; not his, unless he also loves me." Thunder again and lightning that made of the room a cube of cold fire with human figures frozen in it. Sudden darkness, in which the lamp was like a yellow pin-point. Squalls of seething rain, like hail. And then again her quiet voice: "If it were I who created love, I would not ask pardon for it."

"Listen to her. I say, listen to her!" boomed Ram-Chittra Gunga. And the thunder, for a moment, blotted out all other sounds.

Then Rita's voice: "But I am of eternity, not time. I am a prisoner in this body of great yearnings and too narrow limits; and for how long I am sentenced none in this world knows. I have forgotten. All of us forget when we are born into these cages that we call our earth-lives. But those are only moments. They pass; and in death we remember. Eternity always is."

"I say, listen to her!" boomed Ram-Chittra Gunga. But for more than a minute the storm monopolized all sound and all sensation. In the glare of the lightning Poonch-Terai could be seen trying to whisper to Mrs. Beddington, but she seemed unable to catch his words. When the deafening thunder ceased for a moment she spoke, almost screaming, her voice pitched sharp and staggering raw because she was exasperated and afraid:

"I didn't come here to be preached at and I don't intend to listen. Such hypocrisy is wasted on me."

Bruce objected before Joe had time to get a word in: "Come now, fair play! Silence, please. It's hard enough to listen without interruptions."

Poonch-Terai promptly upheld Mrs. Beddington: "Take my advice and clear out of here, Captain Bruce. Did you ever hear of black art? This is where they teach it. Haven't you any brains? You know the monsoon isn't due for four weeks, yet here's a thunderstorm. Never mind the rain; my carriage is outside; help me get Mrs. Beddington out of here before—"

"You shut up," Hawkes advised him, "or I'll knock your teeth out!"

Volleying thunder. Poonch-Terai backed out of range of Hawkes' fist. Lightning showed far too much white in his eyes, and he was glaring at Ram-Chittra Gunga as if the Yogi had him by the throat. But the length of the room lay between them. The Yogi was calm. When the squall had spent its momentary fury Rita continued as if there had been no comments:

"Eternity is life. The substance of eternity is love, and love is affluent. I have no need to make demands on anyone. And least of all will I bend the rays of circumstance to make misfortune for the one I love most. I have not made—I will not make one claim on Joe. I love him. He is more free than if I did not love him. Because love enlarges; it is not cruel; it is no python strangling what it seizes. Love sets free."

She had to pause a moment to let another thunder-squall explode its fury. Then she continued:

"Joe and I have loved each other long before we met in this life. But it will need a gentler curiosity than yours to unveil that secret, and a harder heart than mine to bring down ruin on him merely because I am young, and a woman, and yearn for him—"

Thunder interrupted her. Then Joe's voice:

"Rita—"

But she gestured to him to be still; and because he loved her, and knew she was saying what was sacred, he obeyed.

"—merely because," she continued, "destiny delivered him at my door—wounded him at my feet—gave me charge of him to watch and wait on and to clutch back from the gates of death. My duty that I did confers on me no right to claim him into poverty and what you would consider disgrace." She choked a little. "So I set Joe free from any claim that even he may think I have on him."

Joe answered her. Thunder and rain and shrieking wind swallowed his words. He could not even hear his own voice. And strangely stronger though he felt, as if the Yogi were sending him rays of energy, he could not get up from the bed without assistance. He was wild to go and take her in his arms. He would have led her out into the storm to any destiny that might await them. He could have killed his mother when the squall lulled suddenly and her voice, tart and catty, interrupted:

"Did you hear that, all of you? She makes no claim on him. She can't bring suit for breach of promise after that. You heard her, Joe? You needn't be quixotic now. You can act sensibly and come away."

"Speak about forgetting," boomed the Yogi, "when her tale is finished. Then let him or her forget whose right that is. I challenge judgment."

Poonch-Terai spoke hoarsely: "He is making magic. I tell you, this storm is his doing! He is a black magician! It is the wrong time of the year for storms—"

Whatever else he said was drowned in thunder. There was no other sound than the storm, until the Yogi answered him:

"I wonder there is not an earthquake."

"Did you hear him?" Poonch-Terai protested. But the Yogi's calm commanding voice retorted:

"Hear *her*. I have challenged judgment."

"There is not much that I need to tell," said Rita. "I am accused of low birth and of looseness. The only parents I have known were Sri Ram-Chittra Gunga and Miss Annie Weems. My nurse was Amal. They three told me I was born in India. So Indian I am. And I am grateful to the tired and troubled land that gave me all I know of kindness and experience. If I am loose—then I am false to all the teaching I have had. If I am loose—it must have been a dream I dreamed that Annie Weems has always known my inmost secrets, and has praised me, and that Sri Ram-Chittra Gunga has examined my inmost consciousness before he taught such secrets as are not told to the unregenerate. I must have dreamed that I was saving all I have to give for him whom I would infinitely rather die than offer less than my whole self. If I am Eurasian—"

"She said it!" exclaimed Mrs. Beddington.

"—then I am so in spirit. Spirit is universal. Spiritually I claim kinship with all life, everywhere. But as for this body—"

"You needn't insult our intelligence," Mrs. Beddington interrupted. "Besides, you have admitted what you are."

"—there is not in me one drop of Indian blood."

The thunder crashed as if in confirmation of her words, but Mrs. Beddington saw fit to retort:

"Mere assertions prove nothing. All I can say is—"

"You have said too much," Ram-Chittra Gunga interrupted. "Let her speak, on whom your malice is as wasted as the spit of fools who hear the name of wisdom."

Suddenly he raised his right hand. As if even thunder-storms obeyed him a terrific flash of lightning split the darkness into fragments—again and again. Wind shrieked and the rain seethed past the open doorway, almost parallel to earth. The whole earth seemed to tremble under blows of thunder. Mrs. Beddington screamed. But the squall overspent its fury and paused as if panting for breath. In the ensuing sea of sound that felt like silence Poonch-Terai lifted his voice to a strained, excited challenge:

"Liar!" He used English, perhaps because he hoped

that Bruce would sympathize. "You pretend to govern nature! You employ foul devils, do you? The truth is, that you are their servant! Yours is idiots' magic! You're ridiculous!"

"You hold your jaw unless you want it broke!" Hawkes interrupted angrily; but there was more than anger in his voice; the lightning showed fear on his face.

"Magic?" Mrs. Beddington's was the insolence of fear that knows it is found out, and that has no weapon except ridicule. "Any charlatan with nerves could have known a thunderstorm was coming. Only children would believe you started it."

"Children would know better," the Yogi answered. "Does a rock raise winds that whip the sea against it?"

Through the rumble of new thunder Poonch-Terai laughed excitedly:

"Show us some more of your magic!"

Three terrific, shuddering stabs of lightning showed what Hawkes was doing and even the thunder did not drown out Bruce's voice:

"Hawkes! Give that pistol to me!"

"Free love—blackmail—and now murder!" said Mrs. Beddington. "Is this the act of an innocent man to try to prove a case by shooting? Joe—" But thunder silenced her.

Then Poonch-Terai resumed the offensive: "That is an old trick. Any wayside fakir can make a weak-willed drunkard commit murder. That old fool is using wayside magic, that's all. He would have let them hang Hawkes because Hawkes knows too much."

The Yogi was silent. Mrs. Beddington hurled her Parthian shot: "The madhouse would be much too merciful for—"

Rita interrupted: "You?" Her voice changed; it had a note of authority now. It was masterful. "You dare to insult my teacher? You, who have allied yourself with all the evil elementals in the universe! You, who have used black arts to try to govern your own son! You, who have lent yourself to a conspiracy against him, and against me! You, who have become the tool of a devil! Do you dare to mock my teacher?"

Poonch-Terai laughed. "It is I who mock him! Bah! He has used all his magic against me—and he couldn't even make that sergeant pull the trigger!"

"On your own head be your mockery," said Rita. "You, who were too cowardly to come and seize me! You, who used bribery, threats and all the black art that you know! You, who have used lies and deceit and violence to get me in your clutches because you hoped to make me tell you secrets that you think I have learned at the feet of Sri Ram-Chittra Gunga! You, who sent your men from Poonch to bind and gag me! You, who plotted with Joe's mother—"

Mrs. Beddington jumped to her feet. "Do you dare—"

But Bruce objected. "Order, please. It was you who first accused her. Let her answer."

Mrs. Beddington sat down. There was something about Bruce's level-voiced restraint that disarmed her. But Poonch-Terai was as excited as a tiger at bay.

"She is simply lying," he objected. "She is making random accusations—" Thunder silenced him—thunder, wind, rain and lightning-flashes that revealed him looking like a swordsman at bay and alert but not too sure of his advantage. And then Rita's voice, stronger than his:

"You, who challenge truth, are those two men from Poonch not your men? Order them to stand up and relate how they obeyed you—and then disobeyed you! Let them tell their story."

The two coachmen stood up because she pointed to them. But they hesitated. They were scared out of their wits. They stared at her, and then at Poonch-Terai. The maharajah strode toward them. He said something to them in an undertone. Then he faced about and strode back to his place near Mrs. Beddington, murmuring something to her too.

"Make them speak if you can!" he sneered at Rita. "You can lie about me and my men. But what proof have you?"

She turned toward the Yogi, saying nothing. But her gesture was suppliant, as if she asked a favor in extremity. The Yogi's answer boomed forth like an oracle from some Delphic underworld:

"Is memory imprisoned in the words that terror holds unspoken? And is speech the whole of wisdom? Is thought powerless, that it must limp with words, as lame men lean on crutches?"

He commanded with a gesture. Rita turned the lamp out. Then she closed the courtyard door and sat down near the Yogi's feet. He, with his thumb and finger, extinguished the night light. Stifling, pitch-black darkness filled the room as if there never had been light, and all was breathless silence, save for the thunder rumbling as if Dyan Chohans were re-massing their artillery on hurrying wheels.

FROM THE BOOK OF THE YOGI-ASTROLOGER
RAM-CHITTRA GUNGA SINGH

My son, at the root of all contempt lies ignorance; and there is nothing of less importance in the universe than the contempt of learned men and their sycophants, who brand as superstition all experience whatsoever that escapes their shallow understanding. What they think is depth, is surface; what they think is wisdom, is the heaping of dry fact on fact until the Truth, of which the facts are evidence, is lost to them beneath the sanddrifts of their windy blowing. Lo, they blow dry. Which of them will not assure you that I am a knave or an ignorant fool when I say I know at least some portion of the law of Karma, and that I have some little understanding of the law of birth and rebirth of the Soul in matter unto countless incarnations—aye, and of the comfort that the knowledge gives, because I see that Justice reigns and in the end there is neither hell nor heaven but an universal ecstasy! Which of them, nevertheless, has given one ten-thousandth of the thought to it that he has brought to bear on such a simple thing as water? And does the wisest of them know what water is? They are like the sharks that swim in water, slaying one another and all smaller fish, the while they wonder what water may be. Or they resemble rich men in a desert of dry knowledge, wherein water is not to be bought with any coin that they have.

Jesus—and they will tell you Jesus never lived—spoke wisdom concerning rich men; and I tell you, they who are rich in so-called scientific knowledge, but who do not know what Jesus meant by water and the spirit, are of the stuff of which gibbering ghosts are made; because their brains die with them, even as they themselves declare, and their pride dies also. What is left? A consciousness so thoroughly convinced of death that the Soul cannot awaken it, perhaps, for centuries; a thing that lives, not knowing that it lives; a naked, houseless entity that may be likened to the worms which burrowed in the bark. They burrowed in the bark of knowledge, but the bark is stripped away; and what then?

Nay, I tell you, all the scholarship and science in the world is worthless, and is doomed along with dreams, unless a man learn, first, at least a little understanding of his own Soul, ere he bury consciousness in matter. Else he is like a madman seeing clouds reflected in a pool, who plunges in the pool to learn to fly. But his Soul, if he seek his Soul first, shall inspire him with wisdom; wisdom shall give him guidance; guidance, understanding; understanding, courage—so that he shall even dare, in the end, to confess that the love of one bird for another is more than all science, art, invention and philosophy.

Then Love shall teach him and his own Soul shall interpret meanings; then the field of science, that to others may be no more than a drifting sand of facts, shall be a mirror to him wherein he shall seek and find the secrets of Eternal life.

XXVI

> *"I have demanded judgment.
> If it fall on my head, let it."*

Then weird things happened. Faculties, which Joe did not know that he had, possessed him, as they do in dreams, where time and space imblend into a new dimension that unites them both and transcends both. Nevertheless, he knew he was not dreaming. He could smell, for instance, the sour smoke of the night-light wick that the Yogi had extinguished. He could feel the sharp pain below his shoulder-blade that always tortured him unless he leaned his weight to one side. He could hear Annie Weems nervously moving a foot inside her slipper, where she sat on the floor beside Amal's body. He could taste the salt sweat on his own hand when he pressed his lips against it. He could count the buttons on his pajama jacket. But for a length of time that he guessed was sixty seconds he could not see.

Then, however, he saw Rita very clearly, although there was no light. She emerged out of the darkness like the image on a photographic plate, only in color, life-size, and in relief, not flat. She was sitting near the Yogi's feet, quite motionless except that he could see her breathing. Her outline, it appeared to Joe, was silver, but her head and body were of the color of fiery opal and the colors were not motionless, although it would be equally incorrect to say that they were moving. The strangest part of all was, that he could see her also in her natural color. There was a small red flame, brighter than blood, that seemed to leap from the crown of her head, and there was another one over her heart. He could see her white dress quite distinctly.

He realized that he had been looking at the Yogi, too, for several seconds before he became actually conscious of him. Then he saw him peacock-colored, only infinitely more bright and fiery than any peacock in the world. Him, too, he could see in his natural color, bearded and with hair down to his shoulders; but when he looked at him the other way he seemed to be a young man, clean-shaven, with a flame on the crown of his head that shone with every color in the prism. The Yogi sat quite still and did not seem to breathe, but the flames moved constantly, although their motion was indescribable.

Joe coughed. He was awake; he could hear himself cough. But when he did that he found he could see much less distinctly for several moments.

He wondered whether the others could see what he did and since thought, like emotion, obeys habit, he looked around him, not remembering how absolutely dark the room was, until he began to see the others one by one, in outline first, then more or less filled in with color, each one different. Annie Weems was mostly silver, blue and yellow—bright, but shot with sad-gray. Bruce was a golden walnut color, edged with bright green. Hawkes was crimson, although there were other colors lurking in him that seemed to change their hue at intervals. Then he looked at his mother.

He found her—sulky saffron, shot with dull blood-red;

and around her, what might be an aura of the color of floating petroleum seen in slanting light; there was a sort of background, too, of gray-blue steel—a cruel color that made Joe shudder, and made him also feel ashamed of himself because of his reaction to her cruelty. His predominant sensation was one of shame. It seemed to him that, with the exception of the men from Poonch, who were khaki-tinted and almost invisible, he was the only person in the room not burning like an incandescent flame with zeal of one kind or another. He could not see himself. He could not even see his own hands.

The silence was broken awesomely by Poonch-Terai. In a strange, excited, hoarse half-whisper he sneered at the Yogi—in English, again, no doubt, for Bruce's benefit:

"You don't dare! If you do, you take the consequences!"

Suddenly Joe saw him. He was jet-black. It was a mystery how jet-black could be visible in that intense darkness. Even after several seconds, when burnt-orange and vermilion appeared around the region of his eyes, he still seemed jet-black and distinctly outlined. But the outline grew, perhaps in Joe's imagination. Things like spider's legs were added to him—or they might be the arms of an octopus. They were the sort of horrors that a man in delirium tremens sees. Joe glanced at Rita, wondering whether she, too, saw what he did. But he could not guess. She sat stock-still. And it appeared to Joe as if the Yogi's aura, or whatever it was, had extended until it included Rita within its incandescent rays. At the same time he felt, although he could not have described the feeling, a compelling inhibition against speech—against sound of any sort, or even movement. He hardly breathed.

Then light, that somehow was not light, stole slowly on the senses and the room was not there. It was like a dream in which forces seemed at war with one another. There was chaos. Poonch-Terai appeared on horseback, but a dark cloud swallowed him almost instantly. He appeared again; and again the dark cloud. Then Mrs. Beddington emerged in mid-room out of nothing. Suddenly she screamed, so that Joe knew she had seen herself. Her scream took effect. The vision vanished. The room was again in pitch-darkness—nothing visible, not even the Yogi's aura.

Poonch-Terai spoke hoarsely: "You—Bruce—you're the only other sane man in this room." It sounded strained; he was either in deadly fear or else so angry that he could hardly control himself. "Bruce, I warn you. This is dangerous. You've probably heard how men go mad when they get a glimpse of things they shouldn't see. I vote we stop this—you and I. Let's light that lamp. Have you a match? He can only do his tricks in darkness."

"Why, yes," said Bruce. "I've matches. How do other people feel about it?"

"Feel afraid?" Joe asked him.

"Scared, yes. But I don't feel called upon to interfere."

"Hawkes has matches!" said Mrs. Beddington sharply; her voice was like a cracker going off.

"What's mine is mine," Hawkes answered. "Try to get 'em!"

"Light that lamp or I'll make trouble!" she retorted. She was on the edge of hysteria. Joe heard her tugging at something. "I've a pistol. I warn you all. I'll use it unless there's light before I count ten!"

Bruce struck one match—Hawkes another. Bruce crossed over to her. "Give that pistol to me," he commanded. He took it from her, turned his back and returned to his seat. "Now—are there any other firearms?" he demanded. He struck another match; its flare showed Poonch-Terai in mid-room making swiftly toward the courtyard door. "Sit down, Hawkes!" He struck a third match. Poonch-Terai drew the bolt and threw the door wide open. The match blew out instantly. Poonch-Terai suddenly screamed and bit the scream off as if strangled. Wind slammed the door shut and again there was utter darkness. Someone slid the bolt, and Poonch-Terai swore in his own tongue, using gutturals that sounded like boiling volcanic mud. Then, in English:

"Damn—I might have foreseen that!"

Bruce crushed an empty match-box in his fist. "Where are yours, Hawkes? Hand them over."

Hawkes struck one and Bruce took the box from him.

"Quick now—take the chimney off that lamp while I light it."

But Poonch-Terai interrupted: "No, no. Give him darkness. Let him work his magic. I will give him twenty minutes. After that—"

"If you don't light that lamp, I will!" said Mrs. Beddington.

"You sit still!" Poonch-Terai retorted; and he seemed to say it through his set teeth. "Go mad—go to the devil—only sit still! Bruce—"

"Yes?"

"If you light that lamp, I'll smash it. Sit down. You have twenty minutes. I will sit here."

"What's the matter with you?" Bruce asked.

"Nothing. Not a dam' thing."

"Then why did you scream?"

"I didn't."

"Who did?"

"Oh, well, if I did, do you have to keep on reminding me? Nerves—that's all. Caught my finger when the door slammed. Didn't hurt much. I was frightened. There—are you satisfied?"

Joe, for one, doubted him. He had a feeling that Bruce and Hawkes did, too, but no one spoke. However, he distinctly heard Bruce cock two automatics. The feeling of tension was terrific. Mrs. Beddington gulped as she started to scream and checked herself:

"Joe!" she blurted, "this is nothing but a plot to hocus-pocus *me!* I'll not forgive it—do you hear me?"

Before Joe could answer her, the Yogi's voice boomed through the dark:

"There is a time for all things. Speak about forgiveness when the tale is finished. You, who judged another—be judged in the Black Light."

"I will have you punished." She was almost over the edge of one of her hysterical fits, deliberately brought on as a last resource, or last but one, when she felt her will frustrated. Joe knew the symptoms—recognized the catch in her voice—felt half ashamed, from habit, of his own indifference—and wondered what the Yogi would do to quell her tantrum. She gulped twice. "Wait until Mr. Cummings learns you have kept me a prisoner here in the dark!"

Joe saw her then. He saw the color of a coming tantrum, just as clearly as he heard the rumble of dying thunder and the wind-borne swish of rain. She was all smoky crimson, shot with a disgusting greenish violet that he knew was self-pity, although he did not know how he knew it. But the smoky red glowed into passionate crimson when Poonch-Terai's voice answered her:

"I gave you twenty minutes. Why waste time with that fool?"

"Your Highness—!"

"Shut up!" he retorted. Then, either to the Yogi or to everyone: "Go ahead. Can't you feel I'm making no resistance? I could easily ruffle the mirror. But I want to see her shown up."

"You! You traitor!" she exploded. "Shall I tell them—" But she suddenly lapsed into silence.

"Judgment! I have demanded judgment!" said the Yogi. "If it fall on my head, let it."

Not a sound then, except heavy breathing from Poonch-Terai's direction. Presently something moved in mid-room—vague—noiseless—fishy—grey-green—gradually taking shape. Then suddenly, as if it gathered atoms to itself and by force of will, it grew darker. It seemed to grow solid. It swayed. It was a cobra, ten times bigger than the biggest ever seen—erect—its hood raised—in a sort of pool of smoky dim-green light that cast no shadow. It struck, with the speed of lightning, toward where Rita and the Yogi sat. It struck at Joe, but seemed unable to get near him. It struck three times toward where Annie Weems sat, and Joe heard her saying the Lord's Prayer, so he knew she saw it. Then, its forked tongue flicking in and out, it gradually faded as if withdrawn into infinity from whence it came.

"Like unto like!" said the Yogi. "None can summon that who loves not malice. If he can tame malice, he can tame that. If not, though it strike at others, shall it spare him?"

Poonch-Terai groaned aloud. "Make haste!" he urged. He sounded like a man in agony. It was hard to believe he was not. But he had said he was all right.

"What's the matter with you?" Joe asked.

Silence. Then strange sounds, stealthy, as of someone creeping on his hands and knees. A sudden blow—and two oaths, one in English. Bruce struck a match.

Hawkes was on his knees between Rita and the maharajah, who had been knocked down and was crawling away; he reached the darkness by the courtyard door before the match burned Bruce's fingers and Bruce dropped it.

Rita: "Did you hurt him, Hawkesey?"

"No, Miss. Couldn't see him, or I'd ha' hit him proper. You black blackguard! Something told me you were sneaking up on her."

Bruce struck two matches, but the head fell off one and the other spluttered and went out.

"Light that lamp!" commanded Mrs. Beddington. "Dammit—I say, dammit, light that lamp, you—"

"Hold your horses! Very well," said Bruce. "Be patient while I find the thing." His fingers fumbled with the match-box and a match broke, making hardly a spark.

"Sir, beg pardon, sir," said Hawkes, "but may I offer a suggestion?"

"Go ahead. What is it?"

"See this to a finish. See it through in the dark, sir. I mayn't tell no secrets, but I've seen this kind o' thing before. With your permission, sir, I'll stay here. If the nineteen-gun black magician moves I'll butt him in the nose."

Bruce did not trouble to answer him. His fingers fumbled with the match-box and a match broke.

"Damn!" he muttered. "That's the last one."

Rita's voice: "I don't believe the lamp would burn if you should try to light it."

Joe's mother: "I'm going to scream!"

Joe: "No she isn't. She never screams when she says she's going to. See this through, Bruce. I'll go bond that these are decent people. I've had opportunity to get to know them. And I know my mother. She has made a lot of rotten accusations—damned lies—"

"Joe! How dare you!"

"—and as I understand it, the Yogi—"

"Captain Bruce, I'm fainting!"

"No, she isn't. She never faints when she says she's going to. As I understand it, the Yogi proposes to show us the truth in some strange way. I vote we let him."

Annie Weems sighed: "It is no use trying to prevent him! Captain Bruce, I dread this—I believe it's wicked. But they don't think it's wicked. And I know that Rita wouldn't lend herself to harming an insect."

"And there's nobody shan't harm *her*—not unless he gets me previous," said Hawkes.

"Ram-Chittra Gunga is a gentleman," said Annie

Weems, "who knows more than is right that any human being should. He knows terrible things."

"Bah! Why talk?" Poonch-Terai's voice held a note of horror. "Let him show what he knows!"

"Let him?" Annie Weems sounded patiently resigned. "Can you or anyone prevent him? Captain Bruce, I intend to close my eyes, and I advise you to close yours."

"Thanks, no, I'll stay awake," Bruce answered. "All right, carry on. Hawkes, you stay where you are; and if anyone moves, speak. I warn whomever it concerns that I am holding two cocked automatics, one in each hand."

"But I don't think they would go off," Rita answered. "If they make you feel less frightened it will do no harm to hold them."

Bruce was silent, but Joe heard him moving the slide of an automatic as if he felt there were something wrong with it.

Then Mrs. Beddington did scream—hoarsely—horribly—three times. Poonch-Terai laughed, like a man on a rack whose agony is eased by the sound of someone else's.

"What's wrong, Mater?" Joe asked. It was temper. He knew it. He had heard her scream like that a hundred times. But he could not shed fear of her temper. It turned him cold, inside.

"Joe, don't you dare believe this! It's a lie! It's trickery! It's—"

Silence. She had seen something before Joe did. So had Bruce; he was breathing in snorts through his nose. Joe stared into utter darkness. An eternity—perhaps the space of ten breaths—passed before he saw anything.

FROM THE BOOK OF THE YOGI-ASTROLOGER RAM-CHITTRA GUNGA SINGH

My son, it would be wonderful if many very learned men did NOT make mock of spiritual things, maintaining that if such indeed were actual, themselves could verify them. Like unto like, is the Law; and what does it say in your Book of Revelation? He that is unjust, let him be unjust still. I ask you: Can a horse learn languages? Or can a tone-deaf man draw music from a violin? Or can a tree run?

It is so with many very learned men; they are incapable of understanding that which the much less learned sometimes understand with great ease. Big-bellied are they with a surfeit of facts, and leaden-footed with the pride of scholarship; they seek to drag the mountain summits down toward them. But I tell you, he who climbs unburdened to a mountain summit needs no guidance from a pundit ploughing—plough he learnedly or not—in the sands and the mud on the plane of facts, each one of which is as imaginary as the motion of the sun around the earth. Though he be thrice as learned as the three most learned scientists who ever lived if he shall plough for spirit on the plane of matter, what shall he find—save molecules? And though he learn to split the molecules asunder and to label all the fragments one by one, shall that upraise him to the realm of spirit?

They were very learned men who persecuted Jesus. They knew all the laws and all the prophecies. They sought with weighted feet and bellies full of pride to climb by matter—ladders into spiritual understanding. And there is a venom known as jealousy, my son. He who would know the ruthlessness of jealousy in all its plausible disguises—aye, and in its hypocritical rôle of guardian of the unenlightened—let him tempt the very learned, and the fools who feed out of that trough they fill, with one small proof of spiritual knowledge. Better to speak concerning books to horses; they can only kick.

Better to speak of music to a man tone-deaf, for he will only blaspheme. Speak of motion to a tree, and it can only send forth hornets from the nest it hides. But prove one scrap of spiritual knowledge to the men who plough the sands of matter and their sycophants who pounce like crows upon the worms they lay bare—they will crucify you, and then bid you prove it to them lovingkindly from the cross; and should you do that, they will turn their backs and neither see nor listen.

XXVII

> *"Shall not justice justify itself without your mouthings?"*

Joe could hear his own heart beat and when he dug his nails into his skin it hurt him. But when he rubbed his eyes he discovered that he could see equally well with them shut or open. He had a sense of time, space, form and color; and yet, what he saw, took place so rapidly that a year passed while he was drawing two breaths. He saw himself—his own upbringing—every event in his own life until he came to India. And he knew he blushed that everyone else in the room should see him so victimized and so incapable of breaking his mother's tyranny; until it occurred to him—although he did not know how—that every individual in the room was seeing his or her own life in intimate review. Even so, he was not pleased with his own record, although he noticed an extraordinary patience, of which his mother took tireless advantage; and the strength of character beneath the patience seemed to Joe, who watched it, to develop and grow stronger the more his mother ground him down and heaped one imposition on another, until at last he was astonished at the vision of his own strength.

He was wondering how one measured strength, and how it was he recognized it, and how one told strength from weakness, when the nature of the vision changed. It ceased to concern only himself. Hitherto, it might have been his own subconscious memory reflected after the manner of dreams—whatever that is—who knows what a dream is, or how it functions? But now, events that he could not possibly remember began to stage themselves in mid-room, as if the memories of all those present were being projected in three dimensions on some sort of mirror to which time and space were interchangeable, or else the same thing, or perhaps did not exist.

It was the hotel verandah. Mrs. Beddington sat in a wicker chair at a tea-table and conversed with Poonch-Terai, who laughed at something which perplexed her very much indeed. There was no sound—none whatever; and yet it was perfectly clear, not only what each was saying, but what each was thinking and how each was seeking to manipulate the other. Amal came, scared almost out of her senses because she knew that Poonch-Terai knew it was she who had stabbed Joe Beddington. She told all she knew about Rita's birth; as swiftly as in a dream her thought took form and all the details of her flight from dacoits with the new-born child recurred before Joe's vision, until she reached the temple and Ram-Chittra Gunga took the infant in his arms.

Mrs. Beddington was disturbed. She offered Amal money—quantities of money—more than an ayah could ever have dreamed of. Amal was not even tempted, and Poonch-Terai laughed. He hinted that he was the only person who could deal with Amal in such way as to suppress her evidence. And it was absolutely clear, not only that he had murder in his mind but that Mrs. Beddington suspected it and was indifferent provided she should get what she wanted and not be involved.

But Poonch-Terai, too, wanted something—several things; among them Rita, and the temple revenues; but he seemed to know how to get those. What he wanted from Mrs. Beddington was protection. Vague at first, but presently more distinct, the form of Albert Cummings seemed to hover in the neighborhood of both their minds. Darkly at first, and then in plain speech, because she was too cunning to commit herself until he came out from behind his mask of hint and innuendo, he demanded that she should use her influence with Cummings to prevent any hue and cry or official inquiry if he should kidnap Rita, and also to prevent any search for Amal. Hovering in Poonch-Terai's thought were the shapes of Indian policemen, who would take their cue from Cummings, whether he might legally or not restrain them from sleuthing on Poonch-Terai's trail.

Mrs. Beddington promised. She was already entirely sure of her control of Albert Cummings. He appeared in her thought in a glamour of high romance as someone vastly more important than he ever could be and possessing more authority than he could ever dream of having—but obedient to her, beholden to her, subject to her, blinded by her money and as easy to manipulate as any chairman of the board of one of her trust-bound corporations. Poonch-Terai assured her that Amal should not cause her another moment's worry, and that he would very effectively deal with Rita. Murder and rape were in his mind—murder and rape in hers; but she had not said so, and besides, there were no witnesses. Poonch-Terai rode away on horseback, and she ordered champagne when his back was turned; she drank two glasses of it dashed with cognac.

Poonch-Terai overtook Amal trudging along a dusty lane. He drew rein and chaffed her cunningly because her knife had failed, she sullenly refusing to admit that it was her knife that had stabbed Joe. However, he told her no one else suspected her and that she need have no anxiety on his account, he would keep the secret. Then he told her to return to the temple, and watch Rita, and spy on Joe, who was convalescent and undoubtedly involved in some conspiracy to take Rita away to foreign lands.

Rita appeared in Amal's thought as a glittering goddess, certainly not human, and at the same time as a helpless child to be protected and fought for with dogged ferocity. Foreign lands were a thirsty wilderness beyond a raging sea in which monsters swam—horribly hot deserts in which Joe owned packs of tigers and every hole in the earth held a venomous snake. Joe loomed in her imagination as a king who dragged weak women by the hair and beat them horribly unless they prayed in a frame-church, painted chocolate, that had a sheet-iron roof. So Amal turned her face toward the temple, and as she thought of Rita she exuded rays of deep-red rose. But as she thought of Joe, rose changed to hell-red.

Poonch-Terai found Chandri Lal, the man of cobras in a flat reed basket. It was not quite clear how Chandri Lal was brought into his presence; however, Poonch-Terai was seated in a garden between a fountain and a clump of bougainvillea, and Chandri Lal sat at his feet with his basket of snakes on the ground beside him. Wordlessly and indescribably, but nonetheless clearly, it was evident that Poonch-Terai was puzzled how to deal with Chandri Lal, whose mood was mildly mercenary, due to tramping on an empty stomach.

Chandri Lal himself at last supplied the missing clue. He began to beg for money, saying he had been in hiding and had earned nothing, so that even his snakes were starving. Promptly Poonch-Terai demanded to know why he had been hiding. Chandri Lal became evasive, Amal looming in his thoughts. Poonch-Terai accused him of having stabbed Joe Beddington. Chandri Lal denied it. Poonch-Terai informed him that his guilt was well known: Amal had betrayed him—had accused him of the crime and had been rewarded by Mrs. Beddington for the information.

Chandri Lal grew livid with indignation. Through his thought, in a stream of pictures, flashed the crime as he had witnessed it—he, faithful as a dog to Amal, half enamored of her, half believing her a seeress. Joe, staring into darkness, saw himself stabbed and fall at Rita's feet—saw it through the memory of Chandri Lal, projected in the man's own absence—saw—felt—almost tasted the fear that dried up Chandri Lal's throat. He, Joe, saw the very splurge of agony that rushed through his own brain like liquid fire when the knife struck deep beneath his shoulder-blade. More marvelous—he saw the thought that shot through Rita's mind as she knelt to try to stanch the bleeding. He saw that she knew Amal did it; and through Rita's thought he saw the smiling face of Poonch-Terai. He knew then certainly, what Rita knew but Amal did not, that the maharajah's was the mind behind that knife; his was the will, the impulse, the obsessing malice. Amal had reacted to the trained dynamic will of Poonch-Terai more simply and with less resistance than Joe himself had sometimes acted on the impulse of his mother's unvoiced urging.

Now he watched the maharajah set another impulse surging in a consciousness unable to protect itself, though this time he was using words as well as metaphysical suggestion. He told Chandri Lal that his only safety lay in killing Amal, who had gone now to the temple to accuse him to the priests, who would be saved from a great deal of embarrassment at the hands of the police if they could only indicate a likely suspect. He must hurry and kill Amal, whom the temple servants would probably admit without much argument; and once inside the temple she would take her story to the high priest. Why not scale the wall at the place where the baobab formed a bridge that any active man could use? And if a cobra should bite Amal, what then? Could they prove whose cobra did it?

Chandri Lal, unfed and unrewarded because hungry men are more light-headed and amenable to impulse than are men with money and a square meal, went his way. And Poonch-Terai sat thinking, smiling, flattering his thought with pictures of the priests' embarrassment when Amal should be found dead within their sacred walls. They would understand perfectly what had happened and whose the guiding mind was. But could they prove it? On the contrary, it would only make them nervous. Then a tip to the police—a temple scandal—what chance would the priests have of rescuing Rita, with themselves on the defensive and the fatuous Cummings reined in by the plutocratic hand of Joe's determined mother?

His thought was as plain as a motion-picture. He amused himself for several minutes with the prospect of the entertainment he would wring, in the not so distant future, out of Cummings and his fabulously wealthy bride. He would make their wedding wretched. He would hint at blackmail. He would torture them so that Cummings would not dare resign for fear lest his successor might stumble on clues that would lead to indictment. He had many a bone to pick with Cummings—pompously insufferable little Cockney; he would pick them all. And Mrs. Beddington had dared to try to patronize him—him, a nineteen-gun maharajah. She had dared to pose as a pious moralist, who scorned polygamy; as a superior Nordic intellectual whose high ideals no mere Indian could understand. She had insulted him to the marrow with every smirking attempt at flattery, each snobbish gesture of familiarity and each unconscious breach of etiquette. He would make her pay. So help him all the gods he disbelieved in and the forces that he knew were potent, he would make her pay in nervousness until she yelled to him for mercy. And the thought of his mercy amused him still more.

He began to think of Rita. It was then that Joe's jaws set and he knew, to the last hair-trigger tremor of emotion, how it feels to hunger to do bloody murder with your bare hands. He had heard of Sadists; he had even read about them, in a book suppressed by magistrates but pirated through boot-leg channels; he had sometimes thought his mother was one, in a civilized, reserved and hypocritically prudent fashion. But when the plans that Poonch-Terai let float before his mind concerning Rita met Joe's gaze, he knew himself as ignorant of evil as a baa-lamb is of butchers. He had been in brothels. He had witnessed vivisection. He had seen bull-fights. He had even seen a baby born. Joe was not particularly squeamish. He could see such sights and almost straightway forget them. But when he witnessed the pictured thoughts of Poonch-Terai, their object Rita or any other woman, he could not keep silence.

"Mater," he said grimly, "do you see now what your scheming might have led to?"

Sound seemed to shatter the mirror. The vision vanished. Joe's mother gurgled and tried to speak, but her throat seemed dry and Joe imagined her with dropped jaw staring into darkness.

Bruce broke silence: "Beddington, for God's sake don't discuss it. We have seen into hell, if the rest of you saw what I did."

Hawkes then: "Captain Bruce, sir—if you'll pass me one o' them there automatics, I'll do my duty. 'Tain't an officer's job to muck up. Let me kill him. I'll say nothing at court martial. I'll die proud to have sent him where he came from."

But the Yogi's voice boomed forth from darkness before Bruce could answer:

"Silence—lest ye darken judgment! Shall not justice justify itself without your mouthings?"

An eternity—perhaps a dozen breaths—prolonged itself until the light that cast no shadow stole again upon the darkness. There sat Poonch-Terai again, but he was now on horseback. He was speaking to the same two men from Poonch who crouched now, trembling, in a corner of the room. One of them gasped as he saw himself holding the horses harnessed to a carriage that had ventilating slats in place of windows. The gasp disturbed the picture for a moment, in the way a light breeze breaks up the reflections in a forest pool. But that was momentary. Six men joined the others and all listened to what Poonch-Terai was saying.

The carriage vanished in a cloud of dust, with two men on the box and six inside it. Poonch-Terai then rode a long way to the hotel, where he talked with Mrs. Beddington again on the verandah. They discussed Joe; he could see himself like a helpless smoke-shape being tossed from mind to mind. They two reached an understanding, and the thought expressed by Mrs. Beddington was that she would presently have Joe in her control again, where she could bully and persuade him until Rita should become a mere past episode. But the thought in Poonch-Terai's mind was that he would have Joe in his summer palace as a guest beneath the same roof as he raped, humiliated and imprisoned Rita. He anticipated exquisite amusement from the conversation he would hold with Joe and all the vain hope he would stir in him by offering to help him find his ladylove. And even while he talked with Mrs. Beddington his mind was busy searching for a means to let Joe learn the truth at last, but without incriminating Poonch-Terai himself. That was a problem that intrigued his malice exquisitely.

It was after dark when one of the maharajah's open landaus arrived for Mrs. Beddington and waited for her underneath the hotel compound trees. He rode away alone, and presently Joe saw him guide his horse into a gap in a broken wall, where he could wait in total darkness and observe the lamp-lighted jail gate not far distant.

Hawkes sighed noisily, and once again the vision was obliterated by intruding sound. When the picture emerged once more from the darkness Hawkes was waiting near the jail gate with his pipe, not drawing, having to be cleaned with "pop-wire" picked up in the gutter and first thoroughly cleaned of microbes with a burning match.

"Oh, Gawd?" said Hawkes' voice. "Strike me cockeyed! Me a soldier, acting escort!"

And again the vision vanished as the sound-waves stirred its surface. When it reappeared, the small door in the jail gate was in the act of closing behind Rita. There was no one in the sentry box; apparently the man on guard had left his post and was closing the door from the inside. Rita, glancing nervously to right and left, pretended that Hawkes frightened her—perhaps to hide a premonition that she genuinely felt. They walked together, side by side, ten paces.

Then, as sudden as a gun-team, came the two-horsed carriage—horses reined in to a staggering halt that almost threw them—Rita turning to see what it was—Hawkes roughly thrusting her between him and the wall. Six bearded men, like specters, pouring from the carriage—a grim scuffle—one man down, another staggering backward on his heels—then Hawkes knocked senseless. Rita, wrapped in coils of white cloth, seized and thrown into the carriage—the hurt man thrown in after her, five others following. Then the whip, and away as fast as blooded horses could lay hoof to earth—away toward the outskirts of the city—away from the direction of the temple. Dust—wheels vanishing around a corner—darkness.

And then Hawkes' voice, sulky and ashamed: "So now you know I ain't no fighting man. A nurse-girl 'ud ha' done a dam' sight better. Gawd's teeth! I've seen a rabbit show more fight than that. And mind you, I've three medals. I'm paid money for the guts inside my lingerie."

Silence and long darkness, but at last again the weird light. Hawkes lay on his face beside the jail wall. Poonch-Terai, guiding his horse through the gap and pausing to gaze to right and left, rode to where Hawkes lay and stooped from the saddle to see if he moved. He tried to make the horse trample him, but the horse edged away in spite of rein and spur. So Poonch-Terai produced an automatic, cocked it and tried to take aim; but the horse shied frantically and became unmanageable, so Poonch-Terai galloped away, almost dropping the automatic as he tried to reduce the horse to obedience by hitting it hard with the butt-end.

"Blackguard!" Bruce could not keep silence when he saw a horse ill-treated. He would have made other remarks but he saw that his voice had killed the picture. "Damn, I'm sorry. Go on—I won't offend again."

But when the vision reappeared the scene had changed. It was a shadowy courtyard somewhere in the temple area, and Amal crouched beside a fountain chafing tired feet that were not yet dry from washing. Chandri Lal, his basket in his hands, crept stealthily toward her through the shadows at the fountain's edge, the very slight noise that he must have made, obliterated by the splashing water.

Suddenly Amal leaped up, clapping a hand to her left thigh. Apparently she did not scream, but she turned on Chandri Lal and seized him by the throat. She saw his cobra then and snatched it from him, seizing it by the neck below the hood and smashing it to death against the fountain marble. Then, ignoring her agony, she pounced again on Chandri Lal and held him by both shoulders, forcing him to turn toward the light from a chamber window, so that she could see his eyes while she demanded why he did it. There was something more than sentiment between those two, so that even in horror and wrath they understood each other. He accused indignantly. She answered calmly, although she writhed in pain. He stared, incredulous—mocked—cursed her—stared into her eyes. His lips moved. Then he suddenly believed.

He was like a madman then, obsessed by horror. Guilt—remorse—grief froze him until he could think of nothing but to turn destruction on himself. She clutched his basket to prevent him from thrusting his hand amid the cobras, forcing him more by strength of will than of muscles to lay the basket down and listen to her. Then, half crazed, he tried to suck the poison from her wound, she striking him—shaking her head and beating him on neck and shoulders with her clenched fists until at last he obeyed her—sat still—held her head against his breast, and heard her to a finish. There were only two remaining thoughts in Amal's mind—to die at Rita's feet, wherever Rita might be, and to be avenged.

Mrs. Beddington made guttural, protesting noises before she could force speech through a dry throat, banishing the picture: "It was—it was not my doing. I—I swear I had no idea he would have her killed. Joe, I was protecting you. I—"

"Silence, please. I say, let's see this," Bruce insisted.

But the picture changed. It was the shuttered carriage swaying through dusty darkness beneath gathering clouds that blotted out the moon. Two coachmen on the box, one managing the reins, the other acting look-out, stared into deepening gloom. The horses slowed—shied—and the driver flogged them. They reared on their haunches. The other man, his wide eyes white with terror, clutched the driver's arm and pointed. Both men at the same time saw a phantom. Both men recognized it. Several times larger than the living man—long-bearded—naked to the loins and smiling like a statue of an ancient god—Ram-Chittra Gunga, leaning on his long staff, barred the road in front of them. He pointed with his staff toward their right hand. Suddenly the frantic horses lunged and bolted to the right along a pitch-dark road between high walls. And at the end of that, again Ram-Chittra Gunga stood and pointed to the right.

Dumb panic gripped both coachmen and the reins fell slack in terror-loosened hands. The carriage swerved, swayed—and the horses bolted headlong down a road made darker than the Pit by ancient trees—a road that curved like a crescent moon beyond the ancient, ruined city wall and came to an echoing end beneath a huge arch at the temple's almost unused northern gate. It was a gate that creaked on ancient hinges. There was one dim lantern, showing that the gate yawned open hardly a carriage length before the horses reached it. The carriage lurched in, swallowed amid shadows and the gate swung shut behind it.

"Seems to me, you might have used a bit of that stuff to have warned *me*," Hawkes objected, " 'stead of letting me get knocked out. What had I done, to be left to look out for myself?"

But the Yogi made no answer. Bruce commanded silence. There was a long pause before another picture sketched itself in color on impenetrable darkness. Poonch-Terai, on horseback, waited near the lantern at the temple gate where Joe had fallen under Amal's knife. He was pleased with himself. He sat his restless horse with handsome self-assurance, spurring forward presently with a gay laugh at the sound of hoofs and wheels. His open landau, bearing Mrs. Beddington, evolved out of the darkness and the coachman drew rein where the lantern shone directly on Joe's mother's face. She, too, looked confident. They talked, it seemed, in undertones too low for the man on the box to overhear them. But their thoughts took shape. Ram-Chittra Gunga's mirror reproduced them.

Visioned by Poonch-Terai was Rita, gagged and helpless, being carried through a door in the wall of his summer palace and along a pathway leading to a private building amid dense trees. Visioned by Mrs. Beddington was Rita—shamed—crushed, hopeless—stricken dumb by perjured evidence of her half-breed parentage and by proof from the lips of a dozen well paid witnesses to her immorality with Hawkes and with Indian troopers. It was plain enough that Poonch-Terai had promised something of the sort.

Then, smiling confidently, glancing at the sky where lightning was already edging the rolling thunderclouds with blue-white flashes, Poonch-Terai dismounted and, tossing his reins to a carriage footman, strode toward the door where Joe had once lain wounded. There was no bell, so he struck on the door with the butt of his automatic. Instantly the vision disappeared as the thunder of genuine blows on ancient teak reverberated down the passage. Voices and a wail of wind inrushing through an opened door. Then footsteps. Then a pounding on the door near Joe's bed. "Open! Open!"

"Yes, yes. There is a proper time for all things. Open," said the Yogi.

Rita took the big key from his lap and found her way across the room in darkness. She admitted a glare of yellow lantern-light that dazzled strained eyes, splitting shadows into fragments. Albert Cummings crossed the threshold, drenched, well frightened by the storm. He stared at Rita—turned and took a flashlight from a dripping servant who stood in the passage behind him. Then the door closed softly—probably a temple servant did that. He switched on the flashlight, searching for Mrs. Beddington—discovered her half fainting—

"Well, well! Frightened? Safe, at any rate. Thank God you weren't caught in the storm—I see you're dry. The maharajah's carriage passed me with the horses going full-pelt—bolted—stampede—terrified by lightning, and small wonder. Inches of rain—never saw such a storm—must be a record—don't know how I found my way—the maharajah's carriage almost ran me down. I started out with four men following my horse, but three of them ran home. Oh, hello, Joe, how are you?"

"How brave of you to come!" said Mrs. Beddington. "And how I prayed you would come!"

Flattery went to his head like laughing-gas. He struck an attitude intended to suggest the heart-of-oak stock that he came from. "Frightened, eh? No wonder! Such a storm was as bad as a battlefield. And unexpected—no one ready for it—not the rainy season—done a world of damage, I'm afraid. But why do you all sit in darkness? No oil? Are you unwise virgins? Hah-hah! Can't resist my little joke, it's so good to have found you safe. Oh, hello, Bruce."

Bruce grunted.

He ignored Hawkes. He almost ostentatiously avoided Rita. He used his flashlight until it framed the Yogi in a luminous disk and the old man looked exactly like a statue, seated, backed against the wall.

"Oh, hello—salaam, Ram-Chittra Gunga—I must thank you, I suppose, for sheltering these people."

Joe could not tell whether the old man bowed acknowledgment or not. He made no sound; and if he lowered his head it was immeasurably. So the flashlight moved again until its rays chanced on the tip of the turban of Poonch-Terai. It wavered—framed the Maharajah, seated, leaning with his back against the teak door, his head drooped forward on his chest.

"Why—hello, Maharajah sahib! Glad to see you. Too bad about your carriage—you'll be lucky, though, if those horses stop before they break their necks."

No answer.

"Is he asleep?"

The flashlight seemed something dim. He switched it off, and switched it on again. "Are you all right, Poonch-Terai?"

No answer.

He approached him, peering, holding the flashlight well in front of him. "Good God! The man's dead! How did it happen? Come here, someone! Bruce—quick—here's a cobra! Come and kill it!"

FROM THE BOOK OF THE YOGI-ASTROLOGER RAM-CHITTRA GUNGA SINGH

The Law, my son, is: Nothing out of nothing; and to that there is no exception, since it is not Law, but false hypothesis, to which there possibly can be exceptions. There is not, and there never was or will be, one effect that had no cause, no matter how remote that cause may now seem. Bitter causes yield not sweet effects; sweet causes do not bring forth bitterness; and though your priests may blaspheme and your scientists may multiply conundrums, they shall neither of them prove the contrary until the end of time. That scientists deny Divine Idea, and that priests bribe angels with monotonous praise and mulcted sacrifice, is only proof that scientists are childish and that priests are venial; they are no worse than yourself, who seek escape from the Wheel by borrowed light. Whom certain scientists deny, but less immodest men call God, may not be taken between tweezers for dissection; neither can His Law be broken; nor is it merciless, unjust or unwise.

But you ask me: Whence then these injustices that anyone may see who looks? You ask not wisely, having looked too well into the mirror wherein pride confuses and desire deceives; however, who am I that I should not repeat that answer which your own great Avatar saw fit to give two thousand years ago, before they nailed his body to a tree to prove how truly they sought Wisdom? I will speak, though you shall nail me also.

Said he not: It needs must be that evil come, but woe unto him through whom it cometh? Said he not also: Thou shalt by no means come out thence—and he spoke of the prison of this world—until thou hast paid the uttermost farthing? Paid unto whom?   Thy creditor. And who then is that creditor but thou, thyself? And whence comes evil, if it creeps not from the secret places of thine own heart?

For I tell you: there is no Law that a man shall not be law unto himself until he weary of it; is there not eternity wherein to suffer anguish, if a man will? Is the Law not: As ye sow, so shall ye reap? It says not: As ye sow, so shall these others reap; although a fool can see that thousands suffer through the malice or stupidity of one, and one may be a source of comfort and enlightenment, aye, and of grace itself, to many. But how shall a man be what he is not, or give what he has not, or get what is not his due?

You know that if you drop one grain of sand into the sea the farthest star shall ultimately feel it, until at last the vibration returns to its source. But you say: I will escape the consequence of this or that wrong thought or cruel deed, by hiding, or by legislation, or with the aid of magic. Idiot! I tell you: though you have to live ten millions of lives on earth, you shall be reborn, and again reborn until your reckoning is clean; and all that you shall ever have, wherewith to repay, is the virtue you shall make your own by dint of good deeds done, not talked about; nor shall you by any means escape before you pay the last debt—to yourself, your creditor.

For I tell you: the wrong that you do to another, you do to yourself; and the good that they do to you, they do to themselves. It needs must be that evil come to you, because in former lives you caused it. Woe unto him through whom it cometh, but who is he? He is yourself, none other. So, when evil comes to you; and this fool tells you it was luck; or that priest talks to you of heaven and hell; or fifty learned hypocrites assure you there is neither cause nor remedy; then seek you Wisdom, and forgive them; they are only seeking, as you yourself have sought ten thousand times, to escape from Law by argument; their time, it may be, is not yet.

Your time is NOW. Pay you your debt with good will; and though you pay in shame and agony, and see no outcome, you shall sow good seed; you shall create new destiny. It shall be said of you: It needs must be that good shall come; all hail to him through whom it cometh.

XXVIII

"No place for a woman of refinement."

Hawkes looked around for a weapon. There was nothing handy. "Here, give me that flashlight." He snatched it away from Cummings without ceremony and stepped nearer, turning it full on the cobra. Bruce stepped beside him, cocking an automatic that appeared to have repaired itself.

"Mind your eye, Hawkes—hold that steady while I blow his head off."

" 'T's all right, sir—good as dead—its back's broke. I'll bet it was caught in the door when it bit his Highness. But can you beat that—him not letting on? I'll say this for the swine: he had a crust on. I've heard it hurts like hell to be bit by one o' them things. Now, Miss Rita, don't you go too near it. Stand back—please, Miss. Wait until I open that door."

"So, that's why he screamed," said Bruce. "I'll help you." Together they lifted Poonch-Terai and laid him on the floor beside Amal, covering him with the same sheet; there was plenty of it; they did not have to expose Amal to anyone's gaze. Then Hawkes opened the door and kicked the writhing cobra outside into the rain. "Kabadar, you! Watch out!" He played the flashlight on the cobra. "Nag—marao jaldee!" Someone in the darkness outside struck a dozen blows swiftly with something heavy. "Pitch it in the fountain." It appeared he was obeyed by someone, whom he watched with the aid of a flash-light. Then, though, other people tried to enter. "Stand back!" He reached for the door to slam it in intruding faces.

"No, no, let them in," said Rita; "it was they who brought me in the maharajah's carriage."

Cummings thought it high time to reassert himself. "No, shut that door and keep them waiting a few minutes. Now, will someone be good enough to tell me what has happened? Why was the room in darkness? Why all this air of mystery? Captain Bruce—"

"One minute, sir." Bruce picked up Cummings' lantern and returned mid-room, but as he walked past Mrs. Beddington he raised the lantern so that her face showed like a cameo against the wall behind her. She looked haggard. She knew it. She raised both hands to hide her face from Cummings. Then Bruce beckoned to the two tall coachmen from the land of Poonch. They strode toward him—nervous, goggle-eyed, reluctant.

"You, Hawkes, can you talk their dialect?"

"A bit, sir."

"Say this to them: they have seen what we saw, and we know it was they who brought this lady—Miss Amrita, I believe her name is—back here to the temple, instead of carrying her off. Do they admit that Poonch-Terai, who lies dead, ordered them to seize her at the jail gate and convey her to his summer palace?"

"They say yes, sir, they admit that."

"Will they put it in writing?"

"They say yes, sir."

"Let those others in."

Hawkes went to obey. Bruce turned to Cummings:

"If you have a fountain pen and notebook with you, why not take those two men's depositions? They're important. Take 'em on oath, you're a magistrate."

Five men, one with split lips, filed into the room and lined up sheepishly in front of Bruce. They looked in vain for the maharajah. He with the injured mouth attempted to conceal it with his hand; he eyed Rita sideways.

"Now, Hawkes, interpret once more. Do these men admit that they came in the maharajah's carriage, seized Miss Amrita, attacked you, and attempted to convey her to the maharajah's summer palace? If so, who told them to do it?"

Hawkes faced the five men, to interpret. He began. But he was interrupted by Joe's mother, who came hurrying forward and seized Cummings' arm.

"Albert!" she objected. "Albert, do you mean to say you'll make me listen to all this nastiness?"

"Why, no, no. But it's raining. Wait—my horse is out there—I'll send someone for a carriage."

"I can't wait in here. The room's too stuffy."

"Yes, it's no place for a woman of refinement. We can put you a chair at the end of the passage. Will you wait there while I—"

"Albert! Will you leave me alone—today of all days? Won't you wait there with me? Haven't you a court where you can try these men tomorrow?"

"Yes, yes; trust you to be practical!" He turned on Bruce and Hawkes. "This is very irregular. Surely you must know that, Bruce. Who is accused of what? We can't take evidence unless we know a crime has been committed. Even so, the right thing is to send for the police and to have the men charged in the regular way."

"I accuse 'em," said Hawkes, "of assault with intent to do grievous bodily harm—and abduction and assault—and—"

"Abduction of whom?" asked Cummings.

"Miss Amrita, sir."

Joe saw his mother whispering in Cummings' ear—saw Cummings' facial expression take on slyness and a certain smug complacency.

"You mean, they took her in the maharajah's carriage?" Cummings asked. Joe's mother nudged him. "Well, I regret to say I can't take that accusation very seriously without a world of proof. My information is that that young woman is habitually free with her person and not at all averse to taking midnight rides to much worse places than a maharajah's palace."

"You're a liar," Joe said simply. "You have no such information."

Cummings tried to carry that off cavalierly. "Joe, I'll overlook that for your mother's sake and because of your injury."

"Overlook nothing," Joe answered. "I called you a liar. Bruce heard me. So did Rita. So did Hawkes. So did Sri Ram-Chittra Gunga. So did Miss Weems. I repeat it. I intend to continue repeating it at every opportunity until—"

Joe's mother interrupted: "Joe, you're acting like a madman!" She pushed Cummings aside and strode toward Joe's bed as if she meant to strike him. Then she whispered hoarsely: "Fool! You'll only get yourself in bad. You've not a scrap of legal evidence."

His inward calm surprised him, and his outward smile exasperated her. "No? None?" he answered. "Well, you saw what I saw, and you know now what I know."

"Much good may it do you! Prove it!"

"Mater, I don't intend to show my hand until it suits me. Get that. Get it good. And then get this: they call it Black Light that produces what we saw a little while ago. If it can do that, it can do a whole lot more. Just think that over."

"Are you threatening me?"

Joe smiled. "I will protect my friends," he answered, "to the limit."

"At the expense of your mother? Joe—won't you see that all I've done was to protect you?" She had raised her voice. Excitement, or it might be fear, had caused her to forget that there were other people in the room. "I've tried to save you."

"Save yourself," he answered.

Cummings took her arm then. He made two of the men from Poonch take a chair for her down to the end of the passage, where there was a little hallway paved with flagstones. But she lingered. She had fought too many battles to retreat now without spoiling the field for the enemy. She treated Cummings to a taste of what he might expect in days to come, and he took it meekly:

"Albert, don't you think a doctor should be sent for?"

"Yes, yes, somebody should certify to snakebite."

"Send for Muldoon," she suggested. Then, with a half-triumphant, half-vindictive smile at Joe she left the room on Albert Cummings' arm.

But the smile undid the threat. Joe knew her too well. If she had been really confident that Muldoon and his lying gossip about Rita would avail her at all she would have held her tongue and would have thoroughly instructed Muldoon first before hurling him into action with the full weight of surprise to increase the effect of his impudence. As she reached the door she glanced back. Joe detected terror in her eyes, or thought he did. He wondered whether she could read the cool indifference in his and judge the strength behind it.

Then he turned his head to stare at Rita. Bruce had made five of the men from Poonch return outside under the cloister to prevent them from conversing with the other two. He was watching them through the doorway and Joe heard him consult with Hawkes as how best to bring the police on the scene.

"They'll be hard to come by," Hawkes advised him. "The police don't kid 'emselves they're submarines."

"Then see if you can find my horse, if it hasn't bolted. Ride in search of the police and bring the first two or three you can find."

"All right, sir. What about that knife, though?"

"Which one?"

"Sticking in the wall over Mr. Joe's bed."

"I'll look at it. May I, Beddington?" Bruce crossed the room and climbed upon the bed. Joe had to look around his legs in order to watch Rita; she and Annie Weems were sitting at the Yogi's feet and he was listening to what looked like whispered argument. Bruce whistled softly. "Come and look, Hawkes." Hawkes, too, climbed on to the bed.

The bearded coachmen, having set the chair for Mrs. Beddington, returned. One of them sat down patiently with his back against a wall, but the other walked straight up to Joe and handed him a folded piece of paper.

"Bring the lantern."

The man brought it, but Bruce supposed the lantern was for him, so he took it to study the knife in the wall. It was a minute or two before Joe could make out what was written on the ruled sheet torn from Cummings' notebook:

"Come and talk to me. This man will help you out here. Mother."

He tore up the paper, gave the pieces to the man and signed to him to take those as his answer. Then he went on watching Rita; somebody had lighted the night-lamp at the Yogi's feet; its dim rays shone on her face and throat. He was determined she should speak first, but he remembered she had said something about all eternity; he hoped she would not keep him waiting that long.

Hawkes' voice: "Yes, sir—his knife—them are his initials." Bruce stepped down to the floor and Hawkes' voice followed him: "I can work it out of the wall all right without breaking the point."

"No, leave it in there. Go and find the police and let them see it the way it is."

Cummings heard that just as he reentered the door. His attitude and gesture suggested worry, Joe thought, like a tradesman's with an important account in jeopardy. His voice, too, sounded decidedly nervous:

"No, Bruce, not yet. Premature, in my opinion. And besides, that is my department—my prerogative; you soldiers have no business in civil matters. Joe, your mother wants to speak to you."

"So her note said."

"Won't you come? Captain Bruce and I can help you down the passage."

"No, thanks."

Cummings hesitated, half turned away, faced Joe again and jumped his hurdle:

"Joe, my boy, you can take this from me without resentment, since I'm so much older than you are. She is after all your mother."

"Oh, no. She has disowned and repudiated me in the presence of witnesses. I am now a free man, absolutely independent of her. She goes her way, I mine."

"She asked me to say that she regrets having spoken unkindly to you."

"Kindest words she ever used to me. Tell her I'm feeling wonderful since I'm free of her yoke."

But Cummings stuck to it and Joe laughed inwardly. "Joe, this isn't a time to pick quarrels or to stand on ceremony. Judging solely by what your mother has just now hinted to me, circumstances might prove most embarrassing unless we three stick together. Your mother realizes that you feel under deep obligation to Miss Weems and Miss Amrita, so she withdraws any adverse criticism that she may have made."

"Yo-yo-yo! Eat crow—eat crow! You'll earn your lackey's income," Joe reflected. Then, aloud, he answered: "I've nothing to withdraw. Do you remember what I called you?"

Even in the lamplight Cummings' face flushed crimson; he was aware that Bruce was listening; Hawkes, too. However, billionairesses don't grow on brambles. He swallowed what resembled pride:

"I, too, withdraw my criticism."

"What do I care for your criticism? I have told you you're a liar. If you're ashamed of that and would like to apologize, go and say so to Rita."

Cummings swallowed something, flinched and fell back on original instructions:

"Then you won't go and talk to your mother?"

"I have nothing to say to her."

Something seemed to have pulled the plug from under Cummings' dignity. He wilted. However, there are traditionally conventional ways of saving face. He shook his head sadly, turned and walked away with his hands behind his back.

Bruce, trying to seem unembarrassed, offered a suggestion: "I say—pretty personal, all this—I can't help overhearing. Would you rather I'd wait outside? There's the courtyard—Hawkes and I could—"

"Not a bit of it. You help me to keep my temper."

"Do I? I admire your guts. Not many men would turn down all those millions. Nine out of any ten in your shoes would behave like Cummings. Can't imagine what she sees in him. He's cheap. He swallows insults like a dog at breakfast."

"He's afraid of her," said Joe. "She sees that."

"Uh-huh. And a fellow feeling makes us wondrous kind, eh? She's afraid, too. You behave as if you held all the high cards; but as she said before she left the room, what we all saw tonight isn't legal evidence. No court would listen to it. However, it's none of my business. Can't help feeling curious about it, though. I say—there's one chap I would like to see go scot-free."

"Feeling fine and free myself!" Joe answered.

"I mean that cobra-wallah. Poor little devil. Just a simple savage—loyal as a dog to Amal. I admit I wasn't dry-eyed when he saw how Poonch-Terai had tricked him into killing Amal with a cobra. Begged her to forgive him—did you get that? I believe she did, too—hope so, anyhow. I suppose there's absolutely no doubt he deliberately murdered Poonch-Terai with that other cobra?"

"None at all," Joe answered. But he hardly heard Bruce. He was watching Rita. She and Annie Weems were pleading, it seemed, with the Yogi, but if he listened to them he was doing so with closed eyes; he seemed almost asleep.

But suddenly Ram-Chittra Gunga came out of his silence and his voice boomed like an oracle:

"I tell you: It is always NOW. And it is now or never. That which was, NOW IS, and none can change it. That which was not, is not; none can bring it into being. That which shall be, now is, or it could not ever be. But fools imagine vain things; they imagine what they please until the time of wakening. And time—what is it? That, too, is imagination. But you imagine it, so you must wait on your imagination. Are you not like someone standing by the river? This comes—that comes—then the thing that you desire comes floating downstream. Shall you not take it ere it passes? Why not? Whose else is it? However, if you grasp too soon, shall you receive it? And if you grasp too late, has it not gone past you? Should you plunge in, can you overtake it? Nay, I say there is a proper time for all things—aye, a proper instant; because time is of the very essence of that river, on whose bank you think you stand and yearn for what you think you have not."

Cummings entered. He was steaming, and his suit had shrunk badly, so he looked less self-important even than he felt; in fact, he looked like a criminal haled to the dock, which Joe thought interesting, since the man lacked a criminal's courage. He was using Joe's mother's magnetic impulse, which was another story. He had another message from her:

"Joe, your mother wishes me to say that she is willing to apologize. She asks you to come and receive her apology. She thinks you can at least make that much effort to meet her half-way."

"I prefer not to meet her at all," Joe answered. "Cummings, you may say this: I have seen her apologize probably twenty times, and I have never known her to do it unless she felt she had to. I have never known her not to exact vengeance for it afterward. Her apologies have teeth in them."

"Joe, should you talk like that about your mother?"

"You oblige me. I prefer to say nothing at all about her."

"Joe, she realizes she has not been altogether fair to

you. She admits you have been devoted to her, and that you have faithfully and skillfully conducted her affairs. She wants you to continue, but under a contract that will give you a much bigger income of your own and more authority."

"No thanks," said Joe. "I've seen what I want, floating down the river. You may say I am not interested."

"That is your answer?"

"Yes, it's final."

Cummings looked almost pleased. He seemed to think his own nest might be better lined without Joe as a competitor. He retired with a symptom of starch in his smile, becoming sorrow as Joe's obstinacy wore thin; optimism perched between his shoulder-blades.

"Should you seize the wrong thing," boomed Ram-Chittra Gunga's voice, "why bother with it? Throw it back into the river. Someone else may need it. And if someone else takes what you crave, permit that. Shall not two destroy what one can cherish? Give, I say—let go of it. Nay, take not that which is not free and clear, or you will find yourself in bond for others' debts."

Joe thrilled at the thought that he owed no debts, except that thousand pounds to Hawkes, and he knew he could scrape that sum together. There were some bonds of his own in a safe-deposit box; he could sell those.

"Rita," he said, "what have I done? Won't you come and talk to me a minute?" He smiled at himself to think how resolutely he had decided she should speak first.

Bruce and Hawkes had manners. They began to talk together instantly — pointedly — noisily — turning their backs. They could hardly vanish into thin air, but they could create a sort of privacy by holding conversation of their own. They even turned their backs on Rita, and that called for self-control, because Rita walking toward Joe with love-light in her eyes was a symphony in line and plane and movement.

Suddenly then, like a stab in the heart, emotion almost split Joe's consciousness in two. He had not guessed himself so capable of feeling—least of all of feeling—simultaneously, love and hatred. It was like life and death at war within him. It seemed even to divide his eyesight. Through his left eye, and with half of his consciousness, he saw his mother entering the doorway; with his right, he saw Rita and nothing but Rita. They approached each other, and Joe's head swam. But brains are inconsistent mechanisms; he could hear with concentrated clearness, as if the unimportant words were etched on bone inside his own skull, Bruce and Hawkes inventing conversation:

"Sir, if I'd a wish-bone worth a rusty tin can, I believe I'd wish a pair o' seven-league boots on Chandri Lal—him wi' the cobras. The poor devil's broke; he can't go far without a fist-full of rupees. If he'd the British Army's luck—but that kind hasn't."

"The police can't do a thing to him," said Bruce.

"Sir, two or three policemen in a dark cell would make a tough one turn his secrets inside out. That little blighter isn't tough; he'd tell what he knew, and what she knew, and what he saw, and heard, and thought about—"

Attention switched its energy to other nerves. Bruce

and Hawkes faded out of the picture. With the keenness, almost of a concentrated pain, Joe read his mother's thought—but not in pictures—he sensed it, feeling her emotions one by one, as if that invisible bond that once united them had not yet snapped, but was drawn taut and rendered ten times vibrant. She had entered the room resolved to make the utmost sacrifice compatible with self-esteem and willing to concede her son the victory if she only might save her face before the world and still cling to a vestige of authority, that she would know how to enlarge as time rolled by. She heard that scrap of conversation and it frightened her. She saw Rita approaching, face to face, and that enraged her so that rage obliterated reason. She trembled. If her hate could kill, then Rita would have fallen dead that instant. She was actually dumb with baffled jealousy and malice. Rita spoke first:

"Yes, Joe?"

Rage found speech then—tight-lipped—grim. "Excuse me. I came in to speak to my son. Will you leave us alone, please?"

"But I'm not your son," Joe answered. "You disowned me before a number of witnesses. I have something to say to Rita; I invited her to come and listen to me. I have nothing whatever to say to you."

Mrs. Beddington glared at Rita. "Will you leave us?" she demanded.

"Joe answered you, Mrs. Beddington. There is nothing that I need add to that."

"Then you shall listen to me! I am this man's mother. I have offended his pride, and perhaps his dignity, by using tactless methods of protecting him against his own boyish romanticism. He is angry with me. He remembers nothing but what he thinks was tyranny. He forgets what a friend I have been. He forgets that he owes me *some* consideration for my patience with him. That is because you, young woman—you have come between us. If you have a spark of decency—a spark of reverence for motherhood—you will make amends to both of us— to him and to me—by never seeing him again!"

She paused for breath, perhaps expecting a retort. But Rita merely stood her ground, observing her with quiet, unwavering eyes, and Joe said nothing; he had already said all he intended to say.

Then passionate, hate-edged speech again: "Is it money you want? I will make you a monthly allowance on condition that you keep a thousand miles away from him."

A quiet, bronze-voiced answer: "Money? No. I want nothing from you, Mrs. Beddington."

"What do you want? Apology? You may have it. I apologize to you for having said things that I can't prove. The man who could have proved them lies, done to death, under that sheet. I know nothing against you—nothing—except that you're not fit to be my son's wife—nor his mistress either."

Joe spoke grimly. "That's all. Mater, there's the door. D'you hear me? Do you want to be shown the way out?"

Rita stilled that outburst. "But I am not your son's wife—nor mistress."

"Hasn't he made love to you? Do you mean to tell me that you and he haven't reached an understanding? Why, I had it from his own lips!"

"Joe loves me. I love him. But we don't yet understand each other."

"Speak plain English! If you and I can understand each other, that's all that's needed."

"I will not take Joe away from someone else. I think he doesn't understand that. I will not bring ruin on him for the sake of my happiness. Happiness isn't won that way."

"Then you surrender him?"

"He is not mine to surrender."

"There! Joe—did you hear that?"

He stared at them—silent—dumb. He was still a sick man. Strong emotion, following a line of least resistance, staggered him as if he had been struck by someone's fist. It was almost as if Rita had struck him. And the cunning that was hers by instinct quickened in his mother's mind, appraising Rita's honesty—discerning how it might be subtly turned against her.

"Joe, dear, I'm only an aging and rather bewildered woman. What I came in here to say was, that I'm sorry I have treated you so niggardly. I did it for your own sake, but I can understand how you've wanted to have control of things, since it was you who attended to everything. You are an excellent business man. You should be; for it was I who trained you. I have made up my mind to put you in the saddle, as you would call it, and from now on you may have whatever income the estate will stand, and I will give you a contract giving you full authority. Now—isn't that better than being obstinate about a case of calf-love? Say good-by to her and come away with me in Mr. Cummings' carriage."

Not a sign or a word from Rita. Truly Joe did not understand her. But he understood his mother; and she was quick to see the dumb resentment in his eyes. She fired her last shot—hypocritical—astute—astonishing—a stroke of genius:

"Joe! Listen to me. If I thought you really loved this woman—and if I believed she really loved you—I would even overlook all the unpleasantness and receive her as one of the family. I would give her the chance to prove that you and she could get along together and that you wouldn't be a social misfit. Can I say more?"

But a last shot, if it misses, leaves the locker empty and no threat to bluff with. It had gone wild. Joe dismissed it with a gesture, too tired and too indifferent even to feign indignation. He knew—and his mother knew—what she would do to Rita if he fell for that suggestion, and if Rita fell for it. Slow murder. One dynamic and relentless will incessantly alert to break, humiliate and kill a gentler one. It was not worth arguing.

He gazed at Rita. And the most discouraged, blindest duffer could have read the sadness in her eyes. He yearned to her, but she gave no sign that she knew that. And she seemed to expect him to speak. So he said it:

"Am I dismissed? You've said your last word?"

"Joe, is there anything else that I *could* say?"

"I suppose not."

He, however, also had a last shot; and he meant to aim it straighter than his mother aimed hers. Physical strength had seeped out and his wound was hurting, but he preferred to fire his final salvo standing up. So he called to Bruce:

"Would you and Hawkes mind helping me a minute?"

So they sat down on the bed on either side of him and he put an arm around each shoulder. Then they stood and raised him to his feet, he feeling weaker than he looked, erect between them. He addressed his mother as a man might speak to an opponent taken in the act of cheating:

"You heard just now what Rita said. So you can't say any longer that I am being influenced by her. I understand—for reasons that I don't quite understand—that I have lost her. I assure you—also, doubtless, for a reason that you will not understand—that you have lost me. I have done my best to serve you loyally, until now. I don't regret that, since it leaves me not in your debt. But I refuse to serve you another minute, in any capacity, on any terms or for any consideration. Good-by."

There seemed nothing else to say. His shot had gone home. It had left him feeling empty and discouraged, but it made his mother angrier than he had ever seen her. He saw no sense in standing up to the fishwife fury that he saw was coming, so he signed to Bruce and Hawkes and let them lower him back on the bed, where he could sit with pillows to support him. He heard Hawkes—not that Joe was interested now in anything, but Hawkes spoke with a growl of mistrust, adding vehemence to nearness:

"Where have those two buzzards been?"

He looked up—saw that the two coachmen from the land of Poonch were entering the room. He had not noticed them go out; they had been squatting with their backs against the end wall, opposite the Yogi. Joe felt it was none of his business, but he was grateful for any interruption since it postponed his mother's speech. Hawkes seemed irritated out of all proportion to the circumstances:

"Speak up. Where have you two blighters been?"

It was Albert Cummings, shrunk but reinflated with a new importance, entering the room, who answered:

"Bruce, is everyone accounted for? These coachmen say that when the maharajah came in through the courtyard door there was a flash of lightning. They say they distinctly saw someone else enter the room. They describe him as a small man, who could hide in a very small space."

"Pipe-dream!" Hawkes was scornful, but the scorn was vaguely unconvincing. Bruce glanced at him sharply. Rita, too. However, Hawkes insisted: "Where could a mouse hide? Under the bed's the only place; there's no one there."

"What is under the sheet?" asked Cummings.

"Corpses, sir. His Highness Maharajah Poonch-Terai—and Amal."

Annie Weems left her place by the Yogi and knelt near the sheet—rearranged it—tidied it a little—made it look less ghastly.

"Are you sure there is no one hiding under there?" asked Cummings. Death seemed dreadful to him; he spared his nerves the horror of a personal inspection.

"You may see if you wish. Am I to raise the sheet?" asked Annie Weems.

"No, no. I'll take your word for it." He strode nearer, glanced swiftly, once at Joe, and then led Mrs. Beddington out of the room. "No place this for a lady."

Rita stood still. Joe kept wondering why she stood there. Did she mean to prolong the parting agony? Well, all right; he would give her any satisfaction in his power. There was not much he could do or say, but he would rather say it standing. Could he? He didn't want witnesses, not even decent ones like Bruce and Hawkes. He staggered to his feet and stood there, swaying.

"Rita. Since it's good-by, and I don't quite understand it, let me say this, lest you misunderstand me. I am a free man, and I have nothing in the world that by any stretch of imagination could be called a fortune. I am beholden to no one—not even to you; because I have offered you all that a man can offer, and you refused it. I've no motive, in fact, for telling anything except the truth. It's this: I love you. And, God pity me, I don't think I can ever even try to love another woman. That's all."

Then he let his knees yield and his weight sway backward until the pillows seemed to rise and meet him midway.

"All is all I need, Joe!"

She was seated on the bed beside him before his head ceased swimming. He discovered himself in her arms. And again, he did not understand, but this was a misunderstanding that he could tolerate. He closed his eyes, marveling—wondering millions of unanswerable questions, of which only one was formulated:

"Had he character enough to make a go of it?"

He decided he neither knew nor cared. He loved her. And he knew, by God, that Rita loved him.

FROM THE BOOK OF THE YOGI-ASTROLOGER RAM-CHITTRA GUNGA SINGH

When I consider then and now, I think I see one universal law, although its consequences are as many as the number of the beings who obey it. I perceive, or so it seems to me, that virtue comes forth only from necessity, as sprouts spring only from the broken husk. It is a mystery to me why people say of this or that one: Yea, he is now virtuous, but was he always?

Lo, I tell you, if he had been always virtuous, he never would have entered this world, which is a place of discipline and growth. The darkest hour precedes the dawn. The darkest horrors of a human character assert themselves and swell into enormity when virtue stirs within. So when I see one revelling in wrong, although I praise not that nor lend it countenance, I bridle accusation: for I know, or think I know, that rampant evil is the movement of the rotted soil that covers a quickening seed; so I observe, that I may see some almost imperceptible, ascending tip of virtue presently. If no wind chills it, and no foot crushes, it may grow big.

XXIX

"I have delivered judgment."

A tart disgusted exclamation from Joe's mother brought him back to reality. Reality, as usual, was irritating, because his mother was rearranging someone's plans. Someone, was Albert Cummings:

"Really I'd rather you'd wait at the end of the passage. This isn't decent. Do go."

"No, I'll sit here. And besides, I've something more to say to Joe before I turn my back on him forever."

There was not much light, because Cummings' lantern had been set down on a table and he was standing between it and Joe. But Joe could see his mother. He could also see Ram-Chittra Gunga, at the opposite end of the room, still perfectly motionless and resembling an ancient carving because of the yellowish dim light and soft rich shadow cast by the night light at his feet. The sight of him offended Mrs. Beddington. She proceeded to give him a piece of her mind:

"You're an old fraud! You can fool people with your tricks, but when you're found out in the end they'll take no pity on you. If there's such a place as hell, you'll go there!"

Cummings puffed importantly to disguise his alarm. "Don't—please don't—for your own sake. You can have no notion what trouble a man like that can make. It sounds ridiculous, but—"

He was interrupted by Ram-Chittra Gunga's voice. The old man answered her.

"Where are you?"

"Hush!" said Cummings. "Hush!"

Then the Yogi again: "Are you in heaven? As much of me as you know anything about is in hell also. It is wise to be partly in hell. Is light not partly in the darkness? It is what you bring to hell, not what you find there, that is important. The effect that you have on hell is more important still."

He relapsed into silence. Cummings fussed pompously: "Please—please don't argue with him. Captain Bruce—my carriage will be here in a few minutes—I have just seen the lamps in the distance. I am going to take Mrs. Beddington back to her hotel. May I ask you to remain here—you and Sergeant Hawkes—until I can send someone to relieve you and to take charge of the prisoners?"

"What prisoners?" Bruce asked him. "I don't know of any."

"Oh, well—if you wish to stand on technicalities—I will arrest them formally." He pointed at the Yogi. "I arrest you! Mr. Beddington, you, too, are under arrest. So are you, Hawkes. So are you, Miss Weems." He avoided even looking at Rita. "So is that young woman, and these two coachmen."

"There are five men out under the cloister," Bruce reminded him.

"Yes, yes. Will you bring them in here?"

"Bring 'em yourself. As you remarked not long ago, the military shouldn't interfere in civil matters. Under protest—if you insist—I will take temporary charge of anyone you choose to tell me is a prisoner. However, it's your responsibility."

"Very well, I will go and arrest them. I will record your protest."

Armed with his flashlight, Cummings chested his way importantly toward the courtyard door.

"What am I charged with?" Joe asked.

"You will be told that at the proper time."

"No good reason that I see for arresting anyone." Bruce grumbled. "And if anyone, why not me too? I was in here when it all happened."

"Why not my mater then? She was in here, too," Joe suggested.

Cummings ignored such farcical objections. He opened the courtyard door and stepped out. Apparently he had to do a little searching amid the cloister shadows. The door swung shut behind him. Mrs. Beddington moved nervously—opened her mouth as if to speak—decided not to—closed it again as if she had swallowed something that did not taste good. Hawkes, with his back like a ramrod and a cast-brass expression, faced Bruce:

"Sir, if you had fifty rupees you could lend me until pay-day—"

"What on earth for?"

"Luck money. There's chances, sir, no officer should take. But if you'd trust me—"

Mrs. Beddington snorted. "Trust that man? I would as soon trust a cobra!" She shuddered.

"All right, here are fifty dibs," said Bruce. "And now what?"

Hawkes walked to the sheet that covered Poonch-Terai and Amal. He stooped and raised one corner of it.

"Come on," he remarked. "Step lively!"

Mrs. Beddington smothered a scream as the sheet moved. Joe's eyes almost popped out of his head. It looked as if Amal had come to life and was sitting upright.

"Come on—nobody won't hurt you."

Chandri Lal, the scrawny, wiry, small-boned man of cobras, crawled out on his hands and knees and was jerked to his feet by Hawkes' hand underneath his armpit. Groping with his foot under the sheet, Hawkes kicked out his circular basket. The lid came off. It was empty. Hawkes stooped and gave it to him.

"Now then. I'm your friend, and nobody arrested you yet. Take this."

Fifty rupees changed hands.

"You can get to hell-and-gone with fifty rupees. Run and hide. You understand that? But the day you come and find me—secretly—at night—there's fifty more—maybe a hundred more. Now—never mind who killed the Maharajah—that's his business and he's busy minding it. But you came in here with him. You came in and hid. What for?"

Chandri Lal's eyes sought Mrs. Beddington.

"Did you come in to kill her? Why?"

"Aren't you leading your witness?" Bruce asked.

"Kindly lock that door, sir. We don't want Mr. Cummings here for half a minute."

Bruce strode to the door and stood there with his hand on the enormous key. The Yogi suddenly broke silence:

"I demand judgment!"

Chandri Lal trembled at the sound of his voice. Hawkes stared at Mrs. Beddington. She stood up.

"Rattled!" Joe whispered to Rita. He felt as suddenly excited as if a bull were in the ring. "I don't believe the snakeman knows a thing against her. How can he? But she thinks he does. Look at her face."

Joe's mother saw him whispering. She started toward him. "Joe," she began, then hesitated. "No, no, I will speak to Albert. Let me pass, please."

"That's right. Go and tell him to arrest you," Hawkes suggested sweetly.

She ignored Hawkes—sailed straight up to Bruce. "Will you open that door?" Bruce opened it. She went out. Bruce closed the door behind her, but they could hear her shouting, "Albert! Albert!"

"Now," said Hawkes, "I'll bet the drinks. We're going to see a perishing proconsul swap sides—sudden! Git, you—git, you heathen! Out there through the front door. You're too innocent. Us criminals are no fit company for a nice little man like you. Go forth, my son, and kill another maharajah. Kill the next one 'fore he gets fresh."

He shoved Chandri Lal by the shoulders. The man was so bewildered that he dropped his basket. Hawkes kicked it along in front of him, bundled him out through the door and along the passage. A door slammed. Hawkes returned, winking at Rita. "It's a nice night now," he said—then faced Bruce and saluted: "Orders, sir?"

Bruce stepped back from the courtyard door. It opened. Cummings entered, closing it behind him. He stood silent, irresolute, awkward, trying to look self-controlled. But his hand, with which he stroked his chin and concealed his mouth, was shaking.

"Was there no one else in here?" he asked.

"There was," said Hawkes.

"Who was he, and where is he?"

"An important witness, sir, for the defense," Hawkes answered. "The defendants will produce him if, as, when and why."

"You're impudent."

"Me and my friends," said Hawkes, "are not so used to being put under arrest for nothing, that we feel too dam' respectful." He was brazenly, deliberately insolent, with an air of a man who has surprises up his sleeve. "I'm on my rights. I ask to know what I'm charged with."

"You are not charged. The arrest is canceled. It was a mistake, due to misunderstanding."

"That apply to me, too?" Joe asked.

"All of you."

Then Rita stood up. Joe had not yet seen her furious, but she was trembling now. He seized her hand and tried to pull her back beside him, but she broke free. Annie Weems got in her way—stammered "Rita, dear!"—was overwhelmed and borne along in a vortex of emotion, until they two, hand-in-hand, stood facing Cummings. Gestureless, stock-still for a moment, mastering her voice, she stood trembling with indignation. She seemed to expect Cummings to speak. Her gaze embarrassed him. He stiffened himself, trying to look dignified.

"You, too," he said. "It was a mistake. You are not—"

She burst in on him, and her voice was cold with concentrated anger. "You arrested Sri Ram-Chittra Gunga! Is there nothing now you wish to say to him?"

Cummings nervously inclined his head toward the Yogi and made a weak, conciliating gesture with his left hand.

"It was a mistake—due to misunderstanding," he stammered.

"Is that all?"

Cummings stroked his chin. "What else? I canceled it."

"You? Who are you to wipe out with a word an insult paid to Sri Ram-Chittra Gunga?" Cummings shrunk away from her. He almost raised an elbow as if afraid she might strike him. But she was stock-still. "You have insulted Annie Weems, and Mr. Beddington, and Sergeant Hawkes—and me. I can forgive that. I can pity you for that. But you have blasphemed Sri Ram-Chittra Gunga. You have committed sacrilege. You cur! You yellow dog! You ignorant, presumptuous, cheap official!"

Cummings protested, stammering, spluttering: "I will not be spoken to like this! I—"

Rita interrupted: "Dogs like you have died for lesser blasphemy! Are you much better than the man whose body lies beneath that sheet? Have you his courage? Do you dare to let the Black Light show your record? You, who have set your hunger for a woman's moneybags so high that you despise him—BRING THAT WOMAN IN HERE!"

Ram-Chittra Gunga made no sign or sound. Bruce opened the courtyard door. "Come in, please, Mrs. Beddington. You're wanted."

In she came, not jauntily. She looked terrified.

"I have demanded judgment!" boomed Ram-Chittra Gunga. "If it fall on my head, let it."

Cummings made as if to speak, but Mrs. Beddington forestalled him.

"Joe! I'm your mother! Do you mean you would ruin your mother?"

"I will let things take their course," Joe answered. He had not the slightest notion what was going to happen, except that he trusted Rita, and he doubted that Ram-Chittra Gunga would permit violence, or even malice.

Rita said her say then: "You! Who have accused me. Sri Ram-Chittra Gunga, in his wisdom, saw fit to admit you to the presence of the Black Light. You have seen such measure of your own guilt, as your own soul dared to let you see. Now speak."

Mrs. Beddington stood still, her eyes wild, shame and indignation alternating. Suddenly she spoke past Rita:

"Joe! What am I to do now? Tell me!"

"Come clean," Joe advised her.

"Joe—have you put up that cobra-man to lie about me?"

Joe was silent.

"Speak," said Rita. "You have faced the Black Light. Face me. Face Joe. We are far less dreadful."

Cummings drew out a handkerchief and mopped his face. He had forgotten dignity; he sighed and bit his fingernails, nervously watching the door for a servant to come and announce the carriage. Mrs. Beddington clenched and unclenched her fingers.

"Speak," said Annie Weems, "it's much best."

Then the dam went down and Mrs. Beddington burst into tears. They blinded her. She sobbed into her hands, choking artlessly, and through her hands her words came spluttering and indistinct:

"What shall I say? I've done wrong—all my life—I've done wrong—I admit it—I've been a devil—Joe—where are you, Joe—"

Rita and Annie Weems made way for her. She staggered—stumbled—almost fell on Amal's body—ran then—fell at Joe's feet—groped blindly—raised herself and knelt beside him, burying her face among the blankets:

"Joe, say I'm your mother again. Joe, dear—Joe—my boy—can you forgive me? Joe, I'm broken-hearted. Joe, dear—ask her to forgive me—won't you? I can't ask her. Joe, I loved you so much—I was so proud of you. I was just a vain old woman—I wanted to keep you close to me and—Joe, dear, I've been wrong, I know I have—Joe, listen to me—listen—"

Joe laid his hand on her shoulder. "All right, Mater. Only—"

"Joe, don't say it! I surrender—I give up everything—you have it all—I'll sign that trust deed over to you—Joe, dear, you and Rita—"

Nobody had seen Ram-Chittra Gunga rise to his feet. He stood erect, tall, shadowy, in the dim light, and his voice was startling with a ring of triumph:

"I have done my dharma. I received. I have delivered judgment."

ORDERING

Additional copies of *Black Light* may be ordered for $19.99 each, plus $5 for postage, from Ariel Press. If ordered in quantities of 5 or more copies, the cost per book is $16 plus shipping. When ordered in quantities of 10 or more copies, the cost per book is $12 plus shipping.

Black Light can also be ordered as part of a set of 7 books by Talbot Mundy being issued by Ariel Press. The 7 books are:

Black Light, in print, $19.99.
Caves of Terror, in print, $14.99.
The Thunder Dragon Gate, May 2006, $17.99.
Winds from the East, an anthology of stories
    & poems by Talbot Mundy, June 2006, $17.99.
Old Ugly Face, October 2006, $23.99.
Gunga Sahib, January 2007, $17.99.
C.I.D., April 2007, $17.99.

The full set of seven can be ordered for the special price of $120, postpaid.

To order, send a check or money order to Ariel Press, P.O. Box 297, Marble Hill, GA 30148. Or send your order by email to sales@lightariel.com and charge it to a major credit card. We also accept payment by PayPal. Orders may also be faxed 24/7 to (706) 579-1865 or phoned in to (770) 894-4226 Monday through Wednesday during normal business hours.

OTHER ESOTERIC FICTION

In addition to the writing of Talbot Mundy, we carry an excellent selection of esoteric fiction. including:

The Secrets of Dr. Taverner, by Dion Fortune
$17.99

It's All in the Mind, by Carl Japikse
$15.99

In the Days of the Comet, by H.G. Wells
$13.99

Winged Pharaoh, by Joan Grant
$17.99

Life as Carola, by Joan Grant
$14.99

The Story of the Other Wise Man, by Henry van Dyke
$10.99

The Deodorizer of Dead Dogs, by Ambrose Bierce
$9.99

The Zen of Farting, by Reepah Gud Wan
$11.99

To order, pleaase follow instructions on page 407.